W9-BNS-132

MURDER IN OLD BOMBAY

NEV MARCH

MINOTAUR BOOKS
NEW YORK

This is a work of fiction. All of the characters, organizations, and events portrayed in this novel are either products of the author's imagination or are used fictitiously.

First published in the United States by Minotaur Books,
an imprint of St. Martin's Publishing Group

MURDER IN OLD BOMBAY. Copyright © 2020 by Nawaz Merchant. All rights reserved. Printed in the United States of America. For information, address St. Martin's Publishing Group, 120 Broadway, New York, NY 10271.

www.minotaurbooks.com

Designed by Devan Norman

Library of Congress Cataloging-in-Publication Data

Names: March, Nev, 1967- author.
Title: Murder in old Bombay / Nev March.
Description: First edition. | New York : Minotaur Books, 2020.
Identifiers: LCCN 2020026248 | ISBN 978-1-250-26954-6
(hardcover) | ISBN 978-1-250-75377-9 (ebook)
Subjects: LCSH: Mumbai (India)—Fiction. | GSAFD: Mystery fiction.
Classification: LCC PS3613.A7328 M87 2020 | DDC 813/.6—dc23
LC record available at https://lccn.loc.gov/2020026248

Our books may be purchased in bulk for promotional, educational, or business use. Please contact your local bookseller or the Macmillan Corporate and Premium Sales Department at 1-800-221-7945, extension 5442, or by email at MacmillanSpecialMarkets@macmillan.com.

First Edition: 2020

10 9 8 7 6 5 4 3 2 1

To my parents, Khurshed and Silloo Parakh

GRENADIER'S LAMENT

Two hundred mutineers we called to assembly,
My brothers came, and lined up proper.
They had rifles but no cartridges from ordnance that day.
The command was given. We turned and fired.
Like soft wax, they dropped, still in their ranks.
The rest we tied to cannon, and tore to shreds.

BASED ON A GUJARATI POEM
BY BEJAN FERDON JHANSIWALA (1858, JHANSI, INDIA)

MURDER IN OLD BOMBAY

CHAPTER 1

THE WIDOWER'S LETTER

I turned thirty in hospital, in a quiet, carbolic-scented ward, with little to read but newspapers. Recuperating from my injuries, a slow and tedious business, I'd developed an obsession with a recent story: all of India was shocked by the deaths of two young women who fell from the university clock tower in broad daylight.

The more I read about it, the more this matter puzzled me: two well-to-do young women plunged to their deaths in the heart of Bombay, a bustling city under the much-touted British law and order? Some called it suicide, but there seemed to be more to it. Most suicides die alone. These ladies hadn't. Not exactly. Three men had just been tried for their murder. I wondered, what the hell happened?

Major Stephen Smith of the Fourteenth Light Cavalry Regiment entered the ward, empty but for me, ambling as one accustomed to horseback. Taking off his white pith helmet, he mopped his forehead. It was warm in Poona this February.

I said, "Hullo, Stephen."

He paused, brightened and handed me a package tied in string. "Happy birthday, Jim. How d'you feel?"

The presents I'd received in my life I could count on one hand. Waving him to the bedside chair, I peeled the brown paper back and grinned at the book. Stephen had heard me talk often enough about my hero.

"*The Sign of the Four*—Sherlock Holmes!"

He nodded at the newspapers piled about my bed. "Interested in the case?"

"Mm. Seen this?" I tapped the *Chronicle of India* I'd scoured these past hours. "Trial of the Century, they called it. Blighters were acquitted."

Outside, palm trees swished with a warm tropical gust. He sat, his khaki uniform stark in the whitewashed ward, smoothing a finger over his blond mustache. "Been in the news for weeks. Court returned a verdict of suicide."

I scoffed, "Suicide, bollocks!"

Smith frowned. "Hm? Why ever not?"

"The details don't line up. They didn't fall from the clock tower at the same time but minutes apart. If they'd planned to die together, wouldn't they have leapt from the clock tower together? And look here—the husband of one of the victims wrote to the editor."

I folded the newspaper to the letter and handed it over. It read:

Sir, what you proposed in yesterday's editorial is impossible. Neither my wife Bacha nor my sister Pilloo had any reason to commit suicide. They had simply everything to live for.

Were you to meet Bacha, you could not mistake her vibrant joie de vivre. She left each person she met with more than they had before. No sir, this was not a woman prone to melancholia, as you suggest, but an intensely dutiful and fun-loving beauty, kind in her attention to all she met, generous in her care of elders, and admired by many friends.

Sir, I beg you do not besmirch the memory of my dear wife and sister with foolish rumours. Their loss has taken the life from our family, the joy from our lives. Leave us in peace. They are gone but I remain,

sincerely,
Adi Framji (February 10th, 1892)

As Smith finished reading, I swung my legs over the side of the bed and got up. Or tried to, for the room did a dizzy whirl. I lurched, cursed, grabbed for the bed and missed.

Smith hollered, "Orderly!" and scrambled over.

They got me abed, but it was a struggle. I am not a small man.

"Take it slow, pal," Smith said, his expression odd, as though I'd sprouted horns while he wasn't looking.

"All right, all right," I muttered to the orderly, a stocky Sikh in a grey turban and hospital uniform, who tended to fuss overmuch.

"Sahib has not been well, for many months," the man assured me.

Bollocks. Had it been months? Only a few weeks, surely? I recalled feeling numb from cold, a fog of confusion, unfamiliar faces that came and went. . . .

"Dammit, Jim," said Smith, wincing. "We've got to talk about the Frontier. The Afghans, Karachi."

"Do we?" I asked. A drum began to pound in my head. I lay back and pressed the base of my palm to the aching pulse above my ear.

* * *

In the days that followed, my doctor came by, adding a host of cautions as medicos will. He seemed both pleased and doubtful at my progress. No longer a young man, I lay in bed considering my future and found it bleak. I had no family, just old Father Thomas at the Mission orphanage, who'd raised me. My friends from the Company were buried in the red dust of Karachi. Of the old company, only Smith, Colonel Sutton and I were left.

There was little profit in dwelling on it. Instead I returned again and again to the puzzle of the women's deaths. Could I piece together the dire events of that sunlit October day? The story was starting to fade from the front pages, giving way to news of railway expansion across the Indian subcontinent. Yet that heartfelt letter haunted me: *They are gone but I remain*, the young husband had written. His words cut into me, the sharp burn of his grief. I knew something of his pain, for my brothers-in-arms were gone, yet I remained.

A week later I took medical discharge. Most of my army wages had gone toward my care and I had forty rupees to my name. I needed a job.

Well, perhaps I could write for the papers. Thinking of that snippet, the letter to the editor tucked in my billfold, I decided to call on the editor of the *Chronicle*.

CHAPTER 2

THE INTERVIEW

Four weeks had passed since young Mr. Adi Framji's letter had burned through my fog in army hospital. Having persuaded the editor of the *Chronicle* of my seriousness, I rode a tonga through red gulmohur trees and stately houses to plead my case to the reclusive Mr. Framji. At the entrance to a great white house on Malabar Hill, a turbaned gateman disappeared through an ornate door with my calling card: Captain James Agnihotri, *The Chronicle of India*, Bombay.

Now standing atop a sweep of stairs outside Framji Mansion, I hoped to meet the man whose words would not leave me: *They are gone but I remain.*

Filled with trepidation, I breathed in the crisp morning air. Bougainvillea danced in the breeze beside fluted pillars, and scattered pink petals over smooth marble. The blooms' wasted beauty struck a poignant note, echoing the tragic loss a few months past. Adi Framji's wife and sister had fallen to their deaths from the university clock tower. Had the two women committed suicide, or were they murdered? The trial had failed to resolve the question for lack of evidence. Since young Mr. Framji had never spoken with the press, an interview could be the making of my new career. Hat in hand, I waited.

I'd either be told that Mr. Framji, student of law, son of a Parsee landowner and now the bereaved widower, was "not at home" or I'd be granted the interview I requested last week. He had not replied to my note. I might have waited, but I was eager to establish myself as a journalist.

As I fingered the brim of my hat, the man returned, saying, "Adi Sahib will see you."

I entered a marble foyer, and followed him to a morning room where light filtered through the greenery.

"Hello. I'm Adi."

A thin, pale young man stood beside a wide desk, one hand splayed on the dark wood. Here was no invalid, I saw. He approached with a confident step. His immaculate white shirt and crisp collar framed lean features. A wide, bony forehead rose above narrow nose and clean-shaven jaw. He studied me through wire-rimmed glasses, gaze sharp but not unkind.

He saw a tall fellow with the arms and shoulders of a boxer and short-cropped hair that would not lie flat over one ear. The pale English complexion from my unknown father had weathered during my years on the Frontier. His eyes flickered over my military mustache and plain attire without inflection, yet I felt measured in some undefinable way.

"Jim, sir." I stepped forward to shake hands. "My condolences on your loss."

"Thank you. Military?" His grip was firm, his palm dry and smooth.

"Fourteenth Light Dragoons, until recently. Stationed in Burma and the Northwest Frontier."

"Cavalry. And now a journalist," he said.

I attempted a smile. "Joined the *Chronicle* two weeks ago."

Why the urge to explain my journalistic inexperience? We'd just met, but his pale, almost waxen pallor drew my attention. After the grueling trial and uproar in the press, he had reason to dislike, if not despise, newsmen, yet he'd admitted me. Why?

Waving me to the settee, he took a chair beside it. Behind him, heavy bookshelves lined the wall—thick tomes, dark spines aligned, not ornamental, but substantial. Legal books, I supposed.

I expected the usual pleasantries: weather, how long in Bombay and so on, before I could broach the interview.

Instead, young Mr. Framji asked, "Why did you leave the army, Captain?"

He seemed wary, shuttered somehow, the very quiet of his chamber a rebuke. Of course he'd want to ascertain my credentials. Very well.

"Sir, twelve years was enough." Fifteen, if I counted the years I served officers as a groom for their horses.

"So why join the *Chronicle*?"

This was my cue to introduce my purpose. "I'd done some writing, so I asked the editor Mr. Byram for a job. You had my note last week, requesting an interview?"

He put up a hand as if to say "not yet" and asked, "Who are you, Captain Agnihotri?"

"A soldier, sir." I noticed his keen attention and said, "I'd like to investigate this, ah, matter."

How might I share my interest, no, fascination without sounding ghoulish or insensitive? It was all I thought about these days, for I would not dwell on Karachi.

I'd seen death at Maiwand. Dying friends and dead Afghans. On the road to Khandahar . . . and Karachi. Each time is different, but to me the pain was the same. An ache twists inside when a friend's eyes plead, pleading that gives way to realization, that final contortion as the body fights to hold a soul already breaking free, tearing its way out.

Soldiers trade in death. We give and receive. And we ache. But a pair of young women at the opening of life's adventure? It made no sense. Young Mr. Framji's letter said, *Sir, what you proposed in yesterday's editorial is impossible. Neither my wife Bacha nor my sister Pilloo had any reason to commit suicide. They had simply everything to live for.*

He watched me, the plane of his forehead catching the morning light. Such intensity in his look!

I said, "Sir, I read about the case. Some of the details . . . puzzle me."

"Go on."

I struggled to explain without offending. "Have you perchance read *The Sign of Four* by Conan Doyle? His methods interest me. The use of deduction, observation."

Light reflecting off spectacles hid the young man's eyes.

"The singular, or unusual features of a crime . . . can help explain it. That could be useful in a case like this," I said.

"You want to investigate my wife's death? So why join the *Chronicle*?" When he moved I saw his piercing gaze belied his calm voice.

I explained. "Sir, the *Chronicle* focused on the individuals—the ladies and the accused. I suggested a new approach. Piece together a more complete picture. The sub-editor said there was no story left, but I don't agree. There's more to this matter."

Adi Framji did not speak. I scarcely breathed. Now he would toss me out on my ear. His aristocratic face would stiffen into a polite mask. That's how he'd faced a chaos of reporters at Bombay High Court during the short, inconclusive trial.

"Yes, I wrote to the *Chronicle*," he said at last.

I said, "You wrote that it could not be suicide. Perhaps I can discover what happened."

My words held more confidence than they should, for as yet I had seen no evidence.

His eyes flickered. "How?"

"Examine the evidence methodically, put it together. I'm not sure what I'll find, but I think it can be done."

"You'd like to be . . . Sherlock Holmes," Adi said.

So, he was conversant with Conan Doyle's work. It did not surprise me.

"To use his methods, sir," I hurried to explain. "To investigate what the police . . . might have missed."

He frowned. "You decided you'd had enough of the army? After reading about the trial, and seeing my letter?"

"I'd had enough before that. Your letter caught my attention."

"Hm. You're Anglo-Indian?"

"Yes." My parentage was obvious in my coloring and size. Most Indians are smaller.

"Agnihotri is an Indian name. Your father was Indian?"

So here it was, the fact that dogged my footsteps. "No, sir. Agnihotri is my mother's name. I never knew my father."

I was a bastard. My English father had not stayed long enough to give me his name.

"I see." Adi's face bore no judgement. That was unusual.

I had "grown up army," running errands for soldiers. When I was tall enough, I enlisted and was sent straight to the Northern Frontier. He'd not want to hear about that. Instead I spoke about a case I'd investigated in Madras, involving an officer and the death of a washerman.

"Over several days I observed a Subaltern whose clothes simply didn't fit. His quarters were searched, and evidence found. I wrote a report, and the General was somewhat impressed. So, I considered writing, for the papers."

I'd said more than enough, so I waited.

His gaze did not waver, nor did he seem to find my story trifling. He asked some questions and appeared to reach a decision. "I want to know what happened to Bacha and Pilloo. One way or another. How long do you think it would take?"

I considered. "Six months? If I can't get to the bottom of it, well, I'd be surprised."

He blinked. "What do they pay you, at the *Chronicle*, Captain Agnihotri?"

I looked at him, astonished. He did not explain, but his face was gentle.

"Thirty rupees, sir. Per week." My face warmed. It wasn't much, but enough for a bachelor of modest habits. I remained at "parade rest," face front, shoulders square.

"Work for me instead," he said, "at forty rupees a week."

"For you?"

He nodded.

"What . . . would you have me do?"

He smiled then, and I could not imagine why I had thought him stiff or aristocratic. He was a full decade younger than I. Injured and still shocked from the whole thing, he'd been waiting for some way to drive this mystery to a close. Here was a chance—me.

"Do? Just what you planned to do. Investigate my wife's . . . death." His voice shook with suppressed emotion. "It was no suicide, Captain. Find out what happened, and why. But I don't want anything in the papers. She's had enough of that, poor child. Let her rest."

That's how I became a private investigator.

CHAPTER 3

THE FACTS

Sitting there with Adi Framji, I held back my excitement. I'd set my feet upon a new path. Very well, then. I would play the sleuth, and aid this bereaved husband, this pale young man who'd taken fate's blows with such grim composure.

I pulled out a notebook. "Well, sir, shall we start with the facts."

My client straightened up. I watched him take three breaths. I was to learn that this habit came from his legal training. He was apprenticed to Brown and Batliwala solicitors, and sometimes tasked with taking legal depositions. Thoughtfulness and caution were already his way of life.

Adi said, "Bacha and I wed in 1890, when she was eighteen years old and I twenty. I had just returned from university in England where I'd studied law. We were happy."

That was only two years past. By his distant tone and manner, it seemed very long ago.

"My sisters Pilloo and Diana are younger, and we have three other siblings under the age of ten. So, I'm the oldest of six. Five, now, with Pilloo gone."

Five siblings! I envied him. I wrote quickly. "Who lives here, at the house?"

"My parents and siblings, all but Diana—she'll soon be back from England. . . . We have a staff of eight. Two Gurkha watchmen tend the horses and drive the carriage. Jiji-bai, with her son and daughter, cooks the meals. They attend Mama and the girls, so we have no maids. Three bearers valet us and run errands."

This was a large Indian household, often called a "joint family." Adi and his bride had lived here too.

"Sir, in the days before . . . her death, had your wife been unhappy?"

He shook his head. "She did not appear so. Quiet perhaps, in the weeks before."

"And your sister, Miss Pilloo. What was her demeanor?"

Leaning on his elbows, Adi looked at his hands. "Pilloo had always been rather shy, I suppose, rarely spoke at meals." He sighed. "She was wed just six months before, you know, at fifteen. She'd have gone to her husband when she was eighteen. She was content, I think. But lately, before the tragedy, she seemed . . . withdrawn. Perhaps it only appears so, now that they're gone. Bacha and Pilloo were devoted to each other, you understand."

A lock of hair fell over his forehead, now ridged with grief.

That was my introduction to the victims of this case, the ladies, as I began to think of them. Bacha, nineteen, married a year, and Pilloo, sixteen, just wed, and devoted to her new sister-in-law.

"Is that common among Parsees, sir? To wed at fifteen but remain living at home until later?"

Adi's eyebrows rose. "It's a compromise, I suppose. Tradition dictates girls should marry young, but reformers like our friend Behramji Malabari in Simla have been vocal against it. Diana refused to marry, wanted an education, so Papa sent her to finishing school near London. Pilloo was more domestically inclined."

So, one sister was in England, the other had been married. I knew very little about the Parsees, descendants of medieval refugees from Persia.

I asked, "What can you tell me about the day of the event?"

My client took three breaths and locked his fingers together. "On the twenty-fifth of October, Bacha and Pilloo said they would visit my mother's sister in Churchgate. They set off at about three that afternoon, but . . . never got there. Instead they climbed to the viewing gallery of the university tower."

I'd known this. The university library or reading room was a popular location to meet friends or browse newspapers, filled with students and law clerks most of the day. I said, "Rajabai clock tower, near the reading room. Did they say they would go there?"

"They told no one at home."

Had the ladies hidden their plan to visit the tower, or simply changed their minds midway? Here I was at a disadvantage. Army life taught little about women and their motives. Why would they lie about their whereabouts?

"Who saw them there?" I asked.

"A Havildar, the clock tower guard, escorted them up the stairs. Two siblings—children really—saw them go up to the viewing gallery."

"Their names?'

Adi's brow knotted. "The guard was called Bhimsa. The children are from the Tambey family, I believe."

"And then?"

"Just before four o'clock, Bacha . . . dropped to her death. A short while later, Pilloo also fell from the gallery. I'm told she lived for a few moments."

The gap in time between the women's deaths was puzzling.

"Were there other witnesses?"

"Afterwards, you mean? Oh yes. A librarian—Apte was his name. Francis Enty, the clerk who testified, and Maneck, a Parsee, was charged, along with two Mohammedan accomplices."

I added these to my list. I could visit the university and seek other witnesses, but had little hope of sifting through dozens of students who might have been present.

"How soon did the police arrive?"

"Right away, it seems. Bombay High Court is nearby. Police Superintendent McIntyre testified he got there at ten minutes past four and cordoned off the area."

"Why was Maneck arrested?"

Adi drew a breath. "Maneck appeared unkempt and out of breath, for which he had no explanation. It's in McIntyre's report."

"And the Mohammedan men? Why were they arrested?"

"The Khojas, yes. Before the deaths, Enty, the law clerk, said he saw an altercation in the tower, involving Maneck and two Mohammedan men, Seth Akbar and Saapir Behg. Maneck claimed not to know them. Both had alibis elsewhere."

So, the police had decided Maneck and the Khojas were lying and believed Enty's story. Why? "Behg stood trial but Akbar wasn't found?"

"No," sighed Adi. "It's a famous name—Akbar was an ancient Moghul king, you know? Curious that we don't have his first name, only the title Seth . . . I gathered he's influential. Couldn't be found."

That was odd. "I'll ask Superintendant McIntyre about it."

CHAPTER 4

THE FATHER

The clock tower chimed eight the next morning, its tones ringing as I stepped into the *Chronicle*'s office and found it deserted. Too early for reporters, since the morning papers had gone out at five and the evening blokes had not yet arrived. Eager to begin my investigation, I emptied my desk of belongings and left a note for my sub-editor—matters that required urgent attention—thereby suspending my journalistic career for a while. I would explain in person, of course, but that should do for now.

In the shuttered bazaar street with its empty awnings, upturned carts and tongas, a cow chewed and flicked its tail but otherwise took no notice. I liked the sense of slipping in and out undetected. If one fit into the picture, few people looked closer.

Only just March, a warm breeze came at me. Flagging down a passing victoria carriage, I rode over the coastal way to Malabar Hill. We swung right at Teen-batti and climbed toward Hanging Gardens, where polite society took their evening constitutionals.

At Framji Mansion, the gateman waved me through. In the morning room, Adi nodded a welcome, then noticed my worn khaki trousers, my only white shirt, sleeves rolled up to the elbows, and ubiquitous newspaperman's vest.

"Tea?" he offered.

I accepted. Adi tugged the bell-pull and spoke to a uniformed bearer in a local tongue, Gujarati perhaps, which I did not understand.

Turning back, he said, "Captain, only two people will know of our arrangement. My father, and Tom Byram of the *Chronicle*. He's a close friend of my parents."

So, Adi knew Tom Byram, owner and chief editor of the *Chronicle*. His headlines, "INCOMPETENT AND CONFUSED!" flayed the police investigation of the tower deaths. Prosecution was "BUMBLING AND INCREDULOUS." While other journals were less generous, he'd defended the ladies' reputations. Mr. Byram had also been my employer.

"And when my investigation is done, will I return to the *Chronicle*?"

Adi considered. "Shall I suggest a leave of absence? Six months, do you think? And we can't have you dressed as a reporter."

"That would do," I agreed. "So, if I'm not to be a journalist, what's my story?"

A liveried bearer entered with a large metal platter and poured from a porcelain teapot. The delicate teacup looked tiny in my hand.

Opening a bundle of dark fabric, my client shook out a long black garment.

"It's one of my robes, as student of law. Should fit you, though it might be a tad short. The university clock tower is right by the High Court, so there are always lawyers around."

I smiled, thinking of Sherlock Holmes's penchant for disguise. My assignment had taken a new turn, I thought, warming to the idea of wearing one.

"And those?" I nodded at two squat metal boxes by the table.

"My notes from the trial, Captain. Chief McIntyre provided the witness testimonies. I kept some newspaper reports." Distaste tinged his words. "If asked, you work for Brown and Batliwala, our solicitors. And now," he announced, "my father wants to meet you."

I followed Adi to his father's office, passing thickly curtained windows. White molding surrounded ornate framed portraits. Mustached men in traditional attire gazed down from dark canvases. Here, they seemed to say with pride, was the fruit of several generations' effort and enterprise.

Adi noticed my interest in the portraits and stopped in the hallway. "My grandfather," he said, pointing to a man in dress uniform—a Grenadier, an officer, epaulettes gleaming.

"He was with the East India Company?"

Adi nodded. "He served during the mutiny. We've been staunch sup-
porters of British rule. Law and order, you know."

Curious. Although the Sepoy Mutiny of 1857 had occurred over thirty
years ago, few people mentioned it. Led by the last Mughal emperor, supported by Maratha generals and a fiery queen, Rani Laxmibai, an appalling number of Indian troops had rebelled, murdering British officers and
their families. The Framjis were loyalists, but Adi's morose tone puzzled
me. What was that story?

* * *

Adi's father, Burjor Framji, stood before a desk cluttered with piles of
paper, a thick-set man with a ballooning waistline.

"Adi! And Captain Agnihotri. Come in, come in," he rumbled with an
easy smile. I liked the respected Parsee businessman right away.

Moving quickly for one so rotund, he shook hands with an enthusias-
tic grip, peering at me, curious and open. One could not venture to Bombay without meeting a Parsee, I supposed. Widely respected, they were
everywhere. Enterprising businessmen, affably pro-British, they owned
hotels, newspapers and plantations, ran shipyards and banks.

Burjor named senior officers of his acquaintance, then asked, "Where
were you stationed, Captain? Did Mrs. Agnihotri accompany you?"

"Burma and the Frontier province, and no, I'm not married." Officers'
wives were not permitted on campaign. In fact, the army rather discouraged matrimony.

Burjor said, "Last October, the death of my daughter Pilloo and Bacha, Adi's wife . . . well, it's been a blow, Captain."

I commiserated.

He continued, "Many Parsees supported Maneck Fitter—you know
he's one of us, a Parsee? I don't know him. It's unthinkable that one of our
own could kill two innocent girls. But that verdict of suicide? No."

I understood. Neither father nor son believed it was suicide, but they
lacked evidence to prove it. That's why they'd hired me.

We spoke for a few minutes, then Adi said, "I'm off to lecture, Captain. Use my chambers, all right? I'll see you this afternoon."

Still warm from that courtesy, I returned to Adi's chamber. Stretching out on his settee, fingers steepled, I considered what I'd learned, much as I imagined Holmes might do.

What could I deduce from Burjor's kindly, expansive manner? His whiskers overflowed to join heavy side locks, leaving a bare chin. It was an open face, apple-cheeked with laugh lines that swallowed up his eyes. He wore an expensive dark silk tunic, yet he spoke like a man of humble beginnings. Landowner and patriarch, Burjor had made a name for himself in business. Had he also made dangerous enemies?

Opening Adi's box of papers, I extracted several foolscap sheets. Adi's writing was a flowing script, as elegant as a lady's but sharp, as though he wrote quickly.

Instinct is an odd thing. Wherever I am, I must know the way out—cannot rest easy until I know I'm not boxed in. So before reading, I went to a pair of narrow French doors. They swung open to a long, shady balcony and I stepped through.

The smooth stone bannister felt cool under my hands as I glanced over tropical ferns and banana leaves. The Framjis fascinated me, Adi's quiet courage, Burjor's directness and warmth. Somewhere a myna warbled, "Yes? Yes?" The murmur of distant voices and birdcalls brought back a moment from my childhood. The perfume of incense touched my face with gentle fingers. Why did it feel so poignant, like an old scar that aches for no reason? Then it was gone.

This mansion was larger than any home I'd seen. Curious, I went down the white balcony to my left.

"Adi, are you sure?"

Hearing Burjor's gravelly voice, I stopped. To overhear this private moment between father and son seemed a shoddy way to repay my employer's trust. I should return.

"I am," Adi said. "I want to know. No matter what he finds."

"But he'll ask a lot of questions." Burjor slipped into a local dialect and

I missed a few words. "Can he be trusted? No, not business secrets, that's not what I'm saying, though that can cause problems."

"You think if he found something . . . blackmail?" Adi said, "No, Papa. Not this man."

A rush of affection enveloped me. I felt as though my officer had just vouched for me with his commander. But why was Burjor worried about blackmail? What was he afraid I'd find?

He said, "So we'll tell the family, Mama, Diana, all the staff, that he is your friend."

Adi must have nodded, for Burjor continued. "She won't like it. Mama does not like secrets."

"Just keep them out of it."

"But Adi, he'll question them, no? What will they think? This could be very awkward."

After a moment, Adi replied, "I think he's tactful, Papa. I'll mention it."

Clothing rustled as they rose, and I retreated to my client's office. When Adi returned only moments later, I shifted in my seat. Listening around corners did not sit right with me. Now, Captain, I thought, comes a test of who you are.

A smile flickered in greeting as Adi gathered up his books. "Found anything useful?"

"Sir." I faced him squarely. "I was on the balcony. Overheard your conversation. I apologize." I wanted to say, you can trust me—but what did I know about them really?

Adi stared up at me. "All right."

I liked his steady, forthright manner. He'd mentally reviewed his conversation with his father, and was satisfied. If he had something to hide, he would scarcely have engaged me.

He nodded at the boxes. "So you've made a start?"

I hesitated. "Are you sure about this, sir? What if I find, well, something painful?"

His lips tightened. "Let's have it, whatever it is. I can't just keep . . . attending lectures, writing briefs, without knowing what happened."

What happened to her, to his sister and the pretty young thing he'd just married. And if I succeeded? What then? Another trial?

"Sir, if . . . when, we find the culprit? Will we involve the police?"

Adi did not hesitate. "Yes, Captain. If there's proof."

"And if the culprit is, well, someone you care about?"

"Our family?" He drew a tired breath. "Yes, even then. This must end, so we can go on." He seemed to reclaim himself, as though he had stepped back into the ring and dared fate to knock him down.

With instructions to report in frequently, I left, thinking about Adi's letter in the papers: *They are gone but I remain.* Although pounded and tattered after Karachi, I also remained. Not good for much, perhaps, but wanting something more. A soldier needs to belong, to be part of a continuum. I was thirty, an age when many soldiers were retired and married, with a brood of three or four. But an Anglo-Indian is rarely welcome, and finding a wife would not be easy. No, I needed a job, a direction. I needed this post almost as much as Adi needed to lay his ghosts to rest. I was on the hunt, and it felt good to have a goal.

The next day I sat in Adi's chambers and pored over his copious notes. He had a lawyer's logical sense, describing facts in careful detail, although hearing them must have torn him apart. The Medical Examiner's report said Lady Bacha's body had a fractured skull, cracked ribs and a broken neck. Miss Pilloo's body was scratched on breasts and thighs, with numerous internal injuries and broken bones. All consistent with a fall of two hundred feet.

In the margin Adi had scribbled questions, discrepancies and, once, a sad lament: "Bacha, what was so awful that you couldn't tell me?"

I paused, turning pages back and forth. The end of the medical report was missing.

CHAPTER 5

THE VICTIMS

Next day I returned, and stepping through the foyer where sunlight spilled over checkered tiles, I followed the bearer up a stairway to Adi's apartment and found him immersed at his desk. He rose, greeted me and waved me to a chair.

"What news?" his look demanded, but courtesy required that he play the host before embarking upon business. "Join me," he said, lifting the cover from a platter of sandwiches. As we ate, I asked about the missing pages from the Medical Examiner's report.

Adi raised his eyebrows. "Oh? I didn't notice. You could ask the M.E., Patrick Jameson, or Superintendent McIntyre."

He went on to discuss some points of law. He emphasized one in particular—a principle called double jeopardy, instituted to prevent a person from being tried twice for the same crime.

I asked, "If I find evidence, will that prevent another trial?"

"Depends on the evidence," he said, in true lawyerly fashion.

In the silence, I was distracted by the portrait of a lovely woman on his wall.

Noticing my interest, Adi said, "That's Bacha."

His young wife was dressed in pink saree and headscarf, a long strand of pearls curved over her breast. She looked straight on, composed and steady, dark eyes unsmiling. In newspaper photographs she'd been an elegant socialite in diamonds. This quietly assured person seemed far more substantial.

The book in her lap meant she was educated. Since few women learned to read, she must have had a wealthy guardian, a progressive man. One slender hand clasped an ornamented fan. A macaw blazed forth, green and orange, on the balustrade behind her. A pair of spectacles lay beside some embroidery. The unfinished sewing struck me as ominous somehow, prescient of an unfinished life.

"I'd like to examine the ladies' rooms," I said, "and speak with the staff."

Nodding, Adi opened a narrow door, and I followed into a dark passage. He turned up the gaslight to reveal an anteroom adjoining a lady's bedchamber. A doorway led to a white-tiled bath where I spied a claw-foot tub.

"Bacha's room has not been disturbed, since the . . ." he said, and withdrew, in his grief.

Shadows cloaked the chamber, a stillness with unexpected weight. Stepping past a four-poster with its canopy of lacy white mosquito nets, I parted thick ivory drapes to admit sunlight. The room waited, so quiet I could hear my own breathing.

Starting with the pristine bed, I examined the chamber. No indentation of a head in the embroidered pillows; nothing secreted below it, nor between mattress and frame. The nightstand held books: Shakespeare, Mark Twain, and *A Strange Disappearance* by Anna Katharine Green. A copy of *Wuthering Heights,* by Ellis Bell, curled at the edges. I picked it up and fanned the pages—no notes or letters.

On a dressing table were brushes, combs and perfumes. A neat little secretary by the window had wooden dockets for paper and pens, a dry inkwell.

When Adi returned, composed, I asked, "Was there correspondence? Letters and such?"

"Yes. It's in the legal boxes. Nothing useful, but you're welcome to them."

I crouched by the little desk, slid out a drawer, found sheets of paper and a metal box. "Did she handle money? To pay servants or grocers?"

"Yes. There should be three, perhaps four hundred rupees."

I shook the glossy metal box, which rattled. On the lid a lady in purple bonnet and parasol smiled at a red-uniformed soldier. The name Mackintosh's Toffee De Luxe was embossed upon it. Opening the lid, I held it toward my client—empty except for a few coins and pins.

Adi said, "Mama or Papa likely took it . . . I don't remember much from that time."

Missing cash caused no concern. Unsure what to make of it, I noted down the absence.

"May I?" I motioned to the dresser.

Adi nodded, lips compressed. His pale face said he rarely, if ever, entered this room. The first drawer revealed a set of boxes whose contents I examined and found to be lady's ornaments.

"All accounted for?" I asked.

He nodded.

The next drawer had small clothes, kerchiefs and the like. I moved them with a pencil, searching for letters or notes. None. The bottom drawer held beaded toys, sewing things and a few stuffed objects such as one might keep from childhood. Mourning the girl who had kept her toys, I closed the drawer quietly.

Seeking evidence of the lady's state of mind, I stepped past an ornate, floor-length mirror to a pair of wooden almirahs; armoires—exquisitely carved.

"Sahib?" A small, saree-clad woman with a deeply wrinkled face stood in the doorway. I took her to be Bacha's maid.

Adi said, "Ah. Jiji-bai, we are looking for something."

The woman opened each almirah, revealing dresses and fabrics on shelves. The scent of powder and lavender wafted into the chamber like a physical presence, as though the lady herself had turned and greeted us.

We saw silks, brocades and all manner of lace. Bacha preferred pastels, delicate patterns and richly embroidered borders. Alas, we discovered no letters or journals such as I imagined young women might secret among their clothing.

How might I ask the maid about her mistress? She'd reveal little to me, a stranger. Catching Adi's eye, I slanted my head toward the woman.

Taking the hint, he asked, "Ayah, did she say anything, that last day?"

As the maid launched into an animated whisper, Adi translated Gujarati vernacular in an undertone. "Bacha-bibi was a darling, a precious child, God's own beauty," said the woman. "She loved the gardens, Sahib. I would bring a flower with her tea. She read the papers while I did her hair. Each morning she asked after your sisters and brothers, 'How are the children today?'"

When she ended, Adi asked, "And Maneck, did she ever speak of meeting him?"

"No, no, Sahib!" the woman cried, "Bacha-bibi was pure, and kind and good."

I looked at Adi, and he nodded. Bacha hadn't known young Maneck Fitter.

I sighed. Perhaps we were going about this wrong. What if the other two men, the Mohammedans, were known to Adi's wife?

"Ayah, what of Saapir Behg? Was he a friend?"

The woman did not appear to know that name.

"Seth Akbar?"

She did not know it either. This puzzled me. These two Khoja men were tried as Maneck's accomplices. Surely, she had heard their names? Was she lying to protect her mistress?

"What about Miss Pilloo? Did she know them?" I asked, watching her reflection in the glass.

"I don't know, Sahib." She looked worried. She vouched for Pilloo, but not vehemently. Strange, since Pilloo was of this family and Bacha the new bride. Why the reticence?

Anyone in this household might have a valuable bit of evidence and not know it. One must ask the right questions. A trivial detail might be the key to this mystery. Although I questioned her a bit further, I gleaned no more.

When she left, we sat across from each other, Adi on the dressing chair, and I on the window seat, absorbed in our thoughts. What had I learned? Some cash was missing and the maid seemed doubtful about Pilloo. I regarded the feminine furnishings. Bacha had dressed here, wearing a yellow saree that fateful day. Her slippers were found on the lawn, not far from her body. Her cloth purse had been left on the gallery. What else would she have had with her?

I cleared my throat and asked, "Your wife, could she see, without her spectacles?"

Adi shook his head. "Not well enough to cross a street."

"Were they found?"

He straightened. "No."

And there it was. A single fact pointing at . . . what? In Bacha's portrait, the artist had placed her delicate eyeglasses in the front corner of the painting. Thinking aloud, I said, "If it was suicide, her eyeglasses must be nearby."

Adi said, "They could have fallen from her, you know. Superintendent McIntyre had the university grounds searched. Didn't find them. He checked every inch of the adjacent roof—the roof over the reading room."

I felt excitement stirring. "If she always wore eyeglasses, and they were not on her body, nor at the site, they were taken. Someone was with the ladies at the end."

Adi stiffened, his chiseled features intent.

I asked, "Could someone have picked up her eyeglasses, not knowing they were sought?"

"I doubt it," he said. "The police made quite a to-do, marking off the area, and so on. Why would anyone take them?"

"To remove evidence of a struggle? If a pair of smashed eyeglasses was found on the gallery, no one could doubt it was murder."

Next, Adi and I searched sixteen-year-old Pilloo's room—a smaller chamber with wide windows and a gas lamp by the door.

Three large chests contained linens and lace, mosquito netting, sewing and so on—an extensive trousseau, assembled by an industrious young person about to venture into domesticity and determined to take a sizeable dowry.

One by one I summoned servants and staff. They arrived, curious about the "Captain Sahib," as they called me. First came Jiji-bai's son and daughter, followed by Gurung, the Nepalese gateman I'd met the first day.

He'd been in a Gurkha regiment and took to me right away, snapping out a salute that made me smile.

They all said Pilloo was a quiet child. A photograph on the desk showed a plain, dark-skinned girl, hair parted in the middle. She peeked out from the frame with puzzled timidity.

Back in Adi's chamber, I examined the gateman's account. The ladies had left the house just after three in the afternoon. How long did it take them to reach the tower? This I resolved to test.

I sifted through another report: A Havildar, a clock tower guard, escorted the ladies up to the gallery and left them there. Why on earth would he not wait with them? Was he not retained for exactly that purpose?

Had he remained, would they have been accosted at all? Some altercation must have occurred, serious enough to dislodge and perhaps break Lady Bacha's glasses. The guard did not know what time he'd taken them up.

But wait, Watson, what are the facts? A tower guard would surely keep close watch on the time. Was he not up and down a great big clock all day?

CHAPTER 6

THE SISTER

Sahib, you are requested." Adi's gap-toothed bearer smiled at my door the following afternoon, shifting from one foot to the other, as I sat in Adi's room, my headquarters.

Brushing off my rumpled trousers, I followed the quick-footed lad down the balcony. It ran along one side of the square mansion, overlooking a garden. Birdcalls wafted up to us like distant music. A rear stairwell brought us down to the morning room, where Burjor, Adi's father, shook hands and introduced a tall, angular man standing by the window.

"Captain, you know Mr. Tehmul Byram, of the *Chronicle*?"

"Of course, sir." I shook hands with the editor, who'd been my employer until recently.

"Tom, please. On loan now, eh?" he said, smiling. "What progress?"

His casual air did not deceive me. Here was a man accustomed to power, an erudite man, smooth and well spoken.

"Some, sir." I did not elaborate. If Adi wanted to share developments he had not instructed me to do so.

"Yes?"

The editor had many resources at his disposal. He could be a useful ally.

"Sir, I plan to speak with Maneck Fitter. Where is he? And the two Khoja men, d'you know? Now that they've been acquitted, they may let slip some information."

"Police never found Akbar. The other blighter may be around." Byram reached a bony hand into his jacket and busied himself with gold-plated pen and notepad.

"Hello!" Adi strode in, greeted the older men and smiled. Dapper in a black legal robe, he seemed lively today, a lithe young man with an easy charm, both serious and engaging.

"Adi," said Byram, "do you really think one chap can get to the bottom of this? I've had my entire staff doing little else." He motioned an apology to me. "Excuse my candor, Captain."

I shrugged to show I took no offense.

Adi smiled. "Beg to differ, Uncle." Utterly dissimilar, Byram and Burjor were not brothers. By calling him Uncle, Adi was treating the older man as a family elder. "In just one week, we've learned something already."

Both men looked surprised. Adi went on to describe Bacha's empty cashbox, our search for her spectacles and what it might mean.

"Young man," Byram said to me, "if you solve this, I'll pay a hundred rupees for your report."

"I think not, sir."

Adi hastened to explain the terms of our agreement, complete privacy from the newspapers, "For the girls' sakes."

Byram expressed his sympathy, then chuckled at me. "Remember, Captain, you're on loan. Six months, you say?"

"Yes, sir," I said in short syllables. Life in the military had trained me well.

That pleased him. "Solve this, Captain, and I'll make it a gift. Now what's this about meeting the three accursed chaps?"

I explained my intention to interview them and compare statements.

"They're safe, those blackguards, because of double jeopardy," said Adi. "Difficult to reopen the case."

Silence pooled around us. What would these men do if I found the evidence they wanted? Did Burjor have it in him to kill? Would Tom Byram delegate the job with a stroke of his pen? And Adi? I recalled his fierce intensity.

These men had known the victims, so I turned to Burjor. "Sir? Your daughter Pilloo, can you tell me about her?"

He motioned us to the settee, went to his desk and filled his pipe, which he tapped and fussed over but did not light.

Sitting, he said. "Pilloo came to us in '82, Captain. The flu epidemic, you see. When my brother and his wife died, we fostered their daughter."

I'd suspected that. Pilloo looked little like the rest of her family. She was an orphan, like me.

"She came from?"

"Lahore." It was his turn to be taciturn.

"She was married?"

He brightened. "Six months after Adi and Bacha wed, Pilloo married a nice boy from Jhansi, a year older."

"She had no objection to her intended?"

"No, indeed! The lad's from a good trading family. Pilloo met the boy. They were well suited."

"Yes, but . . . what was she like?"

I turned from Adi's surprise to Burjor's puzzled look as he said, "She was just . . . Pilloo."

I began to form a picture of the elusive Miss Pilloo. A dark-skinned orphan in a grand house of handsome, fair people. Given in marriage to a lad far away, accumulating a trousseau, and much attached to the beautiful Lady Bacha. Yet no one seemed to know her at all.

What had she been hiding? And Burjor . . . his hesitation was curious. I went over our conversation again. Something was off, but I couldn't quite put my finger on it.

CHAPTER 7

THE LIBRARY

I should have been careful not to draw attention, but at the time it seemed insignificant. After all, a hundred pressmen had waded through the university grounds—why not one more? Making ready to depart for the clock tower, I donned Adi's student robe. The windowpane reflected a square jaw, dark mustache and serious face over an ill-fitting black smock. My shoulders felt cramped.

Bombay newspapers had described every detail of the trial, until Police Superintendent Robert McIntyre furiously hollered in open court that the press was ruining his case. Of course, public attention grew stronger after that. The trial's inconclusive end brought two petitions to the High Court. Neither reopened the case. The public was morbidly fascinated, the Parsees still up in arms. Perhaps I should have known, even then, that it wasn't over.

Adi eyed me. "Captain, what do you need?" he asked, a common refrain in the weeks that followed.

Since the trial, no one else had been charged. So, I surmised, the murderer must feel pretty safe at present. That could change, once I started asking questions. Things could get sticky.

"A revolver? And I need to go to Matheran—the hill station. Mr. Byram discovered that Maneck lives there. Apparently something of a recluse."

"Can't say I blame him," said Adi. "Acquitted by the law, but not the public."

Adi's legal mind often overrode his emotion, a curious aspect that I'd come to admire. At such times he appeared more solicitor than bereaved husband, but after reading his notes and scribbles, I knew better. I said, "We need to know what time the ladies reached the tower. How long does it take to get there?"

"Papa had taken the carriage that day. The girls would have got a victoria cab at Hanging Gardens."

Tracing their path, I found a line of carriages as Adi had predicted, and in forty minutes reached the university, a wide expanse of green in the heart of Bombay. Bounded on all sides by thoroughfares filled with carriages and tongas, its stone buildings curved around a well-tended lawn. Proximity to the High Court lent a distinctive air. Men in black jackets and robes strode in animated conversation past clusters of students.

The clock tower dominated the landscape. As I came up the path, a mound of flowers, piled high with wilted bouquets, caught my attention. It lay at an odd angle in the lawn, about ten feet from the tower. A second pile, similarly stacked, showed behind it. So this was where Adi's wife and sister died. I looked up and gauged the awful height.

Violent death is not always quick. It's rarely quiet. It's an ugly moment, the reduction of a person who speaks and thinks to a twisted, crumpled thing on the ground. And there's blood. More blood than one imagines can be contained in a single human frame. It colors the ground long after the body is removed. Someone had covered the stains with flowers as though soft petals could somehow ease the shock of that fall.

The tower loomed, silent, unmoved. An ornate gothic structure with carved buttresses on each corner, it was attached to the library and public reading room. I stepped under the tower into its vaulted vestibule with archways on three sides. It was perceptibly cooler in the shade under its high stone ceiling.

Ahead were two separate entrances: one angling to the right, leading up to the tower. Directly ahead was the library reading room. This I entered first. Stained glass windows curved along one side, their pointed arches giving the room an otherworldly feel. Bookshelves stood like sentries, while long tables straddled the wide floor. A third of the wooden chairs were occupied.

"I'm looking for Mr. Apte," I said at the counter, and was directed to an elderly librarian.

He saw me and stiffened. I had that effect on people. "Army" came through, regardless of my garb. If sleuthing was to be my new vocation, I thought, anonymity might serve it better.

"I am Apte," he said, pronouncing it "Up-teh." A saffron scarf drooped from his neck, over knee-length kurta shirt and baggy trousers. Untidy white hair curled around his head, forming a clumsy halo.

I introduced myself, mentioned the women who died last October and asked, "Were you here that day?"

Removing his wire frames, he nodded. "Sahib, I was at this very desk when it happened."

"Tell me what you saw."

He rubbed his chin. "I saw . . . no, first I heard a sound, an awful thump." He touched things on his table without looking at them. Yes, I thought, there's the sound of it, a sound no one would forget, a hundred soft pounds hitting ground.

He went on, "Along with others, I hurried outside, and what a sight. The poor lady lay just outside the foyer—you saw the flowers?"

I reached for my notebook. "What time was it?"

"The clock was striking four o'clock."

I looked toward the tower vestibule. "How long did it take to reach her?"

He gestured at the distance, a mere fifty feet. "A few seconds?"

"And then?"

He grimaced. "I saw her, lying on her side, twisted. . . ."

"Anyone near her?"

"No, Sahib. I was the first to arrive, I knelt, saw that she was dead. People crowded around."

"How did you know she was dead?"

Apte winced. "There was blood, Sahib. I closed her eyes. I knew young Mrs. Framji. She liked Shakespeare, Byron, Virgil. Classics, mostly."

He'd closed Bacha's eyes. I asked, "Was she wearing spectacles?"

"Spectacles?" he asked, surprised. "No, Sahib."

"What happened next?"

"Soon after that, two or three minutes, Sahib, the second girl fell to the ground. Twenty feet away! A horrible sound. People cried out and clustered around. I went to her. She was alive for a few seconds."

All this was consistent. "Did anyone see them fall?"

"Yes, Sahib. Francis Enty, a clerk who comes often to the university."

Francis Enty, the prosecution's key witness. I resolved to question him soon. Next, I cast about for some way to place Maneck and his accomplices at the scene.

"After the second woman dropped, did you go up the tower?"

"Yes, Sahib, a few minutes later." His head wobbled from side to side.

"Were you the first to go up?"

"We waited until the police arrived, then a few of us went up together. The bank clerk Enty, two police constables and I."

"What did you find?"

"Nothing, Sahib! There was no one."

I frowned. Didn't Adi say Bacha's purse had been found there?

"Nothing? No objects at all?"

"Oh yes. There was a cloth purse. And a shoe. Just one."

One shoe. That suggested foul play. The other had been found near Bacha's foot. "The gallery is not the top, is it? Did anyone go all the way up?"

Apte nodded. "The bell-room, yes, but it is always locked. The police went up."

I'd read their report—nothing out of place. "What did you do next?"

"Sahib, I came back, na? I was terribly upset. People still crowded outside."

Now wait. If the rogues threw the ladies from the gallery, they could not remain there, since a host of witnesses traipsed upstairs. Where would they go? The reading hall had emptied after the first fall. Had the miscreants joined the crowd from the direction of the tower? Surely someone must have seen them come down?

"You returned to the library? What did you find?"

Eyes narrowed, Apte cleaned his glasses. "Two men were seated here, a gentleman and his servant." He gestured to a table by the window. "They asked me what the shouting was about."

Indeed! A hullaballoo outside, and they remained indoors?

"What time was this?"

"Almost five o'clock, Sahib."

"What did they look like?"

He couldn't remember.

"Western clothes, or Indian?"

"Sahib, Indian, I think, I cannot be certain."

Apte said he remembered nothing more. I probed further, to no avail. Thanking him, I turned toward the foyer, planning to climb to the gallery, the scene of the crime. Whatever drove the ladies to death, that's where it transpired.

CHAPTER 8

THE TOWER

The librarian accompanied me out to the vestibule, where the tower rose above us on carved pillars that met in high stone arches. I said farewell, but Apte was not done with me. White hair ruffled by an unruly breeze, he asked, "Where did you say you work, friend?"

"Brown and—"

"Batliwala," he supplied happily. Satisfied with these credentials, he motioned me to a stone step nearby. As we sat, a deep bell sounded, followed by a short melody and two urgent notes. They rang close above us, calling out, exhorting me somehow.

Glancing upward, the librarian asked, "Do you know why it is called Rajabai tower?"

"No."

"It was donated by Premchand Roychand, whose mother, Rajabai, was blind. He built it so she would know the time. It rings every quarter hour." Apte hesitated. "Sahib, there is something else. I did not know whom to tell. I remembered this after the trial, but it was too late, na? The young Mrs. Framji—such a pretty lady. She came here often." To my astonishment, he mentioned an argument between Lady Bacha and an unknown man.

"An argument? Can you describe it?"

The old man scratched his head. "She sat across from a man, upset. Her voice was sharp. It drew my attention, you see. Others also noticed. She was such a kind, soft-spoken miss. The man was holding her wrist. When I went toward them, he left."

Holding her wrist? Had she tried to strike him? "When did this happen?"

The librarian's face wrinkled with effort. "It was in the weeks before the lady's death."

"What did he look like?" This was the closest I'd got to what might be behind these strange doings.

"He wore a green coat. It's all I remember."

Green, a color sufficiently unusual to have remained in his memory. "Had you seen him before?"

"I think he was one of the two men left in the library that day, when the women died. I cannot be sure, I was shaken . . . And another thing . . ." Apte's shoulders hunched against a breeze that picked up leaves and swirled them about like unhappy ghosts. "Something was left in the hall that day."

"The day of the argument?"

"No, Sahib, the day the women died."

"What?" I asked eagerly.

"Two pieces of black clothing," he said, "I gave them to the ragpicker next day. It was nothing, na? Just old clothes left under a reading table."

"Men's clothing?"

"I did not check. The cloth was ragged and torn."

"Where is this ragpicker? Could you find him?"

Alas, Apte had given the clothing to a roving fellow and could not say where he might be. So, no tangible evidence. Suppressing disappointment, I thanked him. The argument he'd witnessed was promising. Who was Mister Green Coat? I did not know what to make of the abandoned clothing or whether it was connected to the ladies. He waved away my thanks, huffed to his feet and took his leave.

Spotting the scrawny Havildar on a stool in drab, lumpy clothes, I pointed at the stairway, a curved set of cast-iron steps leading up into darkness, saying, "Havildar, is the gallery locked?"

He gawked, tripped over his feet and dropped his keys. Recovering, he hurried to lead me upward. I made a few remarks as we climbed, but all he said was, "Hah!" Since "hah" means yes in most local languages, it did not immediately strike me as odd.

"When did they arrive, the ladies?"

"Hah."

"Did you take them up?"

"Hah."

"Why didn't you stay with them?"

"Hah."

Puzzled, I followed him up the narrow coiled stairway, smelling the musty odor of rat droppings. Dissatisfied with our scintillating conversation, I decided to question him on the gallery.

Through two narrow windows, shafts of light broke the darkness and slanted down to us. Footsteps clanging, we passed a doorway open to the first-floor balcony where the altercation with Maneck had been reported. Finally, the latch creaked, the door swung open and we stepped into a sunlit gallery. As the guard began to go, I grabbed his arm, intending to pepper him with questions.

The change in the fellow was awful. He cowered and wailed, and I could make no sense of it.

"All right, all right." I released the poor fool, who quaked in his baggy clothes but made no move to leave. I tried again in Hindustani. "How often did the women come here?"

Terrified, he seemed unable to speak. Did he think I was a policeman? "Hah, hah." His head wobbled, hands joined in supplication. Did he not understand? Perhaps Adi could translate for me.

I need a Watson after all, I thought, letting the frightened fellow stumble off. My pity gave way to frustration. Here was an ideal witness, situated exactly at the time and place of the crime, but he was a bumbling idiot.

On the gallery, a warm breeze engulfed me. It was here that it happened—the ladies had stood on this very gallery against the waist-high parapet.

Resolved to explore the space with Holmes-like thoroughness, I examined the entrance carefully. The door latched from inside the tower. An iron bolt in the doorframe squeaked when I worked it. I ran my fingers down the wood, feeling sharp edges. Holmes would have found a dozen clues. I found only a few dark colored threads snagged low in the doorframe. Folding these into a sheet of paper, I stowed it in my pocket.

The top of the parapet wall was rounded, rather than flat, to dissuade visitors from sitting on it, I supposed. How could petite Lady Bacha have surmounted it? If she'd jumped, she'd have had to propel herself over this wall. In a saree?

I scoured the stone floor for an hour, earning a sunburn and a crick in my back. Where the parapet met the uneven floor, something caught my eye—a single white bead, so small I had to pry it out with the tip of my knife. This minute object also I stowed away.

Next, I looked down in all four directions. The flower memorials were on one side. I pored over the stones in that wall, but they revealed no secrets.

Beneath sky and clouds, the city spread below me in a motley carpet of industry. To the right, Malabar Hill swelled in a green wave that contained Framji Mansion. On the other side, dockyard cranes rose like ugly storks over ships awaiting cargo. Two hundred feet below, students wandered across the university lawn. A quiet scene.

As I stood there, anyone on the grounds or adjacent roads could certainly see me. Here, at the gallery's edge, the girls' plight could have been seen, but standing by the inner wall, I could neither see the ground nor hear sounds below. Nor could anyone down there see me. Could I be heard? I put it to the test.

"Hiy! Hiya!" I cried from near the door. I peered over the parapet, but no one looked up.

"Hiya!" I repeated, now at the parapet. A few surprised faces turned. The tower was not as isolated as I'd imagined. If Lady Bacha or Miss Pilloo had screamed, they would have been heard. Yet the librarian heard nothing.

So why didn't the ladies cry out?

I sighed. What had I learned? Black threads caught in the door? No telling when they'd snagged, since the tower had opened to the public. That tiny white bead might have dropped from anything: a child's toy or ornament.

Memory touched my skin with a cold finger. Wait—had I not recently seen something like this? Where? The sound of my breath filled
the gloom as I stopped on the iron stairs. I waited, searching my memory.
And found nothing. I wound back down the stairs with growing frustration. This was no game. Was I really equal to this task?

CHAPTER 9

A NEW ADDITION

Returning that evening from the clock tower, I came up Malabar Hill through Hanging Gardens. The rear lane to Adi's home had moss-covered walls and overhanging creepers. It offered a secluded stretch, conducive to contemplation.

I'd found two pieces of evidence at the crime scene, a tiny white bead and a few black threads, but could not tie these to the ladies' deaths. Holmes always wanted to be first at the scene. I was months behind. After the tragedy the librarian saw two men in the library, a gentleman and his servant, both nameless. Some black clothing found under a table, discarded. It was not much to go on. I kept wondering—why hadn't the women called for help? It was imperative that I question the law clerk Francis Enty, who'd seen the women fall, and find out who was with them at the time.

Framji Mansion bustled as I passed the kitchen, the cooks all astir. Jiji-bai's daughter hurried past with a platter.

"Salaam, Sahib," she said, looking harried. Did the Framjis have dinner guests?

"Cheerio," I replied, and took the rear stairway to Adi's rooms, where I planned to stash my evidence, then go down and present myself before returning to my rental room on Forgett Street.

As I strode into my client's chamber, a young lady turned from the window, a silhouette against the light. Sunbeams caught the hair that was swept up and piled atop her head. The glow outlined a figure I knew from the portrait of Adi's late wife.

"Oh!" said Lady Bacha, a white-gloved hand to her lips. She wore a blue satin evening dress. A diamond flashed in her earring.

Wait—Lady Bacha was dead. Was I dreaming? My breath locked and the room darkened.

"Captain Jim!" Adi said behind me. "Here, man!" He guided me to a seat. Moments later, he pressed a brandy into my hand.

"Meet Diana," he said, turning up the gaslight. "She arrived this afternoon on the *Ocean Queen* from Liverpool."

I hardly heard anything after his first two words. So, this was his sister, Diana.

"Ah! That's better," he said. Resplendent in black dinner jacket, white waistcoat and tie, he smiled, which I took to indicate that I no longer resembled a dead fish.

I made a weak noise and drank. Fortified, I looked up and found her gaze upon me, surprised and curious.

"When did you last eat, Captain?" asked Adi.

I rubbed my forehead. "Breakfast, sir. I'm all right."

He looked at Diana and a glance passed between them, a language reserved for siblings, mysterious to those like me, who had none. I watched them talk in quick snatches, completing one another's sentences, animated in each other's company. Sitting across from me, Diana's skin glowed against a dark blue neckline. Slender hands rested against an impossibly narrow waist. Her face moved and flowed with her thoughts, appealing in its symmetry and charm. When she caught my glance, her gaze was as direct as Adi's.

Courtesy demanded I make some remark. Try as I might, I found nothing to say.

Adi went to the door and tugged the bell-pull.

"Captain, who did you think I was?" she asked in a soft tone.

Perhaps I flushed. Glancing at Lady Bacha's portrait, I shook my head.

Diana's eyes widened with understanding. "Ah." She smiled, the singular sweetness of her look holding me immobile. Turning to Adi, she said something about dinner.

I heard his voice at a distance, and her quick reply. She did not remark on my foolish mistake. Why? It was no secret. Yet the courtesy of her gesture, the grace of it, was not lost on me. I drew a breath and focused on their conversation.

Both young people sounded very refined. I'd grown up in the army, surrounded by British officers. My commander, Colonel Sutton, had taken a particular interest in me, often sending away for books. Yet I was at a disadvantage under the rapid-fire banter of these two.

After another quiet word with his sister, Adi asked, "Will you stay for dinner?"

"I think not, sir." I grimaced at my trousers, my attire barely adequate for the morning room. But Adi would not have it. He sent a bearer to make arrangements.

While we waited, he told Diana of our investigation, listing my activities and our deduction about the missing spectacles. So Diana was to be part of our inner circle. She listened intently, interjecting questions that revealed a quick intellect. The siblings seemed alike in more than appearance and mannerisms. When she replied to his remarks in fluent Gujarati, I began to see her addition as a tactical advantage.

Adi's manservant brought several garments. As he shepherded me into the anteroom to dress, I wondered whose they were. To my surprise, he followed, gesturing at me to try them on. I complied, somewhat amused, to find that the trousers were either too short or too wide. The fellow clucked and took measurements.

"Very good, Sahib, I will alter," he said in a thick native accent. He laid a white silk shirt and a black coat aside, and bore the trousers away.

When, once dressed, I returned to the siblings and expressed my thanks, Adi waved it away. Diana too seemed to think nothing of it. The Framjis' casual approach to these niceties puzzled me. I had a sense of being managed so deftly that I scarcely noticed it.

Dinner was a formal affair during which I said little, nor needed to, since Adi and Diana held a lively conversation. Burjor's satisfaction in the accomplishments of his oldest daughter was evident. This evening he headed the family table in a grand blue-black tunic and turban-like hat. Adi's mother, a fragile woman in white saree, sat at the other end.

Around her clustered a boy, about ten, wearing a red jacket fashioned like an army uniform, and two curly-haired little girls.

Adi's mother shared his pointed features, the same directness. Lines of grief scored her sallow cheeks. I was presented to her simply as "Captain Jim, a friend of Adi's."

"Welcome, Captain," she said, narrow face revealing little. A silver chain around her neck bore a cameo of two now-familiar faces, Lady Bacha and Miss Pilloo.

After dinner the young children were sent to bed, despite their pleas. The adults moved to a formal parlor, a posh room wallpapered in blue, with white molding. A grand piano dominated one side, by glass-fronted cabinets. Diana and her mother sat close together.

Burjor, in an expansive mood, poured sherry into sparkling crystal globes and handed me one. He clapped his son on the back, smiling.

The scene brought an odd pain to my throat. This I would never have, a sire to thump my shoulder and claim me. With Adi and his father to one side, the ladies on the other, I stiffened. I had no place amid this domestic elegance. I would take my leave.

"Why are you doing this, Adi?" His mother's sharp voice sliced through the banter.

"Oh, Mama!" Diana winced. "We decided to tell you because, well, you should know what's going on. Adi has a right to know the truth."

"Will it change anything?" Her mother's color rose with the tide of her voice. "It's over! For God's sake, Adi. Let her go!"

My client stood still, hands at his side, stoic, like a bust of young Lord Nelson.

"Mother," he sighed, then turned to me, emotions in check. "What do we know, Captain?"

Reminded of my role, I marshaled my evidence.

"It's unlikely to be suicide, sir," I began carefully, "in part because the ladies did not, ah, drop at the same time. Had they planned to jump, for whatever reason, they would have faced it together."

I spoke about how the eyeglasses, always on Lady Bacha's person and now conspicuously missing, led me to believe someone wanted to conceal an altercation.

"So it was murder?" Mrs. Framji's voice trembled. "Someone killed my children?"

A series of facts fell into place all at once. I said, as gently as I could, "It was likely two men, although a third may have held the door."

Adi stared. I'd not had time to apprise him of this.

"Go on, Captain," he said.

"The viewing gallery surrounds the tower. I noticed this morning that one . . . assailant could not confine two active young ladies, as they would simply retreat around the gallery and escape. So there must be more than one."

"Two?" Diana asked. "Or more than two?"

I considered. "Had there been three or more, they should have been noticed going up the tower. Three could certainly have, ah, restrained the ladies, and they were not restrained. So two, then."

"Oh, child!" Mrs. Framji's face creased, her head dropped into her hands. Her voice rose, riddled with sobs. "I forbade them to go about alone! Every day I read in the papers . . . young women go missing. They didn't listen. Oh, my Pilloo, my Bacha."

At her lament, Burjor winced. "Let's see what the captain discovers. Now come, dear, it's late." He helped his wife to her feet.

We stood, Diana staring after her parents, affection and sorrow in the tilt of her head.

After a moment, Adi said, "All right. What's next?"

I pulled out my notebook.

"Miss," I said to Diana. "Did you know Maneck, the Parsee who stood trial? Had you ever met him?"

"Oh," she said, settling back on the settee. "We've known him, Pilloo and me, for ages."

Adi looked as astonished as I felt.

"Please explain."

Taking a breath, Diana began, "Captain, we had a carefree childhood.

Grand trips in the carriage, across the new causeway, or down the sea face. You remember, Adi? How I loved going to the races! That's where Pilloo and I met Maneck."

I said, "Tell me about him."

Diana extracted a slim silver case from her pocket and toyed with it, saying, "Maneck's uncle owns orchards near Bombay. He sells to hotels and establishments through a number of agents. Maneck is one of them."

"Where does he live?" I knew Maneck had removed himself to Matheran, a hill station where soldiers often recuperated, but hoped to discover more clues at his residence in Bombay.

"He boarded at a guesthouse on Ripley Street. I think it's run by a Christian widow."

"Did you and Pilloo ever call on him there?"

"Oh no. We'd never do that. He's a bachelor. But my dressmaker's on the same street. We often met Maneck in passing."

While I took that down, Adi asked, "What next, Captain Jim?"

I considered my list. Questions multiplied on each page, but I had few leads.

"Sir, I asked Apte whether he heard anyone call for help, before either Lady Bacha or Miss Pilloo fell. He heard nothing. Now he was indoors when Lady Bacha fell. I'm going to meet Enty next, so I'll ask him too—did he hear either one cry out?"

Adi said, "Right after Bacha . . . died, the clock struck four. Pilloo fell soon after."

"Righto!" I said, "And in the commotion, it would be difficult to hear Miss Pilloo. But Lady Bacha?"

Adi shook his head, palms wide.

"So only Enty was outside when Bacha fell," Diana said. Then her eyes gleamed. "You said Lady Bacha? When did she become a peeress?"

Seeing Adi's shoulders relax at her gentle teasing, I smiled.

CHAPTER 10

THE KEY WITNESS

Next evening, I visited Francis Enty, the bank clerk upon whose testimony the trial had centered. An unremarkable, middle-aged man with sparse, oily hair parted in the center, Enty had a guarded manner as he invited me into a small parlor. His dwelling was furnished simply. Old pieces covered with floral fabric denoted a small but well-managed budget. A chipped ceramic frame held a picture of two small boys and their mother. Two boys, about six years old, scampered off upon his command.

After introducing myself—Brown and Batliwala, investigating the Framji case, etc.—I asked whether his life had been much changed by the trial.

"Not really," he said. "My daily routine is unchanged. Copy files, prepare letters and so on."

Enty seemed content with humble clerical duties. Noting my close attention, his gaze narrowed. "Who sent you, did you say?"

Enty was sharp. I saw at once why Superintendent McIntyre found him such a credible witness. "Brown and Batliwala. I'm retained to make some inquiries," I repeated.

Before he could protest, I launched upon my questions, leading him through his statement as recorded by Superintendent McIntyre. The entire case against Maneck rested on his account. A key witness indeed!

"Mr. Enty, what did you see on the twenty-fifth of October?"

Looking unhappy, he leaned into an old wingback chair. "I was outside the library, walking toward the clock tower entrance, you know it? I heard an argument—raised voices. I saw three men at the first-floor balcony—it opens to the reading room. I was just below, see?"

I wrote quickly. If true, here at last was a timetable of that day.

"Did you hear what was said?"

He shifted. "No . . . I don't recall specific words now."

I watched him closely. "What time was that?"

"Shortly after three fifteen."

That was interesting. The ladies could not have reached the tower before three forty.

"You're sure of that?"

"The clock had just struck the quarter hour."

"Could you see their faces?"

He nodded.

"Who was it?"

"Maneck Fitter—arguing with two Khojas—Mohammedans. I did not know them. I'd seen Mr. Maneck in the library. We had spoken in passing. Morning, the weather, that sort of thing."

"The two men—how did you know they were Khojas?"

"Their clothing. Long kurta-khamiz in the Indian style. Their turbans."

"Could you identify them?"

"No. Both were taller than Mr. Maneck."

"Did you see them at the trial?"

His face closed. "No."

He seemed irritable now, so I changed direction. "During the . . . argument you witnessed from the ground, did you see the ladies at all?"

"No indeed. But I saw Mr. Maneck clearly. One man caught his collar, shook him."

Police had recorded Maneck's appearance as disheveled, noting his torn coat. I considered Enty's stiff demeanor. While his testimony was consistent, it made Maneck the liar, since Maneck claimed not to know the other two at all.

"What happened next?"

"At a few minutes before four I left the library. When the first woman dropped, I was right there, thirty feet down the path." He grimaced, shaking his head.

This was the closest I would get to an eyewitness account of the women's deaths. Had he left the scene or remained? "Did you summon the police?"

"No. I don't know who called them."

My next questions would either confirm the path I was following or set me on a different one altogether. "Did you hear anything before she fell?"

He shook his head. "I did not."

"No cries, no call for help?"

"None."

"And after she, ah, dropped, Miss Pilloo was still on the gallery. Did you hear anything?"

"When she fell, sir, people cried out, all around. I was shocked. I went to the poor lady. People crowded. What confusion. Calling out questions, exclaiming."

I watched him closely. "What did you do?"

"I went to her. She lay on her side. Apte, from the library, got there before me. We knelt on either side." He winced. "Blood seeped . . . around her head."

I absorbed that. "Did you see Miss Pilloo fall?"

"Indeed I did not! I was trying to find a pulse on the first woman's wrist." He shuddered, and mopped his brow with his scarf. "It was awful, that sound, right behind me. So close."

Miss Pilloo fell twenty feet further from the tower, I recollected. It would feel very near. So perhaps the women had not fallen from the same point on the gallery.

"What were they wearing?" The police reports mentioned torn apparel—just how disarrayed was it? Surely a drop through the air could not shred clothing as the defense argued?

"The first woman, Bacha Framji, wore a yellow saree and blouse. It came unraveled, but she was fully clothed. The second girl wore loose trousers, torn at the knee. The jacket was buttoned. Ripped . . . at the shoulder."

Trousers on women? That was unusual, very modern. Perhaps Miss Pilloo fought longer, which was reflected in greater disarray.

"Did you look up? After Miss Pilloo fell?"

"No, sir. She was alive. I saw her eyelids move . . ." He grimaced.

"Did she speak?"

"No."

"Could you read her lips?"

His eyebrows rose. No one had asked that before.

"No, sir. Her lips did not move. She trembled . . . convulsed." His lips tightened with emotion.

I asked him about his subsequent movements, whom he'd seen and spoken to. He insisted he could not identify the Khoja men, but named Maneck without hesitation. This testimony could have sent Maneck to the gallows. Had someone bribed or compelled it?

Closing my notebook, I said, "Thank you, Mr. Enty. A last question. Do you visit the races?"

"No sir! Gambling is a sin."

It was a long shot, and went wide. If his testimony was contrived, I saw no evidence of it.

"I've kept you long enough from your family. May I thank Mrs. Enty for her indulgence?"

"My wife is not at home." Looking put out, he stood up. "If there's nothing else?"

Not home, so late in the evening? How odd. Perhaps he meant she was "not at home" to me.

"Is Mrs. Enty unwell?" I asked, still seated.

Startled, he said, "Unwell? No. She's visiting her sister in Poona."

"Papa?" a child's voice called from an inner room.

When Enty excused himself, I rose to retrieve my hat. A ball of crumpled paper lay by a stack of unopened letters. Without much thought, I picked it up.

Hearing Enty return, I dropped the scrap into a pocket, shook his hand and departed. While his testimony had damned Maneck for a liar, it also placed Maneck in opposition to two men, possibly in defense of the ladies. No wonder the Parsee community was divided on Maneck's account, some vehemently against him, while others saw him as a hero.

Returning to my dismal rental on Forgett Street, I mulled over the interview. Enty had not mentioned the four o'clock bells. Understandable, in the turmoil. He'd witnessed an argument where Maneck's coat was torn. What was that about? Maneck was a suspect because of his unkempt appearance and "gasping breath." An altercation explained his torn clothing, but what about the rest? Gasping meant exertion, surely? Or was it distress? After all, he'd known the Framji girls.

The librarian said that after police arrived, he accompanied Enty and two constables to the gallery. Enty concurred. He seemed genuine, but something nagged at me, like a shape seen from the corner of one's eye that is not there when you look again. He'd seemed hurried toward the end of my interview, wanting me gone. Why?

A kerosene lamp cast a dull glow over my run-down lodgings in a disused warehouse. The bakery was closed, but the air still held the soft scent of bread, reminding me that I had not eaten. Last night's dinner came to mind, and with it, Diana—that first glimpse of her against the sunset. When I'd taken her for a ghost, she'd been surprisingly kind.

I stowed my notebook to roll out my pallet-bed, feeling morose. The fine clothes I'd worn last night lay on a chair, crisp white cuffs and satin tie draped over the impeccably cut dinner jacket, utterly out of place in my dusty warehouse. Borrowed finery, just a disguise. No matter, I was hired for a task, and that I would complete.

As I stripped for the night, my thoughts twisted in ever-narrower circles. Who were the two Khoja men, Behg and Akbar? Neither Enty nor the librarian Apte had identified them. So who had? Enty's testimony placed two unknown Khojas in Maneck's company. Why did Maneck deny it? Surely he must know it destroyed his credibility? It was time I questioned him.

CHAPTER 11

LET ME HELP

Next morning, Diana said, "Captain, let me help with the investigation."

Arriving early, I'd been directed to the dining room, where she invited me to partake. Adi and his father had not yet come to breakfast. Surprised at her urgency, I set aside the pretty dish of gooseberry jam.

Sitting very straight, she said, "Adi said you're interviewing witnesses. I can help. I speak both Hindustani and Gujarati."

I did not speak Gujarati, since I'd spent most of my life in the north with Punjabi and Pashto. The Sepoys and Sowars in my regiment spoke in Urdu and its close cousin, Hindustani. That tower guard, I remembered, had been no use at all, since I could not converse with him.

Intrigued, I asked, "Miss Diana, why do you want to do this?"

"I'd like to help," she said, attempting nonchalance. Then she softened. "I think about Bacha and Pilloo constantly. I could, well, be of some use to Adi."

I realized that Diana also felt haunted by the tragedy. Small wonder. Yet it was no occupation for a pretty young thing.

"You'd find it very dull, Miss."

"You need an assistant, don't you? Holmes had Watson, after all."

So Adi had shared with her my interest in Conan Doyle. I sent her a lopsided smile, entertained by her ready wit. "Doctor Watson was a crack shot, wasn't he?"

"You think I'm not?"

That surprised me. Since when were young ladies taught to shoot?

"Miss Diana, you've used a revolver?"

"Yes. And you? Are you quite the marksman?" She held my gaze, a hint of color in her cheeks. "In *Study in Scarlet*, Watson made a list of Holmes's areas of knowledge, and lack thereof. I warn you, I shall do the same!" Diana's laugh was water tumbling over river stones.

I grinned at her conversational bull's-eye. "I'm a terrible shot."

Cavalry is trained to draw sabres and charge. But that tactic was rarely used. More often we were sent off on a fast horse with a message. Mounted infantry, we were called, meant to travel quickly, dismount and fire. But I'd broken some fingers boxing—my hand shook, taking aim, making me a poor shot.

"Oh!" Her eyes were brown velvet.

Taken with her game, I continued against my better judgement. "I've done some boxing, however. Not too shabby on a horse."

Diana chuckled. "Of course, you were with the Dragoons. That's a cavalry regiment. Knowledge of geography?"

"Fair." Colonel Sutton had insisted upon a working knowledge of north Indian terrain, the rivers and foothills of the Himalayas and northern tribes. I thrust away a momentary flash of memory. Dust and smoke, bodies on the ground. Karachi.

Diana stopped buttering toast, her gaze sharp with concern.

When I raised my cup to my lips, she continued. "Know your history?"

"I'm keen on military history, but don't ask about kings of England," I quipped, then sobered. Clear-eyed and pristine, she could have no part of this. "Miss Diana, this may turn rather awful. Sure you want to join the hunt?"

She picked up a napkin and dabbed with a delicate motion. "Quite. So I'm hired?"

I found my mind sharpened by the thrust and parry of our conversation. No one could find Diana just a pretty face. While wide eyes and rosy lips distracted me, the keenness of her mind struck me as a useful asset. Yet detective work must be done firsthand.

"I think not, Miss."

She made a moue with that perfect mouth, a look that told me I'd hear about this again.

To work. I polished off the jam and toast and tossed down my coffee. Hearing that Adi had left early for class, we went to his chamber, my headquarters.

"What were they like, Miss Pilloo and Lady Bacha?" I asked.

"I didn't really know Bacha," said Diana. "I've been in England almost four years."

"You didn't attend their nuptials?"

"No. My aunt in London was unwell. I stayed to tend her, and missed Pilloo's wedding as well. But she wouldn't be sent to her in-laws for a while, so I thought I'd see her before she left."

Instead, Pilloo died before Diana's return.

"Pilloo was tall, bony, really. We told each other everything. It hardly mattered she was a cousin. I wanted a sister, and so did she," Diana said. "But while I was in England, she changed. I could tell from her letters. I didn't know her anymore—certainly not what troubled her." Lips tight, she crumpled a kerchief in her hand.

Surely there was more? Her glance skittered away from mine. I'd need to earn her trust before she came out with it.

"Miss, if you think of something, you will say?"

She nodded with a troubled look.

From Adi's box, I extracted the envelope containing my meager evidence.

"At the clock tower, I found this snagged in the gallery door." I handed her the envelope containing a curl of dark threads.

She took it, frowned and delicately picked up the threads. "Cotton or linen. Too thick to be muslin," she said, rubbing the fragment between her fingers.

"It was caught in the splinters, about a foot from the floor. And the librarian found some clothing under a table the next day. Black clothes, torn. Threw them away, alas."

Diana's dark eyes widened. "You think this came from those garments. Men's clothes?"

I opened my notebook to the relevant page. "Apte didn't know. When he returned to the reading hall, he saw two men reading newspapers. They asked about the ruckus."

"Captain, that's odd. They heard the noise, but didn't go out?"

I'd thought that strange as well. Those two had behaved so oddly that the librarian remembered them months later. "They gave him the impression they'd been there all along."

"The reading room is adjacent to the clock tower." I picked up a pencil and flipped over a sheet of paper. With a few deft strokes I drew a square to represent the tower's vestibule. Across one corner I wrote *Tower*, then *Reading Room* along the side.

I tapped the diagram. "They're connected by a balcony one floor above. The men could have hidden in the reading room until the crowd dispersed."

Diana frowned. "Why would they stay? Surely they'd escape in the confusion?"

"Perhaps they wanted to be rid of that clothing. The police arrived quickly, it seems."

"So they were lawyers?" Diana asked, shocked. "Wearing black robes?"

"Perhaps. Apte did not say what these clothes were. Miss, take a look at this." I handed her the paper with the mysterious white bead.

"Oh!" She raised the tiny object to the light. "Could be beading from a dress, but this is tiny. The work would be very fine. Where . . . ?"

"Found it on the gallery."

Diana drew a breath. "Oh my. From Bacha or Pilloo's clothes?"

I consulted my notes. "Miss Pilloo wore a white blouse and dark, loose trousers. Lady Bacha wore a yellow saree and blouse. Was either one beaded?"

Diana caught a lip between her teeth, thinking. "Don't think so. Their clothes and things were returned to Adi."

"Ah." I had not known that. Diana's assistance was already proving useful.

I flipped to my list of witnesses. "A few interviews remain: a group of children who saw the ladies arrive. I've already met the Havildar but got nothing from him. Poor chap was quite terrified. Not sure he spoke either English or Hindustani."

"Captain, would you like me to try? He might speak Gujarati."

"If your father approves. And I've yet to meet Maneck, the chap accused of the murder."

"Oh, Captain, of course Maneck's innocent. He's a lamb," Diana said. "How could anyone think him capable of murder? Silliest thing I've ever heard!"

She seemed very sure.

"Miss, the verdict was inconclusive. Insufficient evidence, no?"

She waved that away. Shaking her head, Diana went to the window. Framed against a white balustrade and deep green boughs, she made a charming picture. "Maneck didn't defend himself. Didn't say a word. Why?"

"Good question. We mustn't theorize before we have all the evidence—biases the judgement, said Holmes."

Diana marveled, "Why, you've memorized every word."

I grinned, binding up a sheaf of reports to take along. "Some of it. Wasn't much else to read in hospital."

She bent toward me. "Oh? How long were you there?"

"Months," I replied, sorting folders. "Ran out of reading material, and I enjoyed Conan Doyle's book, so I read it several times. Devoured newspapers too, of course."

I felt her stillness and looked up. Dappled sunlight touched Diana's head, atilt as she listened. "Captain," she began, then bit her lip, as though uncertain.

"Miss, is there something else? That might have a bearing on this case?"

She pulled back, wary. "I don't think so."

"Righto, Miss, let's speak tomorrow."

Her dark eyes pensive, she watched me go.

CHAPTER 12

WHO WAS BACHA?

Late the next morning I found Adi in his room, dapper in white shirt and crisp black legal jacket. Last night's deliberations had suggested another motive for Lady Bacha's visit to the clock tower. Had she and Pilloo planned to meet a lover? Was Adi aware of any such dalliance? How could I broach this?

His eyes gleamed as I entered. "Captain Jim! You've been busy! Diana showed me the clues you found at the tower."

"Morning," Diana said, pouring tea into fragile blue and white china. She seemed glum. I suspected that the siblings had just had a disagreement, and Adi had prevailed.

He spread his hands. "Diana has asked . . . for a more active role in the investigation. What do you think?"

"Best not, sir. It's a messy business."

Both siblings turned to me with similar expressions of inquiry.

I shrugged. "Well, sir, we believe the ladies were murdered. This could be dangerous, hm?"

"Indeed." Adi frowned. "Another reason, then."

I wondered, what was the first? The obvious answer: it wasn't appropriate, was it? Perhaps Adi had discouraged Diana from associating with me, an old army chap.

Her chin rose. "Captain, in England, I met a young Indian lady, Miss Cornelia Sorabji. She studied law at Oxford! She's been appointed Lady Assistant to the Court of Wards. Why can't I do something useful too?"

"Ah!" I considered her mutinous look. So this was not about fraternizing with the hired help. "Perhaps when you've settled in? Meanwhile, I need an interpreter."

Her face brightening, a glance passed between the siblings. Was Diana saying, "He agrees with me"? Perhaps in time, I'd learn their silent language.

Turning to business, I questioned Adi about the ladies' clothing returned by the coroner and learned that none were beaded. Convinced that the ladies had been hiding something, I said, "Tell me about Lady Bacha. To form a clearer picture of her."

Adi nodded, and began, "Well, Bacha's parents died years ago. A tragedy at sea. She was brought up by an uncle in Ooty. Her family has coffee estates. Her late uncle managed them."

"When did he die?"

"Last year. He'd been ill long before Bacha and I were wed. He was keen on a quick match—so she'd be cared for, you see."

I wrote: *coffee heiress from Ooty.* A previous suitor? A lover?

"Out with it, Captain," said Adi, his voice amused.

"Was she willful? Impulsive?"

"Goodness, no! Bacha was extremely dutiful. But she was rather progressive."

"Sir?"

Adi said, "She was against Pilloo marrying so young, but it's tradition, you know."

Miss Pilloo again. "Any close friends?"

"Goodness, Captain, I wouldn't know where to start! We entertained constantly. She often met friends at Hanging Gardens or the university reading room." He fell silent as the gloom of the clock tower wove a shadow into his ponderings, caught up in some internal turmoil, a familiar argument that left him desolate.

"Politics? Opinions?" I ventured.

Adi shrugged. "We talked of nationalism, social reform, explorers. . . ." His expression lightened. "Bacha once said that Columbus must have been awfully conceited to lay claim to everything he found." He chuckled, looking like a schoolboy in that rare moment. Yet his sparkling bride had a hidden side. Why hadn't she called out for help?

"Sir, I wonder if she planned to meet someone on the gallery. An old suitor, perhaps?"

Surprised, Adi said, "Impossible, Captain." He expelled a breath, shaking his head. "I thought I knew her well, until this."

I let it go. If Lady Bacha had a lover, Adi might not know of it. Secretive Miss Pilloo would, though. "Did the ladies know each other before?"

"Before I married Bacha? No. Pilloo was Bacha's opposite—no social graces at all. She rarely joined us for outings at the bandstand."

"Really!" Diana's eyebrows rose. "Before I left for school, Pilloo and I often went there! We were too young to dance, but we'd watch for hours. Ladies in exquisite dresses, dashing officers in uniform, like scenes from *Pride and Prejudice*! Pilloo loved it."

Ah! This was an entirely different picture of Miss Pilloo. "That's interesting, Miss Diana. Yet in recent years she was shy, almost a recluse. What changed?"

Diana's face went blank. "I don't know."

Adi looked from his sister to me. "Nor do I."

CHAPTER 13

RIPON CLUB

Next day, I arrived to find the house bustling. As though Framji Mansion had awoken from a long slumber, vases overflowed the foyer with flowers and ferns. Thick drapes parted to admit the sun, and bearers hurried along passageways with wide smiles.

I'd learned something useful the previous day: a pivotal event had occurred in the year before Adi's wedding, which changed Miss Pilloo from a sociable teenage girl to a nervous recluse. That incident could be behind the ladies' daring foray to the clock tower for a secret meeting. Not much, as a clue, but it was a start.

Dressed in a smart grey suit, Adi spotted me and said, "Come join us for breakfast. Diana put her question to Papa last night, you know. He said no. Doesn't want her involved in our investigation. She didn't take it well." He threw me a meaningful look as we entered the dining room.

Adi's father nodded his greeting, deep in conversation with the lanky editor Tom Byram. The pressman ate like he'd been here often, his large, deft hands dwarfing his silverware. At the sideboard Adi piled his plate with poached eggs, sausages and rolls. I followed suit.

"Chaloh dikra!" Mrs. Framji said, entering behind us, calling the children along. The younger children bounced in, clean-scented, wearing embroidered kaftans. At the sight of me, the older boy paused, then spied the sideboard laden with food and pastries and ran to it. Soon, childish voices trilled through the room. Once they had partaken and departed, the coffee came and it was time for business.

Byram slid a folio across the table. "Captain, your railway ticket to Matheran departs next Friday. Trains to Bombay ply only on weekends, so we bought your return for Sunday."

"Thank you." I pocketed the papers, eager at the prospect of finally meeting Maneck. Surely he would tell me his tale, now the trial was done? For if I found those responsible, it would exonerate him.

Adi asked, "Well, Captain, what next?"

I summed up my progress. "By my estimate, the ladies arrived at the tower around three forty, or just after. Enty saw an altercation between Maneck and the Khojas at three fifteen. He's quite solid on that. So the women weren't there yet."

Adi's mother spoke for the first time. "The three men quarreled before Bacha and Pilloo got there? What does it mean?"

"Only that the three were not agreed upon their plan," I said, cautious at the note of hope in her voice. "It's a theory, Marm." I addressed Byram. "Sir, the two suspects, Behg and Akbar. Any idea where they are?"

Tom Byram cleared his throat, looking doubtful. "Sorry, old chap. Wasn't able to locate those two. Probably left Bombay."

"Oh, they could still be here," said Diana. "Well-heeled fellows usually visit the racecourse, I imagine. They won't be at British Clubs since Indians aren't admitted, but you can try the Ripon." She caught my glance and smiled. "Why the surprise? I grew up here."

So it was decided. I would be given business attire to gain entry into the Ripon Club, that male bastion of the rich and powerful. Now all I needed was an excuse to be there.

Byram puffed as he lit his pipe and waved out the match. Pointing the stem at me, he said, "Ask for me! I'm a member. I won't be there, but it will get you in. Then you can seek out the blighters."

❄ ❄ ❄

Dressed to the nines in black suit and top hat, I set off for the Ripon Club. Newspaper clippings of Saapir Behg showed a man with a narrow forehead and untidy beard. McIntyre's notes mentioned a snake tattooed on the back of one hand. In my pocket I carried a picture of Maneck, a reedy youth standing with somber-faced Behg at the dock.

No photograph of Akbar existed. He was said to have a penchant for wearing jewelry, but I had no description. He'd attended the trial "by proxy," a courtesy offered by British law to royal members of an independent Raj (princely state). Neither police reports nor papers said what state he hailed from. Strangely little was known about him.

At the Ripon Club, a stately white structure in the baroque style covering an entire block, I paid off the victoria carriage and descended.

A concierge hurried toward me in white uniform and shocking red cummerbund. His turban, in the same red, sprouted folds of stiff cloth resembling a cock's comb, and he wore it with an air of grave authority. I gave Tom Byram's name and was led to the lounge.

Here, as planned, Byram could not be found. While the concierge sent away to the other floors, I picked up the *Chronicle,* pretended to read and examined the spacious hall. Judging from their attire, the occupants of the all-male establishment were mostly British or Parsee.

"I'll wait," I assured the concierge, gesturing at my periodical, "and pass the time. It's quite cool in this fine building."

He was pleased. "We've had great visitors, sir! The Viceroy, why, General Harding has visited us." His voice held a proprietary pride in that august visitor.

"Fine gentlemen both," I said.

This loosened his demeanor. It was time to inquire about my main quarry, the princeling, Akbar. "What about Rajas, princes, and the like?" I asked.

Here too, the man was happy to report, the Ripon Club excelled. This brought me no closer to my goal. A new tack was required. "I wonder," I said, "whether a friend of mine is here. Smith is his name. Major Stephen Smith."

In fact, Smith was in Madras with the Fourteenth Light Cavalry. However, this ruse might allow me to examine the guest book, which most establishments maintained.

"I regret, sir, the name does not strike. Would you permit, I consult the register?"

Head held high, he led me to a desk, so stiff he seemed to walk leaning backward. Beside a shiny new telephone, a thick register lay open upon the ornate table.

Smith, as expected, was not in the book.

"Would you, sir?" My escort requested that I make an entry.

I diligently added an illegible scrawl. "Would you look for another name? I'd like to meet him, but don't know the chap. Behg. Saapir Behg."

He ran a finger down each page, but Behg was not listed.

I said, "I hear he works for Seth Akbar. Is he here?"

The concierge stiffened. "You are acquainted with the Seth?"

Thakur, Seth and such titles were given to landowners or noblemen, indicating both wealth and influence. The concierge knew Akbar, at least by name.

"I have business with him. Is he here?"

"Seth Akbar has not visited for many months."

"I may have seen him at the races. A short young man, is he not?"

The concierge drew himself up. "No, sir! That is his man of business. The Seth is tall, a pehelvan!"

So Akbar was a strong man, a pehelvan or sportsman, well built and powerful. My host closed the register with an air of finality. Suspicious, his brow creased. To allay his doubts, I mentioned other army officers, then strolled back to the reading area. A wide leather chair provided ample view of his desk. Shaking out the *Bombay Herald*, I watched covertly. If he sent a fellow off with a message, well, I planned to slip out and follow.

The concierge did not oblige but busied himself in a ledger. Air wafted through the lounge from two ancient fans above. Only the rustle of newsprint and shuffling footsteps broke the silence.

"What a to-do," said an elderly lawyer behind me. "It gets worse every day!"

In crusty tones, his companion said, ". . . terrible crime in the city. Gone to the dogs!"

"It's the princely states," the first explained, "No law and order. Police utterly corrupt. The Thakurs are pretty much a law unto themselves. They run the Durbar court so if you have a case against them, they won't give you a sanad to appear!" From this I understood that one required a sanad or permit to plead a legal matter in a princely state.

The second gentleman said, "Surely the army can do something?"

"No, no!" said the first. "Can't just barge into those places, what? Not since the mutiny, for God's sake."

While vast landscapes of India were ruled by the British Raj, numerous pockets, called princely states, were held by local Rajas, or princes. An Indian prince must obtain British approval before he could inherit his throne. If succession was disputed, the British Raj could take control.

The old coves resumed discussing the Sepoy Mutiny of 1857, when armed Sepoys and farmers rebelled against British rule. It was before my time, but I'd heard it discussed in army mess halls. Indian soldiers had been assigned new Enfield rifles, which required tearing cartridge casings with their teeth, casings that were rumored to be greased with pig and cow fat. Mohammedan Sepoys were horrified at the use of pork, which is taboo to their faith, while Hindus were distressed at the use of bovine fat, since the cow is a holy beast.

Gathering support, they had laid siege to a fort in Cawnpore. Although its four hundred English residents surrendered, the rebels slaughtered everyone: men, women, children and Indian servants. By '58, the British army had crushed the uprising and the East India Company was no more. The Crown had ruled India ever since.

A headline in the *Herald* caught my attention. "Bandra fishing village attacked." I read that Bandra was only ten miles north of Bombay. No wonder residents like Mrs. Framji felt unsafe.

An hour later I called it a day. Akbar was known, and possibly feared, at the Ripon Club. Small wonder, since the infamous trial, but it brought me no closer to his whereabouts.

Still outfitted in borrowed finery, I resolved to explore the racecourse next. Electing to walk, since a cloudy sky and brisk wind beckoned, I headed north to the races. At Princess Street, a carriage swerved across the road and came directly at me.

"Hiy!" I pulled back from the snorting filly and carriage, missing its churning wheels by a whisker. My foot landed in a ditch, squishing in a pile of cow dung.

Damn! I stepped out and bent to retrieve my borrowed top hat. In that instant something whispered by my ear with deadly speed.

A blow slammed my shoulder with vicious force.

I cried out, pivoted, but it was too late. I glimpsed a turbaned man, bronzed arms swinging a baton. Two men? Three? They moved fast. Blows rained down hard. I jumped in, swung and landed a few myself.

Darkness descended.

CHAPTER 14

DOCTOR JAMESON'S REVELATION

I awoke in a battleground of pain. I tried to move and my head exploded, a full volley of cannons. My shoulder shrieked a violent protest. Elbow, ribs and knee fired in rapid staccato.

A voice behind me said, "Nice to-do, was it?"

I said, "Go to the devil," and heard a chuckle.

"Not dead yet? Well, young man, you've certainly given it a go."

That required no reply. A physician stood over me, sleeves rolled up baring forearms. He probed my ribs, grumbled and proceeded to bend each of my joints in a most unfriendly manner.

"So," he said, when he'd turned my head a few times and peered into my eyes, "what happened?"

"Mph." My left eye throbbed and I flinched away from his grip. What did happen? Images scattered in my mind: an angry grimace under a wide brown turban, dark limbs, a wooden pole cracking down on my shoulder.

"I've seen fewer broken bones on a corpse," the medico said.

That brought me up cold.

"Not that bad, surely?" I knew the pain of a broken limb, the awful weight of it. Neither shoulder nor elbow seemed quite that bad. Was it my knee then?

The doctor's smile broadened. "No, but you've collected some nice bruises." He tapped my ribs, thumb kneading the knots on my breast-bone. "These mended when you were a lad, I take it? Your forearm is more recent. And the shrapnel?"

"Seen many soldiers, Doctor?" My voice slurred. I could avoid speaking of Karachi, even thinking of it, but that grisly history was etched into my skin.

"Hmm." The physician made some notes, and instructed an orderly to bind my elbow.

The door opened briskly. A thickset English officer in regimental uniform stomped in, filling the infirmary with his presence.

"So this is the blighter!" he said.

Although still groggy, I felt an urge to snap to attention, but my limbs would not obey.

"Name? Rank?" the officer demanded, chin forward. "Regiment?"

Blast. My dratted mustache shouted "army," no matter where I was.

"James Agnihotri, Captain . . . retired. Fourteenth Light Cavalry."

His lips tightened, a common reaction when Englishmen heard my name and realized I was Anglo-Indian. Mixed blood, and all that. Frowned upon by one and all.

On my other side, the doctor greeted him, "Good morning, Chief."

So this was Chief Superintendent McIntyre who had investigated the ladies' deaths. Good heavens.

"Jameson," said McIntyre, irate, "this fellow has been causing trouble all over town. University, Ripon Club." He scowled at me. "Agnihotri, eh? What're you after?"

I made no reply. My brain was slowing, wheels chugging to a halt while the engine puffed weary gusts.

His sandy mustache bristled. "The Governor's sent me a note, sir! 'Why is army looking into a police matter?' You've caused an almighty cock-up! What do you mean by it?"

The Governor of Bombay Presidency knew about me? God Almighty.

"My apologies," I said, wheezing.

"I've a fine mind to arrest you," he growled. "Who d'you work for?"

"Brown and Batliwala."

"Solicitors!" he said. "Doing what?"

"Messages, mostly," I invented. That should get the situation to Adi.

"What d'you know about the clock tower, eh? The clock tower deaths?"

I remained silent. If ever discretion was advised, now was the time.

"Tread carefully, soldier!" said the Superintendent of Police. "Where were you, on the twenty-fifth of October?"

October twenty-fifth. The day Lady Bacha and Miss Pilloo died. I stared at him as well as I could with one eye, since the other was nearly swollen shut, and said, "Poona Cantonment Hospital."

He asked more questions, but sleep beckoned. I closed out the thunder of his voice and tried to welcome it.

"Right, Jameson," the Superintendent growled and stamped away. Silence billowed in his wake, with the pungent smell of carbolic.

The good doctor fidgeted with my bandaged knee, then urged me to sit up so he could bind my shoulder. His attentions swept away the cobwebs of slumber.

"I was on the Framji case, young man, the clock tower deaths," he said conversationally, as he spooled a bandage across my chest. A jolt went through me.

He chuckled. "Interested, are you? Yes, they consulted me about it. I'm Patrick Jameson, by the way."

Damnation! Here was a heaven-sent opportunity and I was ill prepared for it.

"Ye . . . es, indeed," Jameson said cheerfully, as he prepared a needle with my dose. My aching body demanded the medication, but his words were compelling.

"Were you the Medical Examiner?"

"One of five, actually," he said, reaching into a cabinet. "Dawson, the Chief M.E., testified at the trial. Three Indian medicos and I also attended. Big case!"

"Were the women assaulted?" I blurted out. I was not at my best in that moment.

"Hmm." Jameson leaned over me. "I don't know what you're up to, but no, there was no . . . evidence of crime." His needle pierced my forearm. "The Indian doctors disagreed about the ladies' bruises, but one thing was clear. Both young women were . . . of the species Virgo Intacta."

I stared at him. So they had escaped molestation. That was good, was it not?

Tradition dictated an early wedding, but Miss Pilloo had not moved into her husband's home. It explained her innocence.

But Lady Bacha? The question shot through my mind. She and Adi had been married more than a year. Was this what she was hiding? Was my charming and erudite client, in fact . . . homosexual?

Doctor Jameson swabbed my knee, then had me turn while he bound it.

Awash in pain, I scarcely noticed his ministrations, as my mind roiled at his disclosure. I'd wondered whether Lady Bacha was being blackmailed. Now I questioned whether her marriage was a sham.

Sodomy was a crime across the British Empire, punishable by imprisonment, banishment or worse. Was this what Adi's father was afraid I'd uncover? Lady Bacha would be desperate to preserve such a secret. If found out, Adi would be a social pariah, a laughingstock, an object of derision and hate.

What was Holmes's famous line? "When you remove the impossible, whatever remains, however improbable, must be the truth." I considered my client: intense, resolute . . . and reserved. Had he wrestled with indecision, determined to hide this fact but desperate to know whether it was the cause of his wife's demise?

All right. If Adi bore that sad secret, what of it? He'd done nothing wrong, that I knew of. To have married a charming lady and failed to bed her, well, it injured no one. By all accounts, she and Adi had been happy together. Yet that might be the problem. If someone learned Adi's secret and threatened his reputation, well, Lady Bacha and the Framjis could lose a great deal. Here, at last, was reason for blackmail.

Jameson was saying, ". . . not too bad, but careful with that shoulder. Take a few days' rest, soldier." He motioned to someone behind me. "Get him dressed." An orderly helped me into my trousers, now sadly torn and muddied. Ribs aching with each breath, I complied.

The Framjis came with a clatter of footsteps, scattering my sleep like a puff of smoke. Diana burst into the sick room and spotted me with a cry. She and Adi hurried to my side.

"What happened, old chap?" he asked, taking in my appearance.

"I'm all right." For all his quirks, Jameson was competent enough. I'd lost the round, but broken nothing that wouldn't heal.

"Let's get you home," said Adi.

"Ah . . . to my own place," I mumbled, peering at Adi with one eye, since the other, bruised and swollen, had now closed.

"Your rooms, where are they?" Adi demanded, and I told him.

But we had not reckoned with Diana. She promptly overruled the "little room behind a bakery," and went off to arrange my release.

Since I was not to be detained, I tried to stand. Pain flashed with the bite of a whip and my knee buckled. Strong arms supported me. Jameson barked orders. Then his sedative lifted me away.

CHAPTER 15

DAMNED PERSONAL QUESTIONS

I awoke in a large room, dimly lit, to the scent of sandalwood. My fingers touched white scallops embossed on grey wallpaper and drew me from odd dreams where dark objects hurtled toward me. Heavy curtains kept the morning to quiet shadows. The smell of frying wafted from the kitchens. Adi and Diana had brought me to their home.

"Captain, please stay. At least until you recover," Adi's father said, somewhere above me. Clad in a brocade dressing gown, Burjor's girth moved by my bed. How long had he stood there? "Rest now," his low voice rumbled.

"I'll stay with him," said Diana's voice.

He consented and the scent of sandalwood, laundered linen and soap departed. I winced. Just my luck. Graced with Diana's presence, and I was barely capable of coherent thought.

I recalled the doctor's words and felt weighed down with forebodings. I'd suspected that Lady Bacha's death might revolve around some error of her youth, or Miss Pilloo's. But this was no dusty riddle from the past. Her secret still menaced her husband and I was loath to be the instrument of Adi's disgrace.

The attack had taken me by surprise. My inquiries had disturbed, no, threatened someone. I felt a spurt of satisfaction, a sense of having achieved something: the murderer was uneasy. I smiled and my mouth stung, bringing forth an oath.

"Do you need anything?" Diana moved into sight.

I'd forgotten her! "Where's your brother?" I whispered.

She bent to me. "At lecture. He was here this morning. You were clean bowled, Captain." Her smile brightened the chamber. "We had to carry you into the house. My God, you weigh a ton! It took four bearers to lift you."

Daunted by neither my silence nor, apparently, my injuries, she shook out a newspaper.

"What's the news?" I asked, tilting my chin at her paper. That set my head aching so I closed my eyes. For the next hour she read out the headlines and, upon my nod, the accompanying article. At some point I stopped listening to the words, carried by the ebbs and flows of her voice.

Sometime later Adi arrived with the scent of leather and expensive cologne. He greeted me warmly, inquired after my health, then parted the drapes to reveal a burst of red in a gulmohur tree outside. I was in a guest suite somewhere upstairs. The outer rooms of Framji Mansion had an external balcony abutting a palisade of trees, which I glimpsed behind the gulmohur's crimson cascade. This clever configuration let servants run to and from individual apartments without traveling through the house and disturbing other occupants.

Adi dropped into the bedside chair, his mouth set in a grim line. "One of Byram's reporters heard about you—he sent us word. I'm sorry, Captain. I didn't think you'd get hurt."

Gripped by affection, I cracked a smile at his mournful demeanor.

"It's nothing," I said, then sobered as Doctor Jameson's words echoed in my ears. Adi was my friend, my only friend outside the army. The good doctor had revealed that Adi's wife died a virgin. Was that it? The secret she died to protect?

Yet I hesitated to wound my friend. Would my damnably personal question end our association? But it must be done.

"May I speak with you . . . privately?"

Puzzled, Adi said, "Of course. Diana, would you give us a moment?"

She rose to leave, then stopped.

"No," her voice rang out, clear and strong, "I won't. I'm part of this, Adi."

I shook my head. Impossible to speak in her presence.

Adi remonstrated, but Diana would not budge.

I cursed my impatience. If only I'd waited to broach this awkward matter.

"It's all right. Whatever it is." She perched on the foot of my bed.

That honest, determined look, those intelligent eyes. Now I would lose Adi's friendship, as well as her own good opinion.

"Captain," Adi began while I fumbled for an opening, "do you want to stop? Should we cease this . . . inquiry?"

"God no!" burst from me.

His surprised laughter joined Diana's chuckles.

Now, I thought, I must ask now. I caught his forearm. "There's something . . . forgive me."

"Of course! There's nothing to forgive, Captain."

"Forgive the question. Have you . . . lied to me?"

Adi went still. "No. What's this about?"

"You said . . . you were happy. Lady Bacha and you. Was that true?"

Silence froze the air between us. I pushed forward anyway, once more into the breech.

"The Medical Examiner confirmed . . . both ladies were virgins." My throat ached, dry and painful.

Diana cried, "Thank heavens."

Slowly Adi said, "And you're asking me why. Why was Bacha . . . untouched?"

"What?" Diana said, shocked.

"Hush now, Diana," said Adi. He met my gaze without hesitation, "You're asking . . . am I impotent? Or do I prefer . . . men."

Although Diana looked appalled, I nodded with regret. One didn't speak about homosexuals, even in the army. But it happened. I tried to explain. "Lady Bacha was hiding something. If we knew what it was, we might know why she died."

Adi had not replied. A tide of sympathy swept over me for this lad who held himself so upright and met my glance unshaken. He drew a slow breath.

"Neither, Captain," said Adi. "I do not . . . prefer men. Bacha and I, we barely knew each other when we wed. She was so young, a tiny thing. I thought we had time to . . . get to know each other. I thought we had the rest of our lives.

"Women die in childbirth, Captain, because they're too young. . . . I didn't want Bacha to be one of them." His voice trailed off as his look turned inward.

Silence clenched its fist over us, rebuking me. A drop of light from the window reflected on Diana's moist cheek.

"I'm sorry," I said.

Adi nodded absently and left the room. Diana departed soon after. With her went the quiet comfort of that morning, the sense of being safe and cared for. As I feared, my question had thrust a wedge into our trio.

Setting aside the throb in my shoulder, I considered that Adi's answer rang true. My question haunted me, and his response. I had done what needed doing. So why did regret clench my throat, and curse me for a brute?

CHAPTER 16

AN OLD FRIEND

The next morning, Gurung helped me bathe and redress my bandages. Needing clean clothes, I sent him off to my room on Forgett Street and made comfortable with a towel around my waist in the Hindustani style.

While I waited, the gap-toothed servant, Ramu, retrieved my files from Adi's chamber. I settled down to add recent events to my record.

Adi and Diana arrived at nine, with a bearer carrying breakfast. I was glad to see them. Despite my insensitive probing yesterday, Adi did not seem stiff or withdrawn. So, I was relieved to discover, I was not to be cast off.

Were there lines on his forehead that I had not noticed before? He greeted me cordially enough, moved some papers and directed the servant to set down the meal. Somewhat poked up at being found in such a state of undress, still swollen and bruised from yesterday's ambush, I sat up to return his greeting.

Diana took one look at me and said, "Oh!"

While I shrugged a nightshirt over my towel and bandages, Adi said, "Captain, you should be in bed!"

Gurung brought my clothes, but, ravenous since I'd not supped the previous day, I waved him away and sat before the laden platter.

Loading a plate with eggs, I said, "Those thugs took my notebook."

Adi frowned. "Notebook? For the case?"

I tried a grin. "They won't get much. It's in French. My French is terrible."

His guffaw took me by surprise. Not for anything would I break this moment, this mending of our tattered bond.

Diana moved a stack of newspapers and sat in the window seat. Her face flushed, she moved in a business-like manner this morning. I gathered that she had not forgiven my tactless questions last night.

She asked, "Did they get anything else?"

"Money?" Adi inquired.

"Didn't have much."

"Good heavens," said Adi, appalled, "I haven't paid you."

"Haven't needed it. You provide breakfast and dinner." I pointed to the tray with a fork.

"Captain, who did this? Did you recognize them?" asked Diana.

"No." A snatch of memory came to mind. A bare-skinned assailant—was it two?—wearing a checkered cloth over mouth and chin. Another man with angry eyes, thick eyebrows and a round turban. I flexed fingers that felt stiff and bruised from those punches I'd landed. I'd not done too badly.

"Thieves, then?" Diana said. "You were dressed like a toff." Her hands flat on her long grey skirt, she wore a crisp white shirtwaist, sleeves buttoned at her elbows.

"Can't say, Miss." I shrugged. My shoulder protested, but Jameson had assured me it would mend. I rotated it and snapped out a quick punch. That hurt, so I settled down to finish scrambled eggs, jam and toast.

Brother and sister conferred on the balcony while Gurung helped me dress. They returned, saying that my statement to the Constabulary could be made from the house. A message would be sent to that effect.

We discussed what little I remembered, then Adi said, "Carriage driver and hoodlums must be in cahoots. The victoria distracted you so those thugs could creep up."

"Perhaps. I'd planned to try my luck at the raceway. Probably passed them in the street."

"You came from the Ripon Club. Could they have followed you?"

"Probably. But the carriage, that had to be planned." While I'd snooped at the club, my assailants had set a trap, neat as I'd ever seen. What had I done to provoke the ambush?

Mulling it over, I wolfed down a bowl of ripe strawberries, enjoying their tart sweetness. Recuperating at the Framji home had its compensations.

"Captain, your ticket to Matheran!" said Adi, face puckered in distress. "It's in three days. Wouldn't you rather wait?"

"No, sir," I replied, between mouthfuls, "I'll take that train."

Maneck, the man accused of the ladies' murder, was the key to this mystery.

Diana looked worried. "Captain, how can I help?"

Holmes would not have shared details of his investigation, but I wasn't Holmes. And Diana wasn't the sort to sit by until the grand finale. I recalled her reticence a few days ago, how I'd been sure she knew something about Lady Bacha or Miss Pilloo. What was she hiding? When would she trust me enough to share it?

"Not much to do at present, Miss." I pointed to a stack of notes. "Those witnesses remain. Two children saw Maneck and Miss Pilloo at the university gate a few times."

Diana flicked open the report and said, "Why, that's just on Grant Road. I can take my Ayah and see them."

Adi looked doubtful. "Diana, no."

"Miss, if you could read me those. . . ." My right eye could bear some rest.

Adi left us to it. Diana separated out the police reports on the Havildar and the children's testimony and read them out. Medical experts focused on some of the ladies' injuries. Defense counsel claimed buttresses protruding from the tower walls had caused these, so that claim was tested in a highly publicized experiment. In the test, the dummy thrown from the gallery hit nothing on its fall to the ground.

Now that I had met Doctor Jameson, I set the medical history aside. Four witnesses remained: Maneck, two schoolchildren and the frightened tower guard. After Diana read out their testimonies, she remarked that the children lived close by. Time passed as we reviewed them.

When we finished, she lingered at the door.

"Don't go anywhere, will you?"

I crooked an eyebrow at her and her cheeks turned pink.

"It's just that . . . we feel responsible. For your injuries. Won't you rest?"

I bowed in acquiescence, and she left. When she was around, invariably words failed me.

* * *

Toward evening I received another visitor. Gurung entered bearing a platter, upon which lay the card of my friend Major Smith.

"My God, man!" he snorted, upon being admitted. "What the devil have you got into?"

I grinned at his florid square face and mutton chop sideburns. After a quiet day, my meals served by Gurung or the gap-toothed boy, I felt weary of my own company. An evening with my oldest friend was just the thing. Smith settled on the settee and stretched out his legs.

"Nice lodgings you've got."

"What, this old place?" I grinned from my sickbed.

After the usual pleasantries, common friends and acquaintances, the garrison, where he was stationed and so on, he said, "Dash it, Jim. They've got a grand gymkhana here. You could get back to boxing, old chap." He jabbed at the air, knotting his mouth in a mock grimace.

Grinning at his antics, I shook my head. "Don't think so. Not as young as I used to be."

"You were good, man! Won some fine fights . . . they still talk about it in the regiment. Right. Now, me lad." Approaching my bedside, he subjected me to a somber stare. "I'm here for another reason. At the barracks this morning, I met Jameson, the physician, and mentioned you."

"Ah."

"Yes." He rubbed his chin. "I was asked, told really, to see Superintendent McIntyre of Bombay Constabulary. D'you know him?"

"We've met." I saw it coming and met it head-on. "You're here for my statement."

He nodded. "Dashed fine chap, McIntyre. Said it would be—um, more appropriate. Sending me, y'see."

McIntyre rose in my esteem. Constables in uniform would send this household into a tizzy. Yesterday's vision took shape in my mind, solid wheels, step-board and all. "Three thugs attacked me on Princess Street. Tell him to look for a victoria with a red seat. They likely rode off in it." I brushed my bruised knuckles. "They'll be somewhat the worse for wear. The leader wears a round turban, like a Khoja or Maratha."

"By Jove!" Smith exclaimed. "You remember all that!" He reached for the pen on the roll top desk and wrote out his note.

Once it was sent off with Gurung, I asked, "So where's the regiment going next?"

"You miss it, eh?" He grinned. "Not me, 'course. You miss your Arabian, Mullicka."

I admitted it. "Loved that beautiful filly. Colonel Sutton's gift—gave her to me after my last boxing match."

"Lucky sod," Smith said fondly. "Peters has her now. Bought her off me handsomely. His own broke a leg and had to be put down." His face grew serious. "We're going home to England, old chap. Time I took a wife. The Thirty-third Horse went back last year, and will you believe, three lads are already engaged! Imagine that! Sure you won't come?"

"I think not, Major." I looked at the man who'd been a brother to me. Would we meet again in this life? We'd been through the worst of it together, smoke and shelling, panic, trying to reload under fire, running out of cartridges . . . Karachi.

Perhaps he caught the direction of my thoughts, because he got up and shook my hand. As I returned his grip, Adi and Diana arrived. I made introductions.

Diana said to me, "Mother asks whether you're well enough to come down for dinner? Major, you're invited too."

Not wishing to do my old friend out of a splendid meal, I accepted.

Dinner was a quiet affair, dampened by Burjor's unhappy mood. Diana and Adi also seemed somber. Did he regret initiating this investigation? Come what may, I would see it through. Digging in, I savored the superb raisin rice pilaf, sautéed lamb, potatoes and an enormous slice of the fruited pie.

Mrs. Framji, an experienced hostess, took it upon herself to draw out my friend, plying him with questions about England, his family and education. Smith held forth happily and at some length.

Mrs. Framji turned a smile on me. "And you, Captain Jim. Where were you educated?"

I stiffened. "Ah, Poona, Marm." I hoped that would be the end of it and winced inwardly to see Diana's close attention, for truthfully I'd had little education.

Mrs. Framji's face blossomed. "Oh, whereabouts? Bund Garden or Elphinstone? I grew up in Poona!"

I realized the Framjis knew nothing about me. Perhaps this was what Diana needed before she'd trust me with what she knew.

"Coolwar, Marm. An orphanage run by missionaries."

Silence greeted my reply. Across the table Diana looked concerned. Mrs. Framji gazed at me in sorrow.

I shrugged. It was not something that came up often, or that I dwelt upon. To bridge the awkwardness, I said, "I suppose I was a handful. Ran off to tend horses for the regiment. At fifteen I signed on as Sowar. Marm, that's a Sepoy on horseback. My senior officer"—I turned to Smith. "Colonel Sutton, you recall?"—"was rather old-school. What learning I have, I owe to him."

Smith said, "Finest officer I ever served with. Brilliant tactician. But you!" He waved a spoon at me. "This fellow saved my life!"

"Tosh!" I waved it away, but he insisted upon a toast.

Looking pensive, Adi's father joined in drinking to my health. Had it surprised him to learn I was an orphan, and a bastard? Surely not, given my mixed blood. But something had disturbed him, and I could not tell what.

CHAPTER 17

WHERE IS DIANA?

After dinner Smith took his leave with copious compliments on the meal. As host, Adi walked him out in amicable conversation, leaving me with Burjor and the ladies. Gloom knitted Burjor's forehead as he stared, unseeing, at his hands upon the table.

"Sir, may I speak with you?" I asked.

He rose and motioned me to follow. We bid Diana and her mother good night and went to his study, where he dropped into a chair. His brooding filled the room.

I asked, "Is something amiss?"

Burjor looked anxious. "Someone attacked you, Captain. What does it mean?"

"Papa?" Adi said from the door.

"Come." Burjor beckoned. "Adi, I think we should close the . . . inquiry. This feels like a warning. Next time could be worse."

Next time? Why did he fear another assault?

"They could just be thieves," said Adi. "It might have nothing to do with the case."

"Perhaps," I agreed, "but if your father is right, it means I've disturbed someone. There is something to find."

"Give it a chance, Papa. Captain Jim's onto something."

Burjor pressed a fist to his lips. "And if he's killed? We're responsible, Adi!"

He was worried about me. Something inside me blossomed.

I smiled. "Sir, I'll be all right. Let me get further along. But here's a question. Is there someone you suspect? Do you have enemies?"

A look passed between Burjor and Adi that I could not interpret.

Burjor rumbled, "No, Captain. We have business rivals, of course. But none would do a thing like this."

* * *

I slept a large part of the following day. Recuperating is an irksome business, and one that, after the army hospital, I'd hoped not to undertake again. Yet here I was, sore and unable to find any part of my body that didn't ache.

"See, see? See!" Parakeets peeped outside my window, with the murmur of voices in the house below. I remembered Diana's impish smile, the gurgle of her laughter. And I knew, dash it all, that bold, inquisitive girl was too young for the likes of me.

Gurung brought lunch, and proved a quiet, competent batman. Fed, bandaged and dressed, I reviewed what I'd learned so far and prepared to meet the defendant. Maneck's silent defense was not just foolish, it seemed an admission of guilt. First, he claimed not to know his two accomplices at all. When Enty's testimony placed him in their company, he refused to answer, infuriating the Magistrate. Nor did he account for his torn clothing, his "panting breath" or his whereabouts at the time of the ladies' deaths. He escaped the noose only because no one saw him accost the Framji women. If he'd talk, I could get my hands on the real murderers and haul them before McIntyre. With time on my hands, I scoured old newspapers for clues about the two accomplices, Behg and Akbar. While I found no mention of them, gradually a picture of the political landscape emerged.

Three decades after the Sepoy Mutiny of 1857, small kingdoms and principalities were controlled by local nobles, Rajas and Ranis, most of whom accepted a British presence in the form of a British Resident and his household. These states were often mired in unrest. Rajas often married multiple wives, which complicated the matter of succession.

Some retained feudal practices. Many queens could not speak for themselves, because of the tradition of purdah, or seclusion. They were restricted to a zenana, or harem compound, open only to male relatives. To be seen by another man caused noblewomen to "lose caste." They waited upon the Raja's will, losing protection upon his death. An 1830 British law banned suttee, the immolation of widows upon the funeral pyres of their husbands, but it was still practiced in some princedoms.

A queen's lot was rather dismal, I thought. Wealth did not keep a woman safer, nor let her set her own course.

Next, I read about local burglaries, scores of arrests made—Police Superintendent McIntyre had his hands full. All over India, pockets of discontent festered. A recent skirmish was reported in Lahore, which had a large Mohammedan population. Would my old regiment be recalled to duty? Smith might lose his chance to go home. Lahore, I remembered, was where Miss Pilloo was from.

Late that afternoon, fortified with a stream of delicacies sent from the kitchen, I traversed the balcony to test my strength. My knee throbbed, so I bound it up again. It would do.

Adi joined me at six. "Right, Captain, what do you need?"

My list was ready. "A large mirror, some charcoal and money for the trip to Matheran. The rest I have in my rental."

He no longer questioned my peculiar demands, but simply recorded the items, reached into his breast pocket for a wallet and handed me some notes. Then, hoisting a flat box from below the window seat, he extracted a Webley revolver, one of a matched pair. This he handed me, butt first. A box of cartridges followed.

"Something you wanted. I'm sorry it took so long." His mood darkened and he said, "How I wish you had it before!"

I grasped the weapon and liked its weight. It broke smoothly and I nocked in the cartridges. Since I'd handed in my service pistol along with my commission, the revolver felt new in my palm. "Haven't used one of these in a while," I said.

"They're my father's." Adi sounded preoccupied. After a moment he asked, "Have you seen Diana today?"

When he heard I had not, worry creased his forehead. Yanking upon the tapestried bell-pull, he sent someone to find her. The tall bearer brought the news that Diana and her Ayah had taken the carriage out after lunch.

"Did she say where she was going?" Adi questioned.

"No, Sahib."

Adi's lips tightened. "She should know better, after all we've been through."

Where would Diana go? I knew little of her friends and acquaintances. Remembering her determination from the previous day, I searched my papers for the schoolchildren's testimony.

I said, "Those children we spoke of. Where do they live?"

When that particular page could not be found, Adi's face took on a greyish tinge. "She's taken it. They live on Grant Road, don't they? Will you come?"

I was already dressed. The gap-toothed boy appeared with my army shoes, freshly cleaned. I tucked the revolver into my breast pocket, feeling rather grim. Where the devil have you gone, Miss Diana?

Adi and I hurried down the back lane and cut across Hanging Gardens. Ancient jambul trees roped with muscular creepers hung over neatly trimmed hedges. Well-dressed residents of Bombay skirted beds of wide-leaved elephant ear and orange spikes of canna.

"My mother used to meet her friends here," Adi remarked, as we flagged a victoria and climbed in, "but not since . . ."

As he instructed the carriage driver, I spotted a tall fellow in a shiny green coat and matching turban, walking across the road. Just last week, didn't someone mention a man in an ornate green coat?

I remembered. Apte the librarian had seen someone in green arguing with Lady Bacha. While such clothing is unusual on a busy street, it seemed common enough in society circles. In a city this size, no doubt, more than one man sported a green coat. And yet a popinjay who'd accost a woman in a library might well be cool enough to parade his finery under our noses.

"That chap. Green turban. Who is he, d'you know, sir?"

Adi gazed out of the carriage, then settled back as it picked up speed.

"Not sure, Captain. Someone from one of the princely states? They do tend to dress up."

We paid off the carriage at Grant Road, a busy market street. On either side merchants touted their wares. Women in sarees and colored burkhas haggled with vendors or wove through the crowds bearing purchases. Each taking one side, we searched the throng.

Where was Diana? I described her to a fruit seller, who shrugged.

Adi waved me over from across the road.

"Yes, Sahib," said a vendor, deftly hacking the top off a coconut. That blade was as sharp as a razor. He sliced off the bottom with barely a glance at where he struck.

"Very fine horses, black-and-white carriage," he agreed, "stopped there." He gestured at the crossing with his cleaver. "Carriage not moving, big traffic jam some hours ago."

I did not trust his estimate of time, but Diana had been here and not returned home.

Adi pulled out some coins. "Which way did they go?"

"That way." The man pocketed the cash, pointed and went back to his trade. Gazing in that direction, I heard the clock tower chime.

The child witnesses lived on this street. If Diana had learned something of interest, where would it take her? I knew of only one place, close enough that we could hear its bells.

"The university."

Adi set off at a run toward the intersection, where he secured another victoria by the simple expedient of hoisting himself into it. Hampered by my aching knee, I clambered up and we were off.

CHAPTER 18

BACK TO THE CLOCK TOWER

Our cab careened past the university gate toward the library.

A waterfall of bells sang the half hour as Adi leapt out, leaving me to pay. Diana's carriage stood just inside the vestibule. She was here.

My breath came fast, yet I lacked air. Two Framji ladies had died here, and now Diana was in the tower. Limping, I followed Adi as he raced into the tower.

"Diana!" The dark cavern magnified his cry, his terror a fierce thing as he charged up the curved stairway.

I heard raised voices echoed from the gallery above. Adi's, and . . . praise be . . . Diana's. When I reached the gallery and burst through the door, gasping, Diana seemed to be pleading with Adi. They were flanked by the Ayah and Ganju the sais, Adi's groom.

Paying her no mind, Adi glared at three youngsters, the oldest a lanky teenage boy.

"God, Adi, calm down," Diana hissed. She cast a terse glance at me, a warning shot across my bow. Washed in a tide of relief, I hid my smile. Diana was a bricky girl, all fire and intensity today.

Despite her efforts to reassure him, the older boy was anxious. Begging Diana's leave, he shepherded his siblings away.

She skewered Adi and me with an accusing look. "They were just telling me what they saw. Then you barge in like a herd of elephants, and they're frightened all over again. Do you know how long it took to get them to come?"

Neither elephant replied, so she stomped back down the clanging stairs with Adi at her elbow. Her Ayah smiled apologetically and followed, as did the groom.

Alone on the gallery, I saw it now at dusk, one half in the tower's slanting shadow, the other golden from a dying sun. Why did this place hold Lady Bacha in its thrall? Why deceive her household and come up here with Miss Pilloo as her only companion? The silent stones nursed their secret in the still, sullen air.

Descending with careful steps, I caught my breath by the time I reached the carriage. Adi, Diana and her Ayah sat in stiff silence. Unwilling to crowd them and glad, if I was honest, to avoid the awkward tension between siblings, both of whom I admired, I called to our carriage driver, "Hoy, Ganju!" Signalling him to make room, I hauled myself painfully up beside him.

Gaslights threw a golden mist over the white gate of Framji Mansion as our wheels crunched gravel. At the house, amid purple shadows of dusk, bougainvillea boughs cast dappled shapes and swayed, rustling softly.

Burjor and his wife met us on the stairs, their relief warm and heavy as a hot monsoon day. Mrs. Framji embraced Diana. Her children both began to speak, while Burjor's voice rumbled his thunder. Uncomfortable with the to-do, I held back.

When he'd gone a few steps, Adi called, "Captain!"

I resisted, reluctant to give evidence against one or the other. Needs must when the devil drives, I thought, and followed him.

The tableau looked like a court-martial. Diana stood at the window, fingers clenching her skirt. Adi prosecuted before a wide, squat desk where his father leaned forward on thickset arms. Mrs. Framji slumped on the settee. My concern growing, I waited by the door.

"All right, Adi, say it!" Diana burst out. "You were worried. I'm sorry!"

"Diana, you can't do this. You can't go off by yourself." Palms wide, he sought his father's agreement.

Burjor rumbled, "Diana, your mother and I . . . You don't know what it is, to lose a child."

"That's why I went! To help. To find out why." Diana pleaded, "Am I to stay indoors, is that it? We can't invite anyone because of mourning. Now I can't go anywhere either?" Frustration shredded her voice.

Only in such moments did I realize how young Diana was. Her poise and steadfastness made one forget. Now her words seemed strangled with emotion. I paused. Where had I heard that poignant note before? Somewhere in my childhood I'd heard a woman weep like that.

Before I could place it, Diana burst out, "No one else is imprisoned like this! Why, girls in London go to the theater, ride in the park, with just a chaperone." Catching sight of me, she cried, "Captain, tell them!"

She wanted a champion. But I'd seen Adi near the end of his tether today—his headlong dash from the rolling carriage, his cry as he ran up the coiled stairs.

Clearing my throat, I addressed Burjor. "Miss Diana was in no real danger today, with her maid and Ganju, the driver, to accompany her."

When Adi glared at me, I added, "Gurung and he were with a Gurkha regiment. They're scrappy fighters, sir."

"Captain!" Adi protested, "Would you let your sister ride about like that? After what's happened?"

After the deaths of his wife and sister, and my recent ambush, he meant. I drew a breath and considered. "Perhaps, with a larger escort, she'd do all right."

"Burjor," said Mrs. Framji, rising to go to his side. As she conferred with her husband, Diana dropped into the settee. The storm had passed.

She'd been gone six hours. What had Diana learned from the children? As if reading my mind, she caught my glance, then shook her head almost imperceptibly. Not now. Don't remind them of my disappearance.

I'd seen her "speak" to Adi just so and marveled, their discourse mysterious and incomprehensible. Now I heard as though she whispered in my ear. When I dropped my chin a half inch, Diana drew a relieved breath. I will tell you soon, her eyes promised.

Could she read my mind? It was impossible to look away.

A clock began its eight o'clock chime, bringing me back to the present. My train to Matheran departed at six in the morning, and I had yet to collect my valise from my rental.

I asked Adi, "If there's nothing else, sir?"

There was not, so bidding them goodnight I trudged to my lodgings, still musing about that silent conversation with Diana. Something had changed between us, but I could not tell what.

At home, I opened my old valise and rolled up a brown jacket for my trip. It felt oddly lumpy. Had I left something in the breast pocket? Mindful of the need to preserve evidence, all my papers were kept at Adi's. So what was this crumpled sheet?

I smoothed it open on the bedroll. Atop the page, I read, "Dear brother Francis."

Francis? Francis Enty, the clerk at Lloyd's, was the key witness I'd interviewed last week. Called away by a child's voice, he'd left me for a moment. Before he returned, I'd seen a discarded wad of paper—out of place among neat piles of letters—and tucked it into a pocket. Since I'd not had occasion to wear the brown jacket, here it had remained.

I brought the discarded note to the gaslight and read.

As I wrote you last month, it is my dearest wish to care for my sister Jasmine, but you know I have three young ones myself. Now you ask whether I can care for your two sons as well. Francis, please excuse me as I cannot. My mother-in-law is unwell at present, and Raymond is away, so it is all I can do to manage. Please convey my dearest love to Jasmine, and my prayers for her recovery. Francis, you did not mention what exactly is her ailment? Perhaps I can ask the local vaid about it.

It was signed, *Mary Dmitry, Poona Cantonment.*

I stared at the crumpled page and knew I'd been deceived. Enty's wife was not in Poona with her sister as he claimed. He'd lied to me after all.

CHAPTER 19

NIGHT MENACE

I assembled my beat-up valise in short order and looked about the dusty room for my new notebook, having lost the first in my skirmish on Princess Street. There was not much to search. The space I rented was a warehouse of sorts, with sacks of grain along one side, my bedroll and few possessions on the other. Where had I left that notebook?

Realization dawned and, with it, consternation. Of course. It lay by my bed in Adi's home. His frantic search for Diana had dragged me in its wake. Adi saw my ambush as a warning, an ominous message. No wonder his sister's disappearance had struck such a blow. It was not just grief that drove him, but fear.

And what about Enty? Why had he said his wife was in Poona? I should follow him and investigate. But first, I'd visit Maneck in Matheran. Byram had taken a room for me in the hotel where Maneck resided. Dammit, I needed that notebook with my questions. Packing my uniform and a pair of pajamas, I returned to Framji Mansion.

The house was quiet so I slipped upstairs. In the guest chamber the aroma of meat and spice greeted me. Someone, likely Mrs. Framji, had sent up a plate to await my return. Ever since she learned about my childhood, or lack of one, she'd taken it upon herself to feed me. Perhaps she thought a fellow my size needed sustenance, or was moved by my injuries. Not one to complain, I polished off lamb stew, still warm, and fried dumplings called pakoras.

As I climbed into bed, hot wind snaked through the window, brushing my skin with prickles of heat, promising a dire summer. I worked my stiff shoulder as long as I could bear, then unbound my knee to find it bruised and angry. A shot of whiskey might help, but presently I had none.

I had turned down the lamp, but my throbbing shoulder would not let me settle one way or another. Diana had wanted to help with the investigation. What else did she know? She'd watched me with a searching look. A bloke might take that as a mark of interest—I was not fool enough to, was I? Something lay heavy about my mind as well, an ache I could not define. Adi's terror haunted me. The distress in Diana's voice left me feeling raw, unpeeled somehow.

The pattern of darkness in my room shifted. Something had moved. Puzzled, I searched the shadows. Servants often hurried back and forth on the outer balconies, so I only looked to see who it was. Beyond the tiled verandah a branch swung in the moonlight.

My chamber was on the men's side of the house, between Adi's, which faced the front, and his parents' apartment toward the back. Three guest rooms formed the middle, and I had one of them. The women's wing lay on the other side of the building, connected to ours through a passage behind the house, and with a back stairway for servants to bring up hot water.

I heard movement on the balcony. A man's shadow passed my window, headed toward the rear. That height, those sloping shoulders? That was no servant of Adi's. My blood leapt into a rhythm I'd felt before, under fire.

On the verandah I caught a glimpse as he disappeared around the back of the house. I followed, running barefoot in the gloom. At the next corner, the tall figure turned onto the women's balcony. He reached for Diana's door.

I cannot explain what happened next. A rage such as I have never known erupted within me. I ran at him full tilt, my only thought to crush, to utterly obliterate the fiend.

At the last second a glimmer warned me, light reflecting where none should be. I swept his arm aside and slammed into him. It felt like I'd hit a tree. We went down hard. Angry sinew twisted under me.

I scrambled to my feet. We exchanged blows and kicks in the night. He moved fast. Pain exploded at my temple. A jab hit my throat and I reached out in desperation. Cloth tore under my fingers. Here he was!

I swung, felt my punch land on solid muscle. The impact blasted pain into my shoulder.

My assailant grunted. He dove over the parapet and crashed into the ferns below. Feet scrabbled on gravel and he was gone.

Someone exclaimed behind me. Shadows moved and fell away.

In the light of an open doorway, Diana stood ten paces away. I had misjudged her chamber. The door behind me was not hers. My knees buckled, and I sank to the tiles. I heaved, choking and deaf, my heartbeat a train blasting through my chest.

"Captain." Adi helped me to my feet. He rattled the nearest doorknob but it would not open. The chamber I'd defended was locked.

"In here," Diana said, behind me.

Adi half dragged, half carried me into her room. Dropping onto a couch, I leaned back upon soft velvet. In the distance, Burjor's furious voice boomed out, marshaling servants.

"What happened?" asked Adi.

I shook my head, unable to speak, eyes closed to the bright lamps.

Diana answered, "I heard a terrible yell and a thud. It brought me straight up, like a nightmare. I heard . . . God! Thuds and groans, Captain Jim, fighting in the dark. I turned up the lamp. When I went out, the Captain was there."

I heard a click, a familiar sound, like the safety of a revolver. Diana tucked something into a drawer as Burjor's frame filled the doorway. Others entered, a younger son and Mrs. Framji. Whispered questions, eyes wide and shocked. I had well and truly woken the house.

"Are you all right?" Adi asked, placing the quilt from the bed over me.

I nodded and swallowed. A sharp pain stabbed my temple just then, proving me a liar. I touched a hand to my head, saw blood on my palm.

"Adi," I said.

His head snapped around. He spotted the blood and said, "Papa. Call the doctor."

"No," I choked, "check the floor. Knife."

A blade was found, a wicked little thing that could be concealed in a waistband or turban. I'd cut my hand on it, thrusting it away. If I had not, I would have run into it. Colonel Sutton, my old Commander, would be livid at such folly.

"Captain, are you hurt?" Burjor demanded.

I shook my head. With my bruises from Princess Street, I could little tell what ache was new. Fatigue overcame me. Distantly I heard Burjor send the carriage to fetch McIntyre. I bitterly wanted rest, but now I'd get none until the matter was reported. Wrapped in Diana's flowered quilt, I closed my eyes.

In the pause Diana said, "Reminds me of when Pilloo complained about monkeys."

A sentry in my brain cried, "Halt!" I put out a hand to grasp that thought, and rasped, "Was that Pilloo's room? The door he tried to open?"

Silence stilled the chamber. Diana stared. Burjor straightened up, hands on his hips, and said, "Captain, what did you see?"

My throat unlocked at last, I described the man I'd followed: about six feet—as tall as me, and as wide. Not military, no, but there was something familiar about him. I'd run at him, then seen the knife.

Adi glared. "Damn fool thing to do."

I agreed. "He was strong, and trained," I said. "Wore a turban. Escaped over the parapet. Can someone check the bushes?"

"We'll see to it. Go on," said Burjor.

"I hit him." I recalled the solidness of it, how it jarred my shoulder.

The intruder was strong and nimble. Nothing like the three short, lithe men who'd ambushed me in Princess Street. I was accumulating foes, but had no inkling who they were.

"Why did you charge him?" asked Adi. "Why not just shout and scare him off?"

"Don't know. His hand was on the door, the other on the overhang above." A tall man, ensuring he would not bump his head in the dark. I could not explain why I'd found this so menacing. I had feared it was

Diana's door, but that I would not admit. I sighed. Would the dratted constable never come?

Diana had just said something about Pilloo, and monkeys.

"Monkeys?" I asked.

Diana gave a surprised chuckle and curled herself into a chair. Chin resting on her knees, she looked like a child with rumpled hair in a striped blue pajama and jacket.

"It was a great to-do. Almost every week, remember?" she said to Adi, who slouched beside me. He'd had the presence of mind to wear a burgundy bathrobe and was perfectly respectable, like his father. I pulled the quilt over my chest.

"When Pilloo first came to us," Adi recalled, "she had nightmares."

"And she heard monkeys on the roof!" Diana said. Her smile faded as she drew a breath.

"What is it?" Adi said.

"Last week . . . I heard something. On the roof. At first I thought it was jambul fruit, rattling down the shingles. But jambul doesn't ripen 'til monsoon—or at least May. Then I thought it might be monkeys. Such a nuisance, so I called the servants to shoo them away."

Monkeys or jambul fruit rattling on the roof. Something, no, someone. And Diana, alone on the dark balcony in her nightgown. I felt chilled. A long shadow seemed to reach from the clock tower toward Malabar Hill.

Burjor stomped to Diana's rolltop desk and extracted a sheet of paper. Lowering himself onto her tiny white chair, he began to write.

In the silence, Diana bit her lip. "It seems disloyal to say this—Pilloo was really headstrong. Yet she couldn't bear a quarrel."

Just like that, a question popped into my addled brain. Who knew Miss Pilloo better than the sister she wrote to?

I said, "Miss Diana, she wrote you in England, didn't she? May I read her letters?"

She fumbled. "Oh dear. They can't be . . . anyway, I burned them . . . after she died."

Diana was a terrible liar. It was one of the things I liked best about her.

"Before you burn them," I said, "may I read? It may be important."

With bright pink cheeks she fetched them from her dressing room in a show of good faith. I accepted the bundle and assured her that she would have them back.

"Did they quarrel," I asked, "Miss Pilloo and Lady Bacha?"

Adi and Burjor looked at Diana in silence.

She groaned. "Yes, all right. They did. I don't know what it was about. Neither one said! It was a month before they died."

I cannot explain why I knew this was key. Excitement rose fast, billowing sails in a gale. Some event led to the ladies' disagreement, then Lady Bacha tried to fix the problem. I had the thread of an answer in my fist, and must clamp tight to unravel it. But when I leaned forward, the room rocked. Not now, I wanted to shout. The answer was before me, if only I could see.

"That was Miss Pilloo's room next door?"

"No, her room is on the other side of this one." Adi replied. "The first is Bacha's, followed by Pilloo's, then Diana's, a guest room, and lastly the children's."

Why did someone want to break into that empty chamber?

Monkeys on the roof of Pilloo's room. The thief was searching for something in Pilloo's chamber. But he did not know which it was.

"Has this happened before?" I asked. "A burglary, I mean."

"No." Adi replied.

So why now? First the attack on me, with a well-planned departure in the victoria cab, then this attempted burglary. What had I done, to set this in motion? For I knew with utter certainty that I had caused it.

"Well, Holmes?" said Adi, with a pained look.

We were up against a decisive, well-organized foe. I tried to raise a smile.

It did not work, and Adi grew concerned. "What is it? What's coming?"

I shook my head and winced. Would that pounding never cease? I eased carefully through a maze of fact and deduction.

"The killer is afraid, because I'm asking questions. He needs, they need something from Pilloo's room. This thief, tonight . . . that's very quick after Princess Street."

"Go on." Burjor's voice rumbled from the chair.

"I've been too . . . visible. Now they need something that's hidden here."

I had wandered further than I intended. As a boy I'd chased fireflies in a deep blue field, hands outstretched to the twinkling lights. The answer glimmered, just so, beyond my fingertips.

"They need to find it, before . . ."

"Before you do," Diana said softly.

"Yes." I felt bleak. "I think it's why Lady Bacha and Miss Pilloo died."

"But, Captain?" Diana sat up. "That doesn't make sense! If Pilloo or Bacha had it, whatever it was, why go to the tower at all?"

"I don't think they found it. I think they were being blackmailed, Miss Diana," I said, "and the proof is still here, in this house."

CHAPTER 20

MANECK, THE ACCUSED

Exhausted from the midnight skirmish, I fell asleep on Diana's couch before the constable arrived. Accustomed to camping in fields, my pallet tossed into a different tent or barracks each night, I could rest most anywhere.

But sleep did not last. Diana's settee was both softer and smaller than I was accustomed to. I heaved in a breath, felt the ache of bruised ribs and sat up. My inventory of soreness took but a few seconds. Most of last night's blows had fallen on shoulders and arms, but my temple throbbed.

Diana had slept elsewhere, yet her presence permeated the dainty room, flooding me with her lavender scent. Collecting myself off Diana's couch, I hurried from her bedchamber, feeling clumsy to have invaded that intimate space.

A purple dawn painted the low horizon as I trudged down the verandah. Last night's burglar meant more secrets to unearth. I was blind, and the enemy could see. It was taking me too long to work this out, I thought, plodding into my guest room. When my fingers fumbled with the lamp, I noticed bandages encasing my hands. When was that done? Who'd patched me up while I slept? Peeling off the wrappings, my knuckles smelled of peppermint and some medicinal herb. The same greasy stuff covered my face and shoulders.

Every muscle protested. Well, I thought, adopting a limp to ease my knee, I was wounded and a soldier. What better guise for my journey? A wounded soldier I would be.

By lamplight I found the porcelain sink, washed and donned my khaki uniform without ceremony. The clock dinned five o'clock, a solemn, mourning sound, as I picked up my valise and hobbled down the stairs.

A victoria waited by the iron gates of Hanging Gardens. As the sky blushed a wounded pink, I roused the sleeping driver and set off to catch my train. Once aboard, I slept.

"Matheran station, Sahib!" the conductor said in my ear, three hours later. Accustomed to recuperating soldiers, he did not bother me with questions.

That crisp morning, my rickshaw tottered over curved pathways. At dips in the road we passed through dense fog, thick cloud as white as the cotton sheets in Adi's home.

"The name Matheran, what does it mean?" I asked the bare-footed fellow pulling my cart. He twisted around and smiled wide, all wiry sinew and bone, wearing only a dhoti, traditional baggy trousers that ended at his knees.

"Mathey, Sahib, is the head of the mountain. Mathe-raan is the head in the clouds."

Truly, this morning, I had my head in the clouds. Numbed by last night's skirmish, I had forgotten to retrieve my notebook after all.

I was booked at a small hotel, whose blue-tiled verandah gave a magnificent view of the plains. Without a word, a smiling young waiter brought food. The eggs were perfect, over easy, runny just as I like, the sausage hot, the jam sweet and thick over crusty slices of bread. Upon my saucer, a mound of butter had been shaped into a flower, each petal complete with delicate lines. I stared in fascination—how was it made? After the din of Bombay streets, the quiet of the verandah was almost palpable. It poured around me and soaked into my skin long after my meal.

I considered how best to meet Maneck. I would ask the innkeeper. As I hobbled toward the inn, a rumpled youth passed me. His eyes were hollow, skin pale and bloodless and he, like me, had not shaved. That must be Maneck, I realized with a start, the very man I'd come for!

Since my return was booked on a train the next afternoon, I could little afford to wait, and must make his acquaintance. But how? Placing my bruised hands on the railing, I scanned a long sweep of green, indented here and there with patches of silver lake. Dense forest clothed the mountainside in deep shadow over which curled wisps of cloud.

"A nice view," said a young voice by my shoulder.

I nodded and drew a slow breath, rubbing my ribs where they moaned.

"Come from the front?" he asked.

I gave a brief smile and offered my bruised hand. "James Agnihotri, Captain, Dragoons."

"Captain." He took my hand carefully. "Maneck."

I gestured to a pair of wrought-iron chairs. "May we sit? My knee."

"Of course."

He was bony as adolescents are, awkward and high-strung. His prominent Adam's apple moved as he swallowed. He thrust a hand through long unkempt hair, glancing at my forehead. No doubt I appeared worse off than he. My hotel mirror showed that the bruise at my temple had developed colorful streaks.

How to begin? Should I just plow in and ask for his help? Would it alarm him to know that I was not here to recuperate, but to plumb him for secrets?

"Where can a bloke buy a whiskey?" I asked.

He chuckled, a pleasant sound. Saying, "I can help you there, Captain James," he invited me to follow.

Maneck was lonely. I saw that within moments of entering his sparsely furnished chamber. Austere in its neatness, it contained a bed, a dresser and a single chair. In a corner stood an earthen pot for water. Only the clothes slung over the dresser revealed that the chamber was occupied.

My host offered me the only chair, then took a pair of glasses to the window to rinse. His room was suspended over the mountain, and so, probably, was mine.

Pulling out a bottle of White Horse whiskey from the dresser, he raised it at me and poured us two generous shots.

"Cheers." With a murmur of appreciation, I clinked and downed it. It would serve.

Sitting cross-legged on the bed, amused, Maneck leaned forward and refilled my glass.

When I asked about Matheran, he offered generous suggestions: good views, the way to the bazaar and so on. Matheran hill station boasted two sanitariums, a small bazaar street and a waterfall. He, in turn, asked after Bombay.

"How long were you there, Captain?"

I breathed slowly to ease my ribs and watched him, alone and friendless in this silent prison. All at once I pitied him and could no longer hide the truth.

"I'm here for a reason," I said cautiously, "and it has to do with you."

He jerked back, eyes wide.

"Maneck, if you want me to leave, I will," I said, palms wide.

He scrambled to the window and glared at me.

"Are you a newspaperman?" he asked, incredulous.

"No. I work for Adi Framji."

There. It was out.

He opened and closed his mouth. "What do you want?" he whispered at last.

I shook my head. "I mean you no harm. But you know something, about the death of the Framji ladies. I need to know what it is."

His lips twisted into a grimace. "I said nothing when they put me on trial. For murder. Why would I tell you?"

Damn. I needed his help, and had only a day to acquire it. What did he care about? His unkempt distress, his limp beard poking out at all angles were significant. He knew Miss Pilloo and Lady Bacha. Diana said so. Ah. He was still mourning the two girls. After all these months, he was still raw from it.

"You knew the ladies," I said, striving for gentleness, "didn't you?"

Maneck nodded, grudging even that small admission.

"So why didn't you defend yourself during the trial?" I asked. Then I guessed, "You . . . protected them. Their reputations."

His face crumpled like a child's. Dropping to the floor, he wound his arms about his knees and buried his face. Sobs shook his scrawny shoulders. I let the torrent run its course, hoping it might wash away some grief. Weary, I laid my head back upon the chair and closed my eyes.

After a while Maneck quieted. He wiped his cheeks with the back of his hand. "I tried to defend them. And failed," he said bitterly.

"So help me now. Tell me what you know."

Sorrow and fear mingled in hazel eyes. "You don't know . . . they'll kill me."

"They tried to kill me," I said, gesturing at my face.

He gasped, leaning forward to peer at my bruises. "What happened?"

This wasn't what I intended. If I had any plan for this interview surely it did not involve recounting my ambush. Yet something like hope flickered in his eyes. I told him of my visit to the clock tower and the assault on Princess Street. Alert to his growing alarm, I did not mention my skirmish with the burglar.

"Come back to Bombay," I said, "let's finish this together."

"My God." He stared at my injuries, then drew back, shaking his head. "I'm not . . . like you, a soldier."

Maneck knew who had attacked me, or whom they worked for. I clamped down on my frustration and steered a different tack.

"Tell me about the other two, Behg and Akbar? Did you know them?"

These two men were tried as his accomplices but Maneck denied knowing them.

He grew sullen, and shook his head. "I won't talk about that."

I tried another approach, taking him to the day of the tragedy.

Again, he would not budge. McIntyre and the prosecutor for the Crown had interrogated him for months. He'd given them nothing. The police reported Maneck's appearance as "panting." That was the word used. What could account for it?

"Why did you leave the clock tower?" I persisted. "You weren't there, were you, when the women fell?"

For a second it appeared that Maneck would answer, then he covered his face with his hands. In this lonely prison he'd sought a moment of company, invited me to drink with him, and in return I'd subjected him to an interrogation. I pitied the friendless young man, and regretted my broadside of questions when he was already tattered and downed.

"Maneck, I'm sorry. Tell me something. Anything," I pleaded.

His ragged breath filled the room. He said, "Just this, Captain. Ask them about Kasim."

Such bitterness in his young voice. "Kasim?" I had not heard that name in connection with my case. I waited, a question on my face.

Maneck's mouth twisted. "Ask the Framjis, your employers. About the boy Kasim who used to live there. A servant. In their house."

The tension in his wiry frame seemed to accuse Adi's family. This was the first time I'd heard them mentioned in a negative light.

"Did they harm Kasim in some way?" I asked. Had this Kasim killed Lady Bacha and Miss Pilloo for revenge? Was he my unknown foe, the intruder I'd fought last night? Maneck stared at the floor and said no more. As I took my farewell, he shook hands in silence, face shuttered and wary.

"Be careful, Captain," he said, closing his door.

I'd done all I could, and would have to be satisfied with that meager clue. Disappointed and exhausted from more than my injuries, I returned to my room and slept through dinner.

* * *

When I rose, dusk was creeping up the mountain. Birds trilled and crickets called to each other, friendly sounds, yet they reminded me of my solitary state. No wonder Maneck felt alone here. The other guests had supped already, so after a quiet meal I summoned the innkeeper and asked where I might soak in a tub.

"There is a pool in the garden, would that suffice?"

The night was sweet and warm. A pleasant breeze stirred my hair.

"It will do very well," I said, and went to collect a towel.

The blue-and-white tiled pool smelled fresh with running water. Around it the mild sweetness of jacaranda blossoms filled the air. A trickle of water dripped into the pool from a water tank somewhere higher up, some engineering I could not see.

The purple sky dimmed. On the terrace where I'd dined, lanterns were being lit. Screened by willows and peepul trees, I sank into cool water and floated under a cluster of stars, my only companion a chattering squirrel.

That night I lay in a mosquito-netted bed, serenaded by deep-throated frogs. At the end of this, I wanted to clear Maneck's name as well as the ladies' and set Adi's mind at rest. Maneck had stood trial, suffered censure and public vitriol, all to protect the memory of two friends. No one should have to hide, fearful and trembling, after doing something so brave. Diana was right. Here was no monster but a frightened lad, made the patsy of some dark power. No wonder he'd been found innocent.

I drifted off awash in memories of Diana, her elegant composure, her wide smile and lively manner. I'd always planned to marry someday. In my fancies, the figure beside me was someone quiet to walk with at sunset. I imagined I might look up, of an evening, and find her sewing beside me. Now that gentle figure paled beside Diana's diamond sparkle.

I chuckled at my own imaginings. Diana was as far above me as the stars.

CHAPTER 21

DINNER WITH THE POLICE SUPERINTENDENT

I took the train to Bombay the next afternoon. Alone in my compartment, I extracted the package of Miss Pilloo's letters and read them carefully. Writing mostly about books and clothing, she had possessed an active imagination. Only after reading three letters did I realize that the individuals described so passionately were, in fact, characters in books! She spoke of them as though they formed part of her intimate circle. It seemed a lonely life for a girl.

When the train stopped midway to Bombay, I bought a newspaper. As the vendor handed it through the window bars, a headline caught my eye: "Military hero confronts burglar."

Byram, I swore, bloody Byram. This was his doing, damn him. Tom Byram was one of the few people who knew of our private arrangement. Surely he knew that to preserve my story as "Adi's friend," I must avoid public attention. Well, that plan was now blown to smithereens. He'd broadcast my name and business to all of Bombay, if not the entire British Empire.

Captain James Agnihotri, formerly of the Fourteenth Light Dragoons, a guest at the residence of Burjor and Mrs. Framji on the evening of twentieth of March, occasioned to witness a burglar and made short shrift of the intruder. A turban and knife were found at the scene. The Bombay Constabulary is investigating the incident.

I am not quick to anger, despite my odd behavior that night I'd forestalled the burglar. Most things, I find, are temporary and pass into distant memory with the next great event. But this commentary drew blood to my face. How could Byram reveal such important details? How was I to make unobtrusive inquiries now? Damn the man!

Worse still, he'd labeled me a military hero. I cringed, thinking how Smith and my regimental blokes would scoff at such nonsense. We'd all seen action on the Frontier. What a chaffing I should get, next I saw them.

My train pounded out a hollow song as it crossed a bridge overlooking square fields and thatched huts. I thrust my doubts out the open window. A blast of air puffed them back in my face. Dash it all, I was a novice at this career. I'd got very little from Maneck. My association with Adi was all over the papers. I needed a way to ask questions inconspicuously, without revealing my business to all and sundry. I leaned against the window frame, needing the cool air against my heated brow.

* * *

Whatever I expected upon my return, it was not to find lights blazing, and a pair of carriages outside the house. The Framjis were giving a grand dinner. Having already paid off the tonga, I trudged up the path with my valise, feeling as worn and crumpled as my old uniform.

Burjor and Mrs. Framji stood at the top of the stairs to welcome guests. She descended to greet me. A flick of her hand summoned a liveried fellow to take my valise. It was a gracious welcome, observed closely by two gentlemen in white ties and formal evening wear: Byram and Police Superintendent McIntyre.

McIntyre's abrasive stare reminded me of my poor showing on our last acquaintance. Unshaved and weary, no doubt I looked positively rough this time, but at least I was reasonably clean. I set shoulders square, bowed and accepted his hand.

"Evening," he said abruptly. Not disposed to think well of me, then.

"Sir, I'm honored."

McIntyre nodded and went ahead with the Framjis. Dapper in black pipes and tails, Tom Byram smiled, shook my hand, clapped my injured shoulder and invited me inside.

"May I have a word, sir? Right away," I asked.

He shot me a grin, then grew watchful. "Certainly, this way."

He led me to the morning room. There, I rounded on him. "An article, sir. On the front page!" I pulled the *Chronicle* from my jacket and held it up.

Adi entered, startling us. Byram and I swiveled to face him.

"Captain?" Adi saw my grim face, and the paper in my hand. "You've read the article."

"Sir." I drew a breath. "How does this help us? Makes it impossible . . ." I shook my head, irate that I could not articulate it well.

"May I explain?" Byram asked. He grimaced in apology to Adi, spreading his palms. "Adi, at dinner yesterday, we planned Diana's coming out. The ball is in two weeks, and the Captain will still be black and blue. How were you going to explain that? A little piece in the news makes him a hero, and his bruises are accounted for."

Smooth. The man was so composed I disliked and admired him at the same time. Could that really be why he'd done it? It didn't hurt that his was the only paper to carry that story.

"Thank you, Uncle," Adi said, apparently taking him at his word. His gaze flicked to me. "Perhaps if you'd spoken to the Captain first?"

Byram apologized, and was so abashed that it would be churlish not to accept.

"Very well, sir," I said, and begged to be excused from dinner.

But Byram would have none of it. "Nonsense, my boy!" he insisted. "Why, they've come to meet you, of course!"

I stared. What the devil had he done?

"It's all right, Captain." Adi's tone was sympathetic as he motioned me to follow. "Let's get you ready."

In my guest chamber, a set of new evening clothes lay upon the bed. Shirt, tie, black dining jacket, white vest and dark trousers. Adi's man was summoned to dress me.

"A shave first, I think," said Adi to the tall bearer.

Seated before the floor lamp, I pointed to my upper lip. "Right, let's have it off."

Catching Adi's nod, he tsked over my battered face and trimmed away my military whiskers. When he handed me the mirror, I saw that the effect was not displeasing. Some purple bruising remained along my temple and jaw. Clean-shaven for the first time in my adult life, I looked far younger than I felt.

As I dressed, Adi apprised me of events. The prospect of dinner improved when I learned that my friend Major Smith and some of my old regiment had been invited. Besides Byram and McIntyre, the guests included three Ministry coves I did not know.

Smith arrived in fine fettle, his ruddy complexion flushed and beaming. Two friends from the regiment accompanied him, and as I feared, they had a score to settle with me on account of the fuss in the papers. Almost immediately, Smith began to recount tales from my military tenure. Thankfully, Diana and her mother were seated at the opposite end of the table, where I hoped they would neither hear nor understand Smith's less appropriate remarks.

Egged on by Byram, who promised to print none of it without my say-so, Smith chortled, "What about the time Jim was almost court-martialed?"

I choked on my drink, recovered and asked, "Have I harmed you in some way, Major? Do you have some reason to dislike me?"

The fellows guffawed their approval.

"Did it have to do with a woman?" inquired Diana, oh so prim, far down the table.

"Miss!" I protested, "Have a care for my reputation!"

"Of course, Captain," she said demurely.

I looked to Adi for assistance and knew right away it was hopeless. Dash it, he was as eager to roast me as my friend the Major.

"Court-martial? What for?" asked McIntyre, knocking back his third or fourth whiskey—expensive whiskey, for Burjor had good taste in liquor.

"Sir, in present company, it's not a tale I'd care to repeat," I said, but it was no good.

"I'll tell you," said the Major, happily in his cups. "Had to do with a dhobi—a laundryman. The dhobi was found dead, right by the barracks."

"Oh!" said Mrs. Framji, utterly confused.

"In the middle of camp, Madam," Smith explained. "Well, the old cove having died, his people came and took the body, cremated it and that was that." He grinned, stabbing his finger in my direction. "Except this chap wouldn't let it go. Kept asking questions. 'Here's the washerman, where are the clothes? He's either bringing clean clothes, or taking dirty clothes away.'"

I winced, Smith's cavalier manner grating on my nerves. He seemed to forget that a genial old chap was murdered. My face carefully neutral, I wondered, was I that crass?

"And no one can find the clothes!" Smith ended, laughing.

McIntyre glowered, "And the court-martial?"

"Oh!" said Smith, "Jim here went up to a Subedar. Demanded an explanation. Right to his face! Caused a huge to-do, almost came to blows!"

I groaned. "Major, it was an inquiry, not a court-martial."

"Well, you weren't going to tell it," he said.

I addressed Burjor at the head of the table. "Sir, the Subedar flaunted his loot. I simply called him out."

"And you just a lowly Sepoy!" grinned Smith.

I hurried to explain, before Smith did more damage. "The evidence was found in his quarters. He admitted it—he'd struck the dhobi, killed him for clothes that didn't even fit."

My outrage for the poor washerman had nearly ended my military career. Fortunately Colonel Sutton believed me and had the barracks searched in short order. If he hadn't, I'd have faced dishonorable discharge for maligning an officer.

Adi smiled. "Captain, you mentioned it at our first meeting."

Major Smith wasn't done yet. Eager to launch into another story, he announced, "And this chap saved my life . . . twice!" He waved his hands in a magician's flourish.

"If so, I made a mistake, twice," I muttered.

The company erupted into laughter. Across the table Diana caught my eye and raised a glass. God, she was beautiful.

Fortunately, after dinner Smith and his comrades elected to leave, to "put the old chap to bed," as his friend murmured, saying goodnight. When the ladies departed, the men moved to the smoking room. The Ministry gentlemen, Adi and I sat around Burjor and Byram and the talk turned somber.

Byram said, "I've heard rumors of ships carrying human cargo. Any truth to it?"

"It's the slave trade," said the Ministry man. "Possibly from the princely states. They ship 'em through British ports and we're to blame!"

"Which states, sir? Alwar, or Jhansi?" I'd read about them that very morning. "Can the army help?"

"Who knows, Captain? We can't send in troops, not without provocation." He looked keenly at me. "Political, are you?"

"No sir." I declined the compliment, reaching at an elusive train of thought. "The slavers, where do they go?"

"Indentured labor goes to Guyana and Suriname, we're told. Sugar plantations, hm?"

At the Ripon Club I'd overheard talk of disappearances. Now the Ministry chap spoke of ships carrying slaves as labor to Guyana. Of course, Bombay boasted a huge port. Dockyards and shipyards occupied a large portion of the city, with two more docks added recently.

Letting the conversation drift over me, I reflected on my two remaining leads. Maneck implied that the Framjis had harmed a servant named Kasim. "Ask them about Kasim," he'd said, throwing the words at me like a knife. I'd talk to Burjor about this—the fellow might be seeking revenge. And that witness, Francis Enty, who'd lied about his wife's whereabouts. It rankled that he'd got that past me. What else had he lied about?

CHAPTER 22

MISS PILLOO'S LETTERS

My test came at the end of the evening, when only Chief McIntyre and my employers remained in the smoking room.

"Superintendent McIntyre wants a word," said Adi.

Since I'd left for Matheran right after my scuffle with the burglar, I surmised he wanted to ask about it. This was the second time in a week I'd face the brunt of his attention. I did not relish the prospect.

"Shall we?" said McIntyre, plunking his weight into a wingback chair. He motioned me to a chair before him and unfolded a sheet of paper.

I sat, waited.

His voice dry, McIntyre asked, "D'you want a job with the police, young man?"

Was he being sarcastic? Seeing my astonishment, he cracked a smile.

I wanted to look to Adi, but knew that would be a mistake. It was exactly what McIntyre wanted to discover: what was I doing at Framji Mansion?

Evading the question, I said, "At present, sir, I'm not much good for anything." I indicated my shoulder with a wince.

His look held more understanding than I expected. The evening's five shots of whiskey? Either he was a better actor than most, or handled his liquor rather well. He'd seen me return earlier, and I hoped he would not ask where I'd been. Adi wanted to keep my investigation private. So why does an injured man take off to recuperate at a hill station and return right away? I had no reasonable explanation.

Another volley came soon enough. "What did you do, afterwards?"

"After . . . confronting the burglar?" I caught his nod and paused. "Fell asleep, sir. On Miss Diana's couch."

"Hm." His gaze was unnerving.

I held my breath, wishing I had not mentioned Diana.

"And was she there? In the room?" His eyes bored through me.

Was he asking whether I'd spent the night in a bedchamber with Diana? The question alone seemed an impertinence. Was the Superintendent baiting me?

I shrugged, rubbing my shoulder. "Wouldn't know, sir. Expect not."

"So who bound you up, hmm? Bandages?" McIntyre grinned, enjoying himself.

I grimaced, having puzzled about that too. Who had, in fact, bandaged my hands and put that herb on my bruises? "Not a clue. Clean out."

He lost patience quite abruptly. "What are you doing here, Captain?"

I said, "Recuperating? Ah—"

Adi cut me off. "He works for me. To find out why my wife and sister died."

In the long pause that followed, the police chief scratched his head and scowled at me. "You couldn't just say that?"

"Not my prerogative," I replied.

McIntyre had had enough. Flicking at his report, he read through the events of that night as recorded by Burjor. I confirmed each point and answered questions without ado.

"I came by, that night," he said, tucking away the folded page, "while you lay unconscious. Brought Jameson with me—you know him? He confirmed you were breathing, else we'd need a coroner. Bound you up. Again."

I stiffened, having suffered my fair share of dressing-downs in my day.

"This is twice, Mr. Agnihotri, you've taken a beating."

It was deliberate, his use of my name as a civilian, pointing out that I wasn't in the army now. Pointing out to the Framjis that I was vulnerable, and they should not expect so much from me. It stung. I went to parade rest, face immobile.

"Ah, that gets to you." He nodded, leaning forward. "Come to me! To the police, next time," he said, grim, "or I will need a coroner."

It was a warning, delivered as tight as they come.

"Yes, sir." The darn thing was, I didn't know my foes. I knew nothing about them.

"You have a weapon?" His gaze pressed down on me.

I swallowed and nodded.

Adi spoke up, "A Webley revolver. One of a pair. I have the other."

"Know how to use it?" McIntyre asked me.

He knew I'd spent twelve years in the army, damn him. "Yes."

"Right." He got to his feet, and stuck out his hand.

I scrambled up to take it and flinched under his grip, my knuckles still bruised.

He narrowed his eyes at me. "Jameson said you questioned him not ten minutes after you came to. Dash it, man. When you're done here, I could use you. If you want that job, come and get it," he said, and dropped my hand.

Released from the weight of his scrutiny, I felt relieved as he left. Once my investigation was done, I'd consider his offer. But I wasn't done, not even close. Soon I would have to tell McIntyre my suspicions about Enty's missing wife. Where was my proof? Where the devil had I put that incriminating letter? It would help if I knew where she was now.

Once Burjor and the Chief were safely away, I slumped onto the settee and groaned.

"I thought you did rather well," said Adi cheerfully.

"Had an officer like him, Colonel Sutton," I said, eyes closed against the light. "Couldn't get a thing by him either."

On his return, I looked up to see Adi's father glance down at me. "Captain, all right?"

"Of course," I said. "It's nothing."

He scoffed at that, then sobered. "That night you said the thief was searching for something. Do you know what it is?"

"Not yet, sir," I admitted with regret, straightening up. Burjor's frustration was growing stronger, and his enemies bolder. I was running out of time.

I said, "It's troubled me that the burglar knew to try the second floor. He knew the chamber was on the side of the house. Yet he didn't know which room. Someone has told him about this house. Someone who knows it well."

Burjor broke the grim silence. "We'll search each room."

I decided not to mention the servant boy Kasim until I could get Burjor alone. First, this home must be made secure. I said, "Sir, Miss Diana heard something on the roof. Someone could have been here before. How can we prevent them from trying again?"

Now my host was on firm ground, apprising me of changes he'd made. A new police perimeter was set around Malabar Hill, with a watchman at the bottom of the rear lane. A telephone would be installed, whereby he could summon constables if the need arose. He had also hired six retired Sepoys to escort the family and secure the house, reporting to me.

Good news, although it meant I would need to divide my time to supervise the new staff.

"Hullo." Diana strolled into the smoking room wearing a purple dressing gown with the expensive sheen of silk, embroidered with swirling dragons. Carrying a pear in one hand, she curled up on a chair between Adi and me.

"I heard your voices. What's happened?" she asked and took a bite.

Adi chuckled, reached out and rubbed her head. She twisted away and frowned at him. I watched their interplay and wished again for a sibling. The lads in my company had been my brothers, but this easy camaraderie, this freedom to reach out and touch! Diana's curls tumbled in abandon. I pulled away from that dangerous terrain.

Diana asked, "Captain, you know about the dance?"

"In two weeks? I heard."

"Everyone will be there," she said, relishing both the fruit and the prospect of a ball, "our friends and much of high society. Including a Rani and two princes."

I turned to Burjor, surprised.

"Yes, Diana reminded us that . . . well, it's time we begin to entertain again," he said, glancing at Adi. Bombay society would be intensely curious about Adi. Was he up to it?

My client nodded, his face composed.

So the period of mourning had ended. Diana's father had hired a small army while I was away and set up swift communication with the police chief. Now he was addressing Diana's second complaint with a grand party. Thus had Burjor secured his place in their affection, giving his children as much diligence as his most complex business affairs.

If I could have a *pater*, I'd imagined one like Doctor Jameson, brusque yet keen in his care, or Enty, the clerk who spoke to his children with firm tenderness. Burjor was both and more to his offspring. Since I liked both young people well, I felt a deep satisfaction at these familial riches.

Watching Diana take tiny bites from the pear, I recalled her disappearance in search of the child witnesses.

"Miss Diana," I asked, "what did you learn from the children at Grant Road?"

She straightened, holding the fruit with the tips of her fingers. "You remembered. All right." Licking her lips, she began, "There are three children in the Tambey family—you saw them with me at the clock tower. The youngest is just five. The oldest twelve. They had little to say, but the middle child, a girl, well! She noticed Pilloo and Bacha often at the university. Her brother is a messenger boy, and the younger two play on the lawn when he's running errands."

She noticed our keen interest. "Gentlemen, I could get accustomed to all this attention," she said, teasing, taking another bite. Writing quickly in my notebook, I suppressed a smile, for Diana would have no dearth of men, young or old, hanging on every word. When I was done, she resumed, listing facts in a succinct, lawyerly manner that reminded me of Adi.

"Two events are important. One: some weeks before the tragedy at the clock tower, the girl saw Pilloo and Bacha meet Maneck by the jambul tree near the library. Bacha went inside, leaving Maneck with Pilloo. He departed after Bacha returned. The two girls had words—Bacha was angry and Pilloo wept.

"Second, she saw Maneck on the day of the tragedy. He went into the clock tower alone, and there was a ruckus. Voices raised and so on. The children were afraid, so they ran back to the lawn. They saw the quarrel on the first-floor balcony near the reading room—not the gallery, mind—someone holding Maneck by the collar, shaking him."

"She was sure it was Maneck?" I asked.

"Yes." Her voice was definite. "Her brother sometimes ran errands for Maneck, messages and such. That altercation upset the girl, so they left and did not see . . . the tragedy."

Incredible. An eyewitness that the police had ignored, and a perfectly lucid account. I wrote quickly, fountain pen blotting in my haste. "How old is the girl?"

"She's ten. Spoke excellent Gujarati."

"Well done, Miss." I smiled at Diana. This intelligence was priceless. The police would not consider a minor a reliable witness, but it provided a useful picture of events. The child had given Diana far more than she'd told the police. I'd not have got half as much.

Delicate color blossomed on Diana's cheeks. She acknowledged the compliment with a tilt of her head.

Seeing Burjor glance at the grandfather clock, I said, "Miss, before you leave, about Miss Pilloo's letters. She thanked you for your advice. What was it, the advice?"

Pilloo's letters told me she empathized with one Miss Fanny Price, apparently a poor relation in a great house like this one. However, her last letter, apparently dashed off in desperation, alluded to some advice from Diana.

Diana caught my eye. "Oh! It was . . . personal." She shot me a look that I took to mean "Not now, with Father in the room."

But I could not have that. My employers deserved better.

"Now Miss, if you please," I said. "I'm certain Lady Bacha was being blackmailed. What had Miss Pilloo done?"

"Drat!" Diana slumped into her chair.

I had utterly disappointed her. But the thread of the mystery wrapped about my fist, and I could not let go. I recalled my notes. "The librarian Apte witnessed a quarrel between a man in green and Lady Bacha in the reading room. Now according to the child, Miss Pilloo and Maneck waited outside, so perhaps Maneck had brought them . . . to meet the bloke in green?

"Lady Bacha left the library upset and angry. She confronted Miss Pilloo—something so urgent it could not wait for later. Miss Pilloo wept, so it was, perhaps, something she had done."

I turned to Diana. "You kept one letter, didn't you? And burned it? What did the ladies quarrel about?"

Diana scowled at me, her expression approaching dislike.

I winced. "Miss?"

Diana burst out, "Pilloo never said! Only that it was a mistake from years ago, and now it was spoiling everything." She bit her lip. "If it got out, we'd be disgraced, and . . ." She looked at Adi. "You would be ruined."

Adi sat up, startled. "Me! What's it have to do with me?"

"I don't know," Diana said, "but Bacha was furious."

Adi stared at her, shaking his head. "What on earth was Pilloo talking about? I hardly said two words to her! I was in England most of the time she lived here."

Miss Pilloo was fostered by the Framjis. Had she imagined some sort of tryst with Adi, her cousin? If so, it was an imaginary love affair, from the astounded look on his face. If she'd described it, in a journal, perhaps, was that enough for blackmail? Why would anyone kill for something so mundane? The burglar sought it, so it must still hold the power to harm the Framjis.

I said, "If it was something personal, from long ago, why would the burglar try to retrieve it after all this time? No, there's more to this."

One last piece remained. I asked Diana, "And your advice?"

"To tell Mama and Papa," she said, miserable.

Burjor seemed mystified, so that last bit of counsel had gone unheeded.

As I said good night, Diana did not acknowledge me. That hurt more than I expected.

CHAPTER 23

THE DANCE

The following day, I entered the empty morning room to see a splash of color pass outside the window. Through the French door, I saw Diana fleeing along the balcony as though chased by the hound of hell.

Surprised, I called after her. "Miss Diana!" Perhaps I could repair the damage I'd caused with my brusque treatment.

A hand to her mouth, she paused. "Excuse me, Captain. I'm not good company just at present," she said, turning to go.

"Wait, Miss." I reached her in a few long strides. "What's the matter?"

She ducked her head, cheeks flushed. "Nothing." She shook her head, tucking in a wayward lock. Her distress alarmed me. What could have caused it? Who?

"Miss, forgive me. I must know."

Diana slanted me a surprised look, so I explained, "Adi noticed Lady Bacha was withdrawn and quiet. It cuts him cruelly now, that he did not press her for an answer."

She stared. "And you won't make that error."

"Precisely."

Diana took a shaky breath. "It's nothing, Captain. Really. Only that . . . sometimes I fear my parents will sell me to the highest bidder!"

Shocked, I said, "Miss!"

"No. I'm being silly. They only want what's best for me," she sighed. "Papa won't insist I marry right away, but I must prepare for it, meeting eligible young men, their parents."

That was the source of her upset?

"Would that be so terrible?" I ventured.

"No. But . . ." She placed her delicate fingers upon the balustrade and gazed at the lawn without seeing it. "You cannot know what it's like. All my friends are married. Yet I'm afraid. They were so sought after, before. Now one barely sees her husband. Another cannot stand hers. And my friend Jeanie," she whispered, "tries to hide bruises."

Good heavens. "Some are happy, surely?"

"Perhaps," she said, glancing sideways. "Advise me, then, as a disinterested friend."

Disinterested? Here was testament to her innocence.

When I said nothing, she prompted, "Captain Jim?"

"You're very young, Miss," I said at last.

Diana looked affronted. "Whatever can you mean?"

"No one is disinterested, Miss Diana. Self-interest is one thing you can count on, in my experience."

Her serious gaze traced my features. "As a friend, then. Advise me. What should I do?"

I half smiled. "I know nothing of matrimony."

Diana's mood lifted. "But you know men."

That I did, having spent my life amongst all manner of them. At last I said, "The man who wins you will be fortunate above all others. Be sure he earns your regard."

A dimple appeared in Diana's cheek. "Why, Captain, thank you." She searched my face. "So you've forgiven me?"

Surprised, I said, "For what, Miss?"

She said, "Withholding Pilloo's letter, I suppose. I couldn't show it to you. It looked awful for Adi."

"Ah. You feared that Miss Pilloo's letter indicated a relationship with Adi. That her imaginings had been used to blackmail Lady Bacha."

Diana nodded. She was fiercely protective of Adi, and I'd badgered her to give evidence against him in Burjor's presence. How that must have cut. She had pleaded with me to let the matter go, but I'd refused to comply.

I said, "That's why you were upset. I'm sorry."

Her smile as she said goodbye was a cool breeze that lifted my spirits.

Stop, fool, I told myself. You're a bloke with few prospects to recommend him.

* * *

Burjor departed on business that very day, before I could broach the matter of the servant boy Kasim. Entrusted with his family's safety, I worked at securing the house, drilled and worked the new guards into a routine and set them to patrol the grounds. In the days before the dance, I met Mrs. Framji often, but saw little of Diana. Framji Mansion bustled with activity.

Burjor returned just in time for Diana's ball. That evening I donned my regimental red, and strapped on my sabre with some pride. Cleaned and pressed by Adi's houseman, my dress jacket was serviceable enough, the frayed cuff scarcely noticeable. It did not matter, since I'd just keep watch from the background.

Adi, however, had a different plan. As we stood with his parents at the entry to receive guests, he said, "Remember, Captain, you're my friend, not an employee. So don't call me sir. All right?"

"Yes, sir." I grinned at him.

Laughing, he punched my arm.

"Ow!" I feigned a grimace.

When he drew back, startled, I chuckled at his chagrin, for my injuries had healed. I felt quite whole again.

Just then Superintendent McIntyre stepped out of his carriage and caught us grinning like monkeys. His hand went up in a sardonic salute.

The train of carriages came up quickly after that, men in evening wear, ladies ascending in glittering sarees and evening gowns, complete with gloves, to meet Burjor and Mrs. Framji.

I daresay Adi and I made a dashing pair, he in black tails offset by my scarlet. Ladies eyed him with interest, but he simply bowed a welcome, as did I. In truth, I paid the women little heed since they constituted no threat.

I was more wary of the men. Parsee men wore white coats and trousers, or formal black attire. A southern prince, short, dark-skinned and serious, brought two companions, their bejeweled clothing outlandish beside the dark coats and top hats favored by British gentlemen.

Adi said quietly, "That's the prince of Lalkot and his cousins." He named the others, helping me place them with a few quick phrases. I watched closely. Someone meant my kindly hosts harm. Who? Someone in this company?

Our trusted Gurkha guards Ganju and Gurung were bearers tonight, with the new staff positioned out of sight on balconies and grounds. While I had no reason to expect a burglary, these precautions seemed prudent.

Framji Mansion sparkled under crystal chandeliers, all aglow. Guests flowed through the home, filling the ballroom, where music swelled from a violin trio in the corner. Byram entered with a pair of white-haired officers, one of whom spotted me.

"James! I thought you were dead."

"Not yet, sir." I saluted and shook hands. "Glad to see you, Colonel, Sergeant Major."

"Agnihotri, is it? Still boxing?" the officer said. "Saw you fight in Burma."

Adi's eyebrows rose. "Indeed?"

I introduced him and they moved aside, leaving me with the Colonel.

"I'm sorry about the Fourteenth, lad," said the Colonel. "It was a fine regiment."

I hoped he would not mention Karachi. "Thank you, sir." I puzzled over the odd way he'd phrased it. "The regiment . . . where is it?"

He looked sad. "Disbanded. Most joined the Twenty-fourth. You didn't hear?"

"No, sir. Army hospital." Why hadn't Smith told me? Had I not asked about the regiment? Then I remembered—Smith had not answered, talking instead about my horse.

Gurung announced an arrival in his impressive crusty voice. "The Rani Sahiba—Queen of Ranjpoot."

A group of women entered, bejeweled and wearing traditional sarees.

A tall man strode in behind them. I was sure I had seen those great sloping shoulders before, as they passed by my window. *The burglar.*

That strapping frame, corded arms—we had fought in the moonlight. My breath felt tight within my ribs as his gaze skimmed over me. Standing among Smith and other officers in scarlet, I felt fairly well concealed.

Bending to my client's ear, I said, "Adi, the burglar is here."

He gave a start and turned.

"Don't look." I said, tilting my head to the door, "Tall chap in white, with the Rani."

Mrs. Framji greeted the elderly Rani and seated her. The burglar stood behind her chair.

A young woman was presented, and I knew those delicate shoulders, the way she held her head. Hair piled in curls like the first time I saw her, Diana greeted the Rani. I could not bear to watch. Instead I scrutinized the burglar in white turban and finery. Why had he come?

He bent to murmur in the old queen's ear. Wrapped in beaded silver, she unfurled a fan, which obscured my view of their faces.

I had a quick word with Gurung to set our guards on alert, but we need not have worried. The Rani and her retinue behaved impeccably around Superintendent McIntyre and the battalion of Ministry coves. Adi was presented and bore the group's scrutiny with studied politeness.

I hung back, observing the burglar. Like many young men, he watched Diana constantly, scarcely taking his gaze from her. In peach froth, she was particularly lovely tonight, so one could understand the fellow's interest. Yet something about his proud stance worried me. Would he try to dance with her? If so, should I thwart him?

"Who're they?" I asked Adi, tilting my chin at two dandies vying for Diana's attention.

Adi's eyes crinkled. "The Wadia brothers, Percy—in the white jacket— and Soli, who's older. Papa'd be quite pleased if she married one of them."

Diana left the young men to dance with a dashing naval officer I knew, a married chap.

"That's Ratan Wadia, their father, talking to Papa," said Adi. "The other two are McHenry, of Public Works, and Sir Barry Carmichael, the Chief Justice, Papa's friend. He used to visit us often."

Crikey! Sir Barry had presided over Maneck's trial. He was known to the Framjis, and had likely known Bacha and Pilloo too.

Dinner was served under large tents on the lawn, where tables had been draped in white and laid with all manner of delicacies. Not long after, the Rani and her retinue departed. We'd survived without incident.

At evening's end, Adi and I stood by the other gentlemen. Only family, staff and a few close friends remained. Diana had danced all night, her gaiety spilling over the ballroom. A splendid hostess, she crossed the hall often, conversing with other ladies. After bidding her guests goodbye, she flopped into the settee, complaining about tired feet.

"Is it me, or has it grown cooler?" Adi asked, echoing my own relief.

The burglar, I'd learned from a fellow officer, was Nur Suleiman, nephew to the Queen of Ranjpoot. Here was another thread to my case. I would need to learn all I could about him. I told Adi what I'd heard.

"The Rani's nephew?" Adi said. "You're sure?"

"Seems impossible, doesn't it? If he wanted to steal something from this house, wouldn't he send one of his flunkies?"

A hand touched my sleeve.

"Dance with me," Diana's low voice murmured. Her color was unusually high, and her eyes sparkled with mischief as she tugged at my elbow. I hesitated.

"Come, Captain, let's dance."

How much wine had she imbibed? That seemed the only explanation for her request.

"Hmph," Adi choked, turning away in amusement, leaving me to fend for myself.

What can a fellow do when so commanded? Excitement hummed within me. Holding out a hand, I led her to the dance floor.

As violins launched a new tune, I said, "We have two problems, Miss. Your feet hurt, and I don't know how to dance."

Diana paused in dismay. Forehead clearing, she said, "It's all right. Everyone's gone. I'll teach you."

Plucky little thing. She was really quite tiny. I should just return her to her settee and express my regrets. But now we were the only pair on the floor. Although just a few people remained, something was expected of us. Even the servants had stopped to gawk.

Right, I thought. Fortune favors the bold and all that.

I bent toward Diana. "Miss, do you trust me?"

She nodded, a little worried, but game to try whatever I proposed.

"Place your hands on my shoulders," I said.

When she did, I caught her securely around her waist and lifted. She weighed little, and came up easily until we were eye to eye. My shoulder held with just a twinge. Then we were off.

"Oh!" She smiled as I whirled her about. "How nice to be so tall!"

As a dance it was surely ridiculous. But Diana's laugh rippled out and made it fine.

Moments later she sobered and said, "Captain, I have a lot to tell you. Adi said you were interested in the princes?"

We moved sedately around the floor, Diana's feet swaying in time to the melody. To my surprise she began to tell me about the three princely families that had been invited. In a few short hours, she'd compiled more intelligence than I could have extracted in a week.

I swished her to and fro in time to the music, distracted by her proximity and trying to focus on her words. The princedoms of Lalkot and Arkot were to the east, Ranjpoot, to the south. Ranjpoot's Pat-Rani, who attended, was the deceased king's first wife, or head queen. Two younger queens had borne mostly girls. The sole surviving son was just seven years old.

Diana quieted as the melody slowed. The tune drew to a plaintive close.

"Thank you, Miss," I said, taking a long stride that brought us to the settee near her mother. Setting Diana upon it, I prepared to depart. Unexpectedly, she caught my hand and covered it with her own.

I sent her a quizzical look. What's this, Miss?

She gave a small shrug, smiling and shy.

There are moments when a bloke wants to have a brilliant reply, a perfect bon mot, to tell the lady what's in his mind. But no brainy reply came to me. Not a single word formed in my stunned cranium. Mindful of her mother, I raised the hand she'd laid on mine, kissed and released it. Bowing to her and Mrs. Framji, I returned to the gentlemen, feeling astonished and elated.

Breaking away from his guests, Burjor took my elbow. "Captain, let's talk in my study."

His ominous invitation dismayed me. However, this was just the opportunity I wanted, to ask him about Maneck's mysterious clue, the servant boy Kasim.

CHAPTER 24

CONFRONTATION

Have a seat, Captain." Burjor indicated the settee, and dropped into a chair.

I sat down with growing concern. He'd been a generous host all evening, but now his customary bonhomie was conspicuously absent. Had I given cause for rebuke? Searching my memory brought forth no clues. Had something occurred this very evening?

A long pause followed in which he appeared to consider an opening. However, he did not speak. Instead he rose and went to the alcove by his desk that contained his saint's portrait. There he bent his head before it and prayed softly.

Remonstrations I could have managed, even an uncalled-for reprimand. His strange expression was . . . fear? Surely not. Some deep-seated worry, then. My puzzlement melted to compassion for my troubled host.

"Whatever it is, sir. Let's have it," I said into the oppressive quiet.

He returned after a few moments, his footsteps unwilling, and slumped on the brocade seat. His deep-set eyes regarded me steadily.

"Sometimes I'm not sure," he began, "that I'm doing the right thing. It helps, to speak to the prophet." He motioned toward the alcove, saying, "You know we are Parsees, of course."

I nodded, further mystified at his choice of topic.

He continued, "But you may not know what that is. We are Zoroastrians, followers of that ancient prophet Zarathustra." Pointing at the saint's portrait, he went on. "We do not convert anyone to be Zoroastrian.

Centuries ago our ancestors came to Gujarat as refugees, from Pars, in Persia. We are very few—perhaps a hundred thousand in all."

I waited. This history did not explain the ominous tone of his interview.

He said, "So if a son or daughter marries someone who is not Parsee, well, they can no longer continue the race. They are as good as lost to us."

I offered, "I've heard Mrs. Framji speak about it at breakfast."

"Yes!" His voice lifted in palpable relief. "So you see?"

"Well, no."

My words drew him back into a fretful state. He rocked in his chair.

"Captain, you cannot marry Diana," he said, finally.

Whatever I had expected, it was not this. Astonishment gave way to bitterness. I was a mixed breed, a bastard, not worthy of his daughter. Had I not seen that mix of pity and disapproval all my life? Indians did not tolerate the mingling of races any more than the English.

In polite circles, a man who was happy until then to shake my hand would hear my name, James Agnihotri, and pause. His shoulders would stiffen, and he might spot an acquaintance across the room, and need to meet him. Women who seemed perfectly gracious—as they heard my Indian surname, their eyes might widen with understanding. Those quick glances of confirmation, how well I knew them, and the reserve that followed, polite, distant and final.

But this, from Burjor, whom I extolled as an exemplary father! That he thought so little of me cut deep. I wiped emotion from my face, but now he seemed attuned to me and grimaced an apology.

"No, Captain, it's not that. I see great merit in you. We owe you a great deal! You are not responsible for an accident of birth."

His chest swelled with a heavy breath. "No, it is Diana. Two brides were lost to us . . . to my clan, Captain. We cannot lose another!"

The creases around his mouth deepened. His voice dropped to a whisper. "Our customs are all we have." He buried his head in his hands. "This we cannot change . . . But why?"

Surely now he spoke to the saint, rather than to me? I felt winded, out of breath from the unexpected punch to my gut. I hardly dared hope that

Diana might come to care for me. Her lighthearted flirting this evening was no more than an affectation, common surely among young ladies of her class. Yet we had shared a tender moment, as heady as the finest bourbon. I could still feel her closeness, the curve of her waist in my grip. When I moved to leave, her fingers on my hand, staying me, echoed my own reluctance to end our dance.

Clearly Burjor's words were aimed to snuff out that flicker of hope. Moreover, he placed the responsibility upon me to distance myself from Diana. He could have forbade me, even dismissed me, but he had not. He'd simply asked me to leave her be, with a father's prerogative, saying, young man, she's not for you.

My ribs throbbed with a new ache. How could I answer? I felt heavy with regret. As I searched for words to voice my protest, I paused: Who else had he warned off? What else had he done? Burjor had just opened a path for me to ask about Kasim. Since Maneck's obscure remark implied some cruelty on Burjor's part, what better time to put the matter to rest?

"I understand, sir," I said. "May I ask about a different matter?"

He looked up and appeared heartened. "Of course, Captain, anything."

"Who is Kasim?"

Had I struck him in the face, I could not have shocked him more. His lips parted, and his ruddy cheeks paled. Burjor's manner shouted both guilt and remorse. Was Maneck right, then? Had this good man harmed a lowly servant boy?

"What?" he said, then perhaps recalling that it was a common name, "Which Kasim?"

I said, "A lad who worked here, at the house."

Clutching his chair, he hoisted himself up to cross the floor and back. Shoulders hunched into a bull-like posture, planting himself on the carpet before me, he said, "Kasim—can have no bearing on your case. He is dead."

I stared at his face, now creased with distress. "Dead, sir? On the contrary, if he died under suspicious circumstances, that could give someone motive for revenge."

What had Burjor done that was so wrong? I could not believe this gentle soul capable of malice. His staff spoke of him with gratitude and warmth. Jameson and McIntyre called him "Moneybags," yet the moniker was voiced with affection.

Only once had he cut me, by placing Diana beyond my reach. Wait, was that it?

"Did you perhaps warn him away from Diana . . . or Pilloo?" I guessed.

Taken aback, Burjor protested. "It's not the same, Captain! He was a servant, a Khoja!"

A Khoja Mohammedan, like the two conspirators? Was there a link to my case?

Someone knocked on the door. I flinched at the interruption, having forgotten the guests still gathered in the ballroom. So, apparently, had my host.

Adi stepped in, saying, "Papa, the gentlemen have left. Byram sends his compliments." He looked from his father's face to mine. "What's happened?"

His father thumped himself down on the settee. "The Captain asked about Kasim."

"Kasim, who worked here?" Adi did not seem alarmed. So whatever Burjor had done, Adi was not party to it. I was glad of that.

Now Burjor seemed determined to tell the story and have done with it. He said, "All right. It may have some bearing, it may not. Here it is. About ten years ago, my brother and his wife both died in an influenza epidemic. I brought Pilloo from Lahore to live with us. Their servant boy Kasim had no one, so I brought him along. You remember, Adi, it was before you went to England. I hoped that a companion from home would help her . . . not feel so alone."

Adi rubbed his forehead. "I remember him. He was devoted to Pilloo. Followed her everywhere."

"He was a friend, someone to speak Urdu with," Burjor said, "but as she got older, it didn't seem right. He was a servant after all. When she turned twelve, I sent him back to Lahore to learn a trade. The owner of a brick factory took him as an apprentice."

All this seemed reasonable. "So what was the difficulty?" I asked.

"He would not go!" Burjor exclaimed, "He demanded to stay! Made a nuisance of himself, so"—he sounded grim—"I had two bearers take him back to Lahore."

I considered the sad tale. Burjor and his wife had adopted Pilloo as their daughter. A servant boy would be grossly overreaching to imagine himself a suitable match.

"But he died," Adi said. "How did he die?"

Burjor puffed out his lips. "The next year Pilloo was betrothed. Kasim tried to return to Bombay. He was killed in an accident, crossing a railway track."

"How old were they when they came here?" I asked.

"Pilloo was seven; Kasim, about thirteen."

"He's six years older. What year did he leave?"

Calculating, he said, "It was eighty-seven."

He'd said Pilloo was twelve five years ago, so Kasim was eighteen—a young man. His tragic life and untimely death might well be laid at Burjor's door. But who'd want to avenge him?

Burjor rose, saying, "Captain, I regret it. I should have managed it better. But at the time, how could we know?"

I took that to mean it was time for me to leave and got to my feet.

"Thank you, sir. That may prove useful." Because he seemed so pensive, I added, "I will consider what you've said."

Some trace of my bleak mood must have showed, for Adi gave me a sharp look. Perhaps he had a trace of Holmes in him too.

CHAPTER 25

LADY SLEUTH

Both Enty and the burglar Nur Suleiman would bear watching, but at present I had no means to do so. I reviewed Adi's case notes again. Every aspect of it seemed to have been explored, save two: the mysterious servant, Kasim, and the tower guard—that Havildar had been no help at all. Remembering his terror, I realized I needed a way to travel anonymously and seek my answers.

In search of appropriate attire, the next day I took a tonga to Chor bazaar, the thieves' market. Nestled among the wreckage of broken bullock carts was a shabby little shop that fit the bill. Piles of old newspapers framed the entrance. A handwritten sign offered: OLD CLOTHES AND GOODS.

"Used clothes?" I asked the owner, a fat Sindhi, his lips stained red with betel nut.

Curious, he asked, "Yes . . . for who?"

Perhaps he took me for an Englishman. "My servant," I said, "lost his on the train."

"Stolen, no doubt. One should never sleep on a train," said this vendor of the thieves' market. He spat to one side, and beckoned me inside.

"What about this?" He held up a kurta tunic from a pile on the table.

"Something longer."

I sifted through garments in rapid succession, selecting what would fit me.

"How much?" I asked without interest. Any enthusiasm usually doubled the price.

"Two annas each, Janab," he said, "Look around, I have more."

Janab—that was sir, or mister, in the tongues of the north. I chose two khamiz shirts, several cloth strips to wrap into turbans, three baggy trousers, assorted vests and kurtas.

A long black garment caught my eye. A missionary's cassock! A quick rummage produced a priest's white collar. I imagined the discomfiture of some poor *padre* at his loss, and the thief's astonishment when he found he'd stolen a pile of unusable clothes. If I was ever hired to investigate the case of the purloined cassock, these vestments could be just the ticket.

The hem showed a little wear, but no rips or tears. Those black threads I'd found in the door of the tower might belong to a lawyer's black jacket as we surmised, but here was another possibility, a cleric's black robe.

"Do you want that?" the shopkeeper asked. "The priest died, and his man came and sold his things, but I have little use for them."

So much for my speculations, if that was indeed the truth. Struck by the length of the garment, an idea sprang into my mind. The old missionary had been almost as tall as I. His cassock could prove a useful disguise.

"All right." I tossed it on top, then began the process of haggling with the shopkeeper.

He named an amount. I laughed at it.

"For old clothes? Rubbish." I offered to pay a third of what he'd asked. He fussed, then suggested something lower than his initial foray. This went on. To fail to bargain would draw immediate suspicion, but I had a more mundane reason—a depleted wallet.

An hour later I dropped the lot in my rental room behind the Forgett Street bakery. Fortunately, my run-down warehouse came cheap. I had a small pension from the army, scarcely enough to live on, and must establish myself soon. Adi's case was promising, but I seemed no closer to solving it.

For the rest of the day I assembled disguises in which to blend into the city.

* * *

Before I returned to Framji Mansion, I met a friend at Army Ordnance and Supply and procured a map of Lahore. My main lead was Kasim, who died in Lahore, a northern town in the Punjab province. So to Lahore I must go. I sent a note to Byram to reserve my railway ticket.

Spreading my map over Adi's desk, I traced a finger along the main roadways to memorize their features.

"Captain?" Diana stood at the door in a yellow sundress, a ribbon holding back her curls.

My mind went quite blank. When sense returned, I thought Burjor's disapproval of me as a suitor was surely unnecessary. Last night Diana had danced and flirted with several young men. In the light of day, last evening's closeness seemed my own wishful imaginings. She'd collected a wealth of information, but that only proved she was eager to aid her brother.

"I've something . . . to tell you." Her diffident step was a far cry from her usual dainty stride.

I straightened. "Miss?"

"It was all my fault," she said to the carpet, looking about twelve years old.

"What was, Miss Diana?" Sitting on the edge of the desk to avoid towering over her, I smiled to reassure her.

"Don't look at me like that," she muttered, hands clenched at her sides.

Was I so easy to read? I rearranged my face to show only concern. "Like what, Miss Diana?"

Rueful, she took another step. "Like I'm, oh, perfect. I'm not. I try, God knows, but . . ."

Just feet away, her freckles were endearing.

"I hate breaking things," she said, placing her palm flat on the desk.

I felt the weight of it, as though she'd placed her hand upon my chest. Breaking things? What did she mean? I watched, fascinated, as her face tightened with resolve.

"Kasim. It was my fault. Adi said you know about him."

I'd not expected that. Surely Diana was in England at the time? But here at last she might confide what she knew.

"Go on, Miss Diana."

She winced, fisted the hand on the table, and her tale rushed out.

"Ten years ago, when Pilloo came to us, she was seven. I was ten. Everyone made such a fuss of her, poor little orphan. I wouldn't speak with her, play with her. I said awful things."

She seemed determined to paint a harsh picture of herself as a child. Adi would have been a quiet, studious boy, while Diana had the spirit of a thoroughbred. I could well imagine Burjor doting on such a splendid child.

"So many had died in the epidemic," she said in a low voice. "When Papa brought Kasim here, he was three years older than me. I laughed at him because he couldn't read. So Pilloo taught him English. We'd find them together constantly.

"That's why Kasim thought . . . damn fool he was, always making eyes at her, waiting outside her room. He lived here with us but . . . something wasn't right. Pilloo seemed almost afraid of him. I told her to ignore him and she did. They quarreled—Kasim made such a fuss. When Papa heard of it, he sent him away. I felt so sorry for the trouble I'd caused. I tried to make up for it, really I did."

No one could mistake her earnestness and regret. I saw how she might feel guilt over a childhood resentment, now that Miss Pilloo was dead. It also explained why Burjor had felt the need to remove Kasim from his home. In fact, Kasim was older than I had expected. If he'd lived, he would now be twenty-three.

"You didn't pity the boy?"

"No." Diana's tone was sharp. "He . . . I can't quite explain. Kasim was . . . puffed up. He acted like he owned Pilloo."

"How?"

"Oh, a hundred little things—he'd wait for our tutor to leave, demand she come with him. Just little things. He wanted a pocket watch, so Pilloo asked Adi to buy her one. She gave it to Kasim—couldn't refuse him."

"Did she care for him?"

Diana shook her head. "Pilloo was only twelve. Kasim was upset, furious even, about being sent back to Lahore. Everyone felt awkward about it. I think Papa decided I needed discipline too and sent me off to finishing school."

True or not, Diana saw that as a sort of banishment. However, her story convinced me that Kasim was the key to this mystery.

"Is that all?"

Diana nodded, holding my gaze. Troubled, she seemed about to say more. Then her mood shifted.

"You look different without that mustache." She touched my jaw, turning me to examine my faded bruises. Her father's warning rang in my mind, his pained expression as he delivered that plea. My hands clenched on the edge of the table.

"Diana!" Adi exclaimed from the doorway.

"It's only the Captain!" Diana protested over her shoulder. She turned back to me. "You don't mind, do you?"

Only the Captain. How could such innocent words carry such a sting? But it confirmed what I knew. Diana did not consider me a suitor.

I chuckled. "No, Miss."

She grew quiet, repeated my last word. "Miss?" Then said sharply, "Captain, you're not a servant!"

"Am I not, Miss?" I said lightly.

"No!" She looked pained. "You're not."

Why was she so distressed? "What am I, exactly?"

"A friend," she said, raising her chin, "who's gone to ridiculous lengths to keep us safe."

Her fingers rose, touched my bruised temple and stayed to flick a lock of my hair. I tensed, astonished. Diana's touch was breaking rules. Did she understand the allure of her closeness? Her deep brown eyes searched me with a puzzled look.

"Diana!" Adi hissed. "Leave the poor chap alone!"

She glanced back at him, lips compressed at the interruption. I'd learned to beware of this particular mood, and right enough, for the next question knocked me for a six.

"Captain, why did you fight the burglar?"

Her dark-lashed eyes brimmed with determination and something I could not name, a sort of vulnerability. Nothing would do now but the truth.

"Miss Diana, I feared it was your room."

My answer silenced her. Realization dawned in those intelligent eyes. I looked away so she would not see too much.

"Thank you, Captain." Her breath brushed my cheek with warm softness, a touch so light I might have imagined it.

I glimpsed a curious expression on her face, akin to wonder. She'd been about to kiss me, then caught herself, stepped back. A blush crept over her as she ducked her head.

Was Diana interested in me? Adi looked as stunned as I felt. The quiet room waited, breath suspended. Had Adi not been present, would she have kissed me? No, she was just grateful, mistaking my headlong dash on the balcony for chivalry. I strove to read no more into it.

"Righto," I said, clearing my throat, which had gone dry.

Diana had turned away, deep in thought. How to bridge the moment? This morning I'd remembered something to ask her. What was it? Oh, yes.

"Ah, Miss, would you examine these. . . ." I found my foolscap sheets containing her revelations last night and handed them to her. At the top, I'd printed: Ranjpoot.

"The information you collected. Would you complete it? Transcribe it, if you wish."

Eyebrows arched, she took the page. "Did I tell you that much?"

"Yes, Miss. I'm sure I've forgotten some. Would you add what's missing?"

With a brisk nod, she took the sheet and left. I collapsed into the chair behind the desk, knowing Diana was beyond me, yet tangled in threads of amazement and hope. A part of me insisted that Burjor's warning had come too late.

As I leaned my elbows on the desk, Adi's posture caught my attention. Ramrod stiff by the French windows, he stared at me, motionless in the grip of some torment.

"Sir?"

His teeth clenched. "Adi. My name is Adi."

I straightened, disturbed to see emotion twist his gentle face. Only moments before, Diana had taken umbrage just so, at an ordinary term of address. Now Adi too seethed over it. Standing at the window, he tossed a remark over his shoulder. "You've called me Adi before, you know. After you were knifed, Captain. And when you spotted the burglar at the ball."

Something was amiss. Best I got to the bottom of it. I joined him, looking out at the garden.

"Did I?" I did not remember it. But now I needed to know where he stood. I asked, "Does it bother you, that I'm not Parsee?"

He tensed, and his chin stiffened. "As my friend, I don't give a hoot what faith you're from." He sighed, "But Diana's husband . . ."

"Must be Parsee." I finished for him.

Seeing his surprise, I said, "Your father said so. Last night, after the dance."

"Did he, by God!" Adi winced and spread his hands. "Diana . . . you could get hurt."

I wanted to deny it, but his emotion stopped me. All right, I thought. I'd meet him with as much honesty as he offered me.

"Yes."

Adi's eyes widened. He rounded on me. "Captain, why are you so reckless?"

I rocked back on my heels. Reckless? Adi's emotion did not appear directed at me. His angular body tense, he looked ready to do battle on my behalf. A surge of affection lifted me.

"Comes from being a bastard, I suppose. Tends to make one feel rather, ah, dispensable," I replied, repaying him with truth.

His breath huffed. "You are not dispensable."

"Thank you." I smiled at his outrage.

At that, Adi chuckled. I returned to the desk, thinking the strange conversation over. If I hoped to have him as a brother-in-law, pointing out my lack of parentage was not the way to go about it. As it was, I had no chance, so it could not matter.

Adi wasn't done. "Captain, I'm serious. You must guard yourself. Against Diana."

Looking up from the map, I pulled in a breath. "There's not much choice in it, sir. Your sister, she's like the sun. When it's out, there's sunlight."

Adi's face softened.

I placed my fingers on the map. "Now here, I have choices."

He joined me at the table.

"Kasim worked in a brick factory, here perhaps?" I traced the railway lines to the station. "I think that's where he died." I tapped the page. "Here's the army camp."

"You've been there? Returning from the Frontier?"

"No, we went through Karachi Port."

Karachi Port. The words brought back sounds and images, disjointed, vivid, swamping my senses. A horse shrieking. Blood on a turbaned face, eyes vicious, pouring hate. My friends in khaki, crumpled in heaps along a narrow street. Dirt scraping my face. Clouds of dust, dense, white. Gunpowder's sharp reek, choking me. Cannons growling. Walls splintering. Smoke. Fear.

Terror locked hands around my neck. I twisted away from it, blind, reaching for something to hold.

"Captain!" Adi's shocked voice seemed far away. "Are you all right?"

Breathe. Colonel Sutton's deep voice reverberated in my head. When reason returned, I found I'd grasped Adi's arm. He held my shoulders, his worry weaving through his tight grip.

"Captain?"

When I could speak I said, "It was long ago."

I dropped into a chair, exhausted. Strange. I'd not suffered a single nightmare since Adi hired me. Was it a month already? It was the longest I had not dreamt about Karachi.

CHAPTER 26

MAKING PLANS

Adi said no more about my strange episode, although now and again he glanced at me. Recovered, I worked out the details of my trip, planning how we'd communicate and the like.

"Send a telegram every two days," he said. "Papa has a business associate in Lahore. We'll get you a letter of introduction. In case you need help."

He took out a bundle of notes and counted, saying, "Three hundred rupees?"

It was too much. Surely he owed me less? Before I could reply, Adi folded the notes, pulled forward my lapel and tucked them into my pocket. He grinned like a schoolboy. "That's for expenses. When I left for England, Papa did just that. Put a wad of cash into my pocket."

I had no words.

"You'll need it for bribes," he said, "one rupee for clerks and such. Ten for officials."

I'd not considered that. Adi was learning about business from his father.

"Sahib!" Gurung, the gateman, stood at the door. We had not heard his knock.

He handed Adi a note, and touched his forehead to me in greeting. With his slanted eyes and scruffy beard, he resembled Ganju, the other Nepalese Gurkha. That gave me an idea for my visit to Lahore. Thinking of a disguise, I rubbed the stubble on my jaw. Would I have time to grow a beard?

Adi read out the note, his mouth tense. "It's from Byram. His new man says there are no tickets to Lahore for two weeks. Army has commandeered all trains. Trouble brewing, I wonder?" he said, probably weighing whether my journey warranted the risk.

I considered that. The burglar was my only lead in Bombay, but this mystery started with Kasim, who died in Lahore.

"I'll go to Lahore, sir. We need to know who's behind this."

The requisition of trains meant little—the army moved men and equipment routinely for "strategic positioning." Once I'd reassured Adi, we sent Byram word to purchase my ticket on the next available train.

I also needed to learn more about our burglar from Ranjpoot. The audacity of his manner at the ball struck me, his confidence that I could not identify him in his finery! What utter gall to strut about like a peacock, bedecked with all manner of jewels. Adi noticed my grim look and said, "What's the matter?"

"The Rani and her nephew. They came to the dance. The very home he tried to burgle."

"We had to invite them. Papa leases land in Ranjpoot. Palm trees, you know?"

Seeing that I was mystified, Adi smiled. "Ah, Captain, I know something you don't. How nice. Palm trees. We make a local beer from the sap. It's called Toddy."

"Ah!" Toddy was my staple brew in army days, since my purse did not extend to whiskey.

The burglar from Ranjpoot had tried the house twice already: the attempt I'd forestalled, and perhaps when Diana heard a noise on the roof. If this was the enemy, we'd need more than Burjor's watchmen in a skirmish, for the princedom of Ranjpoot had its own standing army. I reluctantly decided to seek Superintendent McIntyre's counsel. No doubt he thought me an upstart, but he held the Framjis in high regard.

In two weeks I'd leave for Lahore. At every turn our foes seemed a step ahead of me. I'd had enough. My plan took shape. Prince Suleiman of Ranjpoot was in Bombay. I'd locate his hotel and follow him.

"Before I leave for Lahore, sir, I'll be away for a few days. Track down the burglar."

Adi drew back, displeased. "How will I get word to you?"

"If you need me, send a note to my room behind the bakery on Forgett Street. It's the warehouse."

"Right." Adi pointed at four sacks by the window. "Those are things you asked for. Do you need to take them there?"

We loaded the sacks into the carriage with Gurung's help, and proceeded to Forgett Street, a short ride from Malabar Hill. Unlocking the rough planked door, I carried two sacks from the carriage onto the mud floor of my rental. I didn't offer Adi a seat, since none seemed nice enough.

At the far side of the warehouse a window leaned over a tiled area, with water in metal buckets. Upon the brick ledge lay my few luxuries: a bar of soap, tooth powder and my fine English razor. Ignoring Adi, who'd grown quiet, I pulled the sacking away to unwrap a large mirror. It would do very well to craft my disguises. Other jute sacks contained charcoal, salt, white ash, jars of resin, collodion and other materials, which I laid along the wall.

"Captain." Adi's voice was pained as he took in the dusty space. In contrast with Framji Mansion, it was a hovel.

"It's got three exits, sir. I come and go quietly. Rent's three rupees a week. The baker leaves me a loaf and potato vadas, for when I return late."

Adi winced. "It won't do, Captain," he said. "Why not stay at the house?"

Thinking of Burjor's sorrowful plea, I went to rinse my hands at the tiled sink.

"Thank you, but this will serve."

We shook hands and made some parting remarks. As he left, Adi took a slow look around, lips tight, as though to ask, "Is this any way to live?"

* * *

I met McIntyre the following day in the stately building on Hornby Road that housed Bombay's Constabulary. Loose and airy, my Indian attire—kurta shirt over trousers—was well suited to the April sun and heat.

McIntyre, of course, was starched upright in full uniform, service revolver buttoned into his shiny leather belt. He glared at my unshaven jaw as though I'd delivered a personal affront. I decided to wait before asking for his help.

He glowered, stood up and said, "Join me for lunch."

Before I could accept, he stalked through hallways, stopping here and there for a word with constables, his remarks cryptic to me but comprehensible to his staff, who cracked salutes left and right. I followed him into a large mess hall, empty in the late morning.

McIntyre called out. "Mess man, two plates. Jaldi! Jaldi!"

His thickly accented Hindustani grated in the quiet hall. The long tables reminded me of army mess halls, places I'd known all my life.

"Counting exits?" McIntyre said, with a smirk.

So the interview had begun. I acknowledged that the Superintendent had reason to resent me. After a very public trial, he'd failed to secure a conviction. Was my investigation a poor reflection on his competence? In hindsight, his concern for my well-being was rather generous. I sent him a brief smile.

His look was strangely kind. "Dragoons. Bombay Regiment?" he said, as an opener.

If I were lunching with a fellow officer, I'd have been glad to get acquainted. However, with danger looming over the Framjis, I felt impatient.

I said, "Sir, that's not why I'm here." Ignoring his steely displeasure, I forged ahead. "I need your help."

His face turning a ruddy pink, he barked out a laugh.

That puzzled me. Had he not asked me to seek his aid? Had he not given me a dire warning should I fail to do so? Or did he just relish seeing me grovel? I pulled out my notebook, flipped to the relevant page and waited.

"All right," he said, dabbing his lips with a white napkin, "let's have it."

"I think this started in Lahore," I said, and gave him a brief history of the servant boy Kasim, who died trying to return to the Framjis. I ended with, "So I'm going to Lahore to find the connection."

He nodded. His gaze had not wavered since I began.

I continued. "That burglar got me thinking. He might have been looking for some journal or papers used last year to blackmail the ladies. We searched every corner of the mansion, found nothing. So I'll go to Lahore. Framji's Gurkha watchmen can secure the house." I described Burjor's new guards, which put our contingent at eleven.

McIntyre frowned. "What's Framji expecting? A war?"

I drew a slow breath. This was the weakest part of my tale. "I believe we have the identity of the burglar."

This annoyed him. "You have? Or you believe?"

I shook my head. "I'm not certain."

McIntyre's lips tightened. "All right, out with it."

"Nur Suleiman, nephew of the Rani of Ranjpoot."

McIntyre glared. "What? The nephew of the Rani? Are you daft, man? Bloke was at Framjis' party, am I right?"

"Yes."

"Damn cheek."

His bland retort did not deceive me. Now he understood why Burjor's staff would not suffice. I said, "The Rani and her nephew command three native regiments."

During the long pause that followed, I massaged my aching shoulder. The mess hall was peaceful. Weary and drooping, I waited.

"Hmph. See Jameson on your way out. Know where to find him?"

Jameson, the physician? I barely recalled leaving his care. "No, sir."

McIntyre directed me with a few lefts and rights, then said, "I don't understand. What do they want with the Framjis?" He tucked a pipe into his mouth, patted his uniform but found no matches or tobacco on his person.

"I don't know yet," I said, "but . . ." I blinked. A fog swirled through my mind, shapes merged and parted as I reached into it. "This is big. It's more than the Framjis, than the two ladies' deaths." I hoped he would leave it at that.

"Big, hmm?" he asked. "Why d'you think so, eh?"

Bollocks, I thought. Holmes never revealed anything before he was good and ready. I'd have to wade into conjecture, and I wasn't prepared for it.

I cleared my throat, thinking aloud. "If it was all over when the ladies died, why attack me? Why seek something in the dead of night, just a few days after that? I'm asking questions, and it's set someone off. Prince Suleiman of Ranjpoot, perhaps. I'm a threat. So there's more going on."

"All right. Find some proof."

"Yes, sir." I paused. "During the trial, the key witness, Enty, did not identify Akbar and Behg, the two conspirators. Apte, the librarian, didn't see them either. What led you to them?"

McIntyre tapped his pipe against the edge of the table. "That's the rub. Enty gave us their names, then withdrew his testimony. Left us with purely circumstantial evidence. Gateman at the university recognized them, placed them in the grounds at the right time. Trouble was, both blighters had an alibi for that afternoon—from the butler at the Ripon Club."

Bloody hell. Enty had refused to identify Akbar and Behg! As for the butler, that was the very concierge I'd questioned. He was Akbar's man! No wonder I'd blundered into a trap. Had he set the gang on me on Princess Street?

McIntyre leaned back. "Captain, something you should know. Akbar hails from Ranjpoot."

I felt a chill. Ranjpoot again. Our burglar, Prince Nur Suleiman, was from Ranjpoot. "You're certain?"

His thick eyebrows descended. "Bloody sure. I tried the case! He's related to the Rani. She wouldn't give him up to face trial."

"Could Akbar be connected with Ranjpoot's prince, Nur Suleiman?"

McIntyre glowered, pipe clenched between his teeth. "May be the very man. Akbar's said to be a tall strapping cove. That's rare in the south. Matches your description of the burglar."

I had identified the burglar as Prince Nur Suleiman. Hadn't the concierge described Akbar as a pehelvan, an athlete? If McIntyre was right, Suleiman could be Akbar himself.

McIntyre asked, "At the dance, did he know who you are?"

"Sir, he could hardly fail to, because of bloody Byram." I mentioned Byram's article that described the attempted burglary.

"I've read it. Did Akbar know you spotted him? Lock eyes or anything?"

I searched my memory of Diana's dance. The prince had watched Diana closely, but so had every man. I'd kept my distance, watching him. Had he noticed me?

"No."

"Good! We have a chance," McIntyre said with relish. "Now. Miss Framji—where does she go?"

I stiffened. "What do you mean?"

"Where does she shop? What friends does she visit? What, now you don't trust me?" McIntyre chortled, mocking me with his knowing look. "To put a bloody Havildar about those places, you dolt. I'm to watch over the Framjis. Isn't that why you're here?"

"Ah." I mentioned Diana's dressmaker on Ripley Street, and her friends, the Petit family.

Our food arrived, and I ate quickly. McIntyre's silence was not harsh, although he continued to examine me. Did the dratted fellow never blink?

When we'd eaten, he clicked his fingers at the mess man and pointed at our dishes, by which I understood I'd been a guest of the Constabulary for lunch. With a jerk of his head that commanded me to follow, McIntyre stalked out.

I lengthened my stride to keep up. We wound about some corridors and ended in a large chamber smelling of familiar carbolic and medicine.

"Jameson," McIntyre barked, tilted his head at me and strode off.

My surgeon ambled over with a gratified smile.

We shook hands. "Thank you, sir, for the bandages."

He took my hand, turned it over and examined the fading bruises on my knuckles.

"Youth!" his cheerful voice boomed. "Best medicine there is."

He directed me to a chair, where he proceeded to turn my head and press upon my shoulder, clucking under his breath. "You'll mend, Agnihotri, if you don't get into any more scrapes."

He bent and peered into my face.

"Still having nightmares?"

CHAPTER 27

RECKONING

"Captain Jim," Diana said, standing at Adi's door, cool and fresh despite the sultry morning.

Folding my notes into Adi's legal boxes, I rose to my feet. "Morning, Miss."

Subdued, she handed me some pages and perched on the settee, smoothing her grey riding skirt. She'd revised my notations on Ranjpoot, transcribing them in her cursive hand. Noting her sober manner, I dabbed perspiration off my forehead with a kerchief and sat to read: Ranjpoot's Rani had no adult heir and must appoint a Regent until her stepson turned eighteen. Like many native rulers, she was negotiating with the Governor of Bombay to approve one. Diana had noted four contenders, including Nur Suleiman, the Rani's nephew.

"Thank you, Miss."

The silence should have warned me.

"Captain, would you drop this investigation? I know it goes against the grain, but please."

I looked up, surprised. She'd been an ardent supporter of my investigation. Now she wanted to end it? Her shoulders cramped and stiff, she looked haunted—by what?

"Good Lord, Miss. Why?"

"I asked Adi to call a halt, to dismiss you," she said. "No one listens."

"Dismiss me!"

"Oh yes, be angry, why don't you? Papa's upset. Adi's furious with me. Why not you too?" Diana leaned back on the sofa, her lips mournful.

"Why are they upset?" I asked, puzzled, thinking back to when I'd last seen them. They'd both seemed at ease.

Diana bit her lip. "After the party, the Wadias asked for a khastegari." She saw my confusion and explained. "It's a formal meeting to discuss marriage. I refused. It's too early! I've only just come home. Mama agreed with me, so it's put off for a few weeks. But then Adi blurted it all out. He's so ridiculously honest! He told Papa, about . . . yesterday. Papa said to me, 'Leave the Captain alone and let him do his job.' He's never spoken to me like that before."

Burjor's rebuke had shaken Diana. Her candor disarmed me. She said, "But Captain, please. Quit this investigation. You could return to the *Chronicle*. You'd still have a job."

I swallowed. "No, Miss. I'll see this through. Even if I'm dismissed."

Her eyes went wide. "For God's sake, why? What's it to you?"

I frowned. "For Adi, Miss. He's lost his wife. Doesn't he deserve to know why? And what of the ladies? Don't they deserve justice?"

Diana winced. "God forgive me. I care more for the living!"

She was afraid. I paused, puzzled by it. "Why, Miss? Why should I stop?"

Her eyes flashed. "Isn't it obvious? So you don't get killed!"

I straightened. This was the source of her anguish? Diana looked away. She seemed certain about some impending danger. What did she know?

"Miss, explain."

Our eyes met. "Adi didn't realize either. You identified the burglar as Nur Suleiman, prince of Ranjpoot. Adi said, 'Thanks to the Captain, we know whom we're up against.' But he doesn't see why this changes everything."

"Does it?"

She grimaced. "If it's Ranjpoot . . . if the Rani's involved and you prove it, well, it would be disastrous for her. The British could send in the army, take control of her entire princedom. It would become part of the British Raj."

I drew a breath. "She would lose Ranjpoot."

Diana nodded. "Adi and my lawyer friend Cornelia spoke about it last week. If a native ruler is incompetent or a minor, as in the Kathiawar estates, well, the Court of Wards manages everything. The Raj controls hundreds of native estates already! No one could fault them for taking over Ranjpoot."

Now our dinner with the Ministry blokes took on a darker hue. "When I returned from Matheran, who were those Englishmen at dinner?"

Her glance skittered away from mine. "Mr. Branwell is with the Home Office. I met him in London, when I lived there with the Channings. The others are on the Governor's council."

Home Office—did that mean the Crown was interested? These gentlemen had assessed me with their questions. If I succeeded, they had much to gain. If I died, they lost nothing.

I said, "If you're right, I'm a pawn in this game. A game of politics between Ranjpoot and the Raj. But, Miss, it doesn't matter. If the Rani is behind this, she must be held to account."

"You still don't see! The Rani would do anything to prevent it. If she's killed two people in broad daylight, well, what's one more?"

Bollocks. She was right. Was that why McIntyre had delivered his warning?

Diana pleaded. "Please don't go to Ranjpoot. There's no law there, no police."

"Hm." I'd visit Ranjpoot, but not until I was ready.

"And Lahore . . . I don't know. Can you take the new guards with you?"

"They're needed to safeguard the house." And you, my dear, I thought.

"Chief McIntyre, then. Could he help?"

I gave her a brief smile. "Alerted him yesterday. Don't worry, Miss. He'll watch over you while I'm away. Give me time to sort this out."

"Time?" Diana gazed at me. "Captain, we have no time. Papa is taking me to Simla in two weeks. To escape this heat."

In two weeks? I set the papers aside. The Framjis were going north to Simla, in the foothills of the Himalayas? Adi said nothing of it yesterday. Burjor must have decided this very morning, in that explosive meeting. "Simla?"

"We have a bungalow on the Mall, before Lowries Hotel."

I understood. Since I proved unable to keep my distance from Diana, her father had found a way to achieve it. I should have expected this.

Diana said, "I could refuse to go."

I straightened. "Don't do that, Miss. When do you get back?"

"July, with the monsoon."

Three months. They loomed, arid until she returned with the season of rain. Yet in Simla, Diana would be away from the threat that hung over us in Bombay.

I nodded. "You should be safer there."

The prince of Ranjpoot could have a long reach, though. I'd have a word with Burjor. He would need adequate staff on the journey.

"It's far. Three days by train," Diana said, glum.

A long silence flowed between us as I watched her worry. Seeing her thoughts flow over her face, I was riveted and devastated at the same time.

What did I reveal in turn? I could not say, but it startled Diana.

She said, "Captain, will you be careful?"

Had I once thought her sophisticated? I strove to reassure with a smile, since speech was impossible.

"You're unlike anyone I've met, Captain Jim," she said, "as quiet, as dependable as furniture! Then that night, what you did . . . Afterwards, waiting for the constable, you fell asleep. Adi and I watched over you. You were so . . . battered and worn. But you're the sort who dives into rivers when people are drowning, aren't you?"

I flinched. "Miss Diana. I'm no hero," I said, my throat thick with pain.

She leaned closer, searching my face, but for what?

The movement rocked a small planter on the window behind us. I steadied it with a hand, her closeness affecting me like wine.

"What is it?" Her gaze dropped to my lips.

All at once, a voice inside me warned, "Have a care! There's no going back!" Diana was curious, but could not really care for me, could she?

She smiled. "You look younger when you sleep." Her hand reached out.

I caught her wrist in midair, held firm. "Miss Diana, don't . . . toy with me."

I had not intended to say that, but it would do.

She stared at me, horrified. "Is that what I'm doing?"

"You know I'm not Parsee." Her wrist was tiny. I loosened my grip.

She pulled her arm away. "Did my mother say something? Or Papa?"

She read the confirmation on my face and cried, "Why do they dictate everything? All my life, I've known my duty. To marry well! Bring forth a new generation! I've always obeyed them. But now? It's my life!"

Cheeks red, she winced. "Bacha died so young. Pilloo, before her life had even begun! What if you . . ."

What if I were killed, hunting the ladies' murderers? A wave of affection caught me unawares.

She looked agonized. "Captain, do you never break the rules?"

I drew a slow breath. "I have. But never without consequences, my dear."

She steadied. Her eyes flickered, registering the endearment. "All right. I'll wait," she said. "Come back soon." How she resembled Adi in that moment, determined and intense!

Come back soon. Those three words lifted my spirits and sent them winging, a kite in a high gale. My God, I thought. What I'd read as willful youth was steadier and more insistent than I'd believed. For some strange reason, Diana might actually oppose her father and choose me!

Then reality set in and emptied the room of air. She was going to Simla, where India's colonial administration and Bombay society flocked to escape the summer heat. Soon she'd be among a host of clever fellows. An heiress, and fair game no matter what her father wished. Reluctant to curb her impetuous nature, yet fearing some headlong dash into uncertain waters, I searched for a way to caution her.

"Miss Diana, you don't know me."

"Of course I do!" she retorted, placing her hand upon my bare forearm.

What new mischief did she have in mind? I raised an eyebrow.

Her laugh was water gurgling over river stones.

She grinned, warm and impish in her delight as she withdrew her fingers, saying, "See? Anyone else would have grabbed my hand and made some sappy remark. You don't do that. One can learn a lot by listening, you see. When you spoke of . . . Mullicka, was it? You said, such power in her, and yet so gentle. That . . . moved me."

"A fine gift from my officer, Colonel Sutton." Sutton had won handsomely, betting on me at a boxing match. I watched Diana, riveted.

She launched into a list, counting on her fingers, "I know that you grew up in a Mission in Poona. You joined the Dragoons. You got injured last year and left the army. And when you met Adi, you were a journalist." She triumphantly concluded the story of my life.

I said, "That's what I've told you. How d'you know it's true?"

She looked puzzled.

"What if I lied?"

"I'd know. I'd just know," she assured me, then said defiantly, "Tell me a lie."

I laughed, shaking my head. I flicked a ribbon that bounced by her ear, and gazed into her eyes, now glinting with amusement.

"Miss, you're a bit like my sister. She's younger, of course, married to a civil service chap in Delhi. She has a three-year-old, David. She used to pepper me with questions, like you."

Diana's lips curved. "What's her name?"

I looked out at the verandah and heaved a sober breath. It was a nice fiction, and for a moment I wished it were true.

"Oh God," Diana whispered. Realization bleached her face, leaving it stark. She swallowed and said, "That was a lie!"

I saw the hurt, and felt like a cad. When she told me about Kasim, she'd said, "I hate to break things." Now I felt the same.

"Can all men lie?" she asked.

"Yes," I said, "though some are better at it."

Diana examined me as though memorizing pages in a book. "I won't forget you, Captain."

"I hope not," I said, striving for a light note, and turned back to her notes.

It would have to do, for I was going to Lahore to sort out the truth of Kasim's death. Despite my fondness for her, and her interest, how could I court Diana? With neither name nor fortune, if she chose me against Burjor's wishes, how could I support our life together?

CHAPTER 28

A PATHAN COMES TO DINNER

Over the next few days, dressed in different disguises, I shadowed Prince Nur Suleiman and some of his cohorts. Experimenting with my new supplies, I copied the appearance of men I'd known. Different turbans and white powder masked my longish hair, while layers of collodion added scars or changed the contours of my face.

Often I followed Prince Suleiman to the dockyard and spent a great deal of time there. One evening Ramu, the Framjis' little gap-toothed boy, brought a note to my room at the bakery. I let him in, grinning through my untidy beard at his astonishment.

Ramu gaped at me. "Sahib?"

I planned to travel to Lahore dressed as a Pathan, an Afghan tribesman from the northwest province. These fighters were generally tall and weather-beaten, so I would not look out of place. I'd known Pathans in the army, illiterate, proud fellows, quick to temper or laughter—one could never be quite sure which—and loyal to the core. Some tribes were friendly to the British army, while others, the Ghazis and Afridis, despised us. I was safer there as a Pathan and more likely to find answers.

"Betho—sit," I said, and took the note to the lamp to read.

Mrs. Framji wrote that it'd been a while since I'd dined with them. Would I come now, before dinner got cold?

I debated leaving for Lahore without meeting the Framjis. Cleaning up for an appearance at the house was out of the question. My beard and worn clothing were ready for my trip.

But I wanted to see Diana before she left for Simla. A plan took form in my mind.

"Who else is coming to dinner?" I asked, pulling a long grey kaftan over my head.

"Just you, Sahib." Ramu remained on his haunches by the door, looking worried.

"Is the carriage here?"

"Hah, Sahib."

Winding a turban around my head, I checked the mirror, then pulled on my comfortable army boots. I washed hands before I set out. Mrs. Framji was rather particular about clean hands.

Here was a chance to test my new guise. If I could get by the Framjis, who knew me well, it would surely pass with anyone else. In *The Sign of Four*, Holmes masqueraded as a sailor, deceiving Watson and Detective Lestrade. Was my disguise as convincing?

When the carriage halted at the gate, three new watchmen rushed up, and it took a while to reassure them. I told them it was a test of their alertness, and they withdrew, looking askance and shaking their heads.

Framji Mansion glowed at the end of the curved drive, where gaslights turned the pillars to silver. I approached in darkness, my footsteps crunching amid a chorus of crickets. The still air was pleasant, yet it held a warning too, some presentiment that this moment was precious and rare, not to be broken with careless words or experiments. Too late to fall back now, I thought. I'd committed to a course of action and would see it through.

Clothes maketh the man, the old adage warns. Did the Framjis' regard depend solely upon my appearance, as someone they'd grown familiar with? Would they know me well enough to see through my exotic costume?

Whom did I want to test? Adi? Burjor and Mrs. Framji? Or was it Diana? How would she react when I revealed myself? For I was more than the British soldier she knew. Would she accept my Indian side with equal aplomb? These two were inseparable within me, after all I'd seen and done.

My pulse quickened as I strode up the clean, porcelain sweep of stairs.

I stomped heavily through the entryway and corridor, thinking to give fair warning to the family waiting for dinner.

It did not suffice. As I stopped in the doorway, a little hunched, and touched my forehead in greeting, Adi bolted up from his chair.

Nor had I reckoned with the children being at dinner. Adi's younger brother pointed at me and yelped. The littlest one wailed. Burjor at the head of the table reached over and scooped her up, hushing and rocking to comfort her. Another child, a girl, dashed out toward the kitchen.

"Oh dear," I said, in my normal voice.

"Captain!" cried Diana and ran to me, eyes bright and amazed. She caught my arm, took in my beard and examined my turban. Her nose wrinkled at the smell of my clothes. The odor of sweat and dust marked me as a working man, a laborer of some sort. I didn't mind the stench, wore it as part of my disguise. A whiff of lavender would turn heads where I was going and draw suspicious stares.

"Turn around!" she commanded.

I did so with a flourish that set the baby to crying again.

Mrs. Framji hurried in from the kitchen, her younger daughter peeking from behind her.

Would she know me? I stepped up, bent and touched her feet in the traditional greeting of elders. "Salaam, Maji." (Mother, I greet you.)

I smiled at the frightened girl hiding behind Mrs. Framji's knees, her brown eyes wide.

"Dikra?" meaning "son," Mrs. Framji said, sounding puzzled. "Who is he?"

I rose to my full height and met her gaze.

She gasped, a hand over her lips. "Captain? What have you done? You've grown so thin!" Her delicate fingers fluttered over my cheek.

Ah, that's where Diana got it from. A wave of comfort lifted and carried me in its wake.

"Thank you for the note, Mrs. Framji," I said. "I've missed your splendid meals."

The clan erupted into laughter and relief. Moments later I was seated, and my plate piled with more food than it could hold. I answered questions between mouthfuls of sausage, sweet potatoes, lamb curry and saffron rice.

Now that his fright was past, Adi's little brother climbed astride my knee to show he was not afraid. Mrs. Framji bid him add another sausage to my plate.

The little one was placed in my arms, to learn that a bearded man was not a fearful thing. Round and warm, she pulled at my beard with tiny fingers, while I explained my plan.

"You look the part, Captain," Diana said, "but can you carry it off?"

"I was a Sowar for three years," I replied. "A Sepoy on horseback. I knew Rashid Khan, the fellow I'm dressed as, quite well."

"Ah!" said Adi. "That's why you're so convincing. He's a real chap. Where is he now?"

"Dead, I'm afraid." I chewed, steering my mind away from Karachi, where Rashid met his end. If only I'd got to him sooner. "Sir, I'm on the eleven o'clock train, so I won't stay long."

Ganju, the Gurkha houseman, set a dish on the sideboard. He'd been watching with concern as I spoke to the Framjis in English. He addressed me now in Gurkhali, his own dialect, "Sahib, I could come with you."

"Your job is here," I said in the same tongue. "Keep them safe, or you answer to me."

The dialect came easily to my lips, and I felt reassured. My new persona would hold.

Ganju stared, and went back to serving pudding.

Hearing me speak, Adi began to laugh. He leaned back in his seat, shoulders shaking.

As I gave the baby to Diana, her arm brushed me. The curve of her throat, the smooth cream of her cheek—ah, how these tugged at me.

Burjor said, "You sound so different. You stand and move like someone else."

Adi said, "You look like an Indian now. A native, as the English would say."

"Sir, I *am* a native," I replied, skewering the last sausage before Ganju replaced my plate with a bowl of pudding.

"No," rumbled his father, "you're not. Like us, you're in between, or both. Neither fully English, nor fully Indian."

I savored a spoonful of Mrs. Framji's pudding, a warm moment of solidarity glowing within me.

After the meal Ganju brought bowls of water in which to wash our fingers. Wiping off on the proffered towel, I reached into my kaftan and handed Adi a wad of papers. "Sir, my report."

He took it with a searching look. "Something new?"

When I nodded, he secured the bundle in his breast pocket. A weight dropped from me then, for I'd given him all I had learned in the last ten days, and what it likely meant.

As I left Framji Mansion that night, my footsteps crunched into the stillness. The scent of jasmine brought the weight of nostalgia. I'd not yet left, and already I felt homesick.

"Captain!" a voice called behind me.

Diana. I swung around.

She dashed down the stairs, skirts fisted in her hands. She'd go to Simla soon, and be away for three months. When next we met she could be engaged to someone else. Yet I had a job to do in Lahore, and wishing would not change it. Did she truly care for me? Could we have a future together? Diana stopped a few feet away, eyes gleaming.

When I said nothing, she burst out, "I know who complained about you to the Governor."

"Do you, now."

"At the Petits last night, I saw Superintendent McIntyre go over to the Governor's secretary. Pandey, I think he's called. So I followed him. They went out to the verandah, so I . . . I stood by the window and listened. McIntyre mentioned you. He asked, 'Who was it that drew the Governor's attention to this?' And Pandey said, 'Oh, that clerk, Francis Enty, of Lloyd's. His lordship banks there. Enty asked why we're still investigating after the case ended months ago.'"

Enty! I pieced it together. "Enty might know I have his letter. He lied about his wife being in Poona."

"Good heavens. Why?"

"Don't know. McIntyre said he withdrew his testimony the very next day. Refused to identify Akbar and Behg, so McIntyre couldn't place them at the scene. It ruined his case."

That was my missing link. Why had Enty refused to identify Akbar and Behg? Could they have abducted the missing Mrs. Enty? Had they held her this long? If so, months after the trial, Prince Suleiman, alias Akbar, still compelled Enty to silence—but how? I'd followed Suleiman for days and seen no contact between them.

I thought of Diana in her evening gown, snooping on government business.

"Miss Diana," I said slowly, "you cannot do this. Listening around corners and such." When she began to protest, I cut her off. "I understand why you did, but please."

"All right," she said. "Captain, I can't get used to this new appearance."

Simla was full of dashing young men. I wanted to tell her to wait, not rush into something she might regret. But what was within me would take longer to say than this stolen moment, and I would not speak the words dressed in another man's clothes.

Diana's fingers knotted at her waist. "Don't change . . . who you are," she said softly.

What was she afraid of? "Hm?"

Indigo shadows played across her cheeks. "Don't let the disguise become you."

Surprised, I said, "It's just clothes."

"It's not." Her voice wobbled. "You sounded different when you spoke to Ganju. Like someone . . . crude and harsh."

The accuracy of that made me pause. It was who I had to be now, a surly Pathan seeking his long-lost brother Kasim. I would wear brusqueness to fend off unwanted questions, retreating into Rashid or my memory of him, so he would not disappear, not entirely. Would it change me? The question sat sharp-edged in my gut. Trust Diana to know where the real threat lay.

"Shhh." I reached for those slender hands and took them in my own. Despite the warm air, her fingers were cold. "I'll be here when you return from Simla."

Would I return? The north bubbled with unrest, and a storm was brewing in the Punjab. I hoped to get in and out, with my answers, before it broke.

Diana was still. Did she know what I was thinking?

"See that you are." She squeezed my hand, pulled away and hurried back to the house.

I watched until she waved from the top stair. She was still standing at the great door when I stepped through the gate.

CHAPTER 29

AWAY TO LAHORE

Huddled in a third-class carriage as my train rumbled across the plains, I considered what I knew of Lahore. Once a walled city in eastern Punjab province, it had long since spilled past the fort to sprawl over a wide tract along the river. Now a two-day train ride north of Bombay, it was a key military supply post, the central point between Delhi and the untamed Frontier.

I'd already learned that my gaze was too mild. It invited conversation and I wanted none. By adopting a scowl, I rebuffed most fellow travelers' attempts to draw me out. Despite this, a Babu—a minor official in a dark jacket that bulged about his middle—took a liking to me. Curious, his gaze lingered upon me, but he did not cause me much concern. Since many Pathans were light-skinned, my color was unlikely to give me away.

When I fell asleep things went awry. Perhaps the smell of the Punjab, sweat, warm hay and horse manure, filtered into my dream. Metallic clanking from the carriage ahead brought memories of army ordnance and munitions. Perhaps the jolting passage over a bridge or a screeching halt at a station misled me, for my mind was back in Karachi.

I felt pain, but could not tell where I hurt. My nightmare twisted around me and tightened, the hammer of wheels joining the pounding in my head. A bloodied face came at me, straining. I froze, grabbed and held him off.

I awoke to a pair of terrified eyes inches away. It was daylight, and the carriage was in an uproar as several travelers strove to restrain me.

Wrinkles radiated down the face of the man I held against the wall of the carriage. Stunned, I pulled my forearm back from his throat. My hand unclenched, releasing his clothes. I slumped into my seat and stared at the fellow I'd assaulted—an old man with thin white whiskers. He doubled over, his turban tumbling to the floor.

What had I done? The faces around me evaded my gaze or met it with suspicion. What had I called out? Had I spoken in English? What of the poor wretch I'd almost strangled? Someone handed the old man his turban.

"Shama karo," I gasped in apology. Weary and woolly-headed, I leaned back against the seat. Someone offered me a tin cup of water. I took it gratefully, spilled some and drank.

"Fauji hai." (He's a soldier.) My fellow travelers had decided I was a Pathan soldier, going home on sick leave.

"What happened?" someone asked in the Punjabi dialect.

The Babu, a clerk or accountant perhaps, appointed himself to answer on my behalf. "This one"—he pointed to the old man huddled across from me—"fell on him. Woke him."

I ignored the puzzled murmurs.

"Bhayah" (brother), he said to me, "you should see a doctor."

He proceeded to list a slew of remedies for various ailments. Ignoring him, I resolved to remain awake for the rest of my journey. I'd almost given myself away. Strange that I did not dream in Adi's home, not once, despite my skirmish in the dark. I felt safe there, clear in my role and my task.

The Babu assured me I would be all right, beaming like a proud mother. I winced at the old man, ashamed to have handled him roughly. Deep creases in his face, he nodded patiently.

* * *

The travelers grew friendly over the next two days, a camaraderie thrust upon them by hours and proximity, but I remained silent, shaking my head when questioned, brushing off sympathetic looks.

We reached Lahore at dusk. The carriage emptied, passengers erupting from their cramped quarters. I hoisted my sack from the floor and slung it over a shoulder, my right arm sore, despite Jameson's assurances. As I dropped from the train to the concrete three feet below, my knee protested that foolhardy decision.

Across the deserted platform, a weak lamp glowed by a small brick building where the call of crickets swelled. Only the Babu and his ingratiating smile remained.

"Bhayah," the round little man addressed me, and made a motion to carry my sack.

I shook my head, thanked him briefly and limped away to find a rickshaw. But I hadn't considered the hospitality innate in my compatriot. Had I approached him in his official capacity, he'd no doubt squeeze a hard bargain in bribes. But confronted with a lonely, broken soldier, he did not just offer assistance, he insisted upon it.

In my pocket was Burjor's letter of introduction to the Talukdar, tax collector of Lahore. I did not expect to use it. Instead I'd find the brick factory where Kasim had lived and worked, and discover who might want to avenge him. I pulled out a crumpled scrap on which I'd written Kasim's address.

"My brother," I said, pointing at the scrawl.

The Babu took the paper with relish, thinking me an illiterate fellow, and said he would accompany me. At the next intersection, a mule-drawn tonga stood under a gaslight.

While I had a comfortable command of the northern dialects, it behooved me to say little, to avoid detection. My lack of local knowledge would expose me. So, resolved to play the stranger, I boarded the tonga with my cheerful companion to rattle over murky, cobbled streets.

The Babu proved a helpful, if garrulous chap. That suited me well. Crowded beside me in the cart, he spoke about the planting season, his village (someplace called Awal), and assured me that he knew all the "big people" of this town. As intelligence it was scattered and random, but might be useful. I pretended not to listen. Since he was evidently content with this arrangement, we proceeded in agreement. Bare, narrow streets gave way to a cluster of light, a bazaar in the distance.

The smokestacks of the brick factory, squat against the sky, blocked out a swath of stars. Seeing a glimmer ahead, we slowed and disembarked before a cluster of low-thatched houses lit with kerosene lanterns. The night had cooled. Marching ahead, the Babu addressed two men who lounged on a charpoy bed in the courtyard. I limped along behind him, with an aching knee that I did not have to feign.

"Kasim's brother?" the older man said.

The younger one, evidently his son, with the same bushy eyebrows and beard, said, "Kasim is dead."

I stopped where I stood, for all three turned to stare at me. "Dead?"

The older man approached and gave me a brief history. "Yes, Janab, Kasim did work here. A hardworking youth. Some years ago, he died in a train accident."

The son brought a dozen or so dark-clothed men and women in shawls, who formed a circle around us. I felt oddly distant, playing a man learning of his brother's death.

I'd paused too long after the man finished speaking. Some of the group moved restlessly while the rest looked on. I questioned the older man. "Where did he die?"

He conferred with those around him and said, "Janab, he died at Moga station, on the way to Bombay."

A frisson of surprise flickered in me. "Was anyone with him? You? Anyone here?"

A sorrowful whisper rose from the perimeter. The older man shook his head.

"Did anyone see his body?"

The balding Babu patted my arm, since I still denied the fact of my loss.

The older man answered with reluctance, "No, Janab, he fell under a train."

Had hapless Kasim, desperate to cross the tracks and catch his train, bled to death from his injuries? I dropped my head and searched for my next question. The group waited, their courtesy no less kind for all its rough simplicity.

"How did you hear of it?"

"A telegram." The older man did not recall any more about it.

"Did he have friends?" I used the Punjabi word for companions.

"All of us," the man said, spreading his hands.

These brickmakers and workmen had known Kasim, and perhaps liked him. It was time to leave, before they began to ask questions. I nodded, placed my hand upon my heart in a gesture of thanks, hefted my sack and began to walk away.

I'd taken a few steps when a voice called out, "Janab!"

Perhaps I made a solitary figure, standing outside the circle, but this seemed my natural place, the wanderer, the man over whom they would puzzle tomorrow.

The older man approached. "My mother says a doctor tended Kasim."

I drew a slow breath. "Does she remember anything else?"

My question was relayed to an old woman. I trudged over, bent to her and waited.

A small, shriveled face peered out from layers of cloth. A bony hand extended from her shawl, and her dry voice warbled, "Janab, during the tragedy, Doctor Aziz took care of Kasim."

"Maji, how do you know?"

"Why, Doctor Aziz told us Kasim is dead. He sent us the telegram!"

"Where is Doctor Aziz now?"

No one knew, but they would not have me leave. "At least take a cup of tea, Janab!"

While I hesitated, the Babu accepted eagerly, and launched into a description of my fracas on the train. A born raconteur, he knew the value of a good tale. This did not overly concern me. My guise held, so if the Babu chose to use our acquaintance for a story, what of it?

Sitting on a charpoy, I accepted a steaming cup of tea and asked, "Why did Kasim leave? Was he not content?"

The older man grimaced, spreading his hands. "Janab, he did not like it here. We are plain folk. Kasim could read! He wanted to be a great man. So he left for Bombay."

The group became more talkative, asking about Kasim's (and my) parents. I described the epidemic in which Kasim's parents perished, and the conversation eddied and drifted. These simple folk could tell me no more.

It was late but I dared not sleep here. I might call out in my sleep and give myself away. A short while later, I thanked them and the surprised Babu, and left.

CHAPTER 30

UNEXPECTED EVENTS

That night I walked dark lanes, toward the bazaar lights in the distance. Lahore was unknown to me, one street much the same as another. My stomach rumbled. I'd not eaten much during the journey, and now the aroma of grilled meat beckoned. Hampered by my stiff knee, I trudged toward it.

Tomorrow I would visit the train station, cable Adi about my progress and seek the whereabouts of Doctor Aziz. This decided, I turned into a bustling street.

The raucous bazaar smelled enticing, with food prepared in little carts all around. Other vendors squatted on their haunches with baskets of fruit, bread or meat. Lit by flickering lanterns, a turbaned Pathan rotated a hunk of beef over a wood fire.

I pointed at the meat, bought some and crouched beside the road to devour slivers of carved meat in a thick disk of naan bread. From this vantage I observed the street. When a fruit seller passed, I bought apples. Next, a boy tried to sell me cheese. Had I not seen a thousand such lean, spry urchins, as willing to ply their wares as to run off with one's purse? When he would not leave, I bought a small cloth-wrapped lump and sent him away.

Diana would not approve of my ill temper. She'd be fascinated by this street, with its smoky lamps that yellowed passersby and sent shadows dancing on the cobbles.

Pockets of young men laughed together. Families clustered, the children all but tripping burkha-clad women by running underfoot. A husband stalked ahead, a small boy abreast, while his wife and another child trailed behind, sharing sweetmeats. Babies, swaddled in homemade blankets. A boy in a smart vest and kurta proudly bore a large kite, followed by his protesting younger brother. No one walked alone. When I tired of this pageantry I crossed a bridge to a quieter street.

Here, pairs of turbaned men leaned against mud and brick walls. They watched me, a solitary stranger, with suspicion. Seeking a safe place to sleep, I plodded along the riverbank.

A large man is, in my experience, generally left alone. Carrying a plain sack and dressed in ordinary garb, I had little cause for concern. Yet I feared to sleep for two reasons: thieves grow bolder when their prey slumbers, and my outburst on the train warned me about my somewhat unsteady frame of mind. Were I to call out in English in my sleep, no guise would protect me. Although the British administered Punjab province, that was still fairly recent, and strangers were not welcome.

Finding a nook under a bridge unoccupied, I ducked into it and waited, my hand curled around the butt of Adi's revolver. As birds rooked and flapped somewhere above, I listened for a footfall, but none came.

A small dinghy moored under the bridge offered shelter, so I pulled it close, peeled back the cloth covering and found it empty. Its boards smelled of rotting fish and river kelp, but I climbed in and stretched out in the small space. Pushing off into the shallows with an oar, I felt content. If anyone should approach, the splash of water would warn me. With that comforting thought, I drifted off.

✳ ✳ ✳

While I slumbered, Lahore burned. I woke, choking on the acrid stench of smoke. I was trapped. Karachi. Panic rising, I felt cloth above me. Some perverse breeze had wrapped the blanket close over the dinghy, and for a few awful moments I struggled to escape. The air was thick and stale. I gasped and choked as remnants of sleep scattered. Rubbing eyes that itched and burned, I remembered where I was, not in Karachi, but Lahore.

A haze of smoke screened the distant shore. Fire? What had happened last night? I waded to the nearest bank, plunked down on its slope and tugged off my boots. As I drained water from them and squeezed out my baggy pants, footsteps and voices sounded on the bridge above.

I climbed the embankment and saw a stream of bedraggled people hurrying over the bridge, their possessions slung in bundles or piled upon their heads. Women carried infants, an arm or leg dangling from a cloth sling. They pushed ahead, stark worry and alarm in their faces.

"What's happened?" I asked a man.

"Pathans are coming! Pakhtuns!" he snarled, hurrying on.

This alarmed me. Pakhtun—soldiers? Were they not an independent princely state, an Afghan tribe in the northern mountains? If they were here, Lahore might soon be under siege as the British vied for control of the city.

Bollocks. I was on a battle line again. I had to get back to Adi.

I asked an old man hunched at the crossroad, "Janab, which way to the station?"

Eyes dull, he pointed to a deserted street.

The station house was silent. I crossed the platform and tried each door without success. Around back, where the single lantern hung last night, someone peered through the slats of a window.

"When's the next train to Bombay?" I called out in Urdu.

A rumpled guard opened half a shutter and squinted out at me.

"Janab, all trains stopped," he said, as if repeating himself.

All trains stopped? I was stranded in Lahore, goddammit. "Why?"

Having had enough of my questions, the guard closed his shutter.

I'd have to wait until the trains resumed. But perhaps I could further my inquiries. A doctor was surely a rarity in these parts. I called to the railway guard. "Do you know Doctor Aziz? Where is he?"

The shutter opened a few more inches. "Doctor Aziz? He's not here. He left years ago!"

"Where did he go?"

"Who knows? He went with the army."

An army doctor! I was on sound footing here. Why not cable McIntyre to find out where the good doctor was posted? I would also telegram Adi as promised.

"Where's the telegraph office?"

"Here in the station. Closed."

I argued with him, demanding to send a cable, but he was adamant. It was no use, he said. The lines were down.

Thinking, I retraced my steps to the crossroad. If the trains had shut down, the Afghan soldiers must be near. A shiver brushed my skin like a column of ants.

Without telegraph, I could not cable news of my delay to the Framjis. Not for anything would I alarm them, but now lacked means to reassure. That reminded me of the introduction in my pocket to Burjor's tax collector friend. He might own a telephone. After a few failed attempts, I gained directions. For the rest of the day I walked through deserted streets and lonely scrub to a suburb of Lahore where the tax collector resided.

Lahore is a maze of streets that curve around so that one might start out east and soon find oneself headed north. I persisted, finding my landmark, a well in a dusty clearing. As I approached, thinking to pull a cool bucket and drink, I noticed flies swarming and a foul odor. Dark smears of blood pooled around the wellhead. Were there bodies down there? What had happened here last night?

Worried, I headed down a wide street bordered by blackened trees. In what was once a fashionable part of town, white fluted pillars and gateposts now protruded like bones from the blackened corpses of once-splendid houses. The mansion I sought looked intact, until I noticed the roof had caved in. The tax collector's home was charred and smoldering.

As I crouched by a stone gatepost to catch my breath, a familiar sound echoed in the hills. Gunfire. The crack of rifles sounded close. Panic swelled, threatening to swamp me.

Breathe. Colonel Sutton's voice growled in my head, low and comforting. I waited, clenched and undecided. Minutes passed before I collected myself. Afghan soldiers were close by. But who were they fighting? The answer brought enormous relief. For I realized the British army was near as well.

Rising to my feet, I moved along the wall toward the gunfire. The hills echoed with it, each nearby crack repeated in bursts of menace. Was the company pinned down? Where were they shooting from? They were close.

Then I remembered—I was dressed as a Pathan. A Sepoy would ask no questions before lifting his musket to shoot. If I were still in the army and a Pathan approached me, speaking English, what would I have done? I'd have no time for his story. At best I'd arrest him and take him back to barracks to sort it out later. No, it would not do. If I wasn't shot on sight, I'd be stuck explaining myself for weeks.

Bombay and safety had never felt so far away.

* * *

For the next two days I joined a river of refugees along the Grand Trunk Road retreating from the stench and smoke of Lahore. At each crossroad a few branched off toward neighboring villages. Others spoke of towns nearby, Amritsar and Jalandhar.

"Where are they going?" I asked a young man beside me.

He shrugged. "Back to their village. When it is safe, they will return."

I applauded this resilience, but was unsurprised. Indians tend to adapt without complaint. And to whom could they protest? The pull and push of factions vying for ascendance was no more startling than the crash of waves in the ebb and flow of tides.

Spotting a railway track, I left the Grand Trunk Road and joined those who climbed over a fence to follow it eastward. At a village station, a map on the wall informed me that Simla was a hundred and fifty miles to the east. Simla! Diana and the Framjis had probably just arrived. I could get there in a day by coach, but no trains chugged up the line. Instead a straggling line of pedestrians tapered into the horizon.

Despite my military boots, my feet ached when at last I reached a little town along the track and shuffled down to the cluster of stalls that formed a market. The deluge of refugees had already stripped produce from carts and shops and what remained was priced outrageously. I supped that night on thin roti bread and an ear of broiled corn that had never tasted sweeter.

I asked the way among a cluster of people buying apples. This set off an excited discussion, as young and old volunteered what they knew of roads, rivers and trails. Their talk continued as I retreated, newcomers inquiring about farther destinations.

The afternoon sun beat down. I wound a rag about my head and chin, to trudge, head down, with other refugees. Walkers struck up conversations on that road, but I could afford no such luxury. For questions invariably turned to "where are you from?" or "where are you going?" and I wanted neither. When conversation threatened, I left my curious companions and hunkered down beside the road to rest. In this way, I traveled alone.

CHAPTER 31

THE PURCHASE

As dusk fell, most groups settled into small camps around cooking fires. Seeing the glow of a settlement ahead, I clumped toward a small railway station house. At a nearby well I drank and washed, then lay down on the cool cement platform for the night.

All day I'd followed the train track, passing fields and thatched huts. Now I slumped in the shadow of the quiet station house, amid the sound of crickets and distant voices from the town. An owl hooted. Lamplight touched leaves in the tall trees, yellowing them.

Footsteps approached from behind me. I tensed. What now?

As I sat up on the station platform, a curious sight approached in the twilight. A thickset man held a rope tied to a shapeless, bundled figure.

"Brother, only two rupees," he said, offering me an ingratiating smirk.

What was it? He tugged the shape out from behind him: a small burkha-clad woman, bound at the wrist.

"Two rupees. For a half hour," said the man, pumping his hips.

Was he offering this woman for my pleasure? I stared, aghast, as he went to his haunches to haggle the price.

Then I heard a sob. Goddammit. Alone in this countryside, I could ill afford to be embroiled in a fracas, but what choice was there?

"How old?" I demanded, outrage swelling in my throat.

"Only twelve!" the fellow grinned, showing crooked teeth.

"Are you her father?"

He drew back, affronted. "What's it to you? No, I bought her."

"What did you pay for her?" I wanted to plant a fist in his well-rounded middle.

His betel-red lips cracked in a wide smile. The fiend knew he had me. For the next few minutes he extolled the virtues of his wares: young, strong, works hard, can bear many children, while I cursed him for a thief and a crook.

"Two hundred," he wheedled. "A wife for only two hundred rupees!"

The belt around my waist held that and a bit more. Yet if I purchased this poor wretch, I must still feed us both until she could be safely sent to relatives, or gain employment.

I suppose from the moment I heard that sob, my decision was made. Perhaps the stream of refugees was in my mind, men and women trudging along, families in little groups. This child belonged with some such companions, not tethered like a dog.

If I could not buy the poor creature I resolved to follow in the gloom and take her from the brute who peddled her. That was assault—it did not worry me overmuch. Here in the wilderness, civilized law seemed prim and distant.

"One hundred," I said, looking away as though done with him.

We went back and forth, until he said, "Hundred and thirty rupees, Janab."

I counted it out. A rope was pressed into my hand and I had bought a human being.

I called her Chutki, which means little one. Once her chuckling master withdrew, I loosed her wrists. Her face was hidden in the dusk, so I handed her an apple, my last, picked up my sack and stepped onto the railway track.

"Come," I said, walking away.

After a moment, she followed.

Not for anything would I remain at the station house. That brigand might return with reinforcements, or knife me while I slept, to regain the girl. Instead, I followed the track east toward Simla. Chutki followed in silence, lagging far behind.

The night deepened into darkness. Impatient with her slow pace, I doubled back and beckoned. When that had no effect, I hoisted her into my arms. She weighed far less than Diana had, when I'd carried her at the ball.

The child did not struggle. After a single gasp, she ducked her head, limp and uncomplaining. Twice we stopped on the moonlit road and hid in shadows. The first time a horse went by, its rider passing in careful search. When the moon rose above the trees, the rider returned at a swift trot. I waited, one hand across Chutki's mouth, my other gripping the revolver, motionless until the sound of hooves faded into distance.

When the horizon glowed purple with distant dawn, a wall beside a stream afforded a secluded place to sleep. I put the child down on the sack that contained little more than a few clothes and settled on the grass, weary and aching. I cursed inwardly, expecting I'd wake to find that she'd robbed me and run off. Well, so be it.

* * *

When daylight broke, the girl was still there. She'd curled up in her black garb where I placed her. Now she sat and glanced about, peeking at me from time to time.

Our track ran along a rivulet. I waded in, still wearing baggy trousers, and scooped up sparkling water. That morning, the cool, clear stream quenched more than my thirst, it restored me. Bathing away the smell of yesterday's fish and grime, my shoulder swung freely. Despite the long trek, my knee held steady as I hauled myself up the pebbled bank to retrieve fresh clothing.

Chutki watched these proceedings from what I later learned was her habitual pose, knees pulled up, hands clasped before her face.

Last night I'd given her my breakfast, and a rummage through the sack produced nothing edible. I turned to the girl.

"Do you speak Pashto?" I asked in that tongue.

She gasped at being addressed directly and hid her face. "Yes."

"Go." I pointed toward the stream. "Get clean."

She stood, looked at me for a long moment, then hobbled toward the water. I finished dressing, counted out my remaining money, placing it in suitable pockets so as to have the required denominations at hand, then checked and reloaded Adi's revolver. We had evaded Chutki's captor last night, but he might yet find us.

She returned, still wearing the burkha, and stopped, staring wide-eyed at my weapon. Pocketing it, I searched the sack for something she might wear. Finding a kurta-shirt that might serve as a floor-length dress, I tossed it to her.

She took it, lifting the hem of her burkha, uncertain.

"Throw that thing away," I said. My disgust at her captor was tied, somehow, to that burkha. Indeed, without it, we'd be harder to find.

"Bao-di" (father), said a small voice, when she was done. Wearing my kurta bunched up and tied about the waist, a young girl with large eyes peeked at me through wet, matted hair.

I patted the stone wall and asked, "How many times did he sell you?"

She perched beside me, ducking her head. "Many times." Her voice was a thin thread, too young to be so weary. Wringing out the wet bur-kha, she draped it over her shoulders to dry.

How on earth would I explain her to Adi and Diana? Adi's father might understand my predicament. Perhaps the boy Kasim had been just such an orphan when Burjor came to Lahore to rescue Miss Pilloo.

When we started down the path between the rail line and the river, Chutki would not walk beside me, but followed six feet behind. I asked questions, and she called out answers.

Although I did not understand some words, I gathered that her parents had died, and her uncle gave her to be married. But the wedding did not happen. Instead she was sold to the "Arkati." Her voice was barely audible, so I said no more about it.

"Do you have relatives? A brother, or sister?" I ventured.

"Yes, Bao-di," she said, "but they would not want me now. It's too late."

"An uncle or aunt, then, who would keep you safe?"

No answer. After a moment, "Are you my husband now?"

I sat cross-legged on the grass until she caught up. As before, she crouched beside me, pensive, overlooking the road.

"Chutki, you are my little sister, all right?" As soon as I spoke, it felt right.

Just days before, Diana had demanded a lie, and I'd supplied one, saying I had a younger sister, married to a civil service bloke in Delhi. Strange that fate should now drop one into my life.

Chutki pressed her face into her knees, skinny arms wrapped around them. She was crying. Since I could think of no way to console her, I listened to the stream's quiet murmur.

Moments later, I noticed Chutki's feet and stiffened. Something oozed and caked between her little toes.

"What's this?" I asked, reaching for a foot.

She pulled away with a whimper and tucked it under her skirt.

"Chutki."

She would not answer.

"Show me!"

My rough tone succeeded where kindness had not. Chutki stuck out her feet toward me. I cupped a small heel to reveal her sole smeared with blood. Brushing off dirt revealed a cut across the ball of her foot. Although not deep, the wound had reopened as she walked. Blood seeped afresh, drops forming in a line that slowly thickened. Her other foot was injured too.

That long trek last night, the path strewn with pebbles. Eager to get the child away from her captor, I'd not questioned why she'd lagged behind. Twice I'd waited for her, then gone back in my impatience, to hurry her along. What had she stepped on, and with both feet?

When understanding dawned, I could not believe it. Her owner's smirk now took on a malevolence I'd not understood at the time. He knew.

He knew she could not walk. Because he'd made it so.

* * *

With Chutki riding upon my back, we crossed ten miles of dirt road and grassy paths, reaching the green fields of Ludhiana at midday. Although bound with strips of cloth torn from the burkha, her feet would take days, even weeks to heal. In the army I'd have whiskey on hand to douse such injuries. Here I had none, and places that sold spirits were unfit for a child.

In the distance, a cluster of brick houses beckoned. Villagers carrying baskets passed us, stopping only when I sought to buy food off them. What little they had, they would not sell. We'd eaten nothing, so my feet quickened toward the bazaar. After a meal, I would buy salt to cleanse Chutki's injured feet.

"Stay here," I said, setting her on a wall by the market.

"Bao-di!" came a piteous cry. Frantic, her little hands flapped in distress. "Let me come with you," she sobbed, "I eat very little, kasam-seh (I promise)."

I huffed at her, but it was no use. She only cried harder, fearing I meant to abandon her.

"Come then," I grumbled, and she limped over. No, she would not be carried, but hobbled behind me.

Pain is a frequent visitor to a soldier. I knew the signs: tight, pale lips, perspiration on a face rigid with concentration. Chutki bore it stoically as we trudged toward the market.

As I bought provisions, I nodded her to a box or stone to sit upon. My sack gained a comfortable weight with the addition of apples, cooked meats wrapped in newspaper and tomatoes, these because Chutki's eyes would not leave their red ripeness.

We ate, then went to a mochi-stall, where a cobbler sat cross-legged by a wall hung with leather footwear.

"Do you have something for the girl?" I asked.

The cobbler frowned at Chutki's bandaged feet. Without looking up, he unhooked a pair of sandals and dropped them before us.

"Three rupees," he said, returning to his repairs.

Chutki made a sound of protest, entreating me—must she unwrap her bandages to wear the slippers? I cursed under my breath, fitted her feet, still wrapped, into the sandals, and paid.

Next, I haggled for a pair of blankets. High up in the hills, Simla is cooler. A small hand touched my back.

"Bao-di," Chutki whispered, and begged me for five rupees.

I handed it over. My transaction completed, I found her still by my side, standing on one foot to halve her pain. "What did you buy?" I asked.

She shook her head and pointed. I must go with her. At a blacksmith's she chose an enormous iron pan with metal feet. I groaned to think of the added weight, and shook my head.

Chutki giggled, a tiny precious sound, muffled by her hand, like Diana chuckling over something Adi had said. Those breakfasts with the Framjis, light filtered by deep green fronds outside, seemed months ago. The sun bore down on me now, grim and dusty.

The small girl beside me tugged my hand, returning me to the present, and the iron-merchant's stare. I had not answered his question. What did we want to buy?

Relenting, Chutki chose a skillet about the size of my hand. After adding a sack of flour, some salt, and three boxes of matches, I scowled at her extravagance and paid. Thus laden, we made poor time that day.

When the railway line turned south, we followed a dusty road eastward. Encumbered with my sack and little Chutki, I kept a careful pace. Goats and bullocks ambled past us.

At sundown we camped out of sight of the road. Chutki lit a fire and the aroma of fresh baked rotis filled the air. My stomach rumbled, recalling Mrs. Framji's rice pilaf and fish curries.

I bit into a disk of Chutki's flatbread, savoring it with the purchased lamb. Thereafter I did not grumble. She could cook. Rather than buy something for herself, she'd chosen a means for our survival.

We were a week out of Simla. Less, if I could beg a ride on some farmer's cart. That might ease us—both Chutki's feet and my shoulder.

Alas, the very next day our troubles grew worse.

CHAPTER 32

AMBUSHED

The next day we stopped on the banks of the Sutlej. We had not seen Chutki's captor since that first night, yet I kept a close watch. I planned to follow the river east until it looped north at Roopnagar, then continue across hills and tea plantations to the safety of Simla.

Days had passed since I left Bombay and said farewell to Diana in the twilight. She'd have reached Simla and likely heard of trouble in Lahore. Adi, awaiting my cable in Bombay, would be worried.

I set Chutki by a low wall bordering the river. She began preparing dinner, while I stripped off my kurta and went down the bank to bathe. All day the sun had burned down on us, and my shoulder ached. The river babbled and eddied around smooth rocks. Standing waist deep, breathing the soft air of evening, I rubbed a handful of sand over myself for soap. Peace reigned.

"Bao-di!" Chutki cried.

Yelling in a high voice, she wiggled and kicked at some small, wild thing—an urchin boy? I scrambled back, sloshing, slipping on rocks, hampered by sopping wet trousers.

Grabbing a handful of clothing, I hauled the scrawny blighter off her. Scarcely more than a bundle of clothes, he landed on his bottom. A spurt of pity flashed through me, even as I dropped to my knees beside Chutki.

"Are you hurt?"

How valiantly she'd defended our meager supplies! She replied in a startled voice, when a sound interrupted, only inches to my left.

Click-click: a weapon cocked to fire.

I looked up into the barrel of a handgun. Adi's revolver, with its safety off. My breath locked in my throat. A boy with green eyes aimed the weapon with both hands.

"Don't shoot," I said, showing him open palms.

About ten years old, tight-faced and scrawny, he'd hidden behind the wall while his brother lured me to Chutki's rescue. Unseen, he'd plucked Adi's revolver from my clothes left by the river and ambushed me.

I could disarm him, snag the weapon with a quick move. But if he squeezed off a shot, Chutki was too close. Even if he missed, it would be heard a great way. Something else held me back—desperation narrowed those green eyes, but pride, too, a boy trying to be a man, caught between fear and resolve.

A handsome youth, he wore a rough turban on his head, his kaftan bunched at the waist. Were they thieves? Part of a tribe? If so, the others would hear and descend upon us.

Chutki's assailant, perhaps seven or eight years old, came to the boy's side.

When I kept still, the boy lowered the pistol and dropped to his haunches. His brother pointed at a roti burning on the pan and mumbled to him. Next, a baby wailed behind us. I turned, astonished. A third boy appeared, holding a bundle. Setting it on the stones, he crawled over the wall.

I stared, disbelieving, at three boys, the youngest carrying a baby. I'd been taken by a band of children!

For long moments no one spoke, while the baby's wail tore and broke in waves. At last the infant's cry drew Chutki out. Taking the babe, she knelt by the griddle. Humming under her breath, she broke off a piece of roti, sucked on it, and fed the little one. Silence dropped over us.

Since I was not yet to be shot, I leaned against the wall in relief. My journey had taken a strange turn. With a rustle of dry leaves, the leader of the scoundrels scooted up beside me.

"Can I have the gun?" I asked in Pashto.

He glowered with suspicion, then handed it over, butt first.

Once I set the safety, my breath slowed at last. By God, when Adi loaned me the weapon he'd surely never foreseen this.

The two younger urchins clustered around us, peering and curious. Where had they come from? Barefoot, shirtless and wearing only a clumsy dhoti for britches, the youngest might have been five. The middle boy, in lumpy trousers and torn kurta shirt, had a mass of freckles over his face. All three were filthy, and quite comfortable in their grime.

"I'm hungry," said the youngest, swiping the back of his hand across his nose. That small motion broke the strange mood that held me.

With growing amusement, I looked over at Chutki. "Sister, do you want to feed them? They are thieves, you know."

The younger boys giggled. The leader grinned and scratched his head, unabashed. Chutki shushed them, rocking the baby. To my dismay, she placed the foul-smelling bundle in my lap. As she slapped a piece of dough between her hands to prepare more roti, her brusque manner held the lads in check with impressive ease.

The baby snuffled and squirmed against my chest. Little hands reached, grasping. Somewhat surprised at the weight of this small parcel, I settled him closer and he quieted. I'd never held one so small before.

"Where do you live?" I asked the pint-sized leader.

He shrugged.

"Where is your father? Your village?"

"Pathankot," he replied.

Wasn't that a mountain fortress farther north? I'd heard of it—an army supply post.

"I am Razak," he said, then pointed. "These are Parimal and Hari."

"Who feeds you?" I asked. They shrugged and grinned in reply.

Chutki handed me the next roti off the stove. I took it one-handed, tossed and blew on it, watching the boys' grimy faces. The youngest, Hari, sniffed, eyes hungry, ribs protruding with each panting breath.

I divided the bread between them. Reaching into the sack for apples, I tossed them at the boys. Once they saw they need not fight for fruit, they leapt and caught with startling agility.

"Whose child is this?" I asked, reluctant to move and awaken the infant.

Razak shrugged. "We found him in the mud. This morning."

"Found him!"

Speaking all at once, they told of searching the refuse behind a stable. They could not name the place. The child was abandoned, so they took it. It would have died, but for them.

"Where is the mother?"

Razak shook his head. "I was curious. Saw a sack moving, so I opened it."

I plied them with questions they could not answer. When I insisted we had to take the child back, the urchins protested, hopping in distress.

Razak cried out, horrified. "We saw soldiers. They don't like us."

"English soldiers?" I pronounced it Ang-rez, as locals did. Hope knotted in my chest.

He shook his head. "Pathan."

Bollocks. The enemy were all around, I didn't have much cash and I'd accumulated three boys, an injured girl and a baby. I needed a new plan.

Watching the lads cavort in the stream I considered—should I take them to a temple in the next village? They'd only return to their roving ways. As we settled to sleep, I learned that Razak had come south with his village kin, but got separated in a skirmish with another tribe. The younger boys had lost their parents in a mela, a festival fair. Razak found them starving. They'd been together since the monsoon. Six months—a long time to live on stolen scraps. They'd hid from soldiers. I asked where. Taking turns to tell their adventures, they fell asleep.

I considered our situation. The oldest boy came from Pathankot. Could I send him to his village? Deep in Afghan-held countryside, that was impossible. I'd have to take them to Simla.

Adi would think me mad. Diana would smile and shake her head. I had come north to solve the riddle of Kasim, to find who might want to avenge him. Now the prospect of finding Doctor Aziz, and some answers, seemed distant.

Next morning Chutki grilled lumpy biscuits, delicious, despite nuggets of salt. Like me, the boys ate whatever she devised. I watched with admiration as she made a thin gruel, soaked the corner of a rag in it and fed the baby.

Shaking our blankets to rid them of ants, we broke camp. Chutki insisted she could walk. I suspected the boys' presence played into this show of independence. Hoisting my depleted sack, I started out. Chutki followed, carrying the baby. The boys ran alongside, chattering and grinning. When Razak came up, I asked, "Are you with us?"

He ducked his head and nodded.

"And you won't shoot me?"

He shook his head, glancing up, wary.

I nodded, maintaining a solemn expression. Behind us, Chutki sniffed, a sound of such derision that I raised my eyebrows. At that, Razak began to laugh, a husky, pleasant sound.

Alas, by midday Chutki lagged behind on her wounded feet and sobbed. Giving the baby to Razak, I hoisted her up. She curled in my arms, her head bouncing against me as I walked.

Ever since the boys' ambush, I'd begun to worry. If the lads had been Afghan soldiers, I'd likely be dead, and Chutki . . . ?

Now I asked Razak, "If we come by soldiers, what will you do?"

Razak crinkled his eyes and said, "We keep them busy—you kill them."

That was how he'd ambushed me. Children grow up quickly in the countryside.

"No, we hide," I said. "How can we quickly tell the boys to hide?"

The little general grinned. Putting two fingers to his lips, he warbled. The two younger urchins dashed into the brush beside the road. Another birdcall sounded and they scrambled out.

By God, even Colonel Sutton would be impressed. Young as Razak was, the army might hire him as a groom or mess boy. If only I could get the children to safety in Simla and find someone to keep them.

CHAPTER 33

ON THE TRAIL

We walked.

Days ago—six? seven?—the trail of refugees trudging east from Lahore had dwindled. We bought coconuts one day, walnuts the next, whatever came our way. When we passed wide cornfields, we tossed ears into my sack until it was all I could carry. Later, Chutki picked out the bugs and roasted these. Watchful for Pathan soldiers, avoiding crossroads when possible, we made slow progress toward Simla.

"What town is this?" I asked a passing shepherd, solemnly herding his animals. His answer—Roopnagar—lifted my spirits: Simla was about sixty miles away. Leaving Razak with Chutki and the baby, I took the younger boys to the bazaar. Provisions were dear now, depleting the funds Adi had given me a lifetime ago in Bombay. Yet I bought the boys sweetmeats, unable to begrudge the few annas that gave them such pleasure.

That night we heard the low growls of cheetahs. Surely the beasts were high in the hills? Hard to tell, with the wind swishing eerie sounds down the slopes. Little Hari shuddered, tiny shoulders quaking. I checked my revolver, added twigs to the fire and decided to keep watch. The children huddled against me, peering. As the smoking embers died, they slept. So did I.

At daylight we begged a ride from a bullock cart that lumbered by. When the driver scratched his head and halted, the boys swarmed over bales of hay with happy cries. I boosted Chutki into the back of the cart and clambered after her, glad to be off my aching knee.

At sundown our cart reached a cluster of huts. The driver, a friendly sort, agreed to let us shelter in his cowshed. We drank from the village well and washed, then flopped down in a shed that smelled of hay and manure to consume our remaining supplies. Exhausted, my little brood lay down to sleep amid the comforting low of bullocks.

* * *

We caught a ride with a milk cart and were spared trudging some twenty miles the next day, leaving the cart when the driver turned south to his market. Simla was eastward, so we headed toward the sunrise the next morning. A goatherd gave us some milk at noon, and the last of my cash went to purchase cheeses that we consumed with grabbing abandon.

We moved slowly now. The day grew hot. As I walked, my thoughts returned to the Framjis. My dance with Diana seemed part of another lifetime, my hunt for Kasim and Doctor Aziz, a distant quest. Yet if I had not undertaken this expedition, Chutki might still be yoked to her captor, farmed out for men's pleasure. Razak and his little band would have thieved their way across the hills until overcome by misadventure.

Soon, the youngest, Hari, began to wilt. Already carrying the baby, Razak could only coax him along. While Chutki hobbled along, I lifted him onto my shoulders. The older boys quarreled and shoved each other. We stopped often.

At last poor freckled Parimal collapsed. He sat in the dust, crying great heaving sobs. I set Hari down, feeling helpless. Then I remembered— when I'd startled the Framjis with my Pathan guise, how had Burjor comforted his child? As he'd done, I pulled the weeping boy into my arms. His despair pulsed into me as I held him.

We had not heard the baby's wail since dawn. Had Chutki fed it milk soaked in a corner of her scarf? I asked her whether that was today or yesterday. She scowled, leaning her head against me. I feared that Simla was too far, that the children would starve before we reached it.

"Bao-di!" Razak leapt up, pointing.

An oxcart ambled toward us. Razak ran to it, calling out, arms waving with all his might.

Dammit. I had no money left.

Chutki tugged at my hand and pressed something narrow into it, rolled up like a cigarette—the five-rupee note I'd given her! She'd saved it.

We would not starve. When I began to laugh, freckle-faced Parimal clung to me, while Hari stared. We hurried to the oxcart, where Razak was already haggling over a basket of apples.

In the late evening we climbed a rise and settled on a hillside overlooking Simla. I watched the setting sun touch purple clouds with silver. A peachy light bathed the bedraggled children, silent in their weariness. Below us, gaslights appeared, flickering, while stars filled the carpet of sky. I remembered Diana's peach dress, her smile, the turn of her head in the twilight. I'd lost track of the days, and didn't even know if she was here, in Simla. Adi would be desperate with worry, since I had not cabled him from Lahore. Well, tomorrow would tell.

* * *

Next morning, we passed a line of carriages and jampans—porters carrying sedan chairs at Simla checkpoint. Ignoring the queue of waiting pedestrians, I strode up carrying Chutki. Razak and the boys followed, still sleepy and confused. A Sepoy in crisp uniform manned the pedestrian gate. I approached him at full tilt.

"Captain Agnihotri, Fourteenth Light Cavalry," I rapped out, shocking the man. "Who commands this garrison?"

"General Greer, sir," he said, staring. Despite my appalling state, he snapped a salute.

"Right. Let us through. Send word I need to see him, about a fellow called Doctor Aziz. Got that?"

He pushed the gate partway open and the children scurried inside. I followed.

"Captain Agnihotri, sir. Where will he find you?"

"At the Framji residence," I said, without breaking stride. Dear God, I hoped they were here.

Bundled in my arms, Chutki gawked. She'd never heard me speak English before.

CHAPTER 34

REUNION

Diana opened the door wearing a striped blue sundress. A white hat dangled from gloved fingertips. She was about to go out. Her lips parted in surprise to see us on the steps below.

"Miss Diana," I said, "I'm sorry, we had nowhere to go."

She stared at the infant in my filthy hands, the bedraggled children standing close.

"Good heavens." Sounding shocked, she pulled the nearest, Razak, into the house. Chutki followed with the others. Limbs leaden, I went after them. A stout woman with an enormous bindi on her forehead took the baby. People spoke, but their words held little meaning.

Feeling weak, now that we'd arrived, now that we were safe, I slumped. Diana flew at me. Stepping back with the rush of it, I felt a wall against my back, anxious hands on my chest. Face upturned, she asked me—was I all right? Her luminous eyes shone, relieved I was here, unhurt. She was all I could see, her relief, her smile, her welcome. I heard a clamor, but distantly—children's voices, high and anxious, the baby bawling.

"What in heaven's name is going on?" Burjor bellowed. The sight of him in his blue dressing gown brought such comfort, it threatened to buckle my knees.

"The Captain, Papa. Captain Jim is here," Diana said.

Was Burjor furious with us, Diana and I, standing so close? He went from irate to concern, and hollered, "Someone catch him!"

Diana's arms went tight around my waist, propping me up. I struggled to keep my feet, lightheaded with gratitude, pleasure at Diana's care and, most of all, relief. I liked Burjor. His opinion mattered.

Servants were called. Mrs. Framji took charge, dismissing my fractured explanations for later. Once Diana and her parents saw that the children could not be separated without breaking into sobs, we came to an agreement. Crowded into a white tiled washroom, we scrubbed hands and faces at a fancy molded sink. As I soaped his face, little Hari licked the foam. Razak kept turning the faucet on and off, dipping his fingers in the cool water, marveling.

The smell, the sizzle of frying tantalized us now. Clustered in an enclosed verandah, we ate large quantities of potato sabzi. A seemingly endless supply of fried pooris came hot from the kitchen. The boys stuffed their cheeks, swallowing so fast that Parimal coughed, choking in his haste.

"Slow down!" I said, in Pashto.

Seated on a charpoy, Diana was cuddling Hari on her lap. Her head snapped around at my command. Still clutching pooris, the boys threw anxious looks at me, but stopped downing the meal like wild beasts.

Razak began to sob. Shoulders shaking, his head drooped, the poori fell from his hand. He was the leader, this shrewd little thief, and the younger lads, seeing his distress, wailed too.

Swearing softly, I hauled the scrawny lad over. Hari tumbled from Diana's lap and threw himself at us. Parimal joined the chaos of limbs and bodies. Diana paused, dismayed.

"Chutki!" I called.

She hobbled in from the kitchen where she had been working the stove. She had not eaten, nor rested her feet. I smiled at her over the entangled children. "A little help?"

Clucking, she pulled a child from the melee, comforted and sent him back to his meal, then another.

As quiet descended. I said, "Eat," and handed her my metal plate. She sat, filled a poori with potato and bit into it.

"What will you do with them?" Diana asked, an odd expression on her face.

"Bathe them first, I think." We stank of manure and sweat, days in the fields.

Her lips curved in a wry smile, nose wrinkled in agreement. "And then?"

I shook my head. "Haven't planned that far, my dear."

A sound from Razak drew my attention. His body stiff, he stared at me.

"What is it?" I asked in Pashto.

"Angrez?" he whispered.

I understood. "No, son, I'm not English," I replied, "nor is this pretty lady." I wasn't sure he was convinced. My switching languages seemed to worry him.

The Framjis asked about my journey from Lahore, commiserating with me on my trek. Sixteen days had passed since I left Bombay. I told them how Razak had accosted me with my own revolver, sending Diana into gurgles of laughter.

I had thirsted for the sound of her.

After the meal Diana took charge of my boys and had a bath prepared. Clothes were found to replace their rags. Now fortified, Razak and I bathed the boys in a large tub, getting sopping wet, the water sloshing. Parimal giggled and blew soapsuds as I scrubbed his hair. Many of his freckles disappeared under our assault. Razak bathed next, insisting he could manage by himself.

Since Chutki had gone with the women, I said something about her feet to Diana and tottered back to the verandah. Stretched out on the low braided charpoy, I slept.

✻ ✻ ✻

I woke in a verandah soft with afternoon light muted through wicker blinds. From the kitchen came dimly heard voices and the aroma of spices. We'd reached Simla. We were with the Framjis. Each breath feeling lighter, I stretched. It felt glorious to settle my shoulders back again, to be Jim again, not Rashid Khan the Pathan or the others I'd been in Bombay.

Someone had removed my boots while I slept, and washed my feet. Had I been still in the army, my batman would have done it.

"You're awake," said Diana, stepping in, her face gentle. Dressed in a pale blue saree, springy curls held back with a band, she made an exotic picture. I'd not seen her in a saree before, nor known she'd wear it so naturally. The baby cooed from her hip, giving her a curiously domestic appearance.

I reached for the infant, but Diana pulled back.

"No! They're all clean. Only you left," she said, tilting her head toward the washroom.

Realizing I must look like a beggar, I started to go, then noticed the quiet and came abruptly alert. "Where are they, actually?"

"Papa took them to see the horses. We felt you should sleep."

How grateful I was for that luxury.

Diana moved the baby to her shoulder and asked, "Captain, what's his name?"

I paused. This could get sticky. "Don't know, my dear."

Her eyebrows shot up. "But . . . how did you come by him?"

When I told her what I'd learned, she said, "Abandoned in a sack!" Pity etched Diana's face. "The children crowded around you, while you were sleeping. The girl kissed your hand. They're very attached to you."

I scratched my beard, sighing. "They slept on blankets, between me and any wall we could find. Made them feel safe. Now, would someone loan me a kurta, d'you think?" I asked, heading to the washroom.

"Oh! Papa sent Gurung to a tailor. . . ."

She pointed at the garments draped over a chair: grey suit and vest, a grey felt hat.

I hesitated, overwhelmed at this generosity, but uncomfortable at what it signified: the children knew me as a Pathan. In Western dress, would I remain their Bao-di?

"Diana, I can't. It's too soon . . . the children."

Her eyes narrowed. "Too soon for them? Or for you?"

That was puzzling, so I just said, "Please. A kurta-khamiz will do."

She floated off to do my bidding. As she gave instructions in the corridor, her voice curled into me. Its hushed timbre, its rhythm rippled across my skin, which absorbed it like a touch. Yet she'd stayed conspicuously distant just now. I remembered the warmth of her welcome and wondered, had I read too much into it?

* * *

As I bathed—sinking into clean warm water, what heaven!—a smooth oval of soap, French perhaps?—I pondered the peculiar events of the past few days. I'd been retained to solve a mystery. It remained my primary goal. But when I'd come upon Chutki and the boys, how could I turn away? Our choices drive who we are, I thought, and who we want to be. If Adi or Diana came upon a child sold into such misery, would they abandon her? I could not imagine it.

After what she'd endured, Chutki surely deserved the Framjis' pity. But would they fault her for her sordid past? I could not say. When I'd described how Razak took me by surprise, Diana chuckled, admiring their pluck. Neither she nor Burjor withdrew their welcome, yet I held back Chutki's history, saying only, "I found Chutki. She needed help." This wasn't just prudery. Her story was not mine to tell. I feared the uncompromising morals of those who would see her as beneath contempt. How could I defend her from that? I winced, remembering her small black shape uncurling, bound and docile. Her sob—I could hear it still, feel its deep despair.

Combing back my bedraggled hair with my fingers, I donned a grey kurta-khamiz, trousers and black vest and went to the dining room.

"Any news from Adi?" I asked Mrs. Framji.

Watching me demolish a stack of sandwiches with evident satisfaction, she smiled. "He's already on the train. He'll be here soon."

I was glad of it, looking forward to his ready wit, his considered attention. It also meant that the train service to Simla was intact. Since my urchins were still away, I asked Mrs. Framji whether someone might take them in.

"Would their parents not search for them?" she asked.

When she heard how I'd found them, she said, "Adopted? I cannot say. Do you know their caste? Hindus are touchy about that. Perhaps we can ask the Christian Mission."

I remembered the quiet, white walls of the Mission where I'd grown up, wooden pews, worn smooth, the smell of old books, my palms chalky from swiping my slate, old Father Thomas's twinkling smile. Would he still be alive?

"Mrs. Framji, I'm sorry about all this trouble."

"No, son, it's no trouble. We must do what's right." She smiled, a look of such sweetness it stayed with me after she'd left the room.

The front door opened, admitting the clamor of childish voices. The pack descended upon me, no longer silent and wide-eyed, but demanding to be heard with all the power of their lungs.

"Quiet!" I rapped out in Pashto, hauled the youngest up and asked him what he'd done.

His round face glowed. "We saw horses. I touched one!" His hair now neatly trimmed, he was a handsome child, thin like the others, shoulder bones protruding.

Along those dusty roads he'd been a light, loose-limbed bundle, little arms about my neck or clutching my hair when he rode on my shoulders. I'd grown accustomed to the boys' banter, giggles as they chased butterflies or caught beetles. That last afternoon was a sharp, painful memory—Parimal's sobs, his exhaustion, the children close to starvation. This little troop had no one, nor did I. Listening to Hari's chatter, I pondered, could I send them to a Mission? Could I part with them at all?

Someone pounded on the door. Hari whimpered, arms clamping around me.

Mrs. Framji returned, worried. "Two soldiers, asking for you."

Carrying Hari, I went to see who'd summoned me.

Belted and gloved, their pith helmets neat, two Sepoys dwarfed the Framjis' living room. They stared, no doubt thinking that I'd "gone native," something the army disapproved. They did not salute. One said, "Captain Agnihotri? General Greer's compliments. He requests your presence, sir."

At the sentry post yesterday, I'd sent word to the garrison commander asking after Doctor Aziz, but scarcely expected such a quick response. Perhaps the good doctor was in Simla!

When I set Hari down, his face crumpled. Patting his head did nothing to reassure.

"Razak, son, see to him," I said, and went to meet the General.

CHAPTER 35

THE TEST

The Simla garrison occupied a large, walled compound, spread across thirty acres. Rows of barracks lined up in strict precision. Lofty mountains overlooked a lake. My Sepoy escort said nothing as our carriage rattled through a heavily guarded gate and stopped before an imposing colonnaded edifice. One of them led me into a wide foyer and through carved teak doors, into a wood-paneled hall that smelled of cigars, oiled leather and brass polish.

"Captain Agnihotri, sir," he said to a group of officers in field uniforms.

A short officer who'd been leaning over a table was obviously in command—General Greer. Fit, well groomed, every brass button gleaming, the General turned astonished blue eyes upon me. Dressed as I was in long kurta-khamiz, bearded, hatless, my hair down my back like a mendicant, I was not the officer he expected, but a native.

Since he did not invite me in, I remained by the door and acknowledged him with a Pathan bow, hand over my heart. One did not salute in civilian clothing.

"Retired?" he demanded, frowning at my casual appearance.

"Yes, sir."

"You served under Brian Sutton?"

"Yes, sir."

"Brought six lads through the front?"

"Five children, sir. The oldest is twelve."

Another officer said something I could not hear. Perhaps the contrast of my English voice and native garb puzzled them.

The General came to the point. "Can you get into Pathankot?"

"Pathankot?" I asked, surprised. His summons had led me to expect some news of Doctor Aziz, but there was more afoot here.

An officer murmured into his ear. That set him right, for he said, "You're looking for Doctor Aziz?"

I straightened. Had they located the medico? "Yes, sir. Where is he?"

After a huddled conversation Greer said, "We need a scout. D'you want a short commission?"

A commission! After our exhausting trek. "No, sir."

I should have been more fulsome, declined with regrets, but I had been taken by surprise. The General's face darkened at my reply. He studied me, scowling. He had no cause to quarrel with me, but that meant little. Commanding the garrison meant his word was law.

He said, "The man you want, Doctor Aziz, is with Major Hadley and the Twenty-first Gurkha Rifles. I want you to bring them back."

That might suit my purpose too. But that huddle, that quick conference gave me pause. "They're in Pathankot?"

Greer burst out, "Dammit man, you're a bloody pain in the rear! Asking Goddamn questions! We're in a spot right now. . . ." Jaw tight, he motioned at a topographic map on the table. Red pins marked the British line of control. I saw that, halfway to Kabul, Pathankot's distinctive roll of hills was deep inside Afghan-occupied territory.

"Pathankot fort? What're they doing there?" I asked.

"Guarding a supply post. Got cut off when this trouble broke out."

I learned that several Afghan tribes were up in arms, and they'd engaged British troops in a series of skirmishes. Outnumbered, the Twenty-first Regiment had retreated west to Lahore, unaware they'd left Captain Hadley's Gurkha Company stranded.

"I've just come a hundred and fifty miles east"—I bridged the distance on the map between two index fingers—"and you want me to go north?"

"About a hundred miles."

I stared. "Where's their relief?"

"That's whom you'll escort."

He smiled grimly at my dismay. I backed away, showing the palms of my hands.

"Can't do it, sir. My term's done. Surely someone else can do this?"

Greer's mustache bristled. It irked him to have me decline. Had he been my commander, he could simply order me to go. He tapped the map. "The front is a mess. I need someone who's just been there. You want Aziz, I want those men back."

Cliff lines swarmed around Pathankot's treacherous terrain. Doctor Aziz was my only link to Kasim, at the root of my puzzle. If Aziz were taken by the enemy, if he died, my last thread would snap. But Pathankot? That was insane.

"How many men?"

"Hadley had ten Gurkhas, and the physician," Greer replied, stroking his mustache.

I examined the contour lines. It meant crossing into the wild Frontier province. Cavalry was known for speed, not stealth. We'd be seen miles away, shot down in any number of craggy passes.

"It's suicide," I said.

But what if it were just me, on a fast mare like Mullicka, without a column of clanking cavalry? She could weave through the passes, get me to Pathankot. But could I get out? With a company of infantrymen? Impossible. How would I even find them?

"Where are they exactly?"

"The supply post was in the old fortress. Lots of tunnels, I'm told."

If they were alive, I could find Doctor Aziz. A finger of hope jabbed my chest. "Did they have horses?"

"Some, last I heard."

"When was that?"

"Four days ago." Greer grimaced. "Hadley got a man out when they came under fire. Had to abandon the magazine. Since then, nothing."

It was the first I'd heard of a skirmish. He'd said nothing of it before. Bloody General—he'd send me out with few facts, utterly ill prepared. Perhaps noticing the direction of my thoughts, Greer thrust out his jaw.

"D'you accept the job? Yes?" Urgent, his voice rose. "Do this, man! You can name your price."

His gaze pushed me, seeking, assessing, making judgements about my character. Something flickered in my memory—Razak, my older boy, was from Pathankot. What had he said about going down to the fort with his father to sell sheep? Would he know the rivers, the passes? The men of his village would, surely.

I found myself breathing hard. Pressing a hand to my ribs, I weighed my odds. They weren't good.

"I'm not well enough to do this," I said, "but it could be done. A fast rider could follow the gorge up to Pathankot, find the troop. If we're quick, we could be in and out, with luck."

Greer exhaled, unclenching his hands. "I wouldn't ask it, Captain," he said, "if I had a choice. They're cut off, trapped. We need to act right away."

Feeling old and weary, I said, without heat, "They could be dead already."

He agreed, but did not budge, his chin thrust forward in challenge. Wasn't this what my old commander, Colonel Sutton, would have done? He'd try every last thing to get you out, bully, bargain, even threaten if he must.

Four days—an eternity to Hadley's troop, waiting for relief. I remembered huddling by a wall with Smith in Karachi, tasting blood, my face pressed against stone. Bloody hell. I couldn't leave them there. Not again. "Four days?"

"Can't be helped," Greer admitted. "Can't risk a full campaign."

I followed his gaze to the trail of red pins on the map. Until reinforcements arrived from the south, he could not spare the troops needed to recover Doctor Aziz.

When my head went down, Greer knew he'd won.

* * *

While the commission was being drawn up, we settled terms.

"Hazard pay as Scout, not Captain, of course," Greer said, writing. "Major Burton will lead. Eight cavalry ought to do it."

That would lead us straight into a skirmish. "No, sir," I said. "I need just two fast horses."

His head snapped up. "What? You'll go alone?"

"No, sir. I'll take a local boy. He knows the area."

While he digested this, I listed the rest of my supplies, and said I'd leave tomorrow.

Nodding, he continued through a list of questions. "Widow's pension?"

"Yes, sir."

He glanced up. "You're married?"

"I hoped to be, sir, until this crusade." My smile faltered. I'd answered spontaneously, thinking of Diana with my band of urchins on her hands. But there was no formal understanding between us. Worse, bereavement pay would mark Diana, and that hardly seemed fair. "Payment to Mr. and Mrs. Framji."

"Did old Moneybags adopt you, eh?" Greer chuckled, writing again.

That sparked an idea for my second request, a just recompense, for if I died Burjor would be burdened with my little band.

When he heard my proposal, Greer grimaced. He brushed his mustache with a knuckle, thinking. "That's unusual. I'll take it up with the War Office." He held up a hand to preempt me. "Can't promise anything, but it could be done."

Once we'd signed the documents, he invited me to dine. I accepted, surprised at this uncommon courtesy, since I was dressed like a native, and a disheveled one, at that.

On the way to the garrison mess hall, Greer amended our agreement with a slap on the back. "Captain, you'll take a soldier with you. Can't let you go solo. Not done, you know." Saddled with an army escort, my task would be an official action. Seeing he was set on it, I considered how best to turn this to my advantage.

"Righto sir, I'll take a fast rider. Someone who speaks Pashto, and isn't British."

"Well, you're English, aren't you?"

This remark on my parentage didn't bother me, accustomed as I was to the jibes of fellow officers. I replied with a shrug.

He laughed, stalking ahead into the mess hall, where his staff were assembled. Officers turned, staring, since natives were rarely invited. Feeling acutely underdressed in my long grey kurta and unkempt hair, I hung back as befitted my lack of rank.

The word "Scout" followed me, as officers moved to their tables.

Then—a shadow, a blur. I saw it in the corner of my eye and slipped a punch that blew past my ear. Turning, I caught a wrist and swung the chap around. Once I had him immobile, I leaned over to have a look. A heavy, turbaned Sikh groaned as his shoulder twisted in my grip.

"Are we acquainted, sir?" I asked, wondering what had got into him to do such a thing.

The Sardar grimaced, and his eyes flickered to someone behind me.

"Let him go," Greer said, with a grim smile.

So it was Greer. Having a laugh on me. Someone had told him I used to box.

I released the poor Sardar, saying, "Sorry about that," and confronted the General with growing resentment, glad that I towered over him. "What the devil was that for?"

Perhaps Adi was right, for that was reckless. Nearby officers looked affronted. I knew I'd overstepped, but found myself reluctant to retreat. Greer had hauled me out to the barracks, blackmailed me into a dangerous task and then set a bloke to hit me. The first two I might forgive, attribute to dire necessity and such, but a punch?

"A test of fitness, Captain," he said, eyes watchful. "Can't send a sick man on the job."

Damn the bloke. If I'd been knocked down, he'd have released me from this task. As it was, I'd just proved I was able.

Seething, I sat at a table where white-gloved mess men waited to serve the meal.

"Jim, me man!" a boisterous voice called out. The familiar lilt belonged to an old comrade, so I welcomed the Irishman who dropped his weight into the next chair.

"Ay, it's a rare pleasure to see you move again," he chortled.

"Why so, O'Connor?" General Greer plonked down before us and signaled the servers.

"Why, he's Sutton's boxer, isn't he? Won some beautiful fights in Rangoon. Don't wager against him, sir."

A steaming plate of soup was placed before me. Damn army protocol,
I thought. Ignoring the others, I dug in. After the obligatory pause for
grace, O'Connor went on. I hoped he'd quit recounting fights I'd won or
lost, and when he seemed to relish telling Greer I'd lost such weight as to
be a shadow of myself, I'd had enough.

"D'you want to paint a target on my back now, friend?" I said. "I'm
done boxing."

Greer guffawed and seemed to accept it as comradely humor.

* * *

Inexplicably, General Greer refused to identify my escort for the impending trip. Since I planned to leave the next morning, this delay deepened
my concern.

Was I as reckless as Adi had once suggested? To ride into Pathan-held
countryside was in itself hazardous. To try to retrieve ten Gurkha infantrymen from hostile territory, well, it defied reason. I'd agreed because I
wanted to find Doctor Aziz. He'd seen Kasim die, and was the only person who might know who was bent on destroying the Framjis.

CHAPTER 36

SETTiNG OFF

General Greer did handsomely by me, providing carte blanche from the quartermaster and use of the chart room to prepare for our ride. At the stable I chose a fine, glossy-haired Arabian filly and got acquainted with her. Evening brought a fog of weariness, which deepened as shadows spread across the lawn and bearers ran with their appointed tasks. I questioned my sanity, but my course was committed.

When I reached Framji villa at sunset, little Hari clung to my knees, begging to be carried. Razak hung back while I calmed the younger boy, then approached, worried. He crouched beside me, full of questions.

"Bao-di, are you hurt? Did they beat you?"

I assured him I was unharmed.

Chutki peeped around the doorway, so I held out a hand.

With Hari on my lap, Parimal and Razak on either side, her cold fingers gripped my hand. She'd been worried at my absence, left behind in a houseful of strangers.

"Are you well?" I asked.

Chutki's head wobbled yes. When Diana and her mother came to collect the children for their supper, she said not a word, but went reluctantly.

Entering the dining room, Diana said, "The children prefer the verandah where you slept. It used to be a baith-khana, literally a room to sit, with cushions and carpets. They'll dine there."

I sat down and stretched out my legs.

Diana's face lit up. "Adi's train from Bombay will soon be here. Papa's gone to the station to receive him."

Quick and graceful, she set the table, each step soothing like cool sherbet in summertime. I looked away, but it made no difference—I was acutely aware of her every motion. Before long she'd be put out at me for leaving again. I hoped to delay that for a bit.

She said, "You're very quiet, Captain."

Adi and Burjor entered amid a clamor of greetings.

"Captain, you didn't cable!" Adi said, the moment he saw me. "It's been sixteen, no, seventeen days without a word."

I described the state of the railways and telegraph.

"Captain Jim is now a one-man orphan patrol," Diana teased, describing my little brood.

Adi listened intently, and asked, "What about Kasim—did you learn anything?"

I reported my progress, and mentioned Doctor Aziz.

"So that's a dead end?"

"Maybe not. Doctor Aziz was an army medic."

Our dinner conversation grew lively. Although reluctant to disrupt it with my plans of imminent departure, as the meal drew to a close, I could delay no more.

"Sir," I addressed Adi, "these are for you." Drawing my commission and the army contract from my vest, I slid them across the table.

Adi examined the contents, the lawyer in him taking hold.

"Why, Captain, it's already signed. By you and a General Greer, for the War Office!"

"I've come to an arrangement with them—a little task they want. They'll help me find Doctor Aziz."

"Goodness!" His eyebrows rose as he read, then he said, "Papa, read this."

While Burjor examined the documents, I savored some gulab jamun, round delicacies drenched in syrup. My little troop was safe, their scrapes and bruises tended with salves, and Mrs. Framji had prepared gulab jamun for the rascals. A flood of gratitude swamped me.

"Good heavens." Burjor cleared his throat, flipping pages of the contract back and forth. Looking astonished, he asked, "How did you get them to agree?"

Diana asked, "What is it, will someone say?"

Burjor grinned broadly. "Captain Jim has got the army to give me a contract for coffee and tea! Price to be agreed upon, it says. That's wonderful! We can sell from our plantation in Ooty as well as up here in Simla."

Adi thumbed through my commission, frowning. "Captain? What's this? Bereavement pay . . . to Mr. and Mrs. Framji . . . in the event of death?"

"A standard clause," I said. "They asked for next of kin."

Adi huffed. "What do they need you for?"

"Not at liberty to say, sir, just a short trip tomorrow."

"Tomorrow!" Diana burst out, sending me a look that did not bode well.

I said, "Miss Diana, I regret I must leave the children with you. I'll take Razak home, though. It's on the way."

"Why tomorrow? Razak's exhausted, you're as pale as a ghost, why not rest a bit?"

"The army decides these things, Miss."

She winced. "So where are you going?"

"Not far—should take about a week."

"Seven days!"

It would take longer. Pathankot was three full days' ride if all went well. Rising to my feet, I said, "I must tell Razak—and hope it does not keep him up all night."

Diana did not return my gaze. "That's why you were so quiet," she said.

Had we been alone I would have spoken then, said something of what I felt for her. But we were not alone, and it seemed a rotten thing to do, with so much uncertain, when it was possible I might not return. I gave her a brief smile and went to find Razak.

"Home! My home? Bao-di, truly?" Delighted with my news, Razak hopped about, bursting with the joy of it.

"It might be dangerous," I cautioned him.

His face shone with excitement.

Chutki, however, wept. Patting her head had no effect. Tears wiped from her cheek were replaced in seconds. She came up behind me and her head rested, a soft weight on my shoulder.

"Bao-di, will you come back?"

"Yes." If I live, I thought. The Framjis would care for her if I did not return. I knew this for a certainty, and that they would see it as no burden. But they'd retained me to solve a mystery. With Mrs. Enty missing, it must go deeper than the murder of the Framji ladies. Worse, I believed that a threat still hung over the Framjis. Why else had I been accosted on Princess Street? I sighed, remembering Akbar, the burglar, the weight of his blows. What was he looking for? Something was hidden in Framji Mansion, something dangerous. If I died in Pathankot, someone must finish my task. Mulling it over, I went in search of Adi and found him in the dining room, brow furrowed, transcribing my contract.

Dropping into the chair beside him, I said, "Sir, if things . . . deteriorate, would you bring Maneck into the investigation?"

Adi looked up, closing his fountain pen. "Deteriorate?"

"If . . . I don't get back."

He paused, measuring my reply. "I knew it. The army has their hooks into you again."

That was a curious phrase. I secured it to examine later. "Maneck. He's afraid, but he knows more than he's saying. Talk to him, show him the notes, the evidence. Offer him my job."

"Are you going back to the army?" Adi asked. When I shook my head, he continued, "So why?" His stare intensified. "Because it's dangerous, this trip. Jim—you must do this?"

At my nod, his face tightened. "For me? You're doing this for me?"

"Not entirely. I want to find Doctor Aziz, but it's more than that."

He did not question me further, but pulled out his wallet and counted out notes. "Keep it. We'll settle accounts when you return."

Diana said, behind me, "Are you going because of what happened in Karachi?"

I'd not known she'd overheard our conversation, so her question took me by surprise. All at once I was back on the front line, cannons thundering, shells exploding, deafening me. I cringed, covering my ears.

"God, Diana!" I heard Adi's voice far away, faint among the screams in my ears. Bullets whined past my head, a horse neighed, panicked and trapped. Smoke and dust filled my nostrils, and my lips tasted metallic salt, the stickiness of blood.

Diana cried, "What's happened to him?"

"Steady, Captain," said Adi, his hands on my shoulders. "Can you breathe?"

I did. Yet I had no air.

"Breathe out!"

I exhaled, hauled in air, and the waking dream released me. The roar of mortar rounds faded, leaving the chirp of crickets at twilight. Adi helped me to a chair.

"Byram called him 'Hero of Karachi,' so I wondered." Diana winced, sorrow and regret in the set of her lips, the tilt of her head. She whisked off to the corner. Water gurgled as she dipped into the earthen pot. She offered me a tumbler of water, but it was no use. My hands shook and I could not take it. Long moments passed as I recovered.

"Has this happened before?" Diana asked. Upon my nod, she said, "Captain, something's stuck, under your skin. Like a thorn or bullet. You've got to get it out."

Adi swiveled toward me. "Can you tell us? About Karachi?"

I wanted to—but then I'd lose Diana. She'd find out what I didn't want to face, to lay bare. How could she understand what I could not, myself, forgive?

CHAPTER 37

TALE OF PORT KARACHI

I got to my feet with nowhere to go, trying to regain myself and some measure of control.

Stepping to the window I opened it to the twilight, where a coppersmith bird called, "Now, now, now, now." A rush of air hit my temples. Right then, I wanted a spread of stars above me, the warm satin of Mullicka's withers moving under my hands.

I skimmed the chamber, finding nothing upon which to rest my eyes: Adi waiting patiently, Diana's parted lips. I avoided her—soon that sweetness would turn startled, draw back in alarm as though she'd seen a snake. Damn that gloss of innocence that made men heroes, damn, damn, damn.

She whispered, her voice aching, "Adi, he's going to leave."

"Captain." Adi spread his hands in a plea. "Whatever happened . . . in Karachi—you've got to put it behind you."

A cuckoo's seductive call sang in the boughs outside, promising a monsoon downpour.

Diana said, "Jim."

It stopped me there, that word, held me at the window. What was that note in her voice? Head bowed, I heard it again, an aching sound, regret and more, a word draped in emotion. Jim. Not Captain, just my name.

I pulled in a breath. "Diana."

We had finally moved beyond Captain and Miss. All right, I thought, so be it. I did not stand a chance with her, never had. But there was something between us and if she was to know me, she must know what demons drove me. Perhaps that was well. I'd seen her awe of the army, the chivalry of uniforms and rank—romantic notions all, illusions. So I would tell her, and lose her. My throat thick and dry, I asked, "Why does it matter?"

"Secrets are like serpents, Jim. They grow in the dark." Her matter-of-fact tone wrung a chuckle from me. What a talent the girl had, of charm and humor. She wanted to know what happened—but could she bear the weight of it?

Eyes wide and earnest she said, "Courage, Jim. It will be all right."

Courage. I winced and said, "It will change things."

It would change everything. But Diana urged me on, steadfast. All right then. Leaning back, I said, "Fifteen years ago, some tribes in the Frontier province banded together. You've heard of the battle of Maiwand, in eighty?"

Adi looked up sharply. "You were at Maiwand?"

"I was a groom, for the officers' horses. My first campaign, with the Gurkha Infantry."

"Go on," said Diana softly.

"The Afghans won at Maiwand, but two thousand were killed or wounded. We lost nine hundred, our worst defeat in decades. Most were Bombay boys. The next year we backed the tribes into a corner at Kandahar, forced them into a treaty . . . but they've broken it, again and again, over the years. Two years ago, my regiment returned to the Afghan Frontier. We had a few skirmishes, lost ground in ninety, and retreated for the winter. I was with Smith and my cavalry company then, pulling back to . . . Karachi, where our ships waited."

Adi said, "At dinner, Major Smith said you saved his life."

Again that illusion of heroism. Time I set it right.

"Not true. Smith and I led the advance guard, riding ahead to the port. His horse lost a shoe, stumbled and threw him. Smith landed hard, tore his knee. The horse was lame, so we bound Smith up, got him behind me on Mullicka. We rode slowly, each step jarred Smith, the pain quite bad. Went through Scinde, a wild countryside, feared ambush at every turn. Nine horses, clipping along, too slow, too loud, could be heard for miles. So I stayed with Smith and a scout, and sent the others on ahead to the port."

At the time this had seemed a good compromise, a simple solution. Whom had I put in charge? Rashid? Suri? I couldn't remember.

I went on, "The company was ambushed—Afridis, an Afghan tribe, cut them off. Fired on them as they rode in. Would have got Smith and me too, except we heard the shots as we entered the city. I remember blood. . . . Smith was bleeding. I sent the scout back on Mullicka to alert the column behind us. Smith and I took shelter."

Now the hard part. There was no escaping it.

"Those Pathan soldiers killed my troop. I heard our chaps return fire. Heard them scream. Didn't know what was happening . . . my friends . . . Jeet, Pathak, Suri, Rashid Khan. Were the Pathans trying to lure me out? We stayed down, hid."

I turned away. There, I'd said it. No need to describe their agony, the shots, shouts, cries, while I remained safe in a lean-to on the outskirts.

After a moment Adi asked softly, "How did you get out?"

I leaned against the desk, hands clenched on its edge, remembering.

"We waited. Too long. I waited too long." I winced at the memory of pain. Wasn't that my choice, to stay with Smith or to leave him? "Worked my way to the lads. Too late. They were surrounded . . . broke through. . . ."

This was a blur in my memory, fragments of fast action. Unable to face Diana, I went on. "Found some of my lads, dead. Searched for the others. Three days later the column caught up, found Smith and me."

Why had I chosen Smith, my English officer, over the lads? I could not explain it, yet I must have done that, for they were dead, while he and I lived. It haunted my dreams—the sound, the taste of fear—acrid, numbing. Unable to think, cringing from it, I had taken too long to reach my friends. A sheen of tears glistened on Diana's cheek. Did she pity me? Did she see me as something broken, now?

"Your first command?" asked Adi.

"No. Smith was the senior officer. I was his second." I groaned as regret choked me, "Don't you see? I should have been with them, my company— I've thought about it a thousand times. Should have left someone with Smith, and gone with them. There had to be some way to prevent that . . . slaughter."

Adi said, "If you'd gone, Captain, you'd be dead too."

"Perhaps." I searched Diana's face, expecting reserve, even revulsion. She looked puzzled.

Adi's jaw clenched, but only sympathy shone upon his face, no trace of that judgement I dreaded. "You survived. Both of you," he said.

The empty evening answered him. Smith and I, well, neither of us was intact.

Diana frowned. "Jim, are you sure of this? You were awarded the Order of Merit. Have you read the official account?"

I shook my head. "My time in hospital is a blur."

She said, "Something's not right, Jim. I don't know much about military affairs, but I know you, I think. If you'd just got command, after Smith's injury, would you hand it off? I doubt that." Sitting by me, she said, "Now this journey. Are you going for Doctor Aziz? Or because you miss the army?"

"Perhaps both."

She sighed. Over her head, I saw Adi's mournful look. It carried no condemnation. I suspected that the siblings did not really see the heart of it—a Captain must not abandon his troop. But they hadn't been "brought up army" as I was, with tales of honor and duty.

Was Diana right? Was that why I'd agreed to go to Pathankot? Or was it guilt that drove me to redeem myself by attempting an impossible rescue? It would not bring back Pathak and Suri, those brave Bombay boys who rode off in the dust. Would I ever forgive it, my negligence, my lack of foreboding as I sent them off, calling, "Don't forget, hold the ship for me!"

Would I ever cease to hear Jeet's joking reply, "Arrey, hurry up, Huzoor! The tide waits for no man!"

* * *

I'd only said we'd depart tomorrow, not that we'd be gone before daybreak, so none was awake when we stole away. I did not say farewell to Diana, neither that night nor in the dawn, when, dressed as Pathans, Razak and

I slipped past the gate. At the checkpoint on Simla Road, our horses and Greer's escort would be waiting.

Why did I not speak to Diana, tell her of my affection for her? In truth, I could not, for she'd have guessed the tenuous nature of my expedition. I would not leave fear clawing her insides while I was gone. If I was killed, let her learn of it quickly and let it be done. Still consumed by the inexplicable death of his wife, Adi looked weary. His sunken eyes told of long nights without sleep, nights that scoured him with their questions. I did not want that for Diana.

At the Simla checkpoint, a horse huffed and snorted, hearing our approach. Two mottled grey mares stood by the magnificent brown Arabian.

"Huzoor." An accented voice spoke. A barrel-chested, turbaned Sikh stepped out. Although dressed plainly in brown and grey, it was the man Greer had set upon me in the mess hall. He did not approach, but watched me as one gauges a cobra, tense and ready to spring back.

Bloody Greer. Trust him to send a man who did not trust me.

"Sardar, I am Rashid Khan, and you are?" I spoke like a Pathan, in the thick tones Razak was accustomed to. Razak grinned and embraced me about the waist.

I rubbed his newly shorn hair and picked up the Arabian's halter.

"Subaltern Ranbir Singh, sir," said the soldier.

"I'm not 'sir,'" I said in English. "Call me Rashid. Or Bao-di, if you must."

The Sardar flinched, his stare more pronounced. In that gloomy morning, he could not tell what I was, for both Pathan and Captain were equally in my mind.

CHAPTER 38

A NEW PARTNERSHIP

We cantered past the Simla border to cleave through the British guard, then my filly wanted her head so I gave in, letting her out as she pleased. I felt at home here, among these hills. Eager to reach Pathankot and find Doctor Aziz, I leaned into the mare, leaving Razak and the Sardar to speed across the curve of a hillside.

The Arabian ran as if power and poetry were one, her hooves eager for wide ground and open skies. Each stride hit the ground and lifted. She stretched forward in a smooth arc, reaching, until she tucked hind legs under and pushed off again. Each bound curved easily, her hoofbeats punctuating the moments we were airborne. She taught me that my weight rode better toward her forelegs, that to change direction took the slightest nudge. To pull on her would be like shouting in a temple. She needed only whispers, altering her gait as though she knew my mind. I'd not ridden in months, and it felt wonderful to fly across the meadow.

Ranbir and Razak caught up some time later as I watched the sunrise from a grassy slope. Head low, the Arabian licked dew off blades of grass. Razak dismounted Pathan-style, leaping from his horse midstride to run alongside. He dropped on the green beside me, grinning, and said that the Sardar was a terrible rider.

Sardar Ranbir Singh brought the horses together, his shoulders tight and anxious. He would not meet my eyes. All right then. I sent Razak down to water the horses by the stream and asked, "Were you ordered to come as a punishment, Sardar?"

"No, Sahib." His mouth drooped at the corners. It would not do. This man and I must come to terms if we were to survive. I hauled myself up and faced him.

"Ranbir Singh," I rapped out.

Now he had to look at me.

"What disturbs you?"

He shook his head, but I had no time for niceties.

"Is it me?" I asked directly.

He glowered, suspicious and angry. "Who are you? What are you?" he demanded. There was no "sir" in his voice.

I nodded. "That's better. I'm Captain Agnihotri, a soldier. Like you."

He shook his head vehemently. "Not like me."

Ah! I defied his notion of an officer, speaking to Razak in Pashto, taking off on the Arabian like an uncouth tribesman. He'd seen me as a Pathan in the mess hall, so a Pathan I must be. But I spoke English, and was called Captain, so which was I?

I tried to explain. "Ranbir, I left the army, but I'm needed as a scout. For this action."

He scanned my crumpled kaftan, turban and beard. "You were a Captain of Infantry?"

"Cavalry. Light Dragoons. Medical discharge."

He liked that. It matched my peculiar appearance, but he wanted to be sure. "Are you Pathan?" he asked, incredulous.

I sighed. Indian hierarchy, dogging me again. At the top, admired, obeyed and watched, always watched, were British officers. Next came "the civil": administrators, Englishmen regardless of education or connections. Then non-coms, followed by native officers of high caste. All high castes, Brahmins—the priestly class—and Shatriya warriors preceded Sikhs and Gurkhas. Parsees might figure with the non-coms, educated, wealthy and influential. At the bottom, ignored at best, often just despised, were the low castes: traders and tribesmen thought to be crude, ignorant carpet peddlers like the Pathans, like me. High castes could escape crimes perpetrated upon lower castes. Low castes could not hope to be promoted, since no one would follow them. Did I expect Ranbir to follow a Pathan?

"Ranbir, I can hardly ride to Pathankot as an officer, can I?" I said. "What did they say about me?"

"Huzoor, I was told, there is a rude Pathan coming to the mess hall. Knock him out. That's all. But . . . I failed." He blushed to have been shamed in front of his officers. "Last night General Sahib summoned me. He said, take three horses to the checkpoint. Go with Captain Sahib, find the Gurkha Company and bring back survivors. I did not know the Captain was you."

Ranbir's shoulders eased. Agreeing to speak only Pashto, he said, "I heard what you did. It is noble, bringing children from Lahore. But how can we find the Gurkha Company?"

"Ranbir, we can do this. Razak's village is near Pathankot."

For the first time, he smiled.

We made good time for the next two days, stopping only to water and spell the horses. We made cold camps after dark. My rank was no longer Captain, but scout. Forgetting that, I gave Ranbir orders. "No fire. Dry provision only. Let the horses at their nose bags."

Then I remembered, and apologized.

Exasperated, Ranbir said, "Bao-di, it is all right!"

"Bao-di?" I grinned. He'd used Razak's name for me—a form of Babuji, meaning father.

Soon we left the banks of the Sutlej, traveling north. The ride would get steeper, more treacherous as we neared Pathankot. We'd have to thread narrow gorges, Afghan territory. Now I regretted not saying farewell to my little troop, and to the Framjis. Diana—it sat heavily on me, that I'd left things so unsettled between us. If I did not return, all I'd left her was silence.

Over the midday meal, Razak questioned our story. If I was his uncle, taking him home, how could Ranbir be my friend? Although he wore native garb, his beard was neat. Like me, Ranbir wore army boots, and an army belt girded his waist.

"Anyone can see he's a soldier," Razak grumbled. He did not say the same of me. Perhaps I was gaunt enough to be taken for a tribesman.

It grew cooler as we rode north. We kept a deliberate pace, fording streams quickly, skirting settlements, stopping only to rest our steeds. Soon we must slow, lest the pounding of fast horses alert the enemy.

I dropped to a trot, twisting in the saddle to find my companions. Unexpectedly, my horse bucked.

Perhaps something startled her, a snake or rabbit. Had I not glanced back, it might have cost me nothing, a tight grip on her reins and a low word would suffice. Without these to calm her, she reared—an enormous wave that flung me off her back

I landed on my right with a blinding shock. Pain speared my shoulder—filling my mind. I recalled Jameson's admonition, "it will heal if you don't get into any more scrapes," and feared he was right. This time I'd surely broken it. My right arm hung heavy and useless under that searing agony.

That night, Ranbir proved his worth. He found me doubled over, speechless, and took charge, setting up camp. My pain numbed both hearing and sight. Would it not ease? Feeling drunk and lightheaded, I longed for the oblivion of sleep. I ran my fingers around the bone, felt no sharp edges. While I crouched by the campfire, Ranbir strapped up my shoulder. With the practical manner of the Punjabis, he unbuckled his leather belt and bound my arm to my waist.

That helped. When I groaned about my previous injury, Ranbir grumbled, "Why, Bao-di? Why take this job, if you were already hurt?"

"I have to take Razak back."

Dark eyes in a pale face, Razak looked anxious. I had to tell him about our mission. Thus crippled by my injury, a greater part would fall to him.

I said, "Razak, tell no one. Our soldiers are trapped in Pathankot. If it was me, I would want someone to get me out. Will you help?"

Eyes wide, he agreed. The night was long. Why had I spoken to Greer so, claiming the Gurkhas could be rescued? Did I want his praise, his respect? I didn't even like him. I just needed to find Doctor Aziz, and determine who killed the Framji women.

* * *

Ranbir the Sardar was strong. I didn't know how strong until the next morning. Aching and dull-headed after a tortured night, I tried to mount, one-handed, a foot in the stirrup. I hopped, groaned, tried again, until Ranbir grabbed my waist and hoisted me into the saddle: I did not plummet off the other side, but it was a near thing.

Since I was little use, Ranbir and Razak conferred upon a hilltop, scanning the crevices, and settled upon a winding path. My right arm bound to my waist, wearing a poultice that Ranbir produced out of herbs that smelled suspiciously like horse dung, I slumped in the saddle. Low cloud spilled over rocks, hiding us from the valley, yet making the ride more treacherous. We rode slowly. As though she knew the price I'd paid for her foolishness, the Arabian walked softly along the edge of the mountain.

Around midday, we climbed an outcrop and there it was: Razak's village. He broke into a lope, and clattered across a wooden bridge toward the houses.

Shouts erupted. Boys, turbaned men, women in dark shalwars ran toward us in surprise. "Razak?" someone cried. I pulled to a halt and drooped over my horse, smelling woodsmoke and cooking and cool mountain air.

"Come, Bao-di," said Ranbir. I lifted a leg across her withers and slid down the Arabian's flank. Ranbir caught me, carrying me like a child.

I heard Razak, questioning. A voice creaked like an old leather saddle. Then darkness.

* * *

Razak's voice, pitched high with worry, woke me. "Dac-tar, will he wake?"

My shoulder had eased to a dull throb. A neatly bearded young man by my side wore a shirt, collar and vest, a white prayer cap atop his head. Seeing he wore a stethoscope, I breathed in relief.

An educated voice asked in Pashto, "Does he understand English?"

Ranbir's dry voice replied, "A little."

Let him have his joke, I thought. My chest was bare, and a dozen or so bearded faces peered down at me.

"Why is he so pale?" someone asked.

"He may be Kashmiri. They are pretty." The creaking leather voice belonged to a wrinkled man with broken teeth.

"This will bring trouble," grumbled a thin man with a pointed beard.

I moved, heard a collective sound of approval and grimaced. My audience pulled back.

The young doctor continued in Pashto, "Your shoulder was dislocated. I have put it back." His hands made a twisting motion. I'd been incredibly fortunate.

"Is he awake?" asked the village elder with broken teeth. He spat to one side, limped up and touched my forehead with the backs of thin fingers.

I croaked, "Salaam." Damn, I could barely speak.

My greeting delighted the old man. He clucked and patted my arm with a leathery hand. "Salaam, Salaam, my guest."

"Bao-di, my father went down to Pathankot"—Razak's voice swelled with pride—"and brought the dac-tar."

"Janab, welcome," a deep voice said behind me. Razak's father, I thought distantly. The voice of a leader, a voice that inspired confidence said, "You brought our son Razak, at some cost to yourself."

Hazel eyes curious, but not demanding, Razak's father, a thickset man in white turban and clean khamiz, grey scarf rolled around his neck, was in his forties. White flecked his dark beard. I'd need his help to find the Gurkha troop. Yet his formal tone held caution. The Afghan army was a militia, assembled from villages spread throughout the mountains. Some villages were at war with the Pakhtun tribe, others allied to it. Was the enemy here?

"Are soldiers here? Pakhtun soldiers?" I choked. A reasonable question, surely? Don't most travelers fear soldiers? If the village, or Razak's father himself, were friendly with that principality, now I'd surely hear of it.

Ranbir stood at my side, scarcely breathing. Did he fear that in my delirium, I might give us away?

"No, they have gone," Razak's father replied, rubbing his chin.

So they had been here. I said, "I regret to burden you, Janab. May we stay . . . a few days?"

He grew concerned. "Are they searching for you?"

He did not like the soldiers. That reassured me. "No. We've had no trouble. My arm . . ."

"You are my guest, Bao-di to my son. You are safe."

I wasn't sure all the curious tribesmen behind him agreed. Would Melmastia—the Pathan tradition of hospitality—protect me if they learned who I really was?

CHAPTER 39

EXPLORING PATHANKOT

I woke each dawn to the Muezzin's distant call to prayer. Ranbir tended me, then accompanied village men on their forays through the hills, taking goats to pasture or down to Pathankot market. In this way, he gathered intelligence while I recovered. Three days passed.

Working the doctor's noxious-smelling medicine into my shoulder, I sat outside a hut, leaned against a wall and greeted passersby, practicing Pashto with local children, much to their shrill amusement. In this way, I too gathered intelligence.

"Look, Bao-di!" A round-faced boy in an oversize khamiz showed me his cupped hands.

Admiring the beetle on his palm, I asked, "Were there strangers here, some days ago?"

"Hah, Bao-di!" an older boy said eagerly, his features already angular, but open. The habitual narrowing of eyes would come later. "They went to Pathankot."

I let the beetle advance to my hand, its touch tickling as it crawled over my knuckles.

"How many were they?"

"Many! Maybe twenty!" Another said, "Fifty!

"How many horses?"

They agreed there were eight horses for riders, and four pulling wagons. A week ago Afghan soldiers had confiscated most of the village's grain, but the livestock had been hidden in time, so they were not found. Children know far more than most adults realize.

Following Pathan custom, women did not enter our hut. At mealtimes, late morning and after sunset, we ate with Razak's family. Thick roti, meat and root vegetables simmered on wooden platters, savory and delicious, spices that lit my mouth in a burst of fireworks. In recompense I winched up buckets of water from the river below and carried them, one-handed, to Razak's hut.

Feeling stronger, I walked to a cliff at the edge of the village, a few boys trailing me. They ran ahead to the bridge to await the menfolk's return. Blue-grey woodsmoke drifted from low thatched houses. I sat on an outcrop, snow-draped mountain slopes at my shoulder. My cliff perch offered a view of the barren road to Pathankot, white stones of the pass brilliant in the sunlight. It wound to a narrow bridge, the entrance to the village, turning it into a perfectly defensible qila—a fortress. There was no sign of any enemy.

Far below, a boy with a long stick herded sheep over a crest. The wind came through mountain crags with a soft, shrill whistle, a warning, ever present. Almost a week had passed since we left my little brood with Diana. We had yet to find the Gurkha troop.

Next morning Ranbir and I prepared to depart for Pathankot. When I told Razak's father I was looking for someone there, he drew in the dust to show us landmarks.

A heated exchange caught my ear. Young Razak, mutinous, argued with his mother.

"I will go! You can't stop me!" he cried, tearing from her grasp. Catching sight of me, he stopped, shaking with emotion. "They won't let me go . . . to Pathankot with you." His voice broke, reminding me that, despite his bravado, he was only ten.

His mother, a young Afghan woman wearing a brown headscarf, creases already etched around her mouth, cast a pleading look at me. She'd only just found her lost boy. What must she think of a pale, haggard bloke that her son called "father"?

"Razak." I caught his shoulders, bent to peer into his face. "Stay. They were without you for so long. This is your home, is it not?"

His mother's relief rewarded me. Little Razak nodded, crestfallen, as I rubbed his head.

"What will happen to Parimal and Hari?" he whispered.

I promised to care for them, adding, "You did well, Razak, son, khuda-hafiz."

At this goodbye, his scrawny arms wound about me. Reluctantly releasing me, he stood by his father while we mounted.

Ranbir and I set off at a walk. Well rested, the Arabian picked her way over rocks and roots down to the wooden bridge. My shoulder eased. I rode, balancing my weight against saddlebags packed with provisions as we stepped downward.

"Bao-di!" Razak called, from high above, a long note of sorrow. I pulled up, craning my neck at what I could see of the little hamlet. Razak's tousled head, narrow shoulders showed briefly. I would miss the little general.

Pathankot was an hour's ride, a bustling town beside a broken fortress. It spread across a valley, between the Chakki River and its main tributary. One bank of the river rose in sharp folds of grey rock. From this high ground, we crossed a stone bridge toward the city.

Ranbir stirred, pointing. Pathan soldiers with distinctive large white turbans guarded the crossroads leading into the city. We followed the bustle of carts and foot-worn villagers.

Most men here carried an old jezail rifle slung over their shoulders. Leather-covered blades hung from their belts. Leading our horses through the crowds, faces muffled in wrappings like other tribesmen, we escaped notice and threaded our way toward the bazaar.

Ranbir grunted. "What now, Bao-di?"

"Now we find the troop. Let's separate and ask questions. Strangers are noticed—say only that we're seeking our friends."

An ironsmith's forge abutted a stable. We bargained, arranged to feed and water our horses, then followed the unmistakable aroma of roasted lamb to the market. Arranging to rendezvous at the stable, Ranbir set off to ask questions at the market. Hours later, having scouted the narrow byways around the fortress, I returned, weary and empty-handed. Ranbir had found kebabs, bread, yogurt and a host of local tales. We sat cross-legged and ate.

Ranbir said he'd avoided several Afghan soldiers, then grinned. "These people are very superstitious! That old palace by the river, in the broken fort? They are all afraid of it. They say the zenana, the women's quarters, is haunted."

"Haunted? Why?" I ate a kebab, wondering what use this knowledge might be.

"An old shoemaker told me the story. Some two hundred years ago a Moghul king tried to capture Pathankot. This town was the stronghold of a Pathan Thakur and his queen the Thakurani." Ranbir mused, "There are many such tales in these mountains."

"Why is it haunted?" I dunked the last kebab into an earthen pot of yogurt and popped it into my mouth.

"The Thakur died bravely in battle. But the Thakurani would not be taken. Rather than become slaves, she and all her court ladies committed Johur. They jumped from the battlements and died."

A shiver ran down my arms. It sounded strangely like the mystery I needed to unravel. Two centuries later, had Lady Bacha and Miss Pilloo faced a similar threat?

"The old man said their ghosts cry out still." Ranbir continued, "Their wails are heard on quiet nights."

Skeptical, I frowned. "From the zenana?"

Dusk was upon us as we decided to search the crumbling fortifications on the edge of town. The Gurkha troop might have secured themselves in its maze of corridors and tunnels, but in the dark, how could we find them?

Ranbir paid the sleepy stableman, who spat sideways on the straw and then untied our horses. I climbed into the saddle and pointed my Arabian to the town outskirts. She walked gently, hooves clip-clopping in the starry night. The market having closed, we wove through a few villagers trudging homeward.

Night comes quickly in the mountains. The air was crisp and still. Navigating cobbles, long since crumbled, that lay loose and uneven in our path, our horses' hooves clinked on stone, high notes interspersed with hoofbeats. I winced—could the sentries at the crossroads hear us?

The fortress loomed, dark and formless. It had been shelled years ago, leaving wide gashes in the wall, a wall that bled piles of stone, great blocks of it slowing our pace.

The outer fortifications towered on my right. I nudged my horse along the perimeter, trusting her to navigate the rubble. Reins slack, she stepped carefully, dropping her head now and again to sniff at stones. Stopping at a dark hollow, a crevice in the wall, she shook her mane as though to ask, "Are you bloody sure you want to do this?"

She'd found the way into the fortress, but could we find our way out?

CHAPTER 40

THE HAUNTED ZENANA

Night is not the time to explore unfamiliar terrain, yet it was all we had—my injury had cost us three days. With a nudge of my knees, the Arabian stepped through the broken archway into the fortress courtyard.

A sliver of moon left the clouds to gleam high above, allowing me a view of vast fortifications. Two turrets loomed at either end of a forward wall, vantage points to pick us off with a bullet. The courtyard offered no shelter between outer and inner walls, a space designed to trap intruders.

"Bao-di," said Ranbir, "this is not a good place."

An archway to one side led to an inner locus, the zenana or women's quarters, marked by narrow windows overlooking a courtyard. I hesitated, reluctant to enter a maze of unfamiliar passages, but there was no help for it. We must find Greer's men and Doctor Aziz. Grateful for moonlight, I searched the shadows for movement. The air was cooler amid the fog and silent stones. Among these walls, one could almost believe in spirits.

Suddenly a plaintive wail wound through the ruin, creeping over bare stones, chilling in its despair. My breath caught, disbelieving. The Arabian lurched sideways, hooves clattering, a familiar sound, comforting in its normalcy, in contrast to the otherworldly cry.

The screech faded, leaving an expectant silence. I held tight to the reins, cold creeping over my skin. We should leave this alien place.

"What is it?" Ranbir whispered.

My hands soothing my mount, rubbing her twitching withers, I said, "Steady, old girl."

There was something peculiar about the torn cry, a familiar quality, despite its eerie resonance. When I nudged the Arabian, she set off at a happy trot. Astonished, I held her back, until I realized that her gait meant something. Could she know that sound?

Then it struck me. Good Lord—that eerie note came from army bagpipes!

I loosed the reins, letting the Arabian find it. Ranbir followed, uttering prayers.

The Arabian sidled to a stairway, her feet dancing, her ears up and alert, eager and high-strung. I dismounted, holding her bridle.

"Rookoh!" A voice commanded me to stop.

I stiffened, heard Ranbir's startled breath and understood. The Sepoys of the Twenty-first Gurkha Rifle Regiment were expert snipers. Only their reluctance to reveal themselves had saved us from a marksman's bullet.

Still clinging to the saddle, I whistled two notes every Sepoy would know.

Someone chuckled. "Mess call," the quiet voice said in English.

We had found the troop. I felt giddy with relief. "Righto. Can you play 'Loch Lomond' on those pipes?"

A short Gurkha in khaki uniform stepped out of the shadows a few feet away, smiling. I admit to a warm rush of relief, even ebullience, then. The troop had survived in the fortress for weeks and surely knew every turn of these blasted passages. Their ruse, those ghostly wails, kept away enemy soldiers and townsfolk by night. With their help we might escape this place.

"I am Seetu. Come," the Sepoy beckoned.

Sending an old bagpiper to hide our horses, Seetu led us to their hideaway. Gurkha infantrymen scrambled to their feet and saluted. Exchanging heartfelt greetings, I asked. "Where's Major Hadley?"

Seetu replied, somber, "Huzoor, he was shot when our post was overrun. We had to blow up the munitions. I assumed command."

"And Doctor Aziz?"

A thin, bearded man in a soiled grey kaftan and vest came forward, saying, "I am Aziz."

At last! I shook his hand gladly as the Gurkhas crowded around us with bright eyes. Seetu distributed our stores among the Sepoys, who consumed them quickly. Huddled together against the cold, we considered different routes of escape. If we left in darkness we'd be at the mercy of the terrain, but waiting for light could bring the enemy.

A plan was devised. We set sentries and lay down on the cold stone floor. Despite that, sleep came quickly.

* * *

Just before daybreak, Ranbir and I set off to the market to buy horses or mules. As we approached the crossroads, leading our horses, I realized that we'd been noticed. A group of Afghan soldiers was pointing at my fine mount. I sighed. There was no help for it but to bluff our way through.

"Irkav!" the leader commanded in Dari.

My pulse sped into a staccato. The filly shifted anxiously.

Just then a high voice called, "Bao-di!" as Razak and his father dropped from their mounts midstride. As they greeted us with the traditional embrace on each shoulder, much to my relief, the soldiers lost interest in the common spectacle of a family reunion.

"Razak would not rest until he found you," Razak's father said. "We watched the crossroads yesterday but you did not return. We have been searching for hours!"

Their arrival greatly improved our prospects. In a brief negotiation I hired his wagon and horses. The village needed grain and supplies, which they would acquire in Simla. Collecting the Sepoys, we began our return with Razak's father and some tribesmen as an escort.

Later, as we prepared for departure, Razak's shoulders slumped, his mouth a crooked curve of dejection. "Bao-di!" he cried.

I'd grown fond of this little thief. I remembered his cool composure that first day as he pinned me with my own pistol. His love for Parimal and Hari, caring for them although still a child himself, how he'd wept when we were safe and fed by the Framjis.

Thin arms went around my waist. I hugged him, caught his shoulders and asked, "Why did you ambush me, that first day? For the food?"

Abashed, he mumbled, "The baby was crying. We hid and followed you. You had a woman making roti."

"Razak, son, why did you take the baby?"

He blinked. "When I found him, Bao-di, he smiled at me. How could I leave him there?"

"Little thief." I grinned at Razak. He was so much more.

As we left, Razak stood in the road, waving to me and his father, until the rocky path dropped out of sight beside the river.

That evening, riding beside Doctor Aziz, I got my chance to question him, at last.

"You were in Lahore some years ago?"

He nodded, puzzled.

"I wonder if you recall—you treated a lad called Kasim? Train accident, I believe."

"Oh!" His eyebrows shot up. "I remember that. Tragedy, of course. Legs sheared at the knees. Femoral arteries severed. Stemmed the bleeding, but it was too late."

"Can you tell me what happened?"

"I heard a great hue and cry, people calling for a doctor, and went to see. The boy had to be carried to the platform. I was summoned, and found the child bleeding. I stayed with him to the end."

"Tell me about it."

Doctor Aziz exhaled. "There were two boys at Moga station, Kasim and a friend. After Kasim died, the other said he had nowhere to go. I brought him with me, as a houseboy for my wife, to help around the house."

Kasim had been traveling with a friend! "Where is he, your houseboy?"

The doctor eyed me in surprise. "This is important to you?" When I affirmed it, he said, "I don't know where he is. He left without a word."

"His name? What did he look like?"

He shrugged. "Sahir? Sabir? A thin youth, morose, always complaining."

A thin youth? Wait. Earlier he'd called Kasim a child. But Diana said Kasim was three years older than herself.

"Kasim and his friend, how old were they, Doctor?"

He frowned, thinking. "Difficult to say. Kasim was perhaps fourteen? His friend was a young man, perhaps twenty years old."

"Which year was this?"

"It was March of eighty-eight. I was leaving Lahore for a rural posting."

Diana was twenty this year, 1892, and she'd been in England four years. That made her sixteen in '88. She'd said Kasim was three years older than her, so the fourteen-year-old who died could not have been Kasim. Was it possible that Kasim was not dead? Was he a twenty-year-old who faked his death by giving a dead boy his name?

"Your posting—where was it?"

"A princedom in the south. You may not have heard of it. Ranjpoot."

I stared. Ranjpoot? Here was my connection at last! Kasim went to Ranjpoot with the doctor, and Akbar and Behg were from there.

We reached Simla at sundown on the second day. I met Greer's scouts, who spotted our approach, so we had no trouble getting through the lines on Simla Road. At the sentry post Greer's officers and Sepoys swarmed toward us. Deep shades of evening washed the surreal scene: Gurkhas dismounted, Sepoys everywhere, officers clustered around the short blond form of General Greer.

Striding toward us, Greer shook my hand, saying, "Good man."

All at once the miles descended, my feet were lead, my eyes burned from the ride. I took my leave of Razak's relatives, raised a hand in fare-well to Greer and the Gurkhas and started toward the Framji villa.

A small tonga pulled up beside me, driven by a young Sepoy with dark skin and flashing teeth who said, "General Greer's compliments, sir. Climb in. I'm to take you home."

CHAPTER 41

SHEARED

I'm told I ran a fierce fever that night, cried out and made rather a nuisance of myself. Voices roused me from sleep only to ply me with a bitter draught that tasted like crushed mosquitoes. I drank and dropped into darkness.

The sound of quick feet running on tile woke me in an unfamiliar bedchamber, a whitewashed affair with teak dressing table and wooden chairs. I'd reached Simla.

Having left Razak with his kin, only two of my urchins, Parimal and little Hari, remained. Seeing me awake, they padded up, all wide eyes and puckered lips.

I could no more resist them than cease breathing. They clambered onto my bed, flinging questions every which way. Time slowed. Each moment precious, each sound etched itself on my senses, like rain after a drought.

"Good morning, Captain," said Mrs. Framji, forehead ridged with worry. She hovered at the door with Diana.

I greeted them. To my surprise they entered. Mrs. Framji gestured at my blanket of boys. "Are they . . . disturbing you?"

I smiled. "No."

Diana shook her head at me, saying, "You gave them the most awful fright. Showing up half-dead. To collapse like that, right at the door!"

"Ah." Gurung had answered the door. . . . I remembered stepping through, then nothing.

I rubbed a hand over Hari's soft head, breathing in the warm feel of them, their clean, soapy smell. It burrowed inside me, mending pieces I'd not known were broken.

"Captain," said Diana, wincing, "would you rather go to the infirmary?"

I looked up in surprise. "That bad?"

She came around to the foot of my bed. "Only if it's better for you. You seemed so . . ." She trailed off, sighing.

"Yes," I said, "but this is what I need." I touched a tousled head, saw round eyes and plump arms, faces whose hollows had filled out. "They look well. Thank you."

Her voice hushed with excitement, Mrs. Framji said, "Captain, Diana has found their parents."

Diana nodded, saying, "You know they're brothers? Well, when Parimal gave his full name, Parimal Vasant Arora, that's his father's name right in there, Vasant Arora. He's from Jalandhar, so I've sent him a telegram. You don't mind?"

I breathed, feeling the boys rise and fall with me. "No. Thank you."

Alas, the quiet moment did not last. Parimal sneezed and tried to push Hari off me. Hari wriggled, raised a chubby hand and delivered a smack to his brother's cheek.

"Buss!" I secured him with an arm about his little body, enveloping his hand to prevent further assault. Although I'd abandoned the lads for a while, Diana had not. Once unrest in the Punjab subsided, perhaps Parimal and Hari could go home.

As Diana whisked them away, a burden lifted that I'd not known I carried. Before I left Razak, he'd extracted my promise to care for them. It said much about the man he would become.

I slept most of that day, waking only to take my fill of Mrs. Framji's superb meals. Whispers from the door alerted me when the boys or Chutki peeked in, but under Diana's admonishments they let me be. Sleep came in an inexorable wave, deep and dreamless, as it had in Framji Mansion. Perhaps that's what home felt like, a sense that I might drop the reins, shelter under Burjor's roof and take what I needed to restore myself.

* * *

Next morning the song of a Muezzin's call to prayer filtered into my dreams. I smelled the crisp tang of mountain pines, the smoke of cooking fires around Razak's village.

A musical sound came from the door, a soft jingle of playful bells. Chutki appeared, her tinkling rhythm telling me she no longer limped. Who'd given her anklets? It both surprised and reassured me that she'd been accepted into this household. She peeked in, dimpled a welcome and left before I could voice my surprise.

Diana swept by in a saree the color of purple dusk, her hair caught up atop her head. She saw me awake and paused, distressed. Thus alerted, I sat up cautiously. Face flushed, she bit her lip in agitation. Diana could not bear to give pain. She had once said she hated to break things. Now she looked fit to throw things, then wring her hands and weep.

I said, "Miss Diana, are you well?"

"I'm glad you rested, Captain, but," Diana said, and sighed, "I must ask . . . about Chutki."

"Yes?" I had provided only the barest details about Chutki, in part to protect her reputation, but also from reluctance to pry into the child's suffering. Diana narrated that her servants had inquired what caste Chutki belonged to. My claim that she was my sister had been met with much curiosity, since we looked nothing alike.

"Of course, I knew that was a ruse," Diana said. Looking determined to take me to account, she asked, "How did she come to be with you?"

Warned by her account of the servants' gossip, I knew I must not reveal Chutki's story. I had to hide her past, in order to give her a future. I asked, "Did she say something? About what happened?"

Diana answered with a long stare. "Why is she with you? How?"

Now I could not believe the accusation in her face. I had not asked

Chutki about when she was a captive. Nor could I tell Diana how Chutki was offered to me. One did not speak of such things.

After a moment, I said, "A bad business, Miss Diana . . . I couldn't leave her there."

"You? Or that awful Pathan?"

"Miss?"

"When you command the children—'Quiet! Enough!'" she hissed, "I hate him."

Him? Fear sputtered in my gut. "Who?"

"The Pathan. That crude person . . . you become," she said.

She walked back and forth, draped in soft lavender fabric, but tougher than many officers I'd known. She'd been afraid my disguise might over-come me. Right. If my guise upset her so, I had no further use for it. Rashid Khan's beard and matted locks must go.

"Miss Diana," I said, "would you summon the barber?"

* * *

The barber, a round fellow, balding, with a fringe of hair at the back of his neck, placed a three-legged stool by the window and greeted me.

Diana marshaled her troops without delay. Fearful perhaps that I might change my mind, she rapped out orders with the ease of a quarter-master. "Bring Captain Sahib's clothes. Heat water for his bath!"

The children begged to stay and watch the barber. Perhaps that was well. They'd know me still, know I was yet their Bao-di. Eager for a spec-tacle, they sat on the floor around the stool.

Chutki giggled from the doorway, a sweet sound I'd thought lost to our misadventure. Shirtless on the low stool, I glanced back to see her duck and hide her face. Behind her, cooks and maids grinned at the morning's entertainment, namely me.

"Military cut, Sahib? All right!" The barber flexed a shiny pair of scis-sors and made short work of shearing me, clumps of hair falling all around.

The smallest boy, Hari, grabbed one off the floor. Round eyes implored, "Can I have it?"

I shrugged. If the little ones found playthings in discarded hair, who was I to refuse?

Diana's maid came in carrying the baby. When she set him down by the boys, he leaned forward and made steady progress on all fours. He could crawl! Had he just learned to do this? He grabbed a fistful of hair. It was headed toward his face, so I lifted him into my lap to disengage fist from mouth. His weight felt comfortable, his familiar, warm roundness curiously satisfying—I'd not known it could give such pride, such pleasure.

"Sahib, look this way," the barber said, soaping my jaw.

Parimal fell over, rolling in delight. "White beard! Old man!" he giggled, pointing.

The infant in my arms crowed and blew, a plump hand reaching for my face. We hadn't named him yet, and the boys were calling him Baby.

When Diana took him from me so that the barber could wield his blade, her face was cautious and closed off. Would she not forget my dratted Pathan guise?

Soon, my face clean-shaved and tingling from his ministrations, I wiped away smears of lather and thrust a hand through hair newly shorn to regimental length.

The boys hung back, quiet and absorbed, their large, dark eyes taking in the change. Surely they'd get accustomed to me soon enough?

I stood, straightening after weeks in the Pathan's studied stoop, and bid farewell to my old friend Rashid Khan the Pathan. I had re-created him in my disguise, from his stoop to his blunt manners. I missed the fiery blighter. But Rashid had been killed last year in Karachi, so I returned him to his grave.

Elsewhere in the house, a deep singsong voice had been praying. When the prayer ended, an odd quiet descended over my chamber. Silent servants grouped at the door. Diana held a hand over her lips, looking as though she might cry. Puzzled, I touched my jaw. What was the matter with everyone?

"Captain!" Adi smiled from the door, dapper in a grey suit. "Welcome back."

I grimaced to be found in such a state of undress, in what was becoming a public spectacle.

"What's this?" Burjor stopped in the doorway, then plowed into the chamber still wearing his prayer cap, broad face wide with satisfaction.

"Captain Jim!" His arms opened and enveloped me.

I stood stock-still. Astonishment gave way to gratitude. Here was the father I'd never had, open and forthright, yet warm in his approval. I grinned and returned the unexpected gift of his embrace.

CHAPTER 42

THE QUARREL

Greer had commanded my presence at ten o'clock the next morning. As Gurung knotted a tie around my neck, I said, "I'm surprised the General waited this long."

From the door, Mrs. Framji said, "My boy, a pair of Sepoys came yesterday while you slept, but Diana sent them back. With some rather unfriendly words, I'm afraid."

I chuckled to imagine how Greer had received that. Since I'd renounced Pathan garb and had left my uniform in Bombay, I wore a formal black coat and trousers, grey silk tie and vest. Pointing at the clock, Mrs. Framji waved away my thanks.

Returning to the map room at Simla headquarters, I encountered blank looks.

"You sent for me, sir?" I said to Greer's back.

When I gave him a Pathan greeting, hand over heart, short bow, he stiffened and said, "Good grief."

Standing among smiling Gurkhas, Ranbir chuckled at my changed appearance. I went over and shook his hand, thanking him for his aid. Words don't comply, at moments like this. They bunch up in my throat and won't form into straight lines. Ranbir's wide smile told me he understood.

"Captain Agnihotri," Greer cut in. "If you please," he said, and went on to review our accounts. "Damnedest thing I ever heard," he said. Mulling it over, he went on, "Fortunately we struck a bargain with the blokes from your lad's village—we have a foothold there now."

But he wasn't done with me. "Captain, you went in with no advance party, no reconnaissance, no fall-back plan and a hundred other blunders. Only God knows how you brought them back alive. Lucky I sent you my best man. Well done, Subaltern Ranbir Singh."

I remained impassive. After McIntyre's dressing-down in Bombay, Greer's was positively mild.

Signaling me to stay, he dismissed the group. As officers and Gurkhas shuffled out, stopping to shake my hand on their way, it brought back pleasant memories of my years in the service. Once they'd gone, Greer said, "A commendation for Singh, eh? What d'you say?"

When I endorsed the idea heartily, he said, "Good. You'll stay to luncheon?"

I declined, reluctant to return to the mess hall. Last time he'd ordered Ranbir to knock me out as a test of my fitness. Being known as a boxer had disadvantages, not least among them the expectation that I actually enjoyed a fight.

He looked put out. "Got somewhere else to be, Captain?"

I pleaded weariness, which he huffed away.

"Right, here it is. Can't put you up for a medal, since you're a civilian. Why not rejoin? How'd you like a commission, as Major? Your, er, name poses a difficulty, but I've a thought we could find a patron for you."

I stared. Indians did not rise above Subedar-Major, equivalent to the rank of Captain, since young Englishmen could not be expected to follow a native. He'd offered me the rank of Major, which came with a fine salary and quarters to boot. But it was too late. I wanted to return to Bombay and finish my investigation.

"I cannot accept, sir," I said, "though I'm deeply grateful, of course."

He nodded, "Expected as much. Medical discharge, Colonel Sutton said."

He'd spoken to my old commander? Had Sutton told him of the slaughter in Karachi? Greer's face gave nothing away, so I rather thought he knew.

An ensign brought in some papers and a wad of cash. Greer counted out some notes and handed them to me. "Took the liberty of sending for your wages: just sixty rupees, for the return of my lads and the doctor." When I'd tucked it away, he bid me goodbye, his face pensive. "If you need anything, you will say?"

Surprised at Greer's emotion, I smiled, saying, "Sir, there is no debt," then picked up my hat and left.

Back at the villa, I wanted only a cool drink and some quiet. In Conan Doyle's imagination, Holmes could hole up for hours, smoke his pipe and scrape at his fiddle. My experience of an investigator's life contained no such pleasantly cerebral pursuits.

As I set down my hat, Diana stepped into the verandah that served as the boys' nursery. It was warm, so I shrugged out of my borrowed coat.

"Hullo, Miss, where are the boys?"

"Captain," Diana said, her voice reserved. "Papa took them to bazaar in a tonga."

"Ah." I pulled off the tie, feeling rather abandoned. "And Chutki, Miss?"

I heard Diana exhale and knew I'd misstepped, but not how. She'd wanted my Pathan guise gone and it was. So what irked her?

She spun around, outlined against the sunlit window. "Why do you call me Miss!"

Why was she so upset? I could not imagine what I'd done to cause it. Her father wanted distance between us, but when I kept that distance, it weighed upon me, and seemed to distress Diana. All through Pathankot I had thought of her. Unaccountably weary, I dropped into a chair.

Diana waited, demanding an answer.

I spoke gently, "Why do you call me Captain?"

She stilled, sunlight catching her hair, weaving it with gold. Her head tilted, as though listening to music I could not hear. Face soft, she said, "Jim."

My name on her lips was an intimate sound. How it affected me! She'd spoken my name before, when I'd told her about Karachi. Yet her presence now held a bittersweet pain. A threshold lay before us, and Burjor had asked me not to cross it.

"Diana." When she did not reply, I asked, "What troubles you?"

Her intake of breath was sharp. She mumbled something, turning away.

But I could no longer wait. I caught her shoulder. "What is it? What have I done?"

"You left!" she said, in a strangled voice, "with no goodbye."

"Ah." How soft her look, how mournful! But in her eyes, turmoil seethed. "I'm sorry, Diana. I had no wish to worry you."

Her brown eyes held flecks of gold. "Oh! No, Jim, not me. You didn't say goodbye to Chutki! To Parimal and Hari! I can't speak Pashto—nobody here can. They woke and found you and Razak gone. I suppose they feared you'd left them . . . or died." Cheeks flushed, her whisper was fierce. "You cannot just pick them up, like objects, then put them aside."

I swallowed against the knot in my throat. Was this rebuke on behalf of the children, or herself? Did she think I put her aside to go off on some mad adventure? I'd had so little time—one evening to regroup.

I wanted to trace the sweet curve of her cheek. Instead I said, "I thought them safe, with you."

"And were you safe? What if you'd not returned? Have they not suffered enough? Eleven days, Captain. They barely ate! They would not leave this room, in case you magically appeared! Mama made gulab jamun, Papa tempted them with puppies. We've had the most terrible time, one or the other crying every night. And Chutki!" She struck my chest with the flat of her hand. "How could you?"

Was this still about not saying goodbye?

"Diana, no one's ever depended upon me like this," I said. "This is new to me. That I might matter to someone."

She pulled away with a cry. "No! You don't tell me anything! It's Chutki. She . . . oh dear!" She flushed. "We feared she might be with child."

I gaped. "She's twelve years old! Is she all right?"

"As it happens, it was only cramps. And she said she's fourteen." She showed ten and then four fingers. "Jim, she's awfully fond of you."

It sounded like an accusation. Was Diana . . . jealous?

I quirked an eyebrow at her, teasing. "Should I ask her to be less fond?"

Diana remained implacable. "You didn't . . . touch her?"

Taken aback, I asked, "Chutki? You're talking about Chutki?"

Diana huffed. "Her regard for you, it's not seemly."

Seemly? I recalled how we'd walked, starving, avoiding soldiers, carrying her, my arms aching. Appearances had mattered not a whit.

I chided, "Tsch. Don't be a prig, Miss."

"A prig! This from an unmarried man with five children!"

Polite society would find this peculiar, I supposed. Would my affection for the children take Diana from me? I struggled to explain. "Should I abandon them . . . as I was abandoned? You have so much, Diana! How can you understand? It is hard, to be without."

"Without . . . money?" she whispered.

I shook my head. "No, Diana, without family."

Looking aghast, she covered her mouth. "Family! Did you marry her?"

"Marry . . . Chutki?"

I caught Diana's arms. As the pieces fell into place, I could barely form the words.

"Chutki . . . when you believed her with child . . . you thought it was mine?" Numbed by Diana's accusation, I whispered, "Diana, you can't believe that."

Her eyes enormous in a pale face, she said, "I don't know him—you, the Pathan. When you're like that." She ducked her head, closing herself off from me.

All at once I could not wait. I choked, desperate with a sort of panic. This moment defined everything. I had no sense of future beyond it.

Gripping her arms, I cried, "Diana! Answer me. You hold a knife to my throat! Would I father Chutki's child?"

Diana searched me with astonishing calm, leaving me adrift, without tether, without compass. Did she not know me at all? That sweet dance at her ball was distant now, part of another lifetime. She took me for a brute. Something in me snapped, some final reserve.

Outrage churned sharp as bile. I demanded, "Even if she wasn't a child. Even if it wasn't an outrage . . . do you imagine I would? That I could?"

"Jim." Diana winced, her delicate throat working. Her brown eyes scorched me.

Feeling wretched, I could not budge. I wanted to cry out, to shake her! No, I wanted her soft voice saying "Jim," wrapping about me like a blanket on a cold night so I could pull her in and close my arms around her. But Diana despised me. How could she think I might harm a child, little Chutki with her torn feet and painful smile, her round, tired eyes and that wispy braid she was so proud of? Feeling gutted, I dropped my hands.

Diana's lips parted. "No. I see that . . . Jim, I'm sorry."

My breathing eased, but the knot inside me remained. Having no heart for this battle and feeling blasted full of holes, I bit out, "You should be, Miss."

Weaving cool fingers through mine, she said, "You could never harm them, Chutki or the boys."

Sunlight streamed through the glass, shimmering on Diana's wan face. She met my glance unafraid.

The tide in me abated, but I'd been hurt and could not forget it. Despite the closeness of our intertwined fingers, I felt . . . ambushed. Why did it hurt so? Because it was unexpected? No. Because I'd trusted her, I believed that therefore she must trust me. I was wrong.

"I've never seen you angry before," Diana said, her voice careful. "There. The clouds depart. Jim, there was something else, wasn't there? Not just Doctor Aziz. Some reason you went to Pathankot, why you had to go?"

She was right. I'd gone to Pathankot for the Sepoys, stranded and alone, fearing detection at any moment.

Diana neared, as though reading my mind, a mournful line to her lips. "I thought so. I call you Captain because it's what you are. You've left the army, but the army hasn't left you."

CHAPTER 43

LEAVING SIMLA

A week later we returned to Bombay on the southbound Frontier Express, traveling first-class, Chutki with Diana and her parents in one coach, Adi and I lounging in another. The servants had the third compartment. I had rested in the interval and eaten well. Although well below my usual weight, I'd even visited the army gymkhana to box.

Stretched out in the railcar, I rubbed my shoulder, thinking of Diana. Ever since our quarrel, a fissure remained: a shadow in her downcast look, a reservation in my mind. No wonder she doubted me, when I would not say how I'd found Chutki. She distrusted my guises, suspecting I behaved differently under their thrall. How little she knew! My guises allowed me entry into places not open to Englishmen. They were dear to me, for I knew them well, my dead brothers-in-arms: Rashid Khan, the rough-mannered Pathan, and Jeet Chaudhary, the dockworker.

Although she continued to call me Jim, I seldom used her name, for it brought the pain of what could have been. She accepted my coolness with calm. From Adi's remarks, I gathered that Soli, the older Wadia brother, had paid marked attentions to Diana in Simla—was my reticence driving her away?

I was a fool, for despite everything, I loved Diana. I knew it was hopeless. A fellow like me, a pauper and a bastard, had no chance at all. And yet it was there, that feeling inside me, a fist that hammered each time she gazed at me with those luminous eyes.

As the train plowed through the undulating hills and plains of

Central India, I dozed, glad of Adi's company but missing the boys' chatter. Little Parimal and Hari were not with us. Summoned by Diana's telegram, their parents arrived, anxious and hopeful. Keen to find an objection, some reason they could not take my lads, I had interrogated the farmer from Jalandhar and his wife, finally hitting upon a simple test: if the boys remembered their parents, I would release them. But if they had forgotten, I would not give them up.

It was all for naught. Parimal saw his mother and bawled. She rushed to him, caressing his face, enveloping him with kisses. The farmer wept and dropped to his knees to thank his gods. Before they took their children home, I held my boys in a bittersweet farewell, breathing in their scent of straw and soap and horses, aching. I'd grown fond of my scruffy band, now restored to their childhoods. All I had left were Chutki and the baby, whom we named Baadal for the impending monsoon.

"Captain?" Adi asked, noticing my malaise. "Once we get back, will you resume the investigation?"

I sat up. "Right, sir. Let's take stock. Here's what we know." I put the events into chronological order. "Some days before October twenty-fifth, Lady Bacha met a man in the library. Apte the librarian saw him grab her wrists. That, and the fact that the ladies came to the tower in secret, suggests that they were being blackmailed. But by whom? And for what? We still don't know.

"So what happened on that fateful day, October twenty-fifth? Francis Enty, the law clerk, saw two men arguing with Maneck but refused to identify them as Akbar and Behg. McIntyre said he went back on his testimony."

Adi started in surprise. "He did? Didn't know that."

"Enty's an odd fish—lied to me about his wife's whereabouts, said she was in Poona. That's a loose end I need to run down." I told Adi about the letter I'd taken from Enty's rooms, which revealed that Enty's wife was not in Poona as he claimed.

Shaking his head, Adi asked, "Why would he lie about that?"

"It will do no good to ask him. He's got something against me. Remember how upset McIntyre was? Enty's the chap who told the Governor I was investigating the case." Diana had discovered this while spying from the shadows. I said, "I should follow him, see what he's about."

Adi considered. "Hmm. That black thread and white bead you found on the gallery floor—can you connect them to Bacha and Pilloo?"

"No," I said, sighing, "but I wonder if it has something to do with the black clothes the librarian found in the reading room. He recalled two men sitting in the reading room despite the commotion outside. Peculiar, no? Again, no one's identified them."

"What about the burglar?"

"Yes. Nur Suleiman, nephew to the Rani of Ranjpoot. McIntyre said he matched Akbar's description."

Adi frowned at that. "When I read that in your report, I could hardly believe it. Akbar who was named in Bacha's trial is actually Prince Nur Suleiman of Ranjpoot? Our Toddy business depends upon Ranjpoot! Papa deals with the Rani and her family."

"Yes. Could he have some personal grudge against you? Or your father? He was searching for something."

Adi looked puzzled. "Can't imagine what. If Akbar was blackmailing Bacha and Pilloo, he must have had something on them. But what?"

"Something the ladies feared. Read through Bacha's papers again. Search for a photograph or document. Could be in a book, hidden in a newspaper, or behind a picture frame."

Adi nodded. "Leave it to me."

I went on. "Akbar also has dealings at the dockyards. I followed him there."

"Before you went to Lahore."

"Mm. And Maneck—I'll have another go at him. He knows more than he's saying. He led me to Kasim, and Doctor Aziz had some rather interesting remarks about Kasim."

As I narrated Doctor Aziz's intelligence, it seemed to me an investigator's job was fairly methodical. Keep running down leads until they tie together. I had a few still: Maneck, the state of Ranjpoot . . . and that terrified Havildar. What the devil did he mean by getting into such a state? Next time I'd take Adi as interpreter.

I needed a break in the case soon. It was almost June—three months since I started working for Adi, confidently claiming I'd get to the bottom of this in six months. That burglar, Prince Suleiman, what was he looking for? It must be valuable to warrant such a risk.

The two sides of my investigation met in the princedom of Ranjpoot. I would go there. First, I'd meet Maneck, who'd sent me after Kasim in the first place. It was time he said what he knew.

CHAPTER 44

MANECK'S STORY

Next morning, dressed in a clean white kurta, I walked to Maneck's boardinghouse on Ripley Street. A maid-servant took my card at the door, bid me wait, and returned with Maneck's landlady, who invited me into a small parlor. Although dressed in Western clothing—modest grey dress and cap—she was undoubtedly Indian. No longer young, she had an arresting face, wide forehead and pointed chin, her wrinkles framing a sharp gaze. She gave an impression of self-reliance and endurance, of being weathered by responsibility.

"Do you want lodgings?" she inquired, fingering a clutch of keys at her waist.

"I'd like to call on Maneck Fitter."

A shadow crossed her face, the sort of caution I'd seen in Diana when she was hiding something. Maneck's landlady looked worried—for him?

"He is not here."

"Does he say when he will return from Matheran?"

"Oh," she said, "is that where he is?"

"Madam, I'm Captain Agnihotri," I said. "I met him there some weeks ago."

"Did you?" she said, her color rising. "I'm not supposed to say where he is."

So she knew! I said, "I mean him no harm. He's had a rum time of it."

"Ah." She paused, undecided. "Is there a message?"

If she was in a position to send him a message, then had he returned to Bombay? She seemed about to speak. When her gaze dropped, I felt a moment of sympathy. He was here.

The landlady's anxiety puzzled me. Did Maneck mean more to her than a lodger? It came to me then, why he was afraid, and whom he was trying to protect.

I said, "Maneck knows me. Give him my name, if you would? I'll return tomorrow."

"Captain." Maneck stepped from behind a curtain.

I started, then shook his hand, saying, "You're a dark horse, aren't you."

Neatly dressed, clean-shaved, unsettled and agitated, with the wiry build that most people underestimate, he paced with the caged frustration of one cooped up too long.

Needing to speak to him alone, I asked the landlady for a cup of tea. When her footsteps receded, I gave Maneck a hard look. Catching his arm, I pulled him to a halt.

"What's her name, your lady?" I asked.

Maneck gave a start. He went quite pale, so I propelled him into a seat. "Yes, lad, it's obvious. You don't want to put her at risk. But you can't get anywhere this way, can you?"

He groaned, buried his head in his hands. "Please, just go. Leave me alone."

"You mentioned Kasim, remember? I followed his trail all over India, even went to Lahore. Now I need the whole story."

He winced. "I swear I had nothing to do with Bacha, all right?"

I absorbed that. "Did Miss Pilloo ask for your help? It's time you came clean."

He looked away, saying, "I can't put Alice at risk too."

So I was right. In the next room someone stirred a teacup.

"Shouldn't you alert her, let her know what this is about?"

As the landlady's footsteps approached, Maneck tensed. She set down her tray and saw his drooping face, exclaiming, "Maneck, what's the matter?"

I pressed my advantage. "Miss Pilloo asked you for assistance. What did she say?"

As Alice perched on the chair, Maneck looked distressed, even angry that I'd put it out in the open like that. I'd have to get Alice away from this mess before he'd help me. I said, "Madam, is there somewhere you can go for a few days? Family elsewhere?"

Puzzled, she said, "Me? A few days . . . why yes. A week?"

"Perhaps two would be advisable." I wasn't as confident as I sounded, but she must be safe, else Maneck would never speak.

"For a couple of weeks, I suppose. I'll go to my cousin. My cook knows what to do, and if you take the rents . . . ?" she asked Maneck.

He brightened. "Of course. Would you be safe there?"

Alice chuckled, a low confident sound that reminded me of Diana. "My cousin's married to a Colonel and lives in the middle of Poona Cantonment. If it's not safe there, why, there's nowhere safe at all!"

Maneck's head came up like a plant revived after a drought. She patted his hand unselfconsciously, telling me theirs was a long association. I glanced at them with sympathy. So Maneck too had a forbidden love. Few would support an intercommunal match between a young Parsee man and an older Christian widow.

I urged him, "Maneck, we have a chance to end this! Tell me, what's this about?"

A long minute he stared at me, then said, "His name is Seth Nur Akbar Suleiman. We met last year. He's some nabob down south, near Mysore. He tried to get Bacha to meet with him, but she wouldn't. Then he told me he had Pilloo's letter, that he could destroy the Framjis—utterly devastate them! The way he spoke—it turned my stomach. He's . . . terrifying."

"I've met him," I said. So this was the man I'd fought on Diana's balcony—that fiend had a letter belonging to Miss Pilloo, a mysterious letter that he'd used to blackmail the ladies. Here at last was confirmation of my theory!

"He said he wanted to speak to her. That was all! So I agreed—to take a message to Pilloo. Diana and she were childhood friends of mine. When she went to her dressmakers', I waited outside and told her about it."

Diana had called Maneck a "lamb." I focused on his tale, imagining how Akbar had terrified Pilloo with his summons. "And? How did she react?"

Maneck moistened his lips, clenching the arms of his chair. "Captain, Pilloo burst into tears. Said 'I knew it! It's all my fault!' She was terribly upset."

Excitement thrummed within me. So Kasim had reached Ranjpoot, possessing an unfortunate letter from Pilloo, something she felt guilty about. Somehow, he'd fallen in with Akbar and Behg, and together blackmailed young Miss Pilloo. Was Akbar still searching for that letter at the Framjis, months later?

"What's in the letter?"

Maneck shook his head. "Never saw it."

"All right. You told Miss Pilloo. She was upset. She went to Lady Bacha for help?"

"Yes. I met them outside the library. It was entirely respectable," he assured Alice.

"On the university grounds, by the jambul tree?"

Maneck froze. "By God, Captain. How on earth do you know that?"

"Some children saw you, gave a pretty clear description. Go on."

"Bacha went inside the library. I waited with Pilloo until she returned. Don't know who she met or what he said, but it frightened Bacha."

It was where Bacha had met the man in the ornate green coat. If Green Coat was Akbar or Behg, my case against him was on solid footing. I sighed—I'd need to make that link, and prove it to Superintendent McIntyre.

Bringing Maneck's attention to the fatal day, I recalled the children who'd witnessed his argument with Akbar and Behg before the two girls arrived. "You were there before them, were you not?"

Looking glum, he said, "Akbar sent me to summon a victoria and hold it at the south entrance. I protested, since I'd told Pilloo and Bacha I'd stay with them. How could I know it would go so wrong? It was afternoon, and in the middle of university."

"You set up the exchange," I guessed. "Miss Pilloo's letter for, how much money?"

Maneck gaped. "How . . . ?"

"A deduction. Three children saw Bacha's quarrel with Pilloo after you left. I had deduced the ladies were being blackmailed. How much?"

"Five hundred rupees."

So the housekeeping money, missing from Lady Bacha's writing table, had gone to pay blackmail. "Right. You left to get a carriage. What time was this?"

"Three fifteen or so."

"But not before you had an altercation with Akbar and Behg."

His pale brown eyes were determined. "I refused to go, but Akbar shoved me."

"And tore your jacket. You were on the first-floor balcony."

"Yes." His Adam's apple bobbed as he swallowed.

"The children saw this, too." I read from my notebook: "A ruckus, two men with Maneck at the first-floor parapet. Tore your shirt . . . or coat, not clear which."

"Tore the collar of my coat. There were witnesses?" His voice reached a place deep within me. I knew that sense of utter despair, of overwhelming darkness, where a glimmer of hope felt so elusive in the tapestry of gloom you doubt it's really there.

I held the thread of the mystery tight, following it carefully. "You left to secure a carriage. The women arrived and went up the clock tower. So what went wrong? Why didn't they pay and retrieve the letter?"

"Oh God!" cried Maneck, jumping up. "I wish I knew! There were no cabs to be found! I ran up and down the street. At last I secured a barouche, begged the driver to wait. He argued, so I gave him ten rupees to do so!

"I rushed back. Imagine what I saw! Both girls, dead on the ground! I had assured them I'd be with them. Captain, it was a public place. Right by the reading room. Make the exchange and leave, we had said. Instead, people crowded around their bodies." He tore at his hair in anguish, then dropped into the chair and covered his face.

Wide-eyed, Alice touched his shoulder in sympathy.

My pulse echoed in my eardrums. Maneck's words clearly implicated

Akbar and Behg in the ladies' deaths. But wait! An important fact lay just beyond the horizon. There was more to this than blackmail. Why not take the cash and demand more later? Why did the women die?

Maneck raised his wet face. "I let them down. All I wanted was to help them through this thing. I even offered to make the exchange for them, but Akbar would not hear of it. It must be them, he said. Kasim deserved that."

Kasim! Here at last was the link to Kasim. "What did he mean?"

Maneck shook his head. "He said Kasim was a servant boy who worked for the Framjis. That's all he said, I swear! It's because of Kasim that Akbar hates them."

"The clock tower—who chose it for the exchange?"

Maneck's face creased. "Akbar. I had suggested the reading room. More public, safer."

"Instead he chose the clock tower," I said, "and got you out of the way."

Maneck said, "So it was revenge, wasn't it? He never intended to give them the letter."

I considered that. Something still did not fit. "Perhaps. But why attack me on Princess Street? Why sneak into the house the very next night?"

My words drew a gasp from Alice. Maneck gaped at me.

"This isn't over," I said, regretting my careless words. "I don't think Akbar has the blackmail letter." I looked at the morose lad. How many months had he borne being questioned in jail? He'd stood at the dock, tight-lipped through the hellish trial.

"Maneck, why didn't you tell the police? Why go through the trial, accused of murder?"

"Because of that letter!" he cried. "Akbar said it would destroy the Framjis. I tell you, he could do it. Why else would Bacha agree to everything? To meet him, to give him the money he wanted. She agreed to the date, the time, everything! And I let them down so completely. Came back too late! Akbar had killed them both. Oh God, I could do nothing!"

I sat back, frowning. *What was in that letter?* Whatever it was, the Framji girls had died for it.

CHAPTER 45

HAVILDAR'S SECRET

Remembering the sight of Alice comforting Maneck, their heads bent close together, I returned to Framji Mansion. Did Maneck's uncle disapprove of the match because Alice wasn't Parsee? I hoped they'd find a way through the maze of social expectations.

I joined the Framjis as dinner was being served. Adi shook hands, inviting me to the meal. It was as good a way to report my progress as any, so schooling my manner with Diana to formal politeness, I accepted.

"Gurung!" Burjor signaled for a place setting. I greeted him, Mrs. Framji and Diana, answering Adi's questions as food was heaped on my plate.

"Bao-di!" Chutki gasped, as she came in with rotis, still smoking from the stove. She beamed a smile, then hurried to her duties, her anklets tinkling.

As she placed a roti before me, I asked in Pashto, "Chutki, how are you?"

"I am well, Bao-di," she whispered, smiling.

"Do you need anything?"

She twisted her lips, then said, "Some money?"

Handing her my billfold, I continued my account of Maneck's story. The Framjis listened in rapt attention as I reported why the ladies went to the clock tower.

When I was done, Burjor looked solemn, pondering Maneck's testimony, which confirmed our suspicions: Akbar had blackmailed Lady Bacha and Miss Pilloo. Adi stared at his plate, motionless.

"Took five rupees, Bao-di." Chutki returned my billfold, stooping to touch my feet.

Uncomfortable, since the gesture is usually reserved for elders, I said, "Tsch! Chutki, what are you doing?" Sitting on the floor, she rested her cheek against my knee. No one spoke, so I touched her hair and asked, "Are you content here?"

"Bao-di. This house is heaven."

I smiled at that silliness, then remembered I'd meant to ask about her anklets.

"Who gave you the payals?"

"Diana Memsahib and Maji Memsahib. They are so kind!" So her name for Mrs. Framji was Mother-Lady. When I sent the Framji ladies a grateful look, Diana seemed surprised.

Overcome, Chutki got up and left without a word.

Returning to my task, I said to Adi, "Sir, about the Havildar—the clock tower guard. I'd like to try him again tomorrow. Would you interpret for me?"

He agreed. Arrangements made, I took my leave. The Framjis needed time to absorb what I'd said. After all these months, perhaps it brought back those awful days, the questions. I wished I had more answers for them.

Seeing me to the door, Diana said, "Jim?"

Our quarrel ached under my skin, a wound, scabbed over but painful still. Keeping carefully neutral, I turned. "Miss?"

"Won't you forgive me? I didn't know it would hurt you like that."

Coming up behind her, Adi broke in, "Diana? What's happened?"

While Diana looked away, perplexed, I said, "A misunderstanding. Nothing of import."

Adi frowned, looking from me to Diana's pallor. He said, "No more secrets. What is it?"

"Miss Diana was concerned for Chutki's welfare." I glanced at Diana. "She was safe in my care. Miss, I do not know what she suffered before that."

Diana said, "Seems she's settled in."

As I left, Adi said, "Diana, that's not the whole story, is it? Let's have it."

* * *

The next day, sitting in the Framjis' new Gharry carriage next to Adi, her chin at a resolute angle, Diana repeated, "So it's agreed? You'll stay out of sight until we call you?"

Still reluctant to let them enter the clock tower without me, I nodded.

Trees rustled. A minivet tweeted to his mate, "Sweet, si-sweet!" In the tower vestibule the Havildar napped, mouth slack, on his three-legged stool.

We needed to know what the Havildar had seen, the day Lady Bacha and Miss Pilloo died. Since my presence terrified him the last time I was at the tower, the siblings proposed to interview him without me. The gallery offered a private space. I could listen, unobserved, from inside the tower door.

Adi clenched his hands, looking acutely uncomfortable.

"Will you be all right?" Diana asked, eyeing his strained face.

"Yes, of course. Don't mind me." His lips in a determined cast, he stepped from the carriage, scanned his surroundings, then handed Diana down. As they approached the tower vestibule, the Havildar scrambled upright.

Holding back for five minutes as agreed, I watched as they followed him into the tower's narrow mouth. Three sets of footsteps clinked upon metal stairs, ascending to where the Framji ladies had spent their last moments.

High above, the tower clock marked time slowly, as dispassionate as when the ladies had stood there. What terror did they face? Had they fought for their lives? As I started upward, the very stones seemed to cry out a warning. Damn foolishness, I knew, but I was wound tight with dread. Stepping quietly, it was a long climb to the gallery.

The wooden door was ajar, bright sunlight glittering through the gap. The Framjis were questioning the guard. Pressed against the wall, I strained to hear.

In Hindustani, Diana asked, "You unlocked this door for the Framji girls. You're sure?"

Farther from the door, a faint voice replied, "Yes, Memsahib."

"So was there anyone here before them?"

"No, Memsahib. Cannot be. Door locked."

"Did you pass anyone on the way down?"

I admired her methodical approach. When the fellow did not reply, she repeated her question.

The Havildar protested, "Why ask this now? It was long ago, no? How can I remember?"

Diana prompted him again, but he'd got his wind up, and wouldn't budge.

She said in English, "Adi, he knows something."

"Now, Captain," called Adi, so I stepped into the sunlight.

Seeing me, the Havildar let out a shriek and dropped to his knees, cowering. "No, Sahib! I swear, I said nothing," he blubbered.

Why did he fear me? I'd met him only once before and he had cringed away just so.

"Why are you afraid?" I asked in Hindustani.

The Havildar raised his head and squinted. "Hai! Cap-tan Sahib! It is you."

Interesting. He knew me, but only after I spoke. The blighter was acutely nearsighted!

"How do you know my name?" I asked.

Reassured by my manner, he said, "I saw you last time. People at the library told me your name." He clasped his hands together in contrition.

"Why did you cry out just now?"

"Because he looks like you, Sahib!" he cried, then clapped a hand over his mouth.

"Who?"

He wrung his hands, weeping. "He held me over the wall, Sahib. If I tell anyone, he will come back and drop me. What can a poor person do?"

"Who is he?"

"Sahib, he will kill me."

"He's tall, like me?"

The Havildar nodded.

"Seth Akbar?"

"Hei Bhagvan!" the guard prayed, covering his face. Yes.

"Was he here, when the Framji women died?"

He moaned, "He was here. But I can say nothing, Sahib!"

That made two witnesses now, neither willing to identify Akbar to the police. Maneck feared Akbar had the means to irreparably damage the Framjis. The Havildar was terrified of Akbar. It wasn't enough for me to prove my case with Superintendent McIntyre. Even if he believed me, we'd need material proof. If only I could find Mrs. Enty!

Returning through the gallery door, I noticed the small passage leading upward to the carillon in the bell-room. On a chance, I entered it. Stone walls angled sharply. The octagonal turret was narrower, so my shoulder brushed the wall. It was dark—I wished I'd left the gallery door open for some light!

Sweating, I trudged twenty steps up, then my outstretched fingers touched a sheet of cold metal. I found the latch and tried it, to no avail. God, it was tight here.

The cleverly engineered carillon played each quarter hour. If Akbar had the key, was this where he'd lain awaiting his prey, the women arriving on the gallery? Had he also secreted himself here afterwards, until it was safe to leave?

Leaving Adi and Diana to ride home in the carriage, I went to the constabulary to apprise Superintendent McIntyre of my progress.

Pieces of this devious business were falling into place, but the gaps in my theory did not please McIntyre. Lips tight, he said, "Spit it out, man!"

I asked instead, "Can you get me into Ranjpoot?"

"What the devil for?" he growled, fierce eyebrows peaked.

"I've connected Akbar and Behg with the ladies' deaths, but since neither the Havildar nor Maneck will give evidence against them, I've no proof! Thought I'd poke around Ranjpoot and learn what Akbar's about."

"Just how d'you connect him to the murders?"

After repeating my conversations with Maneck and the Havildar, I placed my paper with the single white bead upon the table. "This one's from the gallery."

McIntyre grunted, shook his head. "We found a dozen of those on the gallery floor. Doesn't mean a thing."

"Apte, the librarian, saw a man arguing with Miss Bacha a few days before her death. Fellow wore a green embroidered jacket."

"Circumstantial. Could be anyone, any jacket."

"But if I found a garment with beads missing, would that help?"

McIntyre's eyebrows shot up. "Plan to search his wardrobe?"

"Something like that. And I think he's abducted Enty's wife. She may be in Ranjpoot."

He reared back. "Enty's wife? Francis Enty, the clerk?"

I nodded. "He told me she was in Poona with her sister. But take a look at this." I pulled out Enty's crumpled note.

McIntyre smoothed out the creases and read. "She's not in Poona," he said, grim. "Enty wrote to the Governor's office. Did you know? Complained about you."

"Seems he's being pressured."

"Hmph," he grunted, taking out his pipe. "So three witnesses, perhaps. Maneck, the Havildar, and Enty, the clerk. All right. I'll get you an invitation."

But I had another problem—I could not go as myself, nor as Rashid Khan the Pathan.

"Could you invite Father Thomas Watson, a missionary, instead?"

Eyebrows knotted, he asked, "Who the devil is that?"

"Doesn't exist. But I'll travel under his name. Safer, don't you think?"

"Ha!" McIntyre barked a laugh, then sobered. "Have a care, lad. Ranjpoot is not a British protectorate, so we have little say there. The British Resident cannot compel anyone, you understand? When we want something, we have to wait until the Rani needs something from us."

I understood. If I were taken prisoner in Ranjpoot, there would be no rescue.

CHAPTER 46

REVISITING POONA

Shortly thereafter, wearing plain-glass spectacles and the missionary's black cassock purchased at the thieves' market, I boarded a train for Ranjpoot. The spectacles gave me a curiously scholarly appearance. With these and a new goatee, I resembled old Father Thomas, who'd raised me at the Mission in Poona. I suppose I'd planned to impersonate him from the moment I'd seen the cassock in Chor bazaar.

As I waited for the locomotive, I scanned Diana's notes from the dance, tracing her neat, strong handwriting, hoping to devise a plan. I would be a guest of the Resident, representative of the British Raj, courtesy of a well-placed telephone call by Superintendent McIntyre. My invitation extended for a week. I knew Akbar and Behg had blackmailed the Framji ladies, and suspected they'd abducted Mrs. Enty. Now I needed proof, but that posed a problem: Akbar was a bloody prince, and I had just seven days to find evidence of his crimes.

My train would stop tonight at Poona. I remembered a white stone church standing over a grassy slope. Did Father Thomas still run the orphanage? If so, he'd be very old. Would he know anything of my mother? She'd left me with a curious name: James clearly indicated my father was English. But my last name was that of a respectable Brahmin family. Why give me her name? Was it so one day I could find her?

The train arrived, the metallic grind of its brakes like knives being sharpened.

Amid the bustle I boarded with my trunk, thrust it under the seat and dropped into a second-class chair, spare and wood-planked, without cushion or embellishment. The train filled, teeming with hawkers selling newspapers and coconuts, mangoes and chikki—peanuts and sesame seeds candied together with jaggery. Awaiting the station master's whistle, I ran a finger under the cleric's collar, tight around my throat. Despite the hot dust blasting through open windows, my billowy cassock was comfortable, but my goatee itched interminably.

Father Thomas's kind blue eyes came to mind. Perhaps he would lend me a Bible. A cleric should have one, I thought, spirits rising at the prospect of seeing him again. But fifteen years had passed. The old priest could be dead.

* * *

I rode a tonga from Poona Station to Coolwar, passing an enormous construction on my right. "What's that?" I asked the tonga-wala. My Hindustani had a clipped accent that sounded like Father Thomas.

"The new Aga Khan Palace, Sahib. Marble comes to Bombay on great ships! Three thousand people work here."

The Aga Khan was leader of the Khoja sect of Mohammedans. Mostly trading families, they controlled vast holdings in both Bombay and Sind provinces. Known for being secretive and insular, they had their own religious courts and laws. According to police records, Saapir Behg was a Khoja, as well as Akbar and the royal family of Ranjpoot.

The old Mission was smaller than I remembered, a low building appended to a small church, now roped with creepers of sweet-smelling clematis. A crooked lapacho tree spilled pink blooms over the path. Dogs loitered in the yard as I paid the tonga-wala and descended. The bell at the gate rang in the distance, bringing memories of following other ragged boys into a schoolroom, sitting cross-legged and listening to stories when we were supposed to be punished.

A soft voice broke into my reminiscences. "Father? We didn't know you were coming."

The nun at the gate was no older than Chutki. Being called "Father" sent a guilty twinge down my spine. Curious. I'd had no qualms about my other guises. I'd have to get accustomed to this and other expectations of a priest, because it was Father Thomas Watson who was expected at the Resident's House in Ranjpoot.

"Please forgive this intrusion," I said. "Is Father Thomas at worship?"

Shaking her head, she opened a door set inside the gate. "He cannot leave his room anymore, Father, but he likes company. Are you an old friend?"

"I am," I said, and gave her my name.

So Father Thomas was alive! The rush of my joy took me by surprise as I stooped through the opening and followed her. She led me through a white-limed corridor, austere except for blocks of yellow sunlight upon the tiled floor. Pausing at a wooden door, the little nun asked, "Father, will you stay the night? I'll ask Mother Superior if a bed can be spared."

When I accepted gratefully, she tapped on the door. "Father Thomas?"

A weak voice replied.

"He's awake," she said, and left.

My old friend lay in a monk's cell, just six feet across, bare, save for a bed, chair and small table. Two clothes pegs studded one whitewashed wall. A crucifix adorned the other.

"Do I know you?" The old priest, propped up against a pillow, raised a feeble hand, beckoning. I recognized his sharp blue eyes, eyes that missed little, even now. Lines at the corners curved down sunken cheeks. His hair, once dark and unruly, had receded over a shiny domed forehead; what was left was cropped close.

"Yes, you do." I took his hand and was pulled close by a surprisingly strong grip.

Peering into my face, his own creased into a hundred crinkles. "James!"

Here was the friend of my childhood, once tall and energetic, now the size of a child.

"Father Thomas." His fingers felt as fragile as a small bird.

"I wondered . . . why it's taking me . . . so long to die," he breathed. "Now I know. Here you are. At last."

My throat locked. "You remember me."

"Sit down, my boy." He chuckled, patted my hands that still held one of his, then looked surprised. "You were ordained? I cannot believe it."

I moved the chair to face him, sat down and met those penetrating eyes. He deserved honesty, nothing less.

"This is temporary, a disguise. I'm on the hunt for a murderer."

He absorbed that without surprise and wheezed, "How like you . . . to disarm one with the truth. And that"—he pointed to my cassock—"will help you find this man?"

"I hope so."

"So why did you come?"

"I want to borrow a Bible. A cleric should have one, no?"

His blue eyes smiled. "That's not why you're here. You could buy one. From any bookstore. But here." He dug under his pillow to hand me a worn book. "Take it . . . read it."

The knot in my throat thickened. "I'll bring it back."

He waved that away. "There's more to being a priest than looking the part. You could have taken orders . . . at seminary, if you stayed. But I knew you had a different path."

He lay back, closing his eyes. I watched his face in repose, its serenity seeping into me.

He asked, "Do you remember the evenings you read to me? Nelson and Virgil, Shakespeare and Dickens."

"Happiest days of my childhood."

He chuckled. "You were punished . . . for fighting."

That too I remembered. Being tripped, jabbed as I went by. I never asked why, just returned the favor. Was I the only mixed-race boy? I did not think so.

"You were taller than most. Worse, you learned quickly. The others were jealous," said the old priest, reading my stillness.

"I didn't know."

"When you . . . left, James, I searched for you. A milkman saw you in the army camp. I came to the barracks."

Father Thomas had come to the cantonment? "You found me there?"

He nodded, moistened his lips to speak. "I did. Saw you in a stable.

Filthy, but you looked intact. Someone called you and you swung up on the horse. So easy, effortless. Tsch-tsch you told the horse and trotted off. It was . . . poetry. So, I left you there."

I grimaced, thinking of my old friend walking across town to seek his runaway, only to return without speaking to me. Now I wished he had. I wished I'd said goodbye, left with his blessing rather than in the darkness before lauds.

"James, I waited for you all these years," he whispered, "to give you something. The box under my bed, open it."

His wooden trunk slid out easily. He directed me to a small bundle inside.

"It was left by your mother, poor girl."

I stared at him and knew: this was why I'd come.

"Open it."

I unwrapped yellowing linen to reveal a gold pocket watch, scratched and worn with use. On the back was inscribed the name I. Agnihotri.

"It was her father's," said the old priest. "He was dead. Your mother was . . . in a delicate way when she came to us . . . and with consumption. She died when you were two."

That's why I remembered only her touch on my face, and the scent of her, jasmine and incense. "What was her name?"

"Shanti," said Father Thomas. Peace. A simple name.

I ran a finger over the inscription. "And my father? Did she ever say his name?" I questioned, my voice brittle.

"My boy, I never asked."

CHAPTER 47

NEW ALLIES

That night Father Thomas took a turn for the worse. In the early morning, an elderly nun woke me with the whisper, "Come. Now, please."

I sat with him for an hour as dawn broke and sparrows chittered outside. His hand felt thin and dry in mine, its veins blue under papery skin. His eyelids fluttered.

"James." His tranquil face creased into a smile. Watery blue eyes opened, telling me he'd neared journey's end, and was glad of it. "Don't . . . let darkness in."

I leaned closer, fearing that this mention of darkness meant his sight was fading. But even now he had something to teach me.

"Bitterness. Let it go. She was a good child."

My mother. I saw her as a teenage girl, racked with coughing, unmarried and pregnant, clutching an old gold watch that she refused to sell. Coming to the Mission to end her days was a wise choice, as it gave her child a home after she died. How lonely, how desperate she must have been, and how glad of the quiet cloisters in her confinement.

Father Thomas had said she was fascinated by all things English. Only when I was born with such fair skin did he understand why. "She was so curious. Loved, above all, to hear of England," Father Thomas had said. "It must have seemed another world."

Learning this lifted a dead weight off me that I did not know I carried. Had I feared I was a product of violence? If so, his words erased that dread. My English father remained faceless in the shadows.

For the first time I considered the facts as a detective. I was born in 1862 or thereabouts, after the Sepoy Mutiny of 1857. I suppose the tale was common enough—an Englishman found comfort with a young woman and got her pregnant. Such loss of caste dishonored her family, so perhaps she'd run away and found sanctuary at the Mission. I pitied that poor girl, my mother, and hoped she'd found peace. The two halves of me, Indian and English, felt united in this place.

In the late morning I carried my valise down the Coolwar road, leaving Father Thomas in his quiet haven. We would not meet again—I mourned, then gave thanks that I'd come in time to see him.

Tucking the Bible in a pocket of my cassock, I set off for Ranjpoot, home of the mysterious Akbar, alias Prince Nur Suleiman. The train to Mysore was late, crowded, noisy with vendors and uncomfortable. At Mysore, the British Resident sent his carriage to bring me to Ranjpoot. As I arrived at his household, which stood adjacent to the palace, I remembered McIntyre's warning. In princely states, the British government had little authority. Its presence was maintained by a Resident or Agent, who functioned as a liaison between the state and the different entities of British administration. As a guest of the Resident, I had a nominal status in the principality, but it offered no protection if I ran afoul of the rulers.

A mustached bearer greeted me with the news that the Resident and his wife would meet me at dinner. Since it was midafternoon, I had little to do other than dress the part. Father Thomas had furnished me with a hat and another cassock, assuring me that one could not wear the same garment day after day. He'd been shorter than I, so I tugged at the hem, and found I had accurately assessed the cleric's parsimony—it unrolled to reveal more folds, adding four inches to the garment. I had no stockings, so black shoes tidied with a wet rag would have to do.

The shortest way to the palace was a path by the river. Designed with the flair of a medieval fortress, crenellations topped its curved stone walls. High above, a blue-turbaned guard scowled down at me. I doffed my squat cleric's hat to him, and continued. The palace had three levels, each bordered by a terrace. Thick vines tangled over the marble balustrade. A cluster of pink flowers brushed my feet. Lapacho blooms, like those at the Mission. They reminded me of the petals strewn over white stairs at Framji Mansion. Peach, like the dress Diana had worn at her dance. Scooping up a flower, I pressed it into Father Thomas's book.

Turning toward the town center, I saw a group of boys in an open maidaan field, kicking what appeared to be a small pumpkin. Football?

As I watched, the ball came straight at me. I grinned. Had I not done just the same years ago, sent my ball careening toward Father Thomas? Just as he had, I stopped the ball and sent it back to the lads with a well-placed kick. They cried out in appreciation, chased it and sent it back. Apparently, I was standing near their goal.

The day was fine—cloudy and mild, with a cool breeze from the river. What the heck. I put down my hat and glasses, kicked off my shoes and joined the game. Raising the cassock so as not to trip, I raced down the maidaan. When I lost the ball to a young chap who goaled, I thumped him on the back in congratulations.

"Paji!" he chortled, in Hindustani. "You can run!"

It brought me back to the present and my aching knee, so I ruffled the lad's hair and shook hands with the beaming boys.

A young man may do many things without attracting notice. Playing ball while dressed in a priest's robe is not one of them. As I retrieved my hat and spectacles, a pair of carriages caught my eye. Two horse-drawn barouches stood on the road, drapes parted. As I watched, a sais clicked to the mares and set them trotting toward the palace.

* * *

"Was that you playing football, Father?" said Mrs. Gary, the Resident's matronly wife, at dinner that evening.

Choking on the sherry to be seen running about barefoot, I chuckled. "Rather."

While eager to investigate Ranjpoot, I needed to establish myself with the Resident and his wife first. Although reserved, their welcome was polite and undemanding—I'd let down my guard during the lavish meal, served upon magnificent china.

"The Rani noticed you. Did you know?" said Sir Peter Gary, the Resident. An aged, thickset officer, he'd held several diplomatic posts over the last decade. "You're invited to the Durbar tomorrow."

"Indeed!" So I'd get inside the palace. Exploring it was another matter.

"Quite," said Sir Peter, smiling. "I can't call you Father, you know. I'm old enough to be your grandfather."

"At the seminary, we were called Brother," I offered.

"Brother Thomas," said Mrs. Gary, "Mr. McIntyre said you'd been in Lahore recently. What was it like?"

I obliged with a description of my visit to the bazaar, and the chaos when I'd blundered into the frontline. That topic carried us through dessert. Mrs. Gary, a skilled conversationalist, soon had me describing my travels with Razak. I skipped over how I met him as well as General Greer's part in that adventure. Sir Peter, however, noticed the omission.

"The mountain village? Where was that?"

"Near Pathankot." I went on to describe Razak's parents and their joy in recovering the boy, seeing Mrs. Gary's delight in the tale.

After the clock chimed ten, Mrs. Gary rose with a sigh. "Well, gentlemen, I'll leave you to smoke, shall I?" As I rose to my feet, she said, "Such nice manners. Your mother would be proud," and swept out.

"Hmm," said Sir Peter. "You'll have met William Greer of the Simla garrison. He's General Greer now?"

"I've met him."

"Will he remember you?"

Sir Peter might just call Greer on the telephone I'd seen in his study, but Greer would recall no cleric called Thomas Watson. "Possibly. It was a small matter. I recovered something he'd misplaced in Pathankot." I hoped that was enough for Greer to pick up on.

"I see. Mrs. Gary enjoyed your conversation a great deal. We don't have many English visitors here." Sir Peter smiled, eyes crinkling. "You did rather well tonight. Not bad at all. Avoid discussing the royal succession and you'll do all right tomorrow." He met my surprised look. "McIntyre said you were a fake, of course."

Bollocks, I thought. "Did he, now."

Sir Peter sat up. "Aha! There's the real man. So, Watson—that your real name?"

I shook my head but offered no alternative.

He smiled again. "He said you'd been to Pathankot. The great game, eh? To be young again. You're ex-military of course. What was your rank?"

"Captain."

"Should have stayed in service. Chap like you could make Colonel!"

"With an Indian last name?"

Was the old soldier shocked? Would he draw back, lips tight, affronted to know I was Indian? Surprised, he said, "You're . . . er . . ."

"Eurasian," I said.

His face fell, so I made a joke of it. "Half-caste, as they say, touch o' the tar-brush. Coolie. Yellow. Or just chee-chee—dirt." I grinned to show I took no offense.

"Ah. Pity, that." His lips puffed out. "Well, Captain, what're you really after, in this dull little backwater?"

Sir Peter's eyes glowed as he leaned toward me, an old soldier ready to embark on a new adventure. An unexpected ally, and one I might sorely need. Here was the sort of upstanding officer I had grown to admire in the army. Since McIntyre felt he deserved the truth about my subterfuge, I told him about Akbar, and together we formulated a plan. It was well after midnight that we said good night.

I suspected Akbar of kidnapping Mrs. Enty—if she was held in Ranjpoot, how could I find her? Doctor Aziz had brought Kasim to Ranjpoot, but where was Kasim now? And what were the contents of that mysterious letter that Akbar had used to blackmail the Framji ladies?

CHAPTER 48

MAGIC

As I followed Sir Peter and Mrs. Gary into the palace's Durbar Hall the next evening, Akbar was easy to spot. Tall and well built, turbaned and plumed, he stood beside the throne.

Gilt work of striking artistry covered the Durbar's high ceilings and walls. Freshly painted, perhaps? At its center, the Rani perched on a high throne, which glowed on jeweled feet, lit by the slanting rays from a single casement high above. Viziers and members of her household gathered at its base.

I waited behind the Resident and his wife, as a heavily turbaned retainer announced us in sonorous tones, "Sir Peter Gary and Mrs. Gary, and Father Thomas Watson."

We approached, and made our bows: a short nod from Sir Peter and curtsey from his wife. I gave a traditional greeting, hands joined. Other dignitaries followed, wearing ornate finery and outlandish uniforms. More than one bore a sabre at his waist. This went on for half an hour.

The Rani rose, made a short speech of welcome, after which, to my surprise, she shuffled down her stairs and departed.

"Is that all?" I asked Sir Peter.

"No, we'll wait." He sighed. "There's a dinner, but first we mingle."

Sir Peter conferred with a Vizier while Mrs. Gary spotted a pair of Englishwomen. With their help, I acquainted myself with the personages in the hall. Mrs. Gary told me the aging Pat-Rani was eager to name her heir, but the only son her husband had sired was a seven-year-old, born after the Raja's death.

"Big question is," said Mrs. Gary, "who will be Regent, after the Rani?"

"Who are the contenders?"

She pointed them out, the Raja's brothers, standing beside Akbar, and Akbar himself. "Prince Akbar Suleiman's father is the one with the great beard. He's the queen's brother," she said, "but Akbar controls the treasury."

At last the herald called out something long and convoluted, and the audience dispersed. As the contingent to be honored with dinner, we waited.

* * *

Dinner was set up on a wide balcony. Along with the Rani and the royal contenders for the throne, three English couples and a pair of engineers, hired to examine waterways, made up the company.

Head of the table, the Rani was flanked by her kin, attendants standing behind them. Immediately after the soup course, she dropped into a doze. Mrs. Gary shrugged. "Queen Victoria nods off as well, you see. So it's all right." She permitted herself a small smile.

"Father Watson, do you only speak with women?" asked Akbar from across the table. Strikingly handsome, with a dark mustache and flashing eyes, he was about my age. His strong voice had a marked English accent. Was he suspicious of me or simply baiting a young cleric?

Peering through my plain lenses, I smiled. "Indeed no, sir. We of the cloth are happy to speak with all who wish to converse."

"We need no missionaries. We've plenty of priests, Brahmins of the highest caste. And we don't need the Bloody English either."

His comment sent a ripple of discomfiture over our dinner companions. Sir Peter's lips tightened at the slight, but he did not look surprised. So the prince's appalling manners were nothing new.

"We have our Princes, Rajas, Ranis and Ranas, much as you English have your Dukes and Earls. A united Indian monarchy would solve many problems!"

He was referring to the 1857 Sepoy Mutiny—if it had succeeded, Indian nobles would have wrested India from the British. Instead, the co-conspirators were killed, the old Moghul emperor exiled, his sons and grandsons executed. A united Indian monarchy? It was an impossible dream. Princes were barred from making treaties with each other. But Akbar's was no idle remark. To act on it was sedition! Traitors had been jailed, exiled, even executed for less, their families discredited for generations. Designed to shock, his bald statement silenced my dinner companions. A bland observation was called for.

"We each have our role," I said placidly.

"Is that so? What is it you do, Priest?" he snapped.

Seeing this as a good time to implement the plan Sir Peter and I had concocted, I smiled genially around the table. "A cleric's job is to listen, to counsel, and sometimes, to entertain."

This garnered some interest, for the others were eager for a distraction. To begin, I placed Father Thomas's old Bible on the table, pushing it to the center.

Plucking a grape from a bowl of fruit, I held it aloft. "For example," I said, "I can make this grape disappear." When I popped it into my mouth, the company grinned.

I picked up an orange. "A larger object, you agree?" I waved it about, tossed it over my shoulder onto the lawn, making a flourish with the other hand. "And it disappears too."

The ladies chuckled.

"Rather more difficult to bring it back, but I will try," I said. To the man on Sir Peter's right, "Good sir, would you examine the floor by your shoe? Yes? There it is."

He held up an orange, much to the amusement of my dinner companions. Someone clapped. Akbar sneered, singularly unimpressed.

"What, no parable, no lesson?" asked one of the ladies with an indulgent smile.

"I'm rather new at this, Madam," I admitted. "One more? Here I have a rather insignificant object."

I unfolded a piece of paper containing the tiny bead I had found on the floor of the clock tower gallery. This I handed to Mrs. Gary, who examined and handed it to the lady on her right.

"It will appear in a man's pocket. May we have a tray, please?" I asked a bearer, who hurried forward with a silver platter. "Please examine the contents of the pockets of someone wearing . . ." I pinched the bridge of my nose for effect, and said, "green."

"Oh good," said an engineer in black tails. "That's just those two."

The Rani's brother and a young sallow-faced attendant both wore green jackets. The tiny size of the bead had convinced me that it might have lain, all this time, in Behg's or Akbar's pocket. Maneck had mentioned Akbar's fancy clothing on the day the Framji ladies died, but I could not know if he'd wear it today. I was simply shaking trees to see what fell out.

I rose and inquired of the nobleman, "Sir, would you permit the bearer to have a look?"

He agreed in good humor and emptied his pockets onto the silver tray. No bead emerged.

"No?" I said, disheartened, "would you check the lining?"

Unsuccessful, I turned to the young attendant and made my request. But he screwed up his face and refused.

"Come on, Kasim," said Akbar, impatiently, "let him check."

Kasim!

I could scarcely believe it! Akbar had called his attendant Kasim. The Framjis' servant boy Kasim was Akbar's man! So here was the boy who had a hold over Pilloo, who came to Ranjpoot with Doctor Aziz.

He complied sullenly, placing a hand on the table as he disgorged his belongings. On his wrist a cobra was tattooed, head rearing to strike. A Naag, a cobra tattoo! Where had I heard of this? I recalled McIntyre's report, buried in Adi's notes. Akbar's henchman, Saapir Behg, had a snake tattoo on his right hand. For the second time in minutes I felt the thrill of discovery. Perhaps this second revelation should not have surprised me. Kasim was Saapir Behg, Akbar's accomplice. Kasim had not simply met Akbar and Behg, he *was* Behg.

The bearer still stooped, holding the silver tray. Feigning nonchalance,

I asked the servant to examine Kasim's pockets again. Nothing remotely similar to the bead was found. But my magic trick had, in fact, flushed out my quarry. Behg, who carried a Naag tattoo, was the servant boy Kasim.

I felt astonished at the rapidity of these revelations. Since it would not do to draw attention to my discovery, I would close the show as planned. A glance around the table proved that what seemed a long moment to me was no more than an acceptable pause.

"I'm not very good, I'm afraid," I said. "Sometimes the stuff doesn't show up. Mrs. Gary, is that a flower in your brooch?"

"Why yes." She handed the pink bloom over. Sir Peter had followed instructions perfectly.

"And goodbye." I tossed the flower over my shoulder. "Never fear, Madam, it will return. Mrs. Canberry, would you open my book to John, verse ten?" I pointed to my old friend's Bible, into which I'd pressed a bloom. It was found. I handed it to Mrs. Gary to a round of applause.

"Magic—how is it done?" demanded Akbar. "It's a trick, of course."

"Ah, yes," I agreed. "The trick is to seem to break the laws of nature. The laws of man are frail, perhaps, but not those greater laws."

"Rubbish," said Akbar, "I am the law."

The guests paused, glancing at each other. As I searched for a bon mot to lighten the mood, the Rani stirred and picked up the paper containing my bead. The wily old bird. She'd not been asleep at all!

"What is this thing?" she asked, putting on spectacles that were suspended around her neck. "A tiny pearl." She handed it back. "Nephew, we all obey a greater law. We disobey at our peril. So says His Excellency, the Aga Khan Sahib."

From behind my cleric's glasses, I watched Behg, alias Kasim, who knew Miss Pilloo as a child and had lured her to her death.

* * *

I'd bribed servants, waylaid tradesmen near the palace, but found no trace of Mrs. Enty. Remembering an old Urdu saying—"Don't spit in the plate you eat from"—I thought perhaps Akbar kept his nefarious dealings outside Ranjpoot. However, he might keep Lady Bacha's eyeglasses as a trophy.

Three nights later, wearing a black hood over my cassock, I climbed the trellis and crept into the palace. Guards overhead called to each other, spitting tobacco from their high perches. A light breeze covered the rustle of hay I had bound into a sack. I was going to start a fire.

Not that I intended to harm anyone. No, I planned to give the alarm myself. I needed access to Akbar's rooms, and a clear path. What better distraction than something afire? From the shelter of thick vines, I found what I needed—the servants' entryway. For a few annas, a bearer had described the palace layout and Prince Akbar's magnificent chambers.

I'd learned that Prince Akbar had a card game tonight so I waited in a dark alcove overlooking the hall. At last, he and Kasim hurried past toward the Durbar, still talking. Excellent! Moving swiftly down the corridor, I set about my plan.

"Aag! Aag!" I hollered in the local idiom. "Fire!" My shout was taken up. Servants scampered down the stairs, footsteps pounded over the galleries. The palace emptied, as bearers and guards were mustered to haul water from a well in the courtyard. That was all right, because I was already in the men's wing, running through Akbar's things.

By candlelight I searched his desk and wardrobe, a roomful of fancy garments, pearl-encrusted coats and jackets, bejeweled swords and turbans. Although I examined the beading and rummaged through his pockets, I found no wire-frame spectacles, nor tiny beads.

Leaving empty-handed, I spotted branches of blooms, bougainvillea blooms in a giant vase. Reminded of the Framji ladies, outrage rose, thick as bile—he had everything, this popinjay! A life of leisure, a fine education, more wealth than most saw in a hundred lifetimes! Why intimidate delicate Lady Bacha? What manner of man enjoyed terrifying little Miss Pilloo?

Yanking the boughs from the vase, I tossed them on the floor. Let him know I was here, and could return whenever I liked. Petty, perhaps, but

I wanted to shake him, to put the fear of an unseen hand into his mind. This seemed just, because he had dared invade the Framji home.

That's when my plan went wrong.

As I snuffed out my candle and slipped through the corridor, I spotted a woman in a white burkha. She cried out, quaking, standing between me and freedom, the vine-covered balustrade. I'd lit the fire on the other side of the building, so she was alone. White chador curved over her, the small stooped figure clutched a hand to her throat—the Rani!

"I can hear you breathing. Who are you?" asked the familiar, regal tone, peering into the dark. That was brave. Alone at night, a dark shape looming, most would have hollered for help.

Approximating her idiom, I said, "I am not of your household."

Standing in the moonlight, she jerked. "What a strange voice! Who sent you?"

"No one you know. I will not harm you," I said, trying to calm her. I could not be caught here. If she screamed I would have to run for it. But why was she alone in the men's quarter? She gazed around—in fear?—or guilt? Perhaps I could use that. "I know you, Rani Sahiba."

"What are you? Djinn? Demon?" she quavered, her breathing ragged.

Face hidden in my hood, I stepped closer.

"I do not come for you," I said. "But you know why I come."

Suddenly fierce, she whispered, "You come for the wicked, for the evil in my house. Who is it? Who brings this curse upon us?"

Her start of horror upon seeing me was more than surprise. She'd met someone in secret tonight. Superstitious and fearful, was she also party to Akbar's plan? Did she know where Mrs. Enty was? I had to find out. "Those who took the woman from Bombay."

Her mouth dropped open. "Bombay? What woman?"

The Rani was not part of this. Lit by moonlight, wisteria roped the balustrade beside her. Dashing past her, I leapt over the parapet, catching a vine to swing from the creeper into tall ornamental grass. There I waited, trying to breathe softly.

Long moments later she stepped to the parapet, peering out at the darkness, a shriveled old woman with Chutki's grit. She folded her hands, invoking divine protection, then shuffled toward the well-lit courtyard. I wasted no time hotfooting it back to the Resident's home.

* * *

I had found neither Mrs. Enty, the beads, nor Lady Bacha's spectacles, so we tapped Sir Peter's network for some sign of Mrs. Enty, but came up empty. Unable to enter the zenana, I bribed a female servant and palace guards, but none knew of a woman being kept prisoner.

The next day Sir Peter revealed a useful titbit. His palace informant had heard that Kasim, alias Behg, would return to Bombay. I resolved to take the same train—that serpent would bear close watching.

"Take care of yourself, young man," said Sir Peter.

Giving me her hand in farewell, Mrs. Gary said, "You must come back to us."

As the rickshaw trundled me away, I watched the old soldier and his charming wife, standing side by side, hands raised in farewell. Could I be so fortunate in my declining years?

CHAPTER 49

FOLLOWING KASIM

Six days later, dressed as a lowly peanut seller, I followed Kasim down a by-lane toward Dockyard Road. Each morning he stopped at Enty's home, said a brief word, then spent all day on a private vessel moored at Sassoon Dock. Each evening he returned to his bolt-hole on Dockyard Road. Two questions drove me: Where was Mrs. Enty? And what was Akbar exporting by ship?

Maneck had proved amenable to my plan, even eager to aid me, now that his landlady was safe with relatives. I planned to have him watch the house on Dockyard Road.

Face muffled in a checkered cloth, Kasim crossed a narrow bridge, glancing over his shoulder. I plodded along, unconcerned. In me, he would see just a shabby chana-wala, a turbaned vendor of peanuts, carrying a ubiquitous wicker basket. I was nondescript, except for the one feature it was impossible to disguise, my height.

A crossroads is an ideal spot for a peanut vendor, and waiting for customers, ample ruse to observe a street. Narrow homes lined both sides. Dust rose in a cloud of heat and grit. The smell of dried leaves and spices assailed me. Setting down the basket, I crouched by a wall to watch.

Kasim walked halfway down the street and paused, glancing to either side. I fiddled in the basket, paying him no heed. Soon he'd climb the stairs to a brown door. Which one was it? Too far away to see the number, I tried to count doorways.

Footsteps sounded on the bridge. I knew this pattern, familiar from the Framjis' balcony—their houseboy Ramu. As he came even with me, I locked a hand around his ankle. Like a blanket slipped from a horse, he dropped into my arms, his frightened little face crumpled.

"What are you doing, Ramu?" I asked, seating him beside me.

Eyes bulging, he squeaked, "Captain Sahib. I followed you."

"Buy some peanuts," I said, making a cone out of newspaper and scooping peanuts with a practiced motion. His round eyes showed white as he questioned my sanity, rummaging his pockets for a coin.

I passed him his purchase, saying, with a jerk of my chin, "See the man climbing those stairs?" Kasim had knocked, and now awaited a response. In a moment he would disappear.

"Yes, Sahib."

"Run up and see the number on the door, then come back. Do this now."

Ramu returned shortly and sat on the wall beside me, nibbling peanuts.

"He went to number twenty-one."

"Thank you. Why are you here?"

He squirmed. "Memsahib asked me to follow you. I waited at the bakery, and chana-wala comes out. Hai, where is Captain Sahib? Then I saw that the chana-wala is tall. He is you!"

"All right," I said, rising to my feet. "Mrs. Framji was worried about me?"

"No, Captain Sahib." He wiped his nose with the back of his hand. "Diana Memsahib."

Diana had sent a houseboy to follow me? Good heavens. Our last argument no longer rankled, when Diana had all but accused me of forcing myself upon Chutki. But until I solved this mystery I had few prospects, and would not court her against Burjor's wishes. Staying away from Framji Mansion had little effect—it only strengthened my affection for Diana, her humor, her sharp, inquisitive mind, her impish smile. It was time to see her, and Chutki.

* * *

Sometime later, cleaned up, my gift in hand, I strode toward the kitchen.

"Bao-di!" Chutki stopped rolling out bread to swipe her hand across her forehead, smearing it with flour.

I grinned at the curious picture she made, braid dangling down her back, her saree tucked around and secured at the waist. Others in the kitchen stopped to gape. I nodded to them, saying to the cook, "Namaste, Jiji-bai," and tugged Chutki toward the garden.

Three stairs at the back entrance descended into lush greenery. Sitting, I handed Chutki my gift. A peahen gurgled and fluttered away. Curry leaves and peppermint beside a wide pot of aromatic tulsi scented the air.

Wide-eyed, Chutki unwrapped the parcel, winding the string about her hand. Peeling back the paper, she gaped at a blue-green saree I'd bought her.

"Bao-di! It's too soon to give me this. Rakhsha-bandhan is weeks away!" Chutki said in Pashto, her voice soft. Her lips curved. "But I have made something for you."

She untucked the corner of her saree to pry open a knot of fabric. From this she lifted a thick red string, plaited with yellow thread and tassels.

Seeing my surprise, she explained. "It's a Rakhee. Girls give them to their brothers, did you not know? Give me your hand."

As she bound the colored string around my wrist, I admitted, "I never had one before."

Of course I'd seen these ornaments—my friends in the regiment often wore such gifts, taking leave for the festival of Rakhsha-bandhan, the symbolic tying of a Rakhee. Accepting one was a promise to protect a sister. When I'd bought her, Chutki had asked, "Are you my husband now?" I'd said, "I will be your brother." Taking me at my word, she now, with this thread, claimed me as her sibling.

Mindful of Diana's scold when I'd left for Pathankot without a farewell, I said, "Chutki, I will be away some days now. You must not worry."

She drew back, her eyes full of questions.

"It's all right." I assured her, "You are safe, Chutki. I will protect you."

She gazed back steadily. "I will also protect you."

I smiled at that curious idea, then, because she was entirely serious, I nodded.

When we returned to the kitchen Chutki hugged her gift to her chest, beaming her gratitude. I brushed the dusting of flour from her forehead. Siblings could do that, I thought, remembering how Adi had stroked Diana's hair one evening long ago.

"Thank you for the Rakhee," I said, and went to find Adi and Diana. They would not be happy with my plan, but I needed to flush out Akbar and Kasim. There might be scant trail of their past crimes. To catch them in the act, I'd have to force their hand.

* * *

"But why can't you tell us where you'll be?" asked Adi, as we conferred in his chamber.

I chided, "Sherlock Holmes did not share his intentions, did he?"

Adi picked up a book from the coffee table and waved it at me. "*The Sign of the Four*. You've got me reading it now. Did you know Holmes was a boxer?"

"Yes, he's called a gifted amateur."

He grinned. "If you're Holmes, does that make me Watson?"

I chuckled, remembering Diana's insistence weeks, no, months ago now that she would fulfill that role. As though conjured by my thoughts, she swept in wearing a blue saree. Sensible, considering the oppressive heat. I got to my feet, the touch of her smile stroking my skin.

Eyes warm, Diana said, "Holmes, again? He's not a ladies' man, I'm afraid. Rather cold and unfeeling, I thought."

Surprised to hear my hero belittled, I said, "Surely not? Seems a good chap."

Diana waved that off and continued in an animated tone. "Captain, I've been thinking about your visit to Ranjpoot, and the Rani. You said she wore her glasses on a chain? Well, look!" She pointed to Lady Bacha's portrait, where her spectacles were painted at the corner. Attached to them, a thin chain trailed off the table in small white beads, translucent, like the one I had found on the gallery. Lady Bacha's chain had broken there, spilling beads that rolled into tiny crevices.

"Ah," I sighed. But knowing what the bead was did not help, since I could not tie it to Akbar. I had not found the mysterious missing letter, or Mrs. Enty. Enty had lied about his wife being in Poona. Confronted, he would deny it. Why had he lied? I'd need to find out, while Maneck was watching the house on Dockyard Road.

Mulling it over, I said, "I'll be gone a few days."

Adi asked, "How will I get a message to you?"

"Your father has a warehouse on Sassoon Dock. Put a cloth over the door if you want me. A white cloth if it's urgent."

CHAPTER 50

MY GOD, MAN!

Hot on the trail of Akbar and his henchman Kasim, I did not return to Framji Mansion for a while. On the twelfth evening, I saw Adi's signal—a white cloth at Burjor's warehouse. So I left my post near Akbar's ship and hurried toward my room behind the Forgett Street bakery.

I'd learned a great deal about our foes, where they came from and went, and what they were about, but I still didn't know what happened to the Framji ladies. Nor had I found Mrs. Enty. Was she dead, too, her body tossed from Akbar's ship into soundless depths?

From the gloomy patchwork under a jacaranda tree I examined the narrow lane behind me. Was I being followed? A dog howled. Evening fires and cooking scented the warm air. Although the bustle of day was past, night brought little respite from the heat, which rose from the dusty road in sweltering waves. Sweat trickled down my temple as I listened for a footfall. Hearing none, I went on.

A shadow moved behind the bakery. There—by my shutter, beside the barred window, someone waited. A low stone wall concealed my approach as I crept up. It was a moment's work to launch myself at the intruder.

Did he have a knife? My forearm cracked across his—I followed it with my weight.

The intruder gasped as his body slammed into brick. He twisted, grasping at my arm frantically. As I hauled him into the dim light, I caught the shine of eyeglasses askew.

Adi stared at me, shaking. Bloody hell.

"Adi," I hissed. "What the devil are you doing here?"

Shocked at my assault, he struggled to breathe, staring at my matted hair, my face masked in a checkered rag. While he recovered, I unlocked the door and yanked him inside. Leaving him to collect himself, I brightened the place with a kerosene lamp. My blow to his arm would ripen into a nice bruise tomorrow. Why had he not waited at the house?

"What's so urgent, sir?" I asked.

"My God, man," he whispered, "what happened to you?"

Dampening a piece of cloth, I rubbed my teeth to remove the soot I applied there each morning. Good teeth are a dead giveaway, and neat fingernails.

"Charcoal soot," I said. "Rags off a mendicant, manure, rotting fish, local whiskey . . . and dog vomit. A nice touch, no?"

"Inspired," said Adi, as I washed my hands in a bucket. "You look truly hideous."

I grinned at his tone, unwound the rag around my neck to pick up a dish of vada-pav, potatoes and bread, left by the baker on my instructions. Ravenous, I dropped to the floor for a much-needed repast. Adi stalked about, casting dubious looks in my direction.

"When did you last eat?"

"Yesterday," I mumbled, mouth full.

He shook his head—in pity, or was it despair? "Going too far again, Captain?"

That required no reply. A drink of water from the earthen pot went down cool and fresh. I refilled and drank again.

He said, "You were gone two weeks."

"Twelve days. I saw the signal."

His shoulders bore a distinctly unhappy stamp. "Captain, the women are worried. Those Princess Street thugs beat you unconscious, you recall? Could have hauled you off in a victoria, and we'd be none the wiser. Then Lahore. Not a word, for sixteen days. Yes, I know, downed telegraph poles. Now you disappear for weeks," said Adi, his voice sharp. "Are you well?"

I finished my food. "I'm all right, sir. Need some information though."

"Yes?"

That was my friend Adi, prompt to offer his aid.

"SS *Vahid Cruiser*—a small steamship. It's been at Sassoon Dock a long time. That's expensive, to hold a berth that long. It's loading constantly, boxes and crates in dribs and drabs. Guarded night and day by a sentry from Ranjpoot. Why? What's so valuable? What's the cargo?"

"Why are you watching a ship?" he asked. Like Diana, he could not abide my stench of dockyard grime and hung back, revolted.

Stripping off my foul-smelling vest and kurta, I stepped into the tiled sink behind an earthen ledge where the baker had left six buckets of water and soap to slough off my disguise. Scrubbing vigorously, I delivered my report.

"I learned in Ranjpoot that Saapir Behg is really Kasim. He works for Akbar, bringing wagons to Bombay. And he visits Enty every morning with a newspaper. Curious, hm?"

Adi listened intently as I continued.

"I found no sign of Mrs. Enty in Ranjpoot. However, I had a hunch Kasim might lead me to her. So, dressed as a dockworker, I followed him to this ship—*Vahid Cruiser*. He visits it often, sometimes twice a day. And there I've stayed, observing it for days."

"Captain, twelve days!" Adi protested.

"Ah, to hang about that long is no easy matter. One needs a strong-smelling reason to hold a spot like that, without answering questions from dockworkers, officials and the like."

"So you were . . . dead drunk?" cried Adi, disgusted.

I grinned at his expression. "Oh, one can't lie there, passed out, without attracting a Havildar. No. Begging—a drunk dockworker begging for alms."

"Did this dockworker have a name?" Adi asked, shaking his head at my antics.

"Jeet Chaudhary. Before I went to Lahore I tried him out. Trouble was, a dockmaster wanted to hire me . . . loading and unloading ships. That didn't suit, so I had Jeet pick a few quarrels. No one wants a troublesome fellow, hm?"

"No? You surprise me!" said Adi, innocent as a lamb.

I laughed, and emptied a bucket over myself to dispel the smell of fish and manure. Resoaping for good measure, I paid particular attention to my fingers—Mrs. Framji was fastidious about clean hands. My skin glowed pale when stripped of soot and sludge.

Tying a towel about myself, I took the lamp to the mirror and trimmed Jeet Chaudhary's beard. Perhaps I would not need to impersonate my old friend again.

Adi asked, "What's this have to do with Bacha?"

"Holmes says: 'When you have eliminated the impossible, whatever remains, however improbable, must be the truth.' So the missing spectacles? The broken eyeglass chain? These tell us it was not suicide. Two motives occurred to me: revenge or profit. If the motive was a thirst for revenge, well, there are easier ways to kill a young lady—using poison, a riding accident?"

Adi nodded as I went on. "Not revenge, then. Profit? Who stands to gain? Your father pointed out that Lady Bacha's inheritance was already yours by marriage. Her death cannot alter that. Next, I considered Miss Pilloo. Was she the intended target? Again I hit a wall. Her death causes a loss to your family and her husband, but appears to benefit no one. So who gains? That mode of inquiry—who stands to gain—leads nowhere. It's the wrong question, because of these extraordinary circumstances. So I ask, who stands to gain if Lady Bacha does not, er, fall to her death . . . but remains on the tower gallery."

Adi rubbed his forehead. "Captain, I don't understand."

Donning fresh trousers, shirt and vest, I said, "When I found Chutki, sir, she was bound. Her hands were tied before her, and she was hidden under a black garment, a burkha."

"Chutki? The girl you brought from Lahore?"

"As I walked along the rail track, Chutki was, ah, offered for sale."

Adi looked stricken. "That child!" he stammered. "That's why you brought her with you."

"I bought her, sir. No choice, really. Couldn't leave her there."

His eyes gleamed behind his round lenses. "My God."

"The sight of her, hands lashed together, huddled under the burkha, it . . . haunted me. Now I know why. After the ladies died, the librarian found black clothing under a table. Could that be the source of those black threads caught in the tower door? The ladies were, well, prey, much as Chutki was."

"But in broad daylight, Captain? In the middle of the university!" Adi choked.

Lacing up my army boots, I said, "Ah, these cads will stop at nothing to gain their ends. They told the ladies something to prevent them calling out. Perhaps they threatened to expose Miss Pilloo's incriminating letter. Now Akbar's ship, *Vahid Cruiser*, lists its manifest as a cargo of cattle. I followed its seamen to an alehouse each night. Sailors talk, you know, quite loud under the influence. They're bound for British Guyana. But I've seen no cattle loaded."

Adi hunched on the upturned crate, his face waxen.

"Adi, the cattle are women. The seamen mentioned men too, to be sold as slaves. I've alerted the Constabulary. Maneck has been grand these past weeks, watching Kasim's house, running messages to and from McIntyre. The question is, when does *Vahid Cruiser* sail?"

In the army I'd learned to plan a military action. In Pathankot I'd had to lean upon my friends, Ranbir and Razak's clan. Now I depended on McIntyre, who was determined to arrest the slavers. Astonished at all I'd uncovered, he'd agreed to follow my lead.

Adi said, "Let's get back to the house. Uncle Byram can find out anything we need."

Extracting the revolver from my discarded rags, I stowed it, fully loaded, in my breast pocket. "Now Chief McIntyre is not quite ready. He needs a Magistrate's warrant to search the ship. I sent him a note yesterday and have been awaiting a reply. He'll send a constable, since Maneck's watching the house on Dockyard Road."

Adi grunted. "So Maneck's working for you now!"

A rap sounded, repeated, urgent on the wood, a hollow, ominous note. Adi and I jerked at the unexpected interruption. Gun in hand, I yanked open the door.

Ramu, the gap-toothed houseboy, tumbled into my room.

"Sahib, come quick," he panted. "Your sister Chutki is missing."

CHAPTER 51

I'VE BEEN A FOOL

Akbar! How had he got hold of little Chutki? Urging speed, we clambered into the carriage.

"Adi, I've been a fool!" I muttered as we strode into Framji Mansion. While I'd followed Akbar and Kasim around, their flunkies must have been watching Framji Mansion for any sign of weakness. They'd found it in my plucky girl.

Burjor and Diana were in the morning room. Face pale, she looked distraught.

"What happened?" I asked.

Burjor cleared his throat. "The child—Chutki. She went missing in the bazaar. I've sent word to McIntyre."

"When did this happen?"

Diana stammered, "About six thirty? We wanted rolls for dinner. . . ."

Chutki had been abducted at sundown, over an hour ago. "Why was she alone?" Fear made my voice rough.

"She wasn't alone!" Diana protested. "Jiji-bai was with her—left her at the baker's for just a few minutes. When she got back, Chutki wasn't there."

"And then?"

Diana winced. "Jiji-bai was frantic. She asked everyone around. But no one knew."

"Could Chutki have gone elsewhere?"

"Jiji-bai searched for half an hour. She heard the clock tower chime twice. Captain, Chutki wouldn't go off by herself. She's afraid of getting lost."

Think. I forced a slow breath. To escape notice so completely, Chutki might have gone willingly with her captor. How had they gained her compliance? I let my mind follow Chutki from house to bazaar. "Right. Chutki was buying bread . . . nothing out of the ordinary there. What happens next? Someone calls to her."

Eyes wide, Diana asked, "Someone she knows?"

I shook my head. "Don't think so. If it was a known person, then one of ours is in their pay—they would have taken her before, or even you."

"Go on, Jim. Someone calls to her, what then?"

I imagined a bustling bazaar—Chutki turns, eyes searching. "They tell her something that alarms her. Someone is ill? The baby, Baadal? You, perhaps? That gets her attention. She's wanted at the house—a carriage is waiting, a victoria? She steps in and they're away."

Diana's voice dropped into the silence. "Away where?"

I felt chilled. Akbar and Kasim had taken Mrs. Enty to gain a hold over her husband. Now someone had snatched little Chutki—because of me? Tendrils of panic closed my throat.

I addressed Burjor. "Sir, a gang of slavers is at work here. I've been following them for weeks, watching their ship. They could have got Chutki too."

Diana gasped. Burjor dropped into a chair as though his legs could no longer hold him.

"Where would they take her?" asked Adi.

Giving Burjor a moment to absorb what had taken me days to discover, I answered Adi, "The ship, perhaps. Superintendent McIntyre was awaiting a warrant to board the *Vahid Cruiser*. If they've taken Chutki, he may not need one. McIntyre can move up our plan. Ask him to raid the ship tonight."

Burjor rose to his feet. "I'll get McIntyre. There's a big do at the Wadias. We were invited, but I sent regrets. I'll find him." His chin jutted out, outrage and resolve in his shoulders. He'd barely noticed Chutki, but now that my little waif was missing, he was furious.

Glad to have him at my back, I said, "Thank you, sir. They may not wait until the dock opens at dawn. The ship will sail once they're aboard." Then I remembered. "But it's the month of Ramadan. The dockyard closes at sundown for Mohammedans to break their fast."

Adi asked, "If Akbar and Kasim can't get to their ship, where would they go?"

"I followed Kasim to a house on Dockyard Road. It's number twenty-one, by the streetlamp." Was Chutki being held there? I should search it. "Adi, gather the house guards."

He nodded, eyes dark in that pale, narrow face as he yanked the bell-pull by the door.

Burjor eyed me doubtfully. "What do you plan to do?"

"Haven't quite decided, sir."

"I'd tell you to wait for the police, Captain. But that poor child . . . Go. I'll bring McIntyre to the ship." Burjor clamped his lips together, gave me a nod and stomped through the door.

Adi eyed the revolver in my hand.

Laying it on the table, I asked, "Diana, have you more cartridges?"

When she'd gone, Adi said, "Captain, she can't come."

I agreed. Diana could not be part of this, nor Adi himself. I'd not risk my friends in this rescue. Smith, McIntyre and I had seen action. Maneck understood the risk, perhaps even needed to redeem himself. Our house guards were experienced Sepoys. I would risk no one else.

"Adi, I'll take the housemen and search the place on Dockyard Road. The Constabulary can raid a ship when offered just cause. Chutki's abduction gives him that. I just hope they don't sail before he arrives."

Adi cleared his throat. "Captain, the harbor master is a friend of ours. Perhaps he can stop the ship leaving. I'll go to him."

Hope flickered, sending painful thrusts into my chest. "That will do it. Trap them in the bay."

"Right." He clapped me on the shoulder and set off.

It would take a while for Adi to find the harbor master and persuade him. The Framjis had hired me to aid them, but now I depended upon them to find little Chutki. Brave Chutki, who had endured more in her fourteen years than should be asked of anyone. Would I get to her in time?

CHAPTER 52

SS *VAHID CRUISER*

The house on Dockyard Road loomed silent and dark. No light flickered in the windows. Where was Maneck? He was tasked to observe this address from a carriage across the street, yet I saw no sign of him.

With the Gurkhas at my heels, I prepared to demand access to Kasim's house, to threaten violence, since I had no authority to enter it. Ear to the door, I listened, feeling only the weight of silence.

At my signal, Ganju hammered on the door. The sound echoed along the still street. No one answered. The house remained a tomb. Hadn't they brought Chutki here after all?

Our horses snorted, clomping restlessly at the corner, where Ramu held their bridles. Here and there, people appeared in windows, peering out. A drizzle started, and lightning flared overhead, silent and menacing. I paused in an agony of indecision—if Chutki was aboard the ship, we'd waste precious time here. But were they hiding inside?

I motioned to Gurung. "Open it."

The white of his teeth flashed. Thunder belched, as he shot out the lock. He flung open the door, and we crashed into a narrow hallway with doors on both sides.

I heard a thump to our right. Someone was here.

Gurung's hand clamped on my shoulder. He'd heard it too. Slipping ahead, he peered into the chamber and made a startled sound. Someone asked, "What is it?"

Gurung turned up the gas lamp, flooding the small parlor with light.

What looked like a pile of clothes was a man slumped by the settee, his arm bright red, unmistakable. Blood.

"Maneck!"

Why was he here? Damn and blast. I pressed fingers to his neck. Maneck groaned and blinked. Relieved, I tugged off my tie to bind his arm, then checked for other injuries. Finding only a bruise on his forehead, I sat back on my heels.

"It's not mine—the blood," he said, "not all of it anyway." He tried to sit up and swayed.

Propping him against the settee, I said, "You were to watch the house, not enter! What happened?"

"They were here." Maneck's voice wobbled. "I saw them take a girl in, all bundled up. One more slave, right? So I snuck in through a window, tried to get her out the same way. But they found me. I fought . . ."

Chutki had been here! "You fought them?" I said. "Damn foolishness." And incredibly courageous. Although no match for Ranjpoot's guards, he'd put up a good show—dropped unconscious by a blow to his forehead, which now bulged an angry red. It had likely saved his life.

He coughed and groaned, clutching his side. My fingers tightened on his arm.

"Maneck, where did they go?"

"Sassoon Dock."

Sweat dripped down my back, but a chill ran through me. Chutki could already be aboard the ship. I was too far behind. If Akbar sailed, I would lose her forever. Where the devil were McIntyre and his constables?

"You saw Akbar?" My voice sounded rough, unfamiliar.

"No, Saapir Behg—that snake! He's to . . . meet Akbar at the ship."

I left Gurung to care for Maneck and sent young Ramu off with a note to McIntyre. Returning to our horses, I stashed my revolver in a saddlebag. It would not do to lose it on this ride.

The brown mare huffed as I mounted and made for Sassoon Dock, fear pounding inside my chest. Hurry, hurry, hurry.

Ganju and the others clattered behind me, our hooves beating a tattoo along grim cobbled streets. To the north, the clock tower loomed, its face a solitary light that peered down through the gloom.

What was that hullaballoo ahead? As I neared the docks, a mass of people blocked my way. Clad in colorful tunics, the procession followed a large statue of a goddess bedecked in red and gold. Hauling on the reins, I yanked the mare to one side, causing men and women to cry out and leap from my path. Cursing, I drew the mare through gaps in the crowd until she stood, heaving, on the other side. I'd lost track of the date—was it Durga Pooja? The Ganesh festival?

Across the pulsing river of bodies, Adi's house guards pulled up, shouting, "Hoy!" Horses bumped each other. They'd have to wait until the procession crawled past. The wind picked up then, bringing a light drizzle. The monsoon was near—was it already July?

Leaving them, I urged the mare on to the deserted dockyard, only to find its iron gate closed fast with a thick metal chain. Blast.

When would McIntyre's troops get here? Would they reach me before the ship sailed? Adi might find the harbor master, persuade him to close the waterway. Was that even possible at this late hour? Could it keep a steamship in the harbor? I rubbed the mare's neck, her breath puffing like a bellows as she whickered at my indecision.

If *Vahid Cruiser* sailed, so went the abducted women, proof of the crime against Lady Bacha and Miss Pilloo. More than likely, Chutki was already aboard. Little Chutki who walked on torn feet, leaving bloody footprints to glisten in the moonlight.

I could not wait for McIntyre. SS *Vahid Cruiser* must not leave this dock. Some idea of sabotaging the ship's engine ran through my mind, although barricading the engine room would do just as well.

How many men were aboard? I did not know. General Greer would have snarled at me, "All day you watched, goddammit! How many?" In Ranjpoot, Akbar strode about with a troop. At the dock, he had two sturdy guards. What about crew? I could not hope to overcome them all, but I could hide aboard. . . .

The gate was locked, what of it? I'd go over the top.

At my urging, the brown mare sidled up alongside the dockyard wall.

Pulling my feet from the stirrups, I held the pommel, crouched on the mare's back, then launched myself upward. My palms caught the wall's edge. Pain coursed through me, familiar and sharp, taking my breath— like knives cutting my palms. Ignore it, I told my hands, feeling about for a stronger hold. Swearing, I hauled myself up onto shards of broken glass embedded in the top of the wall.

* * *

Steamship *Vahid Cruiser* was still docked where I'd last seen it. Peering out of a nearby warehouse, I breathed in soft hope, thinking of Chutki, bound and gagged in its hold.

The ship bobbed slowly by a pile of mooring timbers, as water sloshed against the pier. Her weight had shifted to the stern since this evening, when I'd watched her loading. Ugly and squat, she sat low in the water, ready to sail with her cargo of stolen women and Chutki, the girl who called me brother.

A turbaned guard stood by the gangplank, which creaked with each swell of the unhappy bilge water. He lowered himself onto a crate and felt about his pockets for a plug of tobacco. Streetlamps glowed at either end of the pier, turning the drizzle into flecks of light that shimmered as they swirled. Ropes clumped beside the moorings in untidy coils. Pallets and broken timbers littered the pier like matchsticks thrown by careless gods.

Only one man barred my way aboard *Vahid Cruiser.*

The guard bit off some tobacco and chewed as I planned my approach through the debris and detritus. That sparked an idea. Why strike and drop him into the depths when I could simply steal his blue uniform and take his place?

I scanned the murky warehouse for some way to distract him. Finding sacks of grain, I hauled open the side door to the warehouse, hefted one over my shoulder and trudged out.

The creaking of the warehouse door had drawn his attention. He looked up, puzzled. Taking a few steps, I dropped the sack with a thump.

"Oi! Give me a hand here. Hurry!" I hollered, using the idiom of Ranjpoot.

The guard gave a start, craned his neck, then ambled toward me. "What, still more?"

As he reached toward the sack, my fist caught his temple. He staggered. Though dazed, he twisted and struggled until a sharp knock told him that wasn't wise. I forced him into the warehouse at knifepoint. Yanking the turban off his head, I hissed, "Undress."

The whites of his eyes gleamed in the dim light. His head bobbed. Wide-eyed, he fumbled at the fastenings of his uniform. He need not have worried—I cut lengths of rope to bind him hand and foot, stuffing a rag in his mouth for good measure. With jagged breath, he watched me don his uniform over my clothes.

I felt my pockets for Adi's pistol, cursed as I remembered—I'd left it in my saddlebag. Wonderful! Greer would have sneered. You're a bleeding one-man show, and you come unarmed. Brilliant, Captain!

My fingers closed on a slip of paper in my pocket—Mrs. Framji's note perhaps, asking me to come to dinner. I had a four-inch blade, now stashed in my boot, and a piece of paper. I slipped it into the cummerbund of the Ranjpoot uniform, over my stomach that heaved like the ship I was about to board.

Just as I took the guard's place, the cruiser's engines chugged to life, spewing smoke from its chute.

No, I swore inwardly. Not bloody yet.

CHAPTER 53

ON BOARD

Vahid Cruiser seemed ready to sail, its coal-fired engines growling. Could I slip aboard to search it? Would the absence of a guard at the gangplank alert those aboard?

Footsteps on the dock drew my attention. A group of people approached, moving briskly. First came a tall turbaned guard, then Akbar, his chin thrust forward, long coat flapping. Flanked between two turbaned men was a shorter, thin man, hatless . . . oh God, it was Adi! How had they got him? He'd gone for his friend the harbor master. Dammit, Adi!

A man in a long kurta followed, sandwiched between them and a guard dragging a girl by her elbow. Chutki. She was alive.

"Excellency." As they came abreast, I imitated the low bow of the Ranjpoot guards. The plume of my borrowed turban hid my face. I was gambling that the upper classes saw only a servant or bearer, not the person inside the uniform. It paid off—Akbar stalked past me. My throat tight, I fell into step behind the group to cross the gangplank. The ship pulsated under my feet, lit only by distant lamps on the wharf.

How in God's name did they get Adi? He'd gone to the harbor master's rooms, had he not? My stomach clenched as realization dawned. The man in rumpled kurta must be that very harbor master, with expert knowledge of the bay. In need of a pilot to weave through the moonlit harbor, Akbar must have waylaid him and nabbed Adi as well. Eager to help me, my friend had walked into the eye of the storm.

The leading guard started up a metal stairway that led to the upper deck. Akbar followed, haughty feet stamping wide.

Adi moved with a sudden spurt, so quickly I barely saw him dart away. Starting up the stairway, he ducked under the guard's outstretched arm and disappeared around the stairs.

Charging down the steps, Akbar bellowed, "Stop!" Mouth twisting into a cruel smile, he grabbed Chutki by the hair. "Come back or the girl dies!"

A weapon glinted in his hand. Desperation wound through me. I could make myself known and distract Akbar. Could Chutki escape in the hubbub? What then? A host of possibilities breathed in and out, each a thread of hope that snapped as I played out Akbar's reaction. In none of them could I see how all three of us, Adi, Chutki and I, might escape.

"All right." Adi reappeared, a silhouette against the gunwale. "You have a choice, Mr. Akbar. If you want to ransom me, let her go."

Akbar chuckled, looking from Adi to Chutki and back. "I think I'll keep you both."

"Don't think so," said Adi, calm as ever. "You see, I can swim."

But Akbar would not lose his prey so easily. Sneering, he pointed the pistol at Adi.

I had to act, and now! As I pressed sticky palms to my waist, they brushed something—the note I'd thrust into my waistband. A mad plan formed in my mind, utterly hopeless, but I had nothing else.

"Excellency!" I pushed forward toward Akbar. "Wait! Message from Rani Sahiba."

I offered the scrap as his retainers did, bowing, arms outstretched, paper held between folded hands. I'd seen his sais, his groom, bring him messages in Ranjpoot. Now, on a ship, ready to depart, would he take the bait? It was a pathetic ploy—it couldn't hope to work.

Yet the habits of privilege are strong. Akbar scowled. "Now? You bring it to me now?"

His right hand lowered the pistol as he reached for the missive with his left. I stepped in close, locked a hand around his weapon, made a fist with the other and slammed it into his face.

It was like hitting a tree. It shook him, but he didn't go down.

"Bao-di!" came Chutki's whisper, shocked and joyful. "You came!"

Akbar turned on me and chaos ensued. Shouts, punches, blows blocked, fingers gouging.

A shot cracked out to my right. Chutki stood there! My head snapped around—a mistake.

That second of distraction cost me dear. Akbar knocked my feet out from under me. I fell, caught at him desperately and dragged him down. We slammed into the deck together. Hearing his expulsion of breath, satisfaction snaked through me, fierce and vicious.

A voice boomed from the wharf, "Prepare to be boarded!"

Twisting under me, Akbar didn't seem to hear it. I grappled, as if I'd captured a python. He was lithe, quick, and he struck hard. For one moment I had the upper hand—but my injured palms were slick with blood and he slipped from my hold, thrusting me back. Feet scrabbled on metal rungs, and he was gone.

Shots cracked out, hitting the boards beside me in a hail of thunder. Instinct drove me to the deck. I caught sight of a spark on the wharf. McIntyre's troops were here and, goddammit, shooting at me! Rescue had arrived, but once again, I was on the wrong side of the firing line.

I curled, huddled tight against the whine and splatter of bullets. I was in Karachi again, amid screams and choking cries. When it ended, I was deafened, chest burning, throat on fire.

Adi. Oh God, Adi had been near the gunwale, closest to the wharf. I shuddered.

"Captain? Jim!" Someone at my shoulder, crying out, shaking me—Adi. His face was strained and pale in the dim light.

"Are you hurt?" he asked. "Are you shot?"

I shook my head, wheezing—I never could talk after a fight. Grabbing his arm, I thrust a word through my throat, pointing at the figures slumped on the deck: "Chutki."

Was one of those rumpled piles little Chutki, my brave girl? Adi turned and headed there.

"Help me!" a man begged from the deck. "I'm bleeding!"

"Good!" Adi said. "Be afraid!" Stepping over the man, he spat out, "That's Kasim, alias Behg. All this started with Kasim."

So I'd been wrong again. The man in the kurta was no harbor master but Kasim, Akbar's partner in the murder of Lady Bacha and Miss Pilloo.

"*Vahid Cruiser*. Stand down." Chief McIntyre's voice, magnified through a blow-horn, boomed across the wharf. "By order of the Viceroy. You will be boarded."

But I was looking for Chutki. I stooped by the nearest figure, saw the turban and stepped over the man. Where was she?

Adi called, "Jim, over here!"

I dropped beside him and bent my head to Chutki's silent chest. Her skin felt warm, but her breath was still. I rubbed her hands, her arms, to no effect, then caught her close. Bending low, I touched my lips to her forehead, choking, my chest aflame.

Chutki's tiny body felt just as it had on our way to Simla, warm, narrow, but slack and loose-boned. I held her, rocking her like a baby, overcome, remembering her last words, "Bao-di, you came!"—so joyful, her surprise woven with delight.

I carried her to McIntyre's impromptu headquarters, set up in the warehouse where I'd left the ship's guard. There I laid her down, covering her peaceful, sleeping face, and the bullet hole in her chest. For just a few weeks, I'd had a sister.

Bright military lanterns lit the wide space. Sepoys brought sailors off the *Vahid Cruiser*, bound and strung together like a prison chain gang. Constables tramped back and forth over the gangplank. Soon a stream of captives staggered from the hold, both men and women, as McIntyre's men emptied the bowels of the slave ship. Bedraggled men and women clustered together, fearful and confused, barefoot and dressed in rags, while McIntyre's booming voice organized assistance. Kasim, alias Saapir Behg, huddled at the center of the warehouse.

"Not a bad day's work!" said McIntyre, surveying the scene, feet planted wide. "Three dead, one civilian . . ." His lips compressed. "Your sister, I'm told. My regrets, Captain. We'll find who's responsible."

The warehouse seemed to move in a ripple, as though I were still aboard a ship.

"Steady on!" Adi caught my arm. "I saw what happened. You clipped Akbar, got into a mix-up with him. When Kasim took a shot at you, Chutki jumped in the way."

I felt numb, a humming sound filled my ears. I'd come for Chutki, and she was dead. The closest thing I'd had to family was gone. My forehead pressed to Adi's shoulder, loss and regret burning a path inside me that I knew well.

Chutki had the sort of pluck no one expects, the courage to endure the unspeakable in Jalandhar, to walk on bloodied feet, to protect a babe and save little scraps to feed it when she had nothing for herself . . . and in the end, to throw herself into the line of fire to save her Bao-di, who showed up, out of nowhere, to get her out of a scrape.

CHAPTER 54

A FUNERAL

Next day while other women prepared for the Rakhsha-bandhan festival, which celebrates siblings, when Chutki should have tied that string about my wrist, we prepared to cremate her.

"May I come with you to the cremation ground?" Diana asked.

"Women aren't allowed," Adi said. "It's an orthodox Hindu place."

Mrs. Framji patted her hand and suggested they pray in their own way. It was agreed—Zoroastrian prayers with flowers and sandalwood would be offered in little Chutki's memory.

"She was a good child," said Mrs. Framji, "and so fond of you. We hadn't seen you for days, and she became rather listless. Diana was teaching her English, did you know? But Chutki would never answer questions about herself."

I sighed. "No. Her history is an unfortunate one, Marm. I couldn't tell you, for fear it might bias some in this household against her."

I glanced at the door, where Jiji-bai and the other servants listened. The Gurkha retainers Gurung and Ganju sat cross-legged against a wall. When I narrated how I'd been offered Chutki, their faces mirrored their distress. They'd come to accept little Chutki, and her death had wounded them. When I told how I'd taken Chutki from her captor, Jiji-bai cried, "Shabaash, Sahib!" praising me.

Diana grimaced, holding back tears. "Why didn't you tell us before!"

I sighed. "I couldn't. Your household would want to know her caste and such. They might look down on her, poor girl, for what she endured. I worried you would not want her here, and might send her away. People aren't kind to such as her."

Diana turned her face into her mother's shoulder and wept.

Rising to their feet, Gurung and Ganju took matters in hand and asked to give Chutki a simple Buddhist funeral as though she were one of their own. I did not protest—Chutki wouldn't mind.

Her body cocooned in a white shroud, Chutki looked like the child she'd never been. Wearing orange clothes, Gurung, Ganju, Adi and I lifted her bier from the cart and carried her to the Shamshan Ghat, the cremation ground on the sands by the Indian Ocean. Burjor followed with his house guards. Maneck's arrival caused a stir, but Adi nodded to say it was all right.

We stepped down a narrow gravel path to the waterside, each holding a corner of the bier. My bandaged hands ached, although Chutki weighed nothing at all.

A stack of wood awaited us by the waterside. Words were spoken, whisked away over the ocean. I lit the pyre with a taper. Flame sputtered, caught, curved around the lower branches and draped them in orange, engulfing the white bundle. My kurta flapped against my knees, echoing the snap and crack of the pyre.

Smoke rose, billowed, curled around me and stung my eyes, wafting toward the setting sun. Standing by the fire, watching the sun dip, my future stretched as wide as the horizon, and as mysterious.

Of the ragtag children I'd found on the road to Simla, Razak was returned to his village, Hari and Parimal to their parents. The Framjis' Bengali cook and her husband had asked to adopt baby Baadal. He needed a mother to love and nurture him, a father to protect him, give him a trade, teach him to be a man. Since I could not offer as much, I agreed.

The girl I called Chutki was my charge for a brief while, a few short weeks. I never learned her real name. As the sun dipped into the horizon, I relinquished her to her maker, whoever that might be.

I'd seen courage in my years, men who rallied their troops or brought off daring feats. Here, instead, it took a quiet form, extraordinary because it came from one untutored to such things. Chutki saw Kasim turn his weapon upon me and used the only shield at hand, her own body. What greater affection could she give me? Her round eyes seemed to chide me now: "Shed these thoughts of unworthiness, Bao-di, and live."

CHAPTER 55

INTERROGATION

The next day, McIntyre summoned us to the Constabulary for the inquest into the deaths of Chutki and two Ranjpoot guards. From his terse note, it seemed he was not pleased with me.

He received us gravely, mopping his forehead, in full uniform despite the heat, his hair plastered to his head. He greeted Adi, then took my bandaged hand carefully, saying, "Glad to see you've recovered, Captain. You'll be questioned first. You've brought the evidence?"

Coming from McIntyre, that was downright civil. We followed him into the courtroom, where the Magistrates' raised dais dominated the chamber. The Framjis' barrister, Mr. J. Batliwala, of Brown and Batliwala, seated us at a wide desk.

A single chair stood in the dock, an ominous island facing a phalanx of pews, every seat filled. Someone rose to make space for Burjor and Mrs. Framji. Diana sat with them, demure in a grey saree.

I set down the box containing my documents, unsure what to expect. I'd barely shaken Batliwala's hand when the Magistrates were announced and the audience rose.

This inquest would precede Kasim's trial. While McIntyre had not arrested me for my part in storming SS *Vahid Cruiser*, he'd told me not to leave Bombay. Whether he'd treat me as a witness or defendant remained to be seen.

McIntyre nodded to the panel. Taking his place, he began, "This is an inquiry into the incident on the nineteenth of June, 1892, which resulted in the deaths of two men originating in Ranjpoot, and one child, a girl named Chutki Agnihotri."

They had given Chutki my last name, because I didn't know hers.

McIntyre called me. I was sworn in, and he cited my military record: "Twelve years in service, Dragoons, Bombay Regiments. Three field promotions. Numerous commendations for action, Maiwand and Rangoon. Three mentions in dispatches. Injured in line of duty, Karachi, June 1890. Nominated for Victoria Cross, awarded Indian Order of Merit. Medical discharge 1892."

Adi glanced at me. The VC was awarded only to those of British descent, so, as an Indian-born native, I'd got the Order of Merit. It lay unopened in a little box at the bottom of my trunk. Reluctant to speak of it, I'd not worn it to Diana's ball.

What had McIntyre just said? Injured in '90? Surely he had it wrong? Hadn't I been wounded last year, 1891?

He said, "Captain, you were hired by Mr. Adi Framji and Mr. Burjor Framji?"

"I was."

"To what end?"

"To uncover the truth behind the deaths of Mrs. Bacha Framji and Mrs. Pilloo Kamdin, née Framji."

"And you have undertaken some investigations to that end?"

I had.

"Very well. Tell us how you came to be on that ship."

This bit was tricky. I had broken into a warehouse, assaulted the ship's guard and stolen his clothes.

I straightened my shoulders, set to parade rest, and said, "I surveilled the ship SS *Vahid Cruiser* for twelve days, watched Akbar and his men load various boxes and crates. Had reason to believe this was a slave ship, carrying women to ports in Guyana. That evening I learned from a witness, Maneck Fitter, that my ward, Chutki, had been abducted and taken to the dockyard. I entered Sassoon Dock to search the ship."

McIntyre's eyes narrowed. "All right, Captain, your steps are marked quite clearly. You cut your hands on glass embedded in the dockyard wall and bled all over the shipyard. A simple matter to follow your path in the light of day. A guard posted to the steamship *Vahid Cruiser* was found beaten, bound and gagged in the warehouse of the Oriental Company. You acknowledge doing this?"

"Yes, sir, to . . . impersonate the guard."

This caused a stir among the audience. My face warmed at this catalog of my brutish conduct. Diana must know that a detective's task entailed the use of force, but I did not care to have it laid bare. Alas, there was no help for it.

"Did you have a weapon?"

"No, sir. My revolver remained in my horse's saddlebag, at the gate."

McIntyre shook his head, then lost patience with me. "Why this ship? Why were you watching *Vahid Cruiser*?"

"I followed the accused, Kasim Khwan, alias Saapir Behg, there from Ranjpoot."

McIntyre frowned. "Why?"

"I went to Ranjpoot to investigate the Framji ladies' murder. You recollect that two individuals, Akbar and Behg, were accused, but acquitted for lack of evidence. Having identified Akbar as the prince of Ranjpoot, I followed him there, and found Behg, who sports a snake tattoo upon his wrist. Akbar called him by the name Kasim. So I followed Kasim to ascertain his movements."

McIntyre looked skeptical. "You met both men in Ranjpoot? Are we to believe you escaped detection?"

"I was dressed as a shortsighted missionary, sir."

McIntyre gave a bark of laughter. Not a shining moment for me.

Yet impersonating Father Thomas had worked. I continued. "Upon his return to Bombay, Kasim frequented an address at Twenty-one Dockyard Road. I followed him to Sassoon Dock, where I took up station for twelve days."

"And escaped notice again? Didn't they spot the old friar sitting there, day after day?"

"Er, this time I dressed as a mendicant, sir. Overheard sailors from SS *Vahid Cruiser* mention cattle to be sold in British Guyana, and the size of the bounty expected from the sale."

"Were cattle loaded onto the ship?"

"No, sir."

McIntyre paused to let the Magistrates absorb that. "No cattle were loaded. Captain, you watched, dressed as a beggar, identified the ship, its cargo and this individual?"

When I confirmed that, McIntyre announced, "The cargo on board this ship, the evidence before the court, is a hundred and thirty-one men and women of various backgrounds, most illiterate, abducted from as far away as Bengal. These persons were rescued from SS *Vahid Cruiser*, where the prisoner, Kasim Khwan, was arrested, having taken part in a scuffle with this officer, Captain Agnihotri. In that action, the girl Chutki was killed."

He signaled me to resume my seat. I did so, checking to see how Adi had received my testimony. He nodded, elbows upon the desk, hands fisted before him.

"Bring in the accused," said a Magistrate.

Kasim was led in, shackled at the wrists. One eye bulged, blue and hideous, as he limped to the dock. He was made to place his hand upon his holy book and sworn in.

I pitied Adi, then. He had endured the arduous trial earlier and now must suffer it again. He'd demanded to know why, and soon we would hear it, the truth of Lady Bacha and Miss Pilloo's last moments.

McIntyre approached the Magistrates, saying, "This has been Captain Agnihotri's investigation. He's asked your indulgence to question the witness himself. Do your lordships agree?"

Good heavens. I had requested permission to question Kasim, and McIntyre had taken me at my word. I'd get my chance to demand answers from Kasim at last.

CHAPTER 56

KASIM'S STORY

One eye swollen shut, Kasim looked thin in his crumpled kurta, hunched over his manacled wrists, elbows tucked in close. Here was Akbar's henchman, the mysterious servant boy Kasim, Chutki's killer. I would need to get him off guard, but how? I recalled that Miss Pilloo had taught him English. He spoke it well.

I asked, "Saapir Behg, you have used the name Kasim Khwan?"

He drew back, alarmed.

"Do we need witnesses, already in this audience, to identify you, or will you admit it? You are Kasim?"

He nodded, wary. "I am."

"You were raised in the Framji household from the age of thirteen? They fed and clothed you, educated you?"

Kasim hung his head. "Yes."

"Were they generous toward you?"

He acknowledged it was so.

I found my lead, a way to take him off course. "How did you come to serve them?"

He blinked rapidly. He'd not expected this, but he rallied. "My mother was a cook, in Pilloo's home."

Not Miss Pilloo, or Pilloo Memsahib. No deference to upper class here. Why? It would bear careful handling. I resolved to take him through each step of this curious business, starting with his childhood.

"You grew up in Lahore. How did you come to Bombay?"

His eyes darted about. "When I was thirteen, my mother and brother died in a terrible epidemic. My father died before, when I was two. At the master's house, all the servants had left. The master was ill—vomiting, coughing. His wife collapsed with fever, begging me to care for Pilloo. She sent us to stay on a rooftop terrace until the disease passed. At night we heard cries and moans all around. We lived there for weeks, buying food with our last coins. The master died first, then his wife, so I cared for Pilloo until Burjor Sahib arrived."

That's why he felt Pilloo owed him! "You saved seven-year-old Pilloo."

"Yes." Kasim straightened, raising his head. He'd be more forthcoming now.

Pressing my advantage, I continued. "Why did you leave the Framjis?"

He started. "I didn't! They cast me off! Burjor Sahib sent me back to Lahore. Because of my friendship with Pilloo."

"Friendship? Did you not demand Miss Pilloo give you things? Clothes? A pocket watch? What else—money?"

His eyes flickered. So I was right.

I continued. "Why did you steal Miss Pilloo's letter?"

Kasim waved his hands, denying it. "No, no! It was not like that. I hid Pilloo's letter as a joke. I meant no harm. Just a game, bargaining for the letter."

He was lying. He'd stolen the letter because it gave him power over her. How did he know its value? Wait, I thought. I had moved too quickly and missed something important. What was it? Pilloo was just a child. What if the letter wasn't something she wrote, but was given?

"You were there when she got the letter," I guessed.

Kasim stiffened. Looking down, he said, "Before the master died, he climbed to the terrace. He was very sick, begged Pilloo not to come close. He gave her something wrapped in cloth and said, 'Child, keep this safe. No one must see it. It could ruin us.'"

Ah! I saw now—that was why Pilloo was so desperate to regain the mysterious letter. Why hadn't she just given it to Burjor? Her father had said it could ruin the Framji clan—no wonder she was frantic to regain it.

That's what changed Miss Pilloo into a frightened recluse—her childhood friend had taken her father's letter.

"So you knew its value. You stole it from Pilloo, to hold over her. Did you read it?"

Kasim rubbed one hand over the other. "I could not."

I watched closely. Was he telling the truth?

"All right. How did you come to Ranjpoot?"

Kasim cleared his throat. "I worked in Lahore, making bricks from dawn till dusk. What life was that? No chance to make anything of myself. No one there could even read!"

He had worked in the brick factory for two years—why leave then? I remembered Burjor saying, "Right after Pilloo was engaged, Kasim was killed on the way to Bombay."

"You left when you heard Miss Pilloo was betrothed. Did you see a chance to make her pay for the letter again? Is that why you changed your identity?"

He licked his lips. "I just needed a fresh start."

I stared at him with an odd presentiment. Pilloo's impending marriage had decided him. That meant more. I guessed: "As Kasim you could never win Miss Pilloo. Did you think a new identity would do it? A new name?"

Seeing Kasim squirm as I exposed his secret, his affection for Pilloo, I pulled in a breath. He and I both loved someone above our station. So how had Miss Pilloo ended up dead?

Sharp-edged, I said, "On the way, you saw an accident. A boy fell under a train. What better way to start fresh? You used that—let the Framjis think you were dead. You told Doctor Aziz, 'That's Kasim.' Did you pretend to weep? He took you under his wing, didn't he?"

Kasim stared. I'd been guessing, but I'd struck true.

"So you left the doctor and hid in Ranjpoot."

Kasim cried out, "No! I came to Ranjpoot to make something of myself, not to be errand boy for the doctor! When he sent me with a note to Prince Akbar, I saw my chance. What a man he is! Akbar had a vision for

Ranjpoot! He accepted me as his servant, giving me great responsibility—I became his man of business."

I could see this was true. At last, one of the ruling classes had respected Kasim's abilities. He was resourceful, ruthless and decisive—a useful man to further the prince's interests. In turn, Kasim admired Akbar, eager for the halo of power that extended to himself. What had he used to gain Akbar's interest? The blackmail letter? What the devil could it contain, to be so valuable?

"How did Akbar learn about Pilloo's letter?"

Kasim bit his lip. "He needed money, for Ranjpoot! For the treasury! I told him about Pilloo's letter. That she would pay something to regain it. He was skeptical—said it was a waste of time."

"But you wanted to see Miss Pilloo again. So you persuaded him."

Kasim spread his hands. "Maneck got a message to Pilloo. She agreed to meet me."

"In the library reading room?"

"Yes. But it all went wrong. That morning, Akbar sent me to Ranjpoot and took my place. And the girls also changed places! Instead of Pilloo, he met Bacha."

So the man in the green coat was Akbar, not Kasim. I recalled the Tambey children had seen Bacha return from that conversation, upset and angry with Pilloo. Akbar had expected to meet with docile, young Pilloo and instead had come up against composed, self-assured Bacha.

I prompted Kasim, "So on October twenty-fifth, on the clock tower gallery, you were going to sell the letter back to Pilloo. You got rid of Maneck—sent him off to secure a carriage. Francis Enty witnessed your altercation at three fifteen. Maneck's coat was torn. Who did that?"

"Akbar," said Kasim.

I understood. If I let him, he would pin everything on Akbar. "Akbar and you hid in the carillon room. Sometime after three thirty, when the Framji ladies entered the gallery, you boxed them in. That's how you got behind the ladies to prevent their exit."

Kasim stared at me. "Yes."

"What happened on the gallery?"

I noticed a movement at the desk. Adi had straightened up. Here was his moment of truth.

Kasim said, "We came in behind the Framji women. The small one, Bacha, scolded Akbar, asked for the letter. He laughed and demanded money. She refused, demanding the letter. She took out a bundle of notes and threw it at him." His face twisted. "She shouldn't have done that. It made him angry. Akbar took the money and told her the price had gone up. The payment was herself and Pilloo! I didn't know, until that moment, what he planned! It was not my fault—"

"You didn't know?" I cut off his whining. The librarian had said the black clothes were worn and frayed. Kasim was lying again. "When you brought the burkhas with you, you didn't realize Akbar was going to abduct the women? These were the same black clothes you'd foisted on other women, other captives you'd taken, yes? Why didn't Lady Bacha shout for help?"

He groaned. "Akbar warned her—if she called out he would give Pilloo's letter to the newspapers! He said, 'Let's see what the world thinks of the fine Framjis then!'"

"Go on," I prompted.

"Pilloo was crying. Akbar told me to put a burkha over her head. He said the girls would come quietly, because we had the letter. But Bacha would not." He looked down at his shackled hands.

"And then?"

"Akbar had boxed Bacha against the wall. She had nowhere left to go. She said, 'You aren't going to return it. You never intended to!' Akbar struck her across the face. Pilloo struggled, weeping. What could I do?"

"Go on."

Kasim continued. "Bacha said, 'No, I won't let you take her. You won't get away with this.' She leaned across the wall and went over."

He slumped in his seat. No one said a word.

I imagined it—tiny Lady Bacha in a yellow sari, facing down the mighty princeling. She'd have pushed herself over the curved parapet. She'd fallen, her sari unraveling, a golden bird in the noonday sun, pure-hearted and free.

A muffled sob sounded on my left. Adi's fist pressed to his lips, his face creased, body shaking. Batliwala patted his arm. Pens scratched on paper as the Magistrates wrote. When they ceased, one of them nodded to me.

I said, "All right. What happened next?"

Kasim shook his head, wordless. He looked defeated. Remembering the black fibers in the wooden doorframe, I prompted, "Pilloo tried to run away. Her burkha caught in the door."

"Yes," he choked.

I understood. Kasim had stopped Pilloo from leaving, damn him.

"So you caught her. You prevented Pilloo's escape."

Kasim cringed, speaking in a rush, mixing English and Urdu. "Akbar was angry. He said, 'Take the burkha off.' I did so—I didn't understand what he wanted. He said, 'We need a distraction.' And . . . he picked her up and threw her over the wall! I swear I did not know he would do that! She was my childhood friend."

So that's why Miss Pilloo hit the ground twenty feet farther from the tower than Lady Bacha. To my left, Adi bowed his head.

Did I believe Kasim? Yes. The guilt was eating at him. Yet I could not pity the vile creature. He'd helped Akbar murder the Framji ladies as surely as if he'd killed them himself.

Feeling vicious, I said, "You prevented Pilloo's escape. Little Pilloo, whom you say you cared for. But that's a lie—as a captive she'd be in your grasp again. That's what you wanted. But Akbar threw her off the gallery. You saw this?"

"I saw it!" Kasim's eyes glittered, wild and feverish, condemning his erstwhile master for a murderer. "It happened so fast. I didn't know what to do. Akbar picked up Bacha's spectacles. I bundled the burkhas under my shirt. We went down the steps. Near the bottom we heard voices. Akbar said, 'Turn around!' We told the people we were just going up and entered the reading room. We sat quietly, pretending to read. We could hear everything. Constables, university people talking. A library clerk came in, and Akbar complained, 'This is a reading room! What is all this noise?'

"We left the burkhas under the table and escaped. When Akbar saw the big carriage waiting at the south gate, he laughed. 'Perfect! We depart in style.'"

So that was it. The ladies crumpled on the ground, Akbar and Kasim calmly walked from the reading room to board the waiting carriage, while the police harangued poor, frightened Maneck about his torn coat.

Seconds ticked by. I asked, "Where is the letter? The letter used to blackmail the Framji ladies."

Looking confused, Kasim blurted, "It must be with Akbar!"

Was that the truth? He'd been abruptly sent off to Lahore—did he have the letter then? If so, why was Akbar searching Framji Mansion?

I said, "No. You hid the letter. That's why Akbar was searching the house when I caught him on the balcony."

Kasim raised his folded hands, admitting his lie. "We could not find it. I swear this."

Had Kasim been the first burglar, the one Diana heard on the roof? Searching in the dark, he had not found what he wanted. When Akbar subsequently looked for it, I accosted him. I felt certain that Kasim knew where the letter was. Could Akbar still intend to use it somehow? I had to find the damn thing.

But I wasn't done with Kasim. Chutki was dead. This was an inquest into her death.

CHAPTER 57

BACHA'S SACRIFICE

Why did you abduct Chutki, my ward?"

Kasim blurted, "Akbar ordered it! We noticed a new girl going to and from the Framji house, and saw the Rakhee tied on your wrist. Akbar said if we had your sister, you would stop pursuing us. He wanted to send you a message."

I understood. Akbar had tried to stop me, just as he'd silenced Enty. "A message? Like the messages you took the law clerk Francis Enty all these weeks?"

Kasim drew back, recoiling. Setting up for a knockout punch, I stepped in, feeling cool, and drove forward.

"Each morning you carried a newspaper to Enty's home. What did it contain?"

Kasim choked, "His wife wrote a note on it under the date. To show she was alive."

I nodded. "And Enty continued to hold his tongue as long as his wife lived. If he identified Akbar and you, that new evidence might reopen the murder case. Well, two days ago, Mrs. Enty was retrieved from the house on Dockyard Road, alive."

The courtroom buzzed with gasps and whispers. My task complete, I felt weary, my limbs heavy, my breath rough. Akbar had taken Chutki in order to control me. By moving up the raid on SS *Vahid Cruiser*, I'd set in motion events that culminated in Chutki's death.

She was gone, yet I remained.

A Magistrate motioned to McIntyre to approach.

After conferring briefly, he turned to me. "A question for you, Captain, if you please. Was the Rani of Ranjpoot involved in this scheme?"

Staring at him, I drew a breath. Here it was, as Diana had predicted. If I implicated the Rani, the British might rule her unfit, place her state under its control. She'd rebuked Akbar's arrogance at dinner. Confronting me in the dark that night, she'd thought I was a djinn. Was she aware of Akbar's schemes? Recalling her puzzlement at my question, I thought not.

"I have no evidence of her involvement," I said carefully.

McIntyre's eyes drilled through me. He repeated the question in different ways, but I maintained a passive stance. The Rani might have benefited from Akbar's crimes, but I could not fault her for them.

"All right, Captain." McIntyre dismissed me.

I sat beside Adi, feeling utterly spent. For the next two hours McIntyre interrogated Kasim about the slave trade, and he admitted everything, revealing all I'd learned about Akbar's dealings: For two years, Akbar's shipments of indentured labor to Guyana had netted him a tidy sum. Kasim, as his man of business, was tasked to identify suitable victims— landless laborers, widows and urchins. They were rendered unconscious and held at Dockyard Road until packed into his ship, which made four runs to Guyana each year.

Next, McIntyre called Adi and questioned him about the death of Chutki. Once Adi gave a succinct account of the action on the deck of *Vahid Cruiser*, her death was deemed manslaughter, not murder, since she was not Kasim's intended target. Kasim would stand trial, but Akbar was not charged, although he remained a suspect. My protest was ignored— McIntyre would not do so "just yet."

* * *

After the inquiry, we returned to Framji Mansion. Burjor and his barrister, J. Batliwala, retreated to his study. I knew I should leave the Framjis to grieve in privacy, yet Adi's red-rimmed glance demanded I remain. We withdrew to the morning room, a quiet group, each immersed in our own thoughts. Diana curled on the carpet by Adi's feet, her cheek against his knee in sorrowful rumination.

Lines etched around Adi's mouth, aging him beyond his years. Slumped on the sofa beside his mother, he gazed at Lady Bacha's portrait, propped against the mantel, draped in a string of white flowers. Miss Pilloo's photograph beside it was similarly adorned.

Touching Diana's head, Adi said, "I keep thinking of Kasim's testimony—Bacha said 'I won't let you take her' . . . that's the answer, isn't it? Bacha tried to prevent Pilloo from being abducted. She could not have known Akbar would resort to outright murder, throwing Pilloo to cover his escape."

I considered it—was that what drove Lady Bacha? What else would she care about? Of course!—Adi.

The seed of an idea taking root, I said, "Sir, I wonder if she had another reason."

"Go on." Adi shook out a white handkerchief and wiped his glasses.

"It puzzled me all along that the ladies didn't cry out for help. That led me to suspect Akbar had a hold over them, threatened to make the compromising letter public. Now Lady Bacha refused to be abducted. Akbar and Kasim could not drag the ladies through the university. An assault was imminent, intended to beat her down, force her into the burkha. Perhaps he held a weapon on Pilloo. If Bacha called out and drew attention, it might save them, but she believed Akbar had that damaging letter.

"That letter may have been uppermost in her mind. If it came out, you, her husband, would face ruin. How could she prevent it? I think she wanted to mark anyone who used it against you."

"Mark them? How?"

"Your family is well liked. If she died, anyone who later harmed the Framjis could be suspected of her murder. Here was a way to save you, and your family, permanently." I studied the painting of Adi's determined young wife. "She intended to render any compromising letters unusable. This was her sacrifice."

A long pause followed. Diana stared up at me. "If someone had cast slurs upon us, and then she died, of course the police would check their alibi closely! But no one had, so far. She was thinking ahead?"

"Yes. If someone made the letter public now, you can bet McIntyre would scrutinize their motives."

Adi sighed. "Yes, it makes sense. That's Bacha's gift, then."

"My poor child," Mrs. Framji whispered, kerchief pressed to her lips.

Adi gazed at the portrait. "She found a way to protect us. But against *what*? What was in Pilloo's letter?"

Indeed, that remained a puzzle. I shook my head in reply.

Mrs. Framji rose, saying, "We thought Kasim was dead. That's why we didn't recognize him at Maneck's trial."

"His beard hid his face, and he rarely looked up," said Adi, remembering. Mrs. Framji left soon after.

I glanced at the portrait of Lady Bacha, that solemn face grown dear, as though I'd once known her. Did Adi want such a constant reminder of his loss? Or did it not matter, since her absence was a prominent silence? He would always miss the sound of her, her smile, her touch.

I asked, "Will you keep the portrait here?"

"Yes," he said, with an air of finality. "I'll make her proud. I need her by me, you see, so I can explain things. Tell her what I'm going to build." As he spoke, his voice gathered purpose. Adi would never be truly young again—the past year had seared that away. The acetic, piercing quality of his gaze had tempered to steadiness, seasoned by events, yet compassionate still.

What of Diana? Her cheeks bloomed with health and vitality, yet those eyes were thoughtful, sometimes mournful. She had an alarming ability to read people's minds, at least to read mine. More than once she'd seen me watching her. At my sheepish half smile, she sent me a questioning look. That low trill of her laugh, always intoxicating, I craved like an opium addict—I heard it, picturing her in the seconds before I dropped into sleep, when I feared dreams would drag me to Karachi. Then I remembered an inadvertent giggle, her gurgle of laughter from our dance, when I'd lifted her off her feet and swung her about to the music. Despite all Burjor's forbidding, the future beckoned.

Yet that missing letter was still a threat. Miss Pilloo's letter again, I thought, rubbing Jameson's stitches that lay across my palm like a row of ants. Akbar had sought that letter the night I'd caught him on the balcony. So where was it? What did it contain?

CHAPTER 58

COLONEL SUTTON'S PROPOSAL

McIntyre had learned from Sir Peter, the British Resident at Ranjpoot, that Akbar was holed up in his palace. Lacking a plan to smoke Akbar out, my investigation had stalled. Undeterred by this, Adi dived into society with a verve that matched Diana's. I enjoyed his company, delighted in Diana's and persuaded myself that close proximity was the best means to keep them safe.

Adi had invited me to join the family at the theater the next day, and I'd accepted. We saw a comedy. Adi and Diana translated for me in whispers, since it was in Gujarati. Then we went to Byram's for dinner, Adi and I all spiffy in tails, top hats and gloves, Diana glowing in a deep purple dress that revealed her delicate collarbones.

Byram's mansion blazed with light and music as we ascended the stairs, Diana's black stole over my arm, her proprietary hand in the crook of my elbow. Victorian manners required that she rest the tips of her fingers on my sleeve, but Diana tugged on my arm, grinning. Ah, how right it felt. Adi looked dapper. Diana sparkled. The three of us made rather an entrance as Byram greeted us in the brightly lit foyer.

Diana was speaking when her gaze shifted behind me and her face changed.

Warned, I turned, but it was too late. I had an instant, a bare second to block Diana with my shoulder. I need not have worried—this greeting was mine alone: a neat clip to the chin that snapped my head around.

No one else had that clean right cut. Rubbing my stinging jaw, I said, "Pleasure to see you again, Colonel."

"Bloody hell, Jim." My commander, Colonel Sutton, caught my shoulder as he gaped at me, our eyes level. "You've gone soft! I haven't landed one on you in years!"

I grinned, then began to laugh. Here was Sutton, my old friend, his sandy hair cut short as usual, pale mustache bristling, not down south in Madras as Smith had said, but standing before me in the flesh.

Diana's grip tightened on my arm. A fierce look passed between her and Adi. What was she upset about—that little tap on my jaw?

"Miss Framji, may I present Colonel Sutton, my commander," I said, remembering my manners. "Colonel, her brother Adi Framji."

Adi and Sutton shook hands.

"Captain," boomed Burjor's voice nearby, so I included him in the introduction.

"Mr. and Mrs. Framji, meet Colonel Brian Sutton, Commander of the Madras Regiment."

When Sutton turned his admiring gaze on Diana, she asked, "Should I be worried, Colonel, or was that how you always welcome Jim?"

Sutton's eyebrows rose at her use of my given name. Cheeks growing rosy, his eyes flashed. "Charmed, Madam!" He made a broad flourish. "The British army at your service."

Bloody ham. He knew. Sutton knew she meant something to me and had set out to charm her. I stifled a smile as he took Diana's hand and raised it to his lips. Behind Sutton, Adi rolled his eyes.

Dinner was a cheerful affair, as most of the company knew each other. McIntyre and Sutton flanked Byram at the head of a long table appointed with all manner of crystal, a full sweep of cutlery and glasses set around each gilt-trimmed plate. Diana was seated by Adi, far across the table from me.

"I see you know the Captain," McIntyre remarked to Sutton. He'd noticed Sutton's peculiar greeting and was curious, in his usual grim way. During a lull in conversation, he asked, "So, Colonel, improvement on the Frontier?"

"Ask the Captain!" replied Sutton. "He was just at the front, don't you know? I've been down south, but I keep an eye on the boy. General Greer, in charge of Simla, said the Captain here pulled off one of the damnedest rescues he'd ever seen."

Mrs. Framji turned to me, concerned. I'd not told the Framjis about it. I sighed. Diana had heard that—would she flay me for this business? Ever since we returned from Simla, something had changed in her. Now and again a pained expression crossed her face, but when I inquired, she denied anything was amiss. What had she heard me cry out, that night I staggered in from Pathankot? She'd look at me, her face soft, yet when I caught her gaze, she'd turn away. I wanted to break this impasse between us, but Burjor's plea, "Captain, she's not for you," kept ringing in my ears.

"Bloody hell," I said. "Beg pardon, Marm." There was no help for it. While Sutton recounted my adventure with Ranbir, placing rather a more romantic light on it than General Greer had, I made inroads through the salmon soufflé and curried lamb.

"Walked straight into an enemy sentry." Sutton paused at the crucial moment of the tale and beamed at me.

Avoiding Diana, I said, "We uh . . . Razak's family, the tribesmen, saved the day. The lads and I got back—that's all that matters."

He grunted. "With ten infantrymen, I'm told. Through Pathan-held countryside."

Sutton's eyes glinted as he raised his glass. "To the lads on the Frontier, and to my boy."

Across the table, Diana melted into a smile. My worries receded, clouds parting after a wretched storm. I caught that radiant look and did not care who noticed.

At evening's end, while the Framjis were saying goodbye to Byram, Colonel Sutton wanted a word, so I joined him at the window. He was trim in uniform, fit, although well past sixty. He'd been a friend when I had none. More than a friend. He'd trained me to box, put me up, bet on me. He'd taught me to win, and then shared his winnings with me. He did not need to do that—just as he didn't have to gift me Mullicka, that bronze Arabian filly who rode as soft as the wind in the clouds and faster than any creature I'd seen.

"Eat up, lad, you're out of shape. You'll train at the camp here," Sutton said.

He waved away my surprise, mistakenly thinking it was on account of my mixed race. "It's all right, I've got you in."

"Train, sir?" I asked. "For what, exactly?"

"A match, 'course!" He grinned. "A real doozy! All lined up. Four weeks away."

A boxing match? I stared. Sutton wanted me for a fight? When the pieces fell into place, disappointment flared. I tamped it down, realizing that was why he'd built me up all evening.

"I'm done with boxing," I said, and felt at peace with it. There, at last I'd said it out loud. Let him find another protégé.

Mustache bristling, Sutton drew an audible breath, huffing, "Come now, lad! I've put some effort into you." Relenting, he went on, "You've been ill, I see that. A few weeks training will get you shipshape." He caught my head between mutton-chop hands. "Boy, you're good. Work at it. You could do it."

My hands had just healed from my wounds at the docks. I pulled back. "Sir, I think not."

He glowered. "How d'you think I paid for those books, eh? Your kit? Your horse, the Arabian? You did for me, I did for you. Once more, eh?"

I understood. What I'd seen as kindness was simply repayment. He'd bet on me, won, and spent some of his windfall on my education. If I ever owed him a debt, it was paid.

I repeated, "No, sir."

"Dammit, Jim!" he growled. "You don't know whom I've got lined up for the fight! Magnificent fellow—champion boxer! The prince of Ranjpoot!"

I stared. "Seth Nur Akbar Suleiman?" That was why Akbar's shape seemed familiar—the shape of a boxer.

Sutton grinned. "That's the chap. Won't come to Bombay, so it will be an hour out, at Palghar, a neighboring independency."

My God. Here was a way to smoke him out! Having lost his ship, Akbar would take the fight to repair his finances. "You've asked him? Does he know my name?"

Sutton chuckled. "He's to fight the best we could put up. You're ex-army but you'll do." He grinned. "So it's yes? Good lad."

CHAPTER 59

DIANA'S CONJECTURE

Diana seethed, her shoulders stiff as she sat between Adi and her mother in the Gharry carriage. "Captain, how could you?" Her voice throbbed with . . . worry? No, something more . . . dread?

Casting a quick look my way, Adi cautioned, "Diana!"

"A boxing match, Adi? Papa, do you think he should do it? With an injured shoulder!" Diana's voice shook. Biting her lip, she gazed out of the window as Mrs. Framji made a shushing motion with her hands.

"The Captain must do as he likes," growled Burjor, giving me the impression that he disliked Sutton's plan intensely.

I explained, "Sir, Colonel Sutton taught me to box. Regiments put up their fellows against each other. Bets are placed. It's an annual competition. Keeps the lads fit, well trained, pride in their colors, that sort of thing."

"Did you win?" asked Adi.

I grinned a reply, then saw that Diana was close to tears. Already upset, she would be livid if she knew my opponent. Yet if there was a chance to bring Akbar to justice, I must take it and put an end to his vendetta against the Framjis. It was a long ride back to the house.

Diana sailed into the morning room, flung her gloves on the table and rounded on me. "Captain, he's using you!"

Mrs. Framji clutched her husband's arm as she and Burjor exchanged a look. Although I'd seen Diana on a tirade before, her flushed cheeks and fiery eyes disconcerted me. On edge, she went to the window and back, her steps stiff and jerky as she crossed the room.

"Go to bed, Diana," said Mrs. Framji, then bid me good night.

"Captain, Adi, it's late," said Burjor, raising his eyebrows toward me, charging Adi to be Diana's chaperone. In her present volatile state, it surprised me that her parents would depart. Reminded of the late hour, I knew I should leave. But first I'd try to calm the lady's fears.

Once her parents had left, I asked, "Miss Diana, what's the matter?"

Her pallor sharp against her dark velvet, Diana said, "My God. You really don't know."

What could she mean?

She whispered, "Your father. Your lousy, rotten father. Colonel bloody Sutton."

I felt chilled, as though my fingers had touched stone and found it icy. Sutton? She was upset about Colonel Sutton? Why had she called him my father?

"Did you not know?" Her voice broke. "He calls you my boy all the time! Jim, just look at him!"

I saw him in my mind's eye. Colonel Sutton stood as tall as I and with a similar build. He had a boxer's square chin and thick neck. But my hair was dark, his the color of honey. I considered the set of his eyes, his jaw, his forehead, how he laid his hands upon my shoulders at every opportunity. I'd seen this as a mark of favor. I'd delighted in it.

"He said nothing," I said, and knew I lied.

Why else had he hired tutors to teach me math, Latin and French? If all he needed was a boxer, why send away for books, fill the evenings talking of Nelson and Trafalgar? Why teach me wayfaring and quiz me on history? He'd seen my love of horses and made it so I joined the Dragoons as an ensign. When I had no means to buy a mare, he gave me one. Not just a mare, but Mullicka, a magnificent Arabian. He'd been a father after all, without ever claiming me as his own. Was he, in fact, my father?

Diana hissed, all hurt and fury. "Colonel Sutton! That man is rotten. Poison! He wants to bet on you like a prize horse. That's all you are to him!" She winced. "Please. You can't fight. Remember what Jameson said. Remember your shoulder! If you hurt it again, oh God!"

She stepped close, beseeching. Adi stepped up, frowning his concern.

The chamber spun around me. I dropped into a chair and gazed at them, two siblings so close to each other, and so distant from me.

"I don't want to, my dear," I said, "but I have to end this. Akbar cannot be allowed to snatch whom he pleases. He took Chutki. Next, he may take a shot at one of you. I can't wait for that. McIntyre has no jurisdiction in Ranjpoot, so he cannot arrest Akbar there. This fight has a large winner's purse. Side bets are enormous. It will lure Akbar out."

"Akbar?" Diana whispered, her voice raw. "You'll fight Prince Suleiman? Damn you, Jim!" Tearing from Adi's side, she fled the room.

I watched her go and feared that this time she might not understand. I had to finish this, once and for all. I was doing it for Diana. But would it cost me her affection?

* * *

At breakfast the next day, Diana seemed quiet and watchful. I explained that the match would be held in Palghar, just outside Bombay. I'd take the train there the night before.

Diana said, "Palghar? I don't like it. Things aren't always what they seem."

Engrossed in his textbook, Adi nodded absently. Called by her mother, Diana left, sending me a glance of worry mixed with some emotion I could not name—one so intense it sharpened her gaze and set her shoulders to soldierly stiffness. This message, if indeed it was one, puzzled me for I could not fathom what she was warning me against.

It got me thinking. She'd suggested Akbar might be at the Ripon Club, and the editor Byram had helped me get in—and then I'd been attacked by Akbar's thugs. The concierge had marked me, sure. I recalled quizzing him at the register—the guest book, by a telephone. How had Akbar put a plan together so quickly? Who'd revealed my steps to him?

I stiffened. Could Byram be a part of this affair? His paper had surely benefited from the tumult and publicity over the girls' deaths. Was it all an act, his charming smile, debonair dash and flair?

A frisson of fear ran over my skin. Not Byram, surely? He was Burjor's particular friend. Such betrayal would wound Burjor. I could only imagine how deeply it would cut Adi.

I recalled a morning Adi and I had met Byram at breakfast. He was reading the papers as I complimented Mrs. Framji on her crepes.

Overcome, Mrs. Framji had broken into sobs. "Pilloo loved crepes," was all she could say. While Adi and I exchanged looks of sympathy, Tom Byram crouched beside the sobbing mother, his arm about her shoulders. Head bent to hers, he whispered consolation. Could a man of such sensitivity plot to murder his friend's children?

But wait. If he had something to do with it, would he have offered me a hundred rupees to solve the mystery? Or was that done simply to bolster his role as Burjor's friend? His distress as he crouched by Mrs. Framji was real. Surely that was him, Tom Byram without his layers of sophistication.

Yet, all along, someone had known my movements and told Akbar.

I cleared my throat and drew Adi's attention.

"Adi, I'm afraid we must set a trap for your friend Tom Byram."

"What! Byram?" Adi sprang up. "Uncle Tom?"

"Akbar has known our plans as soon as we make them," I explained. "I was ambushed on Princess Street—a simple matter, if one simply waited for a gentleman, as I was dressed that day, a gentleman of my height, coming from the Ripon Club. Byram knew I'd go there, since he'd proposed the ruse himself. I was supposed to ask for him, wasn't I? What better way to identify me? While I was laid up with injuries, Akbar the burglar visits by night—a perfect time to search Framji Mansion. When I left for Lahore—on the last train, mind—would Byram not know that Lahore was already under attack? Convenient for Akbar if I'd been trapped there."

Adi groaned. "No, Captain, not Byram!"

Again I remembered Byram's face, consoling Mrs. Framji, his compassion for her grief. What did it mean?

"Did he have a close friendship with your mother, before she wed?"

Adi breathed in, an audible gasp. "They're distant cousins. He's twenty years older, so they couldn't marry." He shook his head, "Captain, it can't be him. He'd give his life for her."

I considered that. "It is a capital mistake to theorize before you have all the evidence. It biases the judgement," I recited.

"Holmes, no doubt," said Adi, glum.

"Mm. I'll craft a test for our friend Byram."

That evening when Tom Byram arrived, I saw a chance to put my plan in action.

"Hello, Tom, will you stay for dinner later?" said Adi.

"'Course, my boy! I heard—a midnight raid! A slave ship! A rescue! Marvelous news—what headlines we'll make," Tom Byram cried, shaking Adi's hand. He kissed Diana's cheek, complimenting her purple silk, then came round to me, holding out a large hand. "The man of the hour. Captain, you've done us proud."

Bloody Byram. Right. Time to see where his loyalty lay.

Taking his hand, I said, "No report, sir. That was our deal. None."

His eyes bulged. "Now wait . . . Surely you don't mean . . . ?"

I tightened my grip. "You said, ask for you at the Ripon Club. An hour later, the Ranjpoot gang accosted me. While I'm in Matheran, you printed details of my investigation—and blew my cover. Got me a ticket to Lahore, and it's the last train—I'm stranded in the middle of a war. You've been helping Akbar. What did he promise? Land? Mining rights?"

Tom Byram's mouth dropped. His lips trembled, the hand in mine shook. Shocked grey eyes holding mine, he staggered.

"But I . . . no. You can't mean that." His voice creaked like old leather. "The Ripon Club . . . no, my boy . . ."

There is a moment when a liar knows he is found out, a moment I knew well. It's written in his eyes, even before I'm done speaking. His eyelids flicker, his face slackens and for an instant his mask drops. I have seen hate, naked and wild, in such men, arrogance and fury. How quickly they spin to accusation or pretense.

"No." Byram looked shaken to the core, but no flicker of awareness came. His weight fell against my arm, and I knew that I'd been wrong.

I helped him to a chair. "I'm sorry, sir."

Adi and Burjor looked appalled. Their friend had aged ten years in just minutes. Diana knelt beside the old man, comforting. "Dear Uncle, it was a test. You passed, of course!"

Byram peered up, his fingers plucking at my sleeve. "Captain. The burglary . . ." he choked, his composure shredded. "I wrote about it. An excuse . . . for your bruises. We were going to have a dance. The rest . . . it wasn't me."

"I see that, sir," I said, repentant.

"Then who?" His jaw dropped. His voice wobbled, uncertain. "No. It can't be."

"Someone who works for you?" asked Adi.

"I'm sorry, Captain." The veins bulging at his temple, Byram clutched my forearm. "It must be my new assistant. He came from the south. Perhaps from Ranjpoot! I didn't realize."

Blast. I had misjudged badly. I patted his hand, giving him a moment to regroup.

Diana's breath hissed in a slow release. She hated breaking things . . . and I had just done as much damage as one can without physical violence. Her saree had been draped over her head, and dropped to her shoulder when she comforted him. As she scooped a handful of silk off her shoulder to pin it over her hair, the smooth skin of her arm, that pointed elbow made me ache.

Crouched beside Byram, I vowed that, come what may, I would see her safe. I'd seen her fight for her place among the Framjis, not a jewel on display but as an equal. God knows I tried to stay distant, to keep myself aloof, but it scarcely mattered where I was. When I was alone, when the world around me paused, my mind returned to her.

"Hm." Byram caught me watching her and exhaled, sorrow drooping his tired face. He left immediately afterwards.

Later, when it was just me and the siblings, I recalled Diana's obscure warning.

"Miss Diana," I said, "you said things aren't what they seem. Did you also suspect Byram?"

She looked startled. "Uncle Tom? Heavens, no! He'd give his life for us."

"So your warning—what did you mean?"

Diana bit her lip, shaking her head. "Jim, people hide things—for all sorts of reasons. You taught me that. Why must you go to Palghar?"

She'd been fretting about my boxing match. A surge of affection lifted me. I cast a glance at Adi and glimpsed the shadow of a smile cross his face. Picking up his textbooks, Adi gave us the morning room, saying, "I'll be next door," a not-so-subtle reminder to maintain a proper distance.

How we talked—her childhood, my years in Burma and the Frontier province—each subject flowed into the next. Diana sparkled, giggling at my tales, telling me her own: escapades, visits to the London School of Medicine for Women. Diana spoke little of her stay in England, but asked me instead about my childhood. When the grandfather clock chimed twelve, I said goodbye, but it was another hour before I left.

She'd known most of my awful history—the rest? How could I tell, when I scarcely knew what was real and what imagined? I did not expect her to understand. But she listened closely, repeating, "Jim, let it go. It's in the past."

CHAPTER 60

BURJOR'S EDICT

That night I dropped into bed, and slipped into a dreamless sleep.

Awakened by parakeets sparring in the lavender dawn, I stretched and grinned, remembering the events of last evening. In the clear light of morning, I relived our conversation, hearing the inflection of Diana's voice, how she signaled curiosity with a sharp tilt to her head. When we spoke of Karachi, I recalled her staunch defense, marveling, buoyed by my relief and elated.

Tonight, I decided. Tonight, I would speak with Burjor and ask his leave to court Diana. He'd forbade it before—but could I change his mind? I'd do whatever he asked. As for the matter of funds, McIntyre's offer of a job could be just the ticket. How much did a police detective earn? I resolved to find out.

Dressing quickly, I went through my usual drill. My knee ached and grumbled, but the shoulder held up all right. Sutton's fight would soon be upon me, so I returned to the gym and spent the rest of the morning being pummeled by younger men. Blocking, weaving, ducking, taking blows on my shoulders and arms—these absorbed me. When I failed to slip the punch, a sharp knock ensured my full attention.

At the gymkhana, I received a note from Maneck requesting an immediate meeting. I found him waiting at my warehouse, looking glum.

"Akbar was seen at the racecourse," he said. "His men laid bets on the upcoming fight. Made quite a statement, all decked out in finery."

It took a while to reassure him. After he departed at noon, I returned to Framji Mansion, called for hot water and spent an hour soaking in a claw-foot tub before Gurung came to dress me for lunch. Ah, the joys of luxury, I thought, as he held out a clean linen shirt and buttoned on a pair of cuffs.

Once we arrested Akbar at the boxing match, my case would be complete. Only the incriminating letter remained—if I could find it, the Framjis would be safe. Still, I could not, in good conscience, continue to live with them. I'd take McIntyre's job and move out of my warehouse hideaway. Chin tilted for Gurung to knot my tie, I resolved to settle accounts with Adi and find suitable lodgings.

In the dining room, Adi smiled a welcome. Handing me a glass of sherry, he said, "New developments, Captain! Byram's discovered how Akbar was getting our plans."

"Found the leak, did he?" I said, sipped and straightened. "Compliments on your father's cellar."

Adi grinned. "Yes," he added, somewhat apologetically, "Byram's new man traded titbits for cash. The blackguard begged our pardon, didn't know anyone would be hurt. . . ."

It did not surprise me: greasing a few palms was the norm, utterly unremarkable. "Just made a pretty penny, eh?" I caught a footfall at the door and swung around.

Looking peeved, Burjor huffed a greeting, then lowered his weight into his chair.

Adi asked, "Are Mama and Diana out for luncheon?"

"Diana won't join us. Mama and she are . . . busy," Burjor said, signaling to Gurung at the door. Lunch was served right away, a splendid swordfish, eggs fried on a bed of spinach, but the air held awkward silences.

"Is something amiss, sir?" I asked, after a particularly long pause. "Perhaps I can help."

My words caused an alarming change in Burjor. His wide face creased in an expression of pain. I feared he'd had a seizure.

"Papa!" Adi cried, leaping to his feet. "What's happened?"

"Sit, Adi. Sit," Burjor ground out, flushed, jowls shaking. "Captain Jim," he sighed. "No. I cannot allow it. After all we have been through—it's too much. The scandal. The papers. People talking. Mama should not have to endure that again."

"Sir?"

"Diana and you," he said, shaking his head.

"What's happened, sir?"

"I met Colonel Sutton at the Governor's. Sutton asked when we're going to announce Diana's engagement to you."

Sutton. That evening after the theater, he'd seen what Diana meant to me, and in his ruddy red-coat blundering, managed to cock it up.

I drew a sharp breath. "I intended to ask your blessing today."

Burjor winced. "You are a good man, Captain," he said. "I'm sorry."

I felt at a loss. "Sir, I care for her . . . deeply."

"Young man, you don't understand . . . a great deal is at stake! The scandal! The Parsees, my brethren, will cease doing business with us."

So that was the end of it? He would not give me leave to court Diana, fearing the scandal it would cause. That's why Diana had not joined us today.

Throat parched, the sherry sour upon my lips, I asked, "May I speak with her?"

"No, Captain," he said, his voice pained. "Best not."

Had he forbidden her to see me? I strove to muster a righteous indignation, but found none. I gaped at him, wanting to persuade, to protest, to rail at this injustice, and could not. His forehead rested upon clasped hands in an attitude of distress that moved me. He was protecting his own. Had he been cold, unfeeling, I could have hated him. Had he pronounced a judgement upon my head, it was easy to reject. But his sorrow, his need to spare his wife further torment, how could I fault that?

* * *

The next week I bunked at Smith's, spending every waking hour at the officers' boxing gymkhana. Although my quandary remained, the match was upon me, so I put my all into preparing for it. The gymkhana afforded a measure of privacy, a gifted Chinese masseur and an excellent hot tub.

Over tedious, painful hours, I rebuilt muscle, gained speed and precision. Eventually, my shoulder proved a greater nuisance than my knee; Jameson scowled at me when next I presented myself.

"When's the fight?" he asked, his hand tight on my chin as he examined a swelling under my eye.

"Two weeks," I mumbled.

"Damn it, lad," Jameson said, probing my shoulder. "Once dislocated, the joint is weak. You understand it could dislocate again, or even break!"

"There's a chance I won't have to fight."

He examined my injured knee as he muttered something about ". . . damn fools who don't know what's good for them." Then he asked, in a clipped voice, "It's Akbar?"

"Yes. He won't be able to stay away. Once he shows, McIntyre will arrest him."

When he was done, I tugged on my shirt. "My shoulder, will it hold?"

He rummaged with his bottles of powders, poured some out and mixed a concoction on a sheet of paper. "One teaspoon, dissolved in milk, twice a day. Build up the bone fast enough," he said, folding it into a packet. "I plan to bet on you."

Pocketing his medication, I grinned at that note of confidence.

"Good," he said, tossing me a tin box emblazoned with the words West Indies Cigar Company. "That's for Framji Senior! See that he gets it tonight."

* * *

At seven o'clock that evening, dressed up and polished like a ceremonial sabre, I trotted up the white stairs and stepped into Framji Mansion again.

I had glimpsed Diana only once last week as she leaned from a carriage that passed me at the gate. While I ached for the sight of her, I dreaded it too, for wanting it too much. I had honored her father's wishes, weighed them greater than my fondness for her sharp wit, her ready compassion, my joy in her smile. And yet, faced with the prospect of telling her so, I balked. I needed to see her, to explain.

As I entered the foyer, Diana slipped out of the morning room. Her blue dress swirled against her ankles. "Captain Jim. I hoped you'd come."

Was she waiting for me? Captain, she'd said, her manner subdued. I felt heavy with regret. "Miss Diana," I said, returning to formal address. Her hair was piled up, as it had been at her ball. "Is there a soiree tonight?"

"No. I've something to tell you. Come." She caught my hand and tugged me to a small door. I followed, mystified, into a chamber without windows, ten feet across. Diana fiddled with a lamp, turned it up and closed the door, saying, "It's the coat room. That side opens to the ball-room."

Having her near was to drink after weeks in the desert. Those delicate fingers, now clenched at her side in folds of pale blue. Her arms, slender and so perfectly shaped, her softly heaving bosom. A pulse flickered in the indentation of her neck. Jewels trembled at her earlobe to send blue flashes flying on the wall.

Diana searching my face, wide eyes dark and questioning.

"Jim, have I done something awful?"

Startled, I said, "No. Why d'you ask?"

Diana winced. "You look so stern. And you've a bruise, there." She pointed to my cheekbone. "I haven't seen you in so long."

"Your father . . ." I began.

She caught my hand, her fingers cool against my skin. "I know. Oh Jim. I'm so sorry."

Her touch unlocked me. I breathed in the sight of her. She knew, and mourned what could not be.

"What did you want to tell me?"

Diana said quietly, "Ranjpoot. Akbar is to be king. His coronation is set for October."

It was the first I'd heard of it. "Is the Rani dead?"

"No. This isn't in the papers. Akbar plans to take the throne," she whispered.

I bent to her. "How do you know?"

Her skin blushed deep rose, from her bosom to the peak of her fore-head.

"At the Petits' last night, when the men went off to smoke, I made an excuse and . . . hid on the balcony outside the smoking room. Overheard the Ministry man tell McIntyre. Akbar's made arrangements to pay the inheritance tax." She broke off and said, "Oh Jim. You're angry with me. I know I shouldn't have. But I had to do something. No one will tell me about you."

Diana had snooped, hoping for news of me.

"I'm not angry." I remembered the gift of cigars in my breast pocket. "Diana, did you speak with Doctor Jameson?"

She bit her lip. "I had to. Just to know you're well."

She had visited the infirmary, alone by the sound of it, to ask Jameson about me. That was why he seemed so exasperated with me. Jameson had seen how it was with her, and sent me to the Framjis with the box of cigars as a pretext. That crafty sod. I owed him!

"Diana."

She looked startled. "Are you all right? You look strange."

The devil with it, I thought. She was the sparkle in my world, the one I waited to tell my discoveries to, whose opinion I valued even over Adi's. With her, each moment turned magical, anticipated all day and savored the next. Not for anything would I cause her parents harm. But I loved Diana—would they not reconcile to it?

"Diana, may I ask you a question?"

I threaded my fingers through hers.

When she said, "Thank heaven," I could no longer hold back. "Diana, I love you. Marry me, sweetheart."

CHAPTER 61

DISCOVERY

Diana looked stunned.

I hurried to explain. "I have some prospects now. McIntyre's come through with the job. Wants me to take an exam next year. Try for a promotion. We'd be all right. Not as grand as this, but comfortable."

"Jim," Diana said, breathing hard, a hand to her lips. "When Cornelia Sorabji's father married a Christian lady and converted, his family cast him out. I've always been proud to be born Parsee. But now . . . I wouldn't be allowed in the Fire-Temple. My friends won't let me in their homes."

I had found a way to earn a living and finance our future, but if we wed, I would gain, and she would lose. How had I not seen this?

I winced. "Does it matter so much to you?"

"Jim, there's more." She struggled with the words, clutching my fingers. "What's worse . . . is to care for someone who . . . lives dangerously. It eats at me, from the inside. I don't know if I can live like that."

What was she saying? Was this about Lahore or Pathankot? Or even Karachi? No, this was about me being a detective, about boxing, she was talking about who I was. She thought I had an appetite for danger!

So it was no.

I'd not known I could hurt like that. Fool that I was, I'd convinced myself I did not hope, but I'd been lying to myself.

She clutched my arm. "Jim. Look at me."

She wanted to see my pain? I met her gaze, hid nothing.

"Jim, no! Don't you see? Despite everything, I have to see you. I need to see you. We'll find a way." Her lips parted in a sad smile. "I care for you, too."

Incredible. Her softness filled my arms, my face against her hair, and for a while, words were unnecessary.

Diana said, "Jim, when you attacked the burglar, I suspected. That you . . . cared. I couldn't quite believe it. These last weeks, after we quarreled, I was miserable." She glanced up, anxious. "I hoped, then. But Papa laid down the law. Jim, I felt so lost. Keeping up appearances, as though nothing's happened. Pretending. It's been awful."

Holding her close, I said, dryly, "Byram covered every soiree. Usually on page four . . . society matters. Described your dresses, whom you danced with."

Her head tucked under my chin, she chuckled at the idea of me scouring the gossip pages. Her soft laugh lifted like mist from a waterfall. We had a chance! Somehow, I had to convince Burjor, find some way to persuade him. Would Adi help me plead my case?

"Jim, this will cause a huge to-do," Diana said. "When we tell my parents—I dread it. If only it was just the two of us. But it will affect everyone."

Her delicate face mirrored each emotion. I nodded, feeling reluctance reflected in her grip. Like her, I wanted to preserve this precious moment, place fortifications around it, secure it somehow—it was so new, so fragile.

"Let's keep this for us, Jim. Just for a while, until I'm . . . not so afraid?"

"Afraid?" I asked. That dratted letter still hung over the Framjis like a specter. Was there something else as well?

"Jim, when we tell them, it will all blow up. Then there's the boxing match. With Akbar. Must you do it? It terrifies me. When you fought him on the balcony, I couldn't breathe. I stepped through the door and you were just feet away. I heard every punch, the sound of it, like a butcher's shop!" She shuddered.

I winced. "Sweetheart."

It was far too late to pull out of the fight, but Chief McIntyre would arrest Akbar and call it off. That was the plan. Perhaps I would not need to fight, I thought, remembering the speed, the heft, the weight of Akbar's blows—he was an ox.

Diana's words sparked a memory—Akbar's shadow passing my window. No hesitation there. He'd known where to go. But what was he actually doing? I'd feared he intended to harm Diana, thought him mistaken, because he stopped at an unoccupied bedroom. But what if Kasim told Akbar where to find that letter? Kasim's hiding place . . . must be in easy reach. How would he escape notice getting to it?

"Pilloo used to hear monkeys on the roof?"

Diana's brow puckered. "Jim, are you feeling all right?"

I touched the pesky curl that bounced by her ear, brushed her soft cheek with the back of my fingers. Was Kasim's hiding place on the roof?

If I found that blasted letter and ended this business, wouldn't Burjor relent? I cupped Diana's cheek, reluctant to break this sweet moment. Here in our secret nook it was just the two of us, a haven sheltering us from the turmoil outside, the storm we'd need to face—could I find a harbor for us?

"Diana, sweetheart, being here with you—it's the happiest I've ever been. Now there's something I must do. Give me a moment, will you?"

Smiling at her astonishment, I traced the softness of her jaw. "Meet me in the morning room. And fetch Adi."

I hurried up the rear stairway to the outer corridor, where I'd fought Akbar that night. His hand had been over the doorframe.

Reaching up, I traced along the curved terra-cotta tiles and felt something move. One was loose. It came away easily. My fingers touched something cold and square. Metal. Pulse hammering, I lifted out a rectangular purple box inscribed with the words Mackintosh's Toffee De Luxe.

CHAPTER 62

THE MISSING LETTER

Miss Pilloo's purloined letter? Lady Bacha had kept household cash in just such a tin box. Curious that both ladies chose similar containers for their valuables!

My pulse thrummed as I slipped the box into my pocket and returned to the morning room. There, Diana and Adi appeared in the midst of an argument. Seeing me, they broke off. Ah! It was about us, Diana and me. Would Adi also oppose our union?

He gave me a wry smile. "I've known for a while, Captain. I spoke to Papa again, but it's no use. My parents dread another scandal."

I knew this, but hearing it ached like a blow upon a wound that was not quite healed.

"Ah. Well, this will interest you." I handed him the purple box. "It was hidden under a tile in the roof—Miss Pilloo's letter, perhaps?"

"Jim," he breathed, "You've read it?"

I shook my head. "Found it a minute ago."

Hinges rusted from many monsoons, the box would not open. Adi used a letter opener to pry it apart. His fingers shook as he extracted an envelope. Fixing his glasses firmly on his nose, he said, frowning. "But . . . this has nothing to do with Pilloo or Bacha! It's from our grandfather to Pilloo's papa, my uncle. Jim, our grandfather died thirty years ago!" He pressed open the folded paper, then looked up. "It's in Gujarati . . . faded . . . I can barely read this. Diana, call Papa. And Mother too. They need to see this."

Shortly after, Burjor hunched over the letter, scouring each page, the letters washed out with age. Mouthing words as he read, he translated for us with painful care.

Two hundred mutineers we called to assembly,
My brothers came, and lined up proper.
They had rifles but no cartridges from ordnance that day.
The command was given. We turned and fired.
Like soft wax, they dropped, limp, still in their ranks.
The rest we tied to cannon, and tore to shreds.

All along the Gwalior road, we marched and no one spoke.
Each tree bore a terrible burden.
My dear, I hope to never see such a thing again.
The mutineers, men, boys, Sepoys, some still wearing our uniforms.
Hung each upon a tree, swaying.
We walked under them, mile upon mile in silence.

"What does it mean?" Diana whispered. "The army? Rebels? Who hanged them?"

His brow creased, Burjor touched the delicate pages. "My father served in the British army during 1857 and '58. It was a terrible time, Diana.

"In Meerut, the Thirty-fourth Bengal Native Infantry rebelled and shot their British officers. Other regiments joined the uprising! Bombay remained loyal to the British, but in Jhansi and Awadh thousands of farmers joined the rebel Sepoys. They asked the old Mughal emperor, Bahadur Shah, to lead them. The Rani of Jhansi brought her army . . . Jagdishpur too. A Peshwa general brought his Maratha army, determined to take back control of India. My father's regiment, Sixty-third Lancers, was dispatched to hunt down these rebels."

He tapped the pages, frowning. "He's written of the things he saw and did. Awful things. He says the army caught sixteen thousand men and boys," Burjor said. "My father calls the mutineers 'my brothers.' He served in the regiment who executed them. Civilians . . . entire villages, he says, townsfolk who pleaded, weeping like babies. Shot, point-blank. He . . . mourns them. This is a sort of a confession."

"Sixteen thousand?" Adi's hushed voice broke in. "I've never heard of this!"

Burjor replied. "It's not widely known. Thirty-four years ago the army was run by the East India Company. After this, the Crown took over."

Diana said, "Thousands of people were slaughtered, Papa? Was there a trial? Was anyone held responsible?"

Burjor shook his head. "Indians don't speak of it." He straightened, looking at me. "Perhaps it's time we did."

Finding myself in the position of defending the army I had served, I said, "Wait. That's not the whole story. Officers used to talk about this. The Rani of Jhansi and the Peshwa army attacked a British camp at Cawnpore. Nine hundred British soldiers, their families and servants . . . three weeks they held out, then surrendered. They were given safe passage. But while they were boarding the boats to safety, the rebels fired on them. Many died right there. Survivors were clubbed to death."

Mrs. Framji shuddered, fingers pressed to her lips.

I continued, "The women and children were taken to Bibi-ghar, imprisoned there, two hundred of them. Then the last straw . . . just as General Havelock's troops approached to rescue them, the mutineers butchered the women—with swords and sabres, children too, their bodies thrown into a well. It devastated the British soldiers." I sighed into the shocked silence. "That's why the reprisal . . . was so harsh."

Diana winced. It was easy to denounce one side as the enemy, when one did not have all the facts. Harder when both sides were vicious, inhuman in their callous slaughter. How did one pick a side then? Diana looked peaked as she caught my glance, a question in her haunted eyes. Were the rebels patriots or cruel fiends? How could they be both?

Burjor nodded. "Such violence on both sides. But this—" He tapped the letter. "Indians need to know what happened. It was hushed up."

"Papa," said Adi, on his feet, eyes wide. "It's worse than that. This contradicts the army's version of events, that the mutineers were shot while trying to escape. Grandpa's called the official story a lie! This letter is . . . sedition!"

Treason.

The word hung between us, an unexploded shell.

The Framjis turned to me, the ladies worried, Adi questioning. Did he really expect me to jump up with a cry of "traitors"?

When I simply met Adi's look, he nodded, understanding that I stood with him.

Thick eyebrows knotted, Burjor cleared his throat to say, "My father wrote this to tell the truth, to leave some evidence of what really happened."

I asked, "Did he come back? After the mutiny?"

"No. He died of malaria on the campaign. I was fifteen years old. My older brother, Pilloo's father, took Papa's place. During the influenza epidemic he must have given the letter to Pilloo, as Kasim said. He would not want this"—he tapped the letter—"to fall into the wrong hands. That's why he warned her to keep it safe."

I asked, "Miss Pilloo could read Gujarati?"

Adi nodded. "We were all taught. She might have read enough to be worried about its meaning."

Diana asked, "Did she think Grandpa joined the mutiny? That he was a rebel?"

Adi said, "Perhaps. But when she showed the letter to Kasim, he took it from her!"

I nodded. "It's possible. He surely understood its value to Pilloo." I frowned. "So why did Kasim leave it behind? Why not take it to Lahore?"

Burjor cleared his throat. "Because I gave him no time. When I told him I was sending him to the brick factory in Lahore, he made a fuss, became rather violent. So I . . . decided not to delay. Sent him off to Lahore that very afternoon."

"And Akbar?" asked Diana, "What did he want with it?"

I said, "It was bait, I think. Although the letter was still hidden under that tile, Akbar pretended to have it to lure the ladies into his trap."

"He killed my girls," Mrs. Framji said bitterly. "But that night . . . did he come to find this letter? Why?"

"So he could blackmail Papa!" said Diana. "Any of us!"

I wondered whether Akbar might have had another motive. I'd met him in Ranjpoot, though he did not recognize me. What had he said? "Bloody British, who needs them?"

I cleared my throat and said, "I think . . . he wants to raise support against the British, even stage another uprising. That would require funds, yes. But it would also need something to catch popular interest, set people afire! A cause to rally around—this letter could do it! Sixteen thousand Sepoys and farmers killed without trial, the murder of prisoners, all hushed up. Kasim must have grasped enough from reading this letter. Akbar knew it could be a useful weapon."

Burjor stared. "Uprising? Captain, you're calling him a nationalist! A patriot!"

"But he abducted women!" Outraged, Adi scoffed. "His own countrymen, sold them into slavery! What kind of patriot is that?"

Was Adi, like many educated young men these days, thinking about Indian home rule and independence? Akbar, however, was far more impatient. More, he was a law unto himself.

I said, "Akbar's sort believes the end justifies the means. He wants a return to Indian monarchy."

"Pshaw!" Burjor scoffed. "The question is, what should we do?"

Mrs. Framji spoke for the first time, her voice strained. "Do, Burjor? With the letter?"

"We have a duty to the truth," Burjor said. He pointed at the small recess in the wall. "Our dharam—our religion bids us so."

"Burjor, no!" Mrs. Framji whispered.

Adi sprang to his feet. "Papa, if this gets out, you're finished. It wasn't our doing, but we'll all be called traitors."

Burjor shook his head slowly. "Even that is small, compared with the truth."

Silence stretched and held as father and son faced each other, one pale and frantic, the other pained, but resolute. Searching for a middle ground,

I went to the alcove where Burjor made his offerings—a silver chalice lay there, containing wood and ash. This I brought to the table and placed between Adi and his father.

Religion. It was central to life in India, with all its festivals and rituals, but I had never seen it put above one's livelihood, or loved ones, or their very life.

Adi said, "Papa, let's weigh this. It's one man's word against scores on the other side. And thirty-five years too late to help those mutineers."

"What should I do?" Burjor muttered.

"Destroy it," said Diana. "Papa, if you want a voice on the Governor's council, this cannot come out. Burn it. Right away, so it can't be used against us."

Shoulders hunched over the letter, Burjor contemplated the paper on which his father's spidery handwriting was fading.

I said, "Sir, Akbar may try to get hold of this letter again. He may have told others about it. As long as it exists, it's a threat. It's my job to protect you—let me do that."

I searched the faces of the Framji clan. I had come to care for them, each in a different way: Burjor, the patriarch, tormented by the choice before him; Adi, fists clenched, pleading; Mrs. Framji, imploring her husband; and Diana? Diana smiled at me.

"No," Burjor said at last. "I cannot burn it. But I will lock it up, until a time when all of this is past. Someday, your children's children have a right to know."

"If we ever seek independence," said Adi, "it should be for the future, not over the past."

Burjor agreed, saying, "Captain, you've been a friend. Protecting us, even from me!"

The surprise in his voice broke the tension among us. Diana's laugh rang out like bells welcoming the New Year.

The mysterious letter found, now all that remained was to arrest Akbar, the devious princeling.

CHAPTER 63

PURPLE MILKWEED FLOWERS

On the Saturday of the match I came early to the boxing hall. My friends were already gathered in the room set aside for contestants. Having been my second many times, Major Smith was in his element as he sat me down to knead my neck and arms.

Superintendent McIntyre repeated his instructions. "Your job is to get Akbar talking. We'll stay out of sight, listen for twenty minutes—that's all. Think you can do it?"

"I'll give it a damned good shot."

Seeing my opponent's carriage arrive in the courtyard, my companions hurried out the side entrance, leaving me alone. Akbar entered with his entourage, saw me and stopped dead.

His attendants hurried past, laying out his things. One put a garland of purple and red flowers on the table, preparing for victory. At the other end of the long room, I rolled my head right and left to stay limber.

"You!" Akbar sneered, thunderous eyebrows and kohled eyes giving him the look of a dacoit prince. In a red satin robe belted with gold rope, all six feet of him was untamed muscle and pride.

"Hullo," I said, lacing up my shoes for the fight. Smith would wrap my hands and help me don my gloves. Gloves were mandatory now, since we followed the Marquess of Queensberry rules. McIntyre had given me twenty minutes to tease a confession from Akbar. He could delay the match only so long. After that, betting closed and the fight would commence. Wagers were high, odds two to one favoring Akbar. Given my history of injury, that was rather generous. Blast, I was in no shape to go against him.

"I know you," Akbar said, in perfectly accented English, as his attendant worked his shoulders with gusto.

"Yes," I agreed. Dressed as a missionary, I'd met him in Ranjpoot. I doubted that he knew that was me. No, he was thinking of our fight on the deck of *Vahid Cruiser*, where he'd downed me and escaped.

"Captain James Agnihotri," he said with an urbane grin, "formerly of the Fourteenth Bombay Regiment, Dragoons. War hero. Injured in Karachi."

I heard the word "Karachi," but no picture swamped my mind, no numbing chill of terror. Nightmares still crept through the windows of my sleep, but hearing the dreaded word no longer squeezed my breath away. Well, now! Diana and Adi were right. I was done hiding from it.

"Yes." I watched Akbar. What did he make of my cool acknowledgement?

Brows haughty, he glowered, assessing me, then snapped to his guards, "Leave us!"

I had to prod Akbar, get him talking, and provoke a confession. Keeping a conversational tone, I asked, "I'm curious. The women on the ship. Why did you abduct them?"

Akbar gave me an affronted stare. Had he denied it, I might have thought less of him. Instead, a corner of his mouth twitched. Then a smile widened across his handsome face.

"Trying to rattle me, Captain?" he chuckled, showing his disdain for such a ploy. "I'm going to beat you to a pulp."

"Maybe," I said, "but why go after the women? Don't you have enough in Ranjpoot?"

His smile dimmed. He shook his head and brushed aside my barb. "You know nothing."

"You're probably right. So tell me. How did it start?"

When Akbar looked at me coldly, I said, "You're an educated man, an Oxford man, so why?"

Akbar strolled across to the enormous garland and pulled out a cluster of purple spikes. "Know what this is, Captain?"

He wanted to talk about flowers? "No."

"It is called purple milkweed," he said. "It makes a fine poison."

More intimidation, I thought irritably. The audience outside sounded restless. I'd have to move Akbar along quicker, but how? I asked, without irony, "You know a great deal. How's it used?"

He gave me a piercing stare. "In drink. It's given to widows, before they become suttee."

Suttee. The ritual burning of Hindu widows upon the funeral pyre of their husbands. Wasn't that archaic custom abolished long ago? What was he on about?

He saw my confusion. Amused, he said, "Did you think, because British law bans it, that it does not happen? I assure you, it does, and not just in the princely states. Well, that's where we started."

"Started what?" I said.

"Sending the women to Guyana and Demerara. Why burn them, when they're toys I could sell?" He spread his hands wide in a flourish. "I just paid off the Brahmins at the Burning Ghat. Instead of milkweed, a sleeping potion was given. Relatives removed to a distance, the woman extracted from the pyre and presto! Set it ablaze. No one's the wiser, and a grateful widow is my prize. They were so keen to escape, they boarded our ship without question."

With growing horror, I understood. He rescued women from immolation and sold them for a tidy profit.

"So what happened? Why try to take the Parsee girls?"

He shrugged. "Supply and demand. Such high demand for fair ones! Light-skinned girls fetch higher prices. Simply had to expand the hunt."

I maintained a puzzled look. "You just lift them off the street?" Like Chutki, my valiant little mite.

"You are Indian, aren't you?" he said. "Agnihotri means you are of Brahmin birth. That is the highest caste, those who tend the temple fire."

"Yes." Dressed as I was today, scruffy beard and unkempt hair, no doubt I appeared a native.

"So why join them? Why fight for the bleedin' English?"

I expressed surprise. "For the purse," I said. "A thousand rupees."

"Tsch." He dismissed it as a paltry sum. "Inquilab! Revolution! That is our destiny. For that we need gold—lots of it. Then we take back what's ours."

I drew a slow breath. This was sedition, as blatant as could be! So where was McIntyre? Had he and his constables not heard?

To keep Akbar talking, I said, "Take back . . . India?"

"Why not?" he said, in his clipped Oxford accent. "The bastards bleed us dry with taxes. Take our cotton for their factories, sell it back to us at a hundred times the price! Too good to drink with us, won't play cricket with us, who needs them? Join us, Agnihotri. Take back your motherland."

My God, he was serious. Akbar was planning another rebellion! Barely thirty years ago, thousands of Indians had paid a terrible price for just such treason. Where was McIntyre?

"How?"

"Throw this fight. Not too soon, though. Third round. There's five hundred in it for you."

Playing for time, I bargained. No Indian worth his salt settles without haggling. I shook my head. "The prize is a thousand."

He grinned. "All right, a thousand rupees if you cede."

I didn't consider it for a second but pretended to work out the mathematics of it. Where the devil was McIntyre? Akbar seemed to enjoy my hesitation.

"Two thousand, Captain!" he hissed. "Decide now!"

"No."

The bell chimed. Outside a roar went up. Akbar smirked, rolling his shoulders.

I'd got his confession, but McIntyre wasn't here to arrest him. The match was on.

* * *

By the end of the second round, I was winded. Akbar's reach exceeded mine, he had a vicious right, and he was fast. I'd kept up with him, backing away, matching blow for blow, watching for a weakness, but it cost. I was tired.

Built like an ox, he was formidable. Twice before, I'd met him, man to man, and both times come off poorly. On the dark balcony near Diana's room, he'd gotten away. When we grappled on the deck of *Vahid Cruiser*, he'd tripped me and escaped. Now he played to the crowd, enjoying their roars when his blows landed.

During introductions and reading of the Queensberry rules, I scanned the crowd for McIntyre. The Superintendent was conspicuously absent. So I boxed.

As the third round started, I took one to the head. Pain flashed. Then I glimpsed my chance. Akbar's guard dropped as he went into his favorite one-two sequence. I danced to my right, and he set up for another go. I went into the gap, and let fly. *For Bacha.*

All my weight packed into a small area on his jaw. It nearly broke my shoulder. Akbar's head snapped back, his eyes lost focus, but he didn't fall. His guard fell away, and I threw myself to doing the most damage possible.

Time. The bell rang the end of the round, breaking into my attention like a thunderclap. We broke apart.

I heard the crowd roar, saw Sutton beaming like a hungry jackal. His smile stiffened into a warning. I started to turn.

Akbar's kick caught me in the small of my back. I slammed into the dirt. Something gave way, sending a spasm down my side. Instinct cried out a warning, demanding, shrieking in my head. Pulling my elbows in, I rolled away from Akbar.

That movement carried me into the referee's knees. He tripped over me with a shout, falling forward.

Cries of "Foul!" erupted, filling the hall. Akbar had not waited for the bell to start the next round. He had followed me, so the referee tumbled into him. They dropped in a tangled heap, Akbar cursing. In the ensuing confusion I climbed to my feet.

Locking away the pain, I bounced to the side and let him come. I'd lost the capacity to duck, so I rolled with his fearsome right, and struck. *For Pilloo.* Hot pain stabbed my shoulder.

Akbar swayed. As prince he had plenty of practice meting out punishment, but few dared to pound him. And I did.

I could not feel my legs now. Each blow cost me at least as much damage as I gave. Sweat singed my eyes. I shook it away, following Akbar, moving in. More! I hit him hard, then again, putting my weight into it. *For Chutki.* My fist landed with a jolt that jarred my teeth.

Akbar slid to his knees. The referee sang out, "One, two . . ."

Jaw slack, Akbar stayed down, seeming insensible to the mounting shouts.

The crowd's roar deafened me. In my corner, both McIntyre and Sutton leapt up, curiously alike, joy and pain creasing their faces. Right, I thought, spat out blood. Time to arrest the princeling.

I turned back . . . the ring was empty! I staggered. Someone caught me about the waist. Sutton, grinning with pride. Where was Akbar? Disbelieving, I shook away the sweat crowding my eyes and searched the raucous crowd. The devil had slipped away.

"My God, Jim," said Adi, flushed, eyes sparkling. "What a fight."

I said, "Akbar. Got away."

He bent closer. "What? Can't understand you, Jim. By God, it hurt to watch you."

Someone unlaced my gloves, pulled them off. Diana cupped my hand in hers. Her tiny fingers shook. "Jim," she said, saw my eyes. "Thank heaven!"

"I'm sorry, lad," said McIntyre. His sandy mustache bristled. "Sutton went over my head. The Viceroy, you see? Said it was too late to stop the match. Told us to get him after. But Akbar's missing."

I spat out blood. Why in heaven hadn't they set a perimeter and caught the blighter? Ah, I realized, Palghar was neutral ground—and the ruler favored Akbar.

"Steady," said Doctor Jameson, out of sight. "Get that splint on him now."

"Akbar's gone? Splendid," said Sutton. "We'll have a rematch!"

Adi and McIntyre both swiveled toward him, glaring.

"All right, all right!" Sutton retreated, showing us his palms in mock surrender.

I hoped he'd wagered a fortune and made a killing on it, because winning it had nearly done me in. Akbar had slipped my trap. Again.

CHAPTER 64

PORT KARACHI REVISITED

The next day, Adi and I settled accounts, much to my advantage, since he was a generous employer. In funds at last, I rented a room at a boardinghouse near Fort Market. Since I was still recovering from the fight, Smith came by to help me move my things.

After packing the clothing the Framjis had gifted me in a trunk, I folded my uniform. A small red box rolled out—my medal.

Tossing it to Smith, I asked, "Stephen, why the devil did they give me this?"

He snatched it from the air, popped it open and grinned. "The Order of Merit. Wondered where it had got to—you didn't wear it at the inquest."

A dull ache grew in my forehead as I stashed my uniform in the trunk. "We survived . . . Karachi. So why? I remember . . . things that don't make sense. A Pathan attacked me—I saw him twisted, crumpled on the ground. How could that be?"

Smith's face froze in an attitude I had not seen before. He pulled in his lips, rubbed his mustache with a knuckle and narrowed his eyes.

His silence disturbed me. Sitting on the bed, I said, "You fell from the horse and got hurt, so I stayed with you. Our lads went ahead. They were trapped and killed."

Smith's mouth opened in surprise. "That's what you recall?"

What was that odd note in his voice? I said, "More or less. I pieced it together."

He drew a slow breath and shook his head. It made me uncomfortable, the way he regarded me, like a dog he wasn't sure was friendly. His fingers twitching, he leaned back.

"Well, do you remember anything?" I asked. "Your knee had you delirious for a bit."

Smith shook his head. "Never broke my leg in my life, Jim. It was you who fell from Mullicka. We left you with the packhorse and a scout, Ram Sinoor, and went on ahead to recon the port. We walked into an ambush."

A knot formed in my throat. "But I heard our chaps . . . yelling, the shots, screams."

"Afghans—came out of nowhere. Afridi tribesmen."

A shudder shook me. I clutched the bedpost, trying to understand. "So I sent Sinoor back to alert the regiment. That part's right. But you weren't with me?"

"Not until later."

"You fought them off?"

Smith stared at me. "You don't remember any of it?"

"No," I said. But that wasn't quite true. I could see twisted figures in doorways, men I'd drunk with, trained with, laughed with, now crumpled in the dust. A Pathan leapt at me, head bloodied. I'd gripped my knife and struck.

Smith said, "You came for us, Jim. It took a while. Only five of us left, then. We held them off, those bloody Pathans, for three days, awaiting relief."

I could not look at him as he continued. "Our chaps started shelling the port, remember? Doctor Jameson said you'd recall it in your own time."

"I don't want to remember, Smith! Just tell me."

"You held them off. That's why Sutton put you up for the VC."

His smile drooped. "Just before relief arrived, you got shot. A head wound, Jim. You weren't yourself for over a year. I visited, off and on. At the sanatorium, you were . . . amenable, obeyed simple instructions. Just sat there. Didn't know me. Then one day you said, 'Hullo, Stephen.' You were reading the papers, cool as you please. Just like that, you were back."

I touched the line above my ear that throbbed at night, the clump of hair that would not comb down flat. "It happened in 1890?"

He nodded, watching me. "Yes. Two years ago."

I'd been out of it for over a year? "Smith, you're sure about this?" Seeing him nod, I said, "The regiment was disbanded. Who survived?"

He stopped a few feet away, mustache bristling. "Well, I joined the Bombay Grenadiers. Pathak and Rashid went to Africa. Suri went home after his term. He grows apples."

Was it true? I searched his beaming face. Four of my friends lived. I felt lighter, filled with unfamiliar buoyancy. "No one told me."

Face flushed, he barked out a laugh. "We did, man, many times! You just. Weren't. There."

I'd injured my knee. That's why I took so long to reach my Company. I remembered that Pathan, the leader perhaps, who came at me with a knife. Unbidden, my hand covered the scar in my side where he'd hit me. Those bloodshot eyes, that turbaned head, the blood running down his face, the man in my nightmares . . . I'd killed him.

So my dreams of mayhem were memories. Dead Pathans demanding to be remembered, my countrymen, insisting I own what I'd done and what I was. Little wonder they haunted me.

I slumped against the bedpost and grimaced as I saw images out of order, my memory a book whose pages I had pulled apart. I'd reached my lads after all, using my rifle as a crutch, hobbling forward on a torn knee.

* * *

In the gymkhana two days later, Smith slouched on a stool as I tapped at the punching bag. My shoulder ached, but working it kept it limber.

"Jim, me lad! Read this," said Smith, grinning as he thrust the *Chronicle* at me. He'd folded it to Byram's editorial.

I left the punching bag swinging and wiped off with a towel, draped it around my neck and raised two fingers to signal a masseur. I threw my leg across a chair, facing the back so the trainer could knead my neck, and read:

The Slave Ship Vahid Cruiser seized last week with ninety-four women and thirty-seven men in shackles was bound for Guyana. Official sources today named its owner as Seth Nur Akbar Suleiman, Crown Prince of Ranjpoot. He has absconded and is presently at large.

When Indians with privilege and power prey upon those of their compatriots who are weak and vulnerable, the dispossessed, the young, orphans and widows, we ought to be ashamed to call them leaders.

"Ashamed to call them leaders?" I said, "Bloody hell. The princes and Rajas won't like that." Akbar would like it even less.

When power is not tempered by wisdom, and greed runs untrammeled over the bodies of our women, the future of society is in peril. If Indians ever seek to share the reins of self-government, then we must be better at policing our own. Wealth and influence must not exempt anyone, English or Untouchable, Educated or Illiterate, from being subject to Law.

Whose Law, you ask? It is our Law together that governs Indians, one that neither the lowliest Chaprasei nor indeed His Excellency the Viceroy Himself can abjure. Neither Prince nor Potentate may trample upon the breast of India but that she rise up and strike him down.

I read the last line aloud: "*Bring Prince Akbar and his cronies to justice! May any man or Rani who shelters him hide their heads in shame.*"

"Great stuff," said Smith, grinning.

"Pompous old chap," I said with affection. Byram had outdone himself, naming Akbar and the Rani directly. It would be harder for him to hide.

McIntyre too would feel the sting of this editorial when the Viceroy and Ministry chaps demanded why Akbar was still at large. Scanning the page, I breathed a grateful sigh. There was no mention of my name.

"The match is on page seven." Smith chuckled. "Sporting news. Right below the Derby winners."

"Mm, imagine that." I sighed as the masseur kneaded my side, still sore from Akbar's kick.

At the door stood a familiar short, uniformed bearer, looking distinctly uncomfortable. Indians were not permitted inside the white-only gymkhana. It was Gurung.

The Durwan intercepted him, hand splayed. "You cannot enter. British officers only!"

"Han-ji! I know!" Gurung's glance searched pairs of bare-chested men pounding at each other. I'd not been to the house, so Adi had probably sent me a message. I handed back Smith's newspaper and went over.

"Captain Sahib!" Gurung touched his forehead, relieved to see me.

"Everything all right?" I asked in Hindustani, dismissing the Durwan.

Gurung grimaced. "Diana Memsahib wants to speak with you. She is waiting in the carriage."

Crikey! No wonder he couldn't give the Durwan that message! I hurried to clean up, wondering what Diana wanted. Fifteen minutes later, I climbed into the Framjis' enclosed Gharry carriage.

Looking rather gaunt, Diana wore a long, divided skirt and white shirtwaist. She wore no gloves. She scanned my face. "How are you?"

"No permanent damage," I replied, trying to gauge her mood.

She would not hold my glance, but examined my bruised jaw and temple. Brushing my shoulder, she said, "Shouldn't you rest?"

Alarmed by her haunted look, I asked, "What's happened?"

Her lips twitched in the semblance of a smile. "I had to see you."

I measured her reply. Her shoulders were tight and stiff. "There's more, isn't there?"

She nodded, her face flushed, secretive. "Akbar. He's been seen. McIntyre's man spotted him at the races. He got away before the Havildar could raise a cry."

"And you know this, how?"

She smiled, a full-blown grin that arrowed into me. "I overheard Papa on the telephone with McIntyre."

"And you snuck away to tell me. Dash it, Diana, your father will be livid."

"He doesn't own me. I had to . . . warn you. Akbar will probably come for you. You beat him. He'll hate that." Her pearly teeth caught her lower lip. "People like him can be vicious. He won't play fair, Jim."

I caught the hand that had clutched my sleeve and raised it to my lips. Her glowing smile churned my insides, because I did not deserve it.

"Diana, don't. Don't look like that. You've got some romantic notion of me. I'm not that man."

"Aren't you? All right. Who are you, then?"

Smith's story echoed in my mind, some of it still missing from my memory. I did not recall firing on the Pathans, nor reaching my comrades. But that last fight with the Pathan leader? I remembered his throat under my palm, the feel of him as he twitched and shook.

Did I deserve to go on, to seek my own happiness? I stared down at my hands. "I've . . . killed . . . natives, my own countrymen."

Her fingers tightened on mine. "You had a duty to the uniform. To your Company. To your friends!"

"I couldn't save them, most of them," I said, remembering Father Thomas, his serene face, now chiding me. Such sorrow in his blue eyes. Had he guessed my tattered inner state? I'd survived skirmishes before, shot at the enemy from a distance. But Karachi was different. Was there a moment when I could have stopped, should have stopped? But I could not think, then, only knew if I released my hold the Pathan would lash out and I had not the strength to overcome him again. Was it self-defense? I did not know. I could not expect her to understand, nor would I speak of it.

Diana squeezed my hands. "Listen to me!" Her fingers touched my jaw, turning me to her. "It was an awful time. You did what you had to. Leave the past behind."

I read her face and found only concern. Determination. She saw me as I am, and did not turn away. Her fingers clutched my coat in fretful impatience.

"Jim, why do you put others above yourself? I cannot understand it!"

I gathered her to me and she came willingly. With her near, only the present mattered. Whatever I had done or left undone faded, regrets slipped away, the burn of self-recriminations eased. Why did she value me so? I stopped questioning it, grateful it was so.

Sometime later the clock tower chimed the quarter hour. It had chimed before, while we spoke. Adi and her parents did not know where she was.

"Let's get you home."

"All right," she said against my chest, then pouted. "You're sweaty."

I laughed out loud, leaned my head out of the window and roused Gurung to action.

Diana clung to me on the short ride back, joyful moments of whispered confessions and endearments. Notwithstanding my malodorous state, we held as close as possible in a carriage that bounced and jolted over cobbles, hitting every stone in the road. Somehow, I had to convince Burjor to let her marry me.

CHAPTER 65

RETURN TO THE CLOCK TOWER

We arrived at the house too soon for my liking. The carriage rocked to a halt and Diana's arms squeezed around my neck, her face warm against mine. I chuckled as she uncurled off my lap and arranged her clothing.

When I stepped out and handed her down, Burjor hurried down the stairs in a panic.

"Diana!" he boomed. "Thank God you're safe!"

Surely that was unwarranted, I thought in confusion. I was no threat to Diana.

"Child, where were you?" Mrs. Framji's voice had a frightened pitch. "Adi got a letter while we were out. He rushed off right away."

Perspiration beading his forehead, Burjor thrust a page at me. "Captain, read this."

In the fading light, I read the note aloud: "Agnihotri, I have the last Miss Framji. Come to the Clock Tower alone. Or she falls, at eight o'clock."

My pocket watch showed it was seven thirty-six. Akbar had left the note unsigned. Byram's editorial had cornered him, so he'd moved against us again. Yet his plot must have gone awry, because Diana was safe with me. Adi, however, did not know that.

Looking pale, Diana said, "I was supposed to go to the theater with friends. I begged off at the last minute because . . ."

Because she had to see me. If she hadn't, she might have stepped into Akbar's trap. The note was addressed to me, and I'd not been at the house in days. Now I feared for Adi, gone to the clock tower in my place. I swore under my breath. Until I stopped Akbar, those I loved would always be at risk.

"You've alerted McIntyre?" I asked Burjor.

He nodded. "I returned ten minutes ago and saw this. Called him right away."

"When did Adi leave?"

He conferred with Gurung and said, "Almost half an hour ago."

Adi could not hope to hold off a beast like Akbar for long. The prince could have killed him already, but I thought not. Akbar was a showman. Why kill Adi without an audience?

Hoping I wasn't too late, I called to Gurung, "Saddle the horses. You're coming with me. Ganju's to secure the house."

As I took my leave, Burjor stood, tight-lipped, clenching and unclenching his hands.

Diana said, "Jim, I'm coming. Last time you sent me off for cartridges and left. Not this time!"

Burjor frowned, aghast. "Child, are you mad? You cannot!"

Agreeing with him, I said, "Diana, no."

She cried, "Papa, Adi's in trouble! I can help. Jim, don't treat me like a child!"

Did she not understand? If she came, my mind would be divided. I needed to think of Adi. "Think what you will of me, Diana, I cannot risk you."

As I turned away, Diana caught my arm. "Jim! Think like a General! I can take orders as well as any man."

Seeing my hesitation, Burjor clenched a fist in his hair and groaned. Lips tight, Diana was fierce in her resolve. Adi was in trouble, so she would follow anyway. With or without me. Better to keep her where I had a smidgen of control.

"Right," I sighed, wondering how to keep her safe.

"Captain!" cried Burjor. "Here, you'll need this." Barreling down to me, he pressed a revolver into my hand. Adi's Webley, the twin of my own. It was loaded.

Grateful, I stashed it securely. I would not leave it in my saddlebag this time.

"What's our plan?" cried Diana as we ran to the stables.

Plan? I didn't have one.

Akbar's note was addressed to me. He wanted me, not Adi. This was personal. It wasn't just losing the fight—Byram's editorial made Akbar a hunted man. His ship impounded, his finances in tatters from betting heavily on the certain outcome of our match, he'd lost both reputation and fortune. He could still hide away, but he wouldn't. He was furious. It made him more dangerous.

What was my plan? I improvised. "I'll hold Akbar off until McIntyre arrives." Hold him off and try not to get Adi or myself killed.

We mounted quickly. Over my shoulder, I told Diana, "Wait for McIntyre. Whatever happens, Diana! Stay with Gurung."

Once I ensured Gurung understood his charge, I dug in my heels and sent the mare bounding down the path, leaving Diana and Gurung to follow.

The clock tower chimed seven as I sped over the causeway, urging the mare on.

Surely not? Surely it was not yet eight?

It rang again—as I charged down Queens Necklace, the coastal road. Then eight again. What the devil?

Adi. He was alive. He'd got into the carillon room and sent a warning I could not possibly miss.

I bolted across the maidaan, yanked the mare around a bullock cart to clatter past the High Court, my heart thudding away. What was the time? Tree limbs obscured the clock face, high above. At the tower vestibule I leapt off the mare and left her snorting as I pounded up the narrow, coiled stairway, revolver in hand. I ran stooped, for the ceiling was low. To either side, cold stone brushed my arms.

The bells were silent when I reached the door to the gallery. Where was Adi? No sound but my own breathing filled the narrow space. I peered through the half-open door, trying to see what I was walking into.

"Come out, Captain!" called Akbar from the gallery outside. He'd heard me.

There was really no choice, after all. I stepped out, weapon at the ready.

Against a splendid crimson sky, Adi sat astride the parapet, one leg over the side. His hands were bound together before him.

Akbar stood beside him in a neat suit, as dapper as a Bond Street gentleman.

"Here you are," he said. "Barely in time!"

I clicked off the safety and pointed my revolver. "Let him go."

Akbar's smile broadened. One hand lay flat on Adi's chest. "So we have an impasse, eh? You have a revolver; I have your friend. It should be the girl, but no matter. He'll do."

Adi said, "Dammit, Jim." Blood dripped from his chin, anguish in the twist of his mouth. He hated being the bait. He'd got away from Akbar to send me a warning and taken a blow to his face as punishment. One push, and Akbar would send my friend over the edge to join his dead bride. Nothing could break his fall.

Nothing? I saw a way for him to hold on, but how could I tell him?

I called out, "Adi, Diana's safe. I held her. Her arms around my neck."

Adi stared. Did he understand? I could not tell.

"You!" Akbar spat, livid. "A half-breed! And Diana—the Parsee princess."

His hand clenched in Adi's shirt. His face twitched, close to madness—why? He'd not known about Diana and me! How could I pull him back, barter with him? I flicked the safety back on and held up the pistol. "It's me you want. Let him go."

Akbar's eyes glittered as he calculated his next move. "Put the gun down. Kick it away." To make good the threat, he extended his arm, holding Adi over the drop by his shirt.

Adi leaned sideways, trying to hug the parapet with his knees. That would not help if Akbar thrust him over.

"All right!" I held up the pistol, bent and set it on the ground. "Here! You win."

Instead of appeasing Akbar, it seemed to enrage him.

"You should have left well enough alone! I had a chance to take back India!" he bit out, his face a mask of fury. "You interfered with my ship. I should have had you killed on Princess Street."

To distract him, I cried, "My sister, Chutki. Why did you take her?"

He grinned, teeth showing in a snarl. "That hurt, eh? You should have stopped then." Mouth twisting in rage, he said, "I was named for an emperor! It was my destiny!"

His palm shot out and shoved Adi in the chest.

I had a choice, I truly did. I could snap off a shot, or try to catch my friend.

"No!" I raced forward as Adi fell.

But Adi had understood my message, or perhaps he acted upon instinct. His arms, bound at the wrist, went over Akbar's head, catching around his neck. Adi's unexpected weight pulled Akbar forward over the parapet.

It bought me time—just enough time to reach out, grab a fistful of Adi's clothes and haul him back over the edge. Entangled, Adi struggled to free himself of Akbar.

Akbar bellowed his frustration, butted against us like a tethered bull. He grappled in fury, pummeled, thrusting and gouging at me while I strove to pull Adi away. At last Adi came free. I shoved him to the side. But now Akbar had me in a headlock, his elbow tight around my neck.

Helpless, choking, I met Adi's horrified glance. My fingers tore uselessly at Akbar's iron arm. Such pressure on my throat. My vision dimmed—I could not stand it much longer.

Stand it. Stand. Could not stand. I slumped, let my full weight fall on Akbar's arm. Unbalanced, he dropped forward, breaking his hold.

I twisted, heaving, my lungs screaming for air. Breathe! My throat on fire, I staggered up, backed away. Akbar did not take his eyes off me.

We circled, gauging the distance and each other. Akbar advanced, his hand pulling something from his waist, while I retreated, gasping.

Hooves rattled on the cobbles below. McIntyre? He was taking his own bloody time getting here.

Akbar's arm lashed out in a curve. Damn. He had a knife.

I jerked back just in time. His blade sliced across my chin, stinging. Blood dripped, warm down my throat.

The parapet hit the back of my hip, bringing me up short. I'd run out of room.

His fist cracked down on my wounded shoulder. Pain drove me now—all I could see was Akbar.

He smiled. "I'm going to take you apart." His blade sliced, missing me by a hair, swung back for another pass.

I grabbed his wrist, sliding my forearm against his as I held him off.

We might have been evenly matched at the start, but now Akbar held the advantage. He had the blade. My shoulder shrieked from the weight of my useless right arm.

In the army I'd heard the whine of bullets that buzz by with a deadly sting, known they'd be the last thing I'd feel. Now my ears hummed as I strained, one-armed against Akbar's fearsome bulk, too weak to push him away.

His eyes flashed as he understood my predicament.

In my early boxing days, I lost many fights. There was a moment when I knew how it would go, the inevitability of it plain, immutable even. I had that sense now, of how this would end. Akbar would kill me, then turn on my friend Adi crouched by the door.

"Adi," I said, choking, "Go! Get away."

I could hold Akbar off no more. Exhausted, I shuddered against the press of his bulk. I would die here. Had Lady Bacha felt this when she made her last stand on these stones? She'd chosen how she would die—no one could take that from her. So would I. I still held a final card, one I did not want to use. Already we teetered against the tower wall, leaned out over it, pressed ever further by Akbar's prodigious strength. I would turn sideways and take us both over.

Trouble was, I didn't want Adi to see it. With the blade at my neck, I could not move to spot him. Instead I listened for a footfall toward the door. Go, Adi. Go.

"Checkmate," Akbar hissed.

"Why did you do it? The Framji girls. Why kill them?" I cried, in a last-ditch attempt to distract him.

He sneered, "The women? Why do you care? Just useless women."

His blade neared, touched my skin with its cold kiss. His breath huffed into my face.

I heard the unmistakable click of a pistol cocked to fire. Adi? Had he found my weapon near the door?

Diana's voice cut the air. "Let him go."

Akbar's smile widened, revealing perfect teeth, inches away. "I warned you, Diana."

"And I told you! Stay away from my family!" Diana cried.

I told you? Diana knew him. She knew Akbar! I weakened, felt the blade's bite.

A shot boomed nearby, deafening me.

Akbar looked astonished. He crumpled, pulling me sideways. Meshed to him, awash in pain, I saw darkness. Hands tugged at me, rolled me over. My head hit a flagstone. A voice barked words that echoed and faded.

I was awash in emotion. All my life I had longed for a family, someone to love. Now I loved, and it hurt. It burned inside me, tearing its way out, cutting sharper than the twinge in my neck. The thickness inside me felt heavier, filling, choking, pouring inside, pouring out. I loved not just Diana but all of them: my cool-headed friend Adi; Burjor—my staunch ally even when I did not obey him; the trust in Mrs. Framji's warm look; Chutki, who would always be with me; Razak's fervent grin, the warm weight of those little chaps Parimal and Hari, and that sweet-smelling infant Baadal. They were with me still. I had not left them.

A handful of stars lay scattered in the twilit sky. Distant and weary, I watched streaks of red and gold in the blue curtain above. Hands touched my face, my neck.

Diana.

Light splintered across her face. I watched her lips move, hearing almost nothing. Diana's lips said, "Jim!" then, "Adi, he's bleeding!"

Her hands trembled upon me. Something pressed to my neck, pinching with urgency. Voices cracked and rattled around the gallery, dropping and rolling like pebbles. I'd learned something awful just before I fell. What was it? I drew a shaking breath, raised a hand to touch her, and remembered. It cut me deeper than Akbar's blade, reached that thickness inside, told me, no, you're wrong, this is a lie.

My words formed slowly, came out slurred. "Akbar. You knew him. All this time."

I had ached to belong, to be part of them, part of her. But Diana was not who I thought she was.

I let go.

CHAPTER 66

MELTDOWN

Doctor Jameson kept me in hospital the next day, while Superintendent McIntyre prodded me with questions. I slept, dropping off midsentence, cursing the hypodermic that was never far from Jameson's reach.

The monsoon broke over Bombay in a low rumble of thunder, followed by a mighty crash. Rain beat the roof and hammered the windows as I swore at Jameson, trying to leave hospital.

"Dammit, Captain, the Viceroy needs answers!" cried McIntyre.

Head throbbing, my shoulder bound tight and immovable, I made slow progress with it.

All the while, Diana's betrayal burned. She must have met Akbar in England. He'd attended Oxford—how had I not seen that they could have met abroad? She'd deliberately hidden their association. Why? The question slithered about my mind, dark and ominous.

Next morning, seeing I was set on going, Jameson sent an orderly to accompany me to my boardinghouse. My things were still in boxes, so I spent some time unpacking, one-armed, with little interest. My bottles of charcoal dust, face paint, white chalk, mirror and brushes used for my guises, I left in their crates.

At noon the boardinghouse sent up a boy to ask me down to supper. I declined, having neither appetite nor desire for company. At four, the kitchen sent up some tea. I sipped it by the window, gazing out at the gloom, where rain bounced off shingles and shattered in the street.

When I was hired, Diana had been eager to aid my inquiry. Now I saw that her searching looks spoke not of interest in me but questioning. Could she trust me with her private intelligence? She had not shared it.

She'd known all along the threat came from Akbar. Had they been friends, or more? At Diana's ball, Akbar had watched her incessantly—had he been in love with her? Diana had not acknowledged him, not the smallest nod, not even when she was presented to the Rani and he stood five feet away. Had they agreed to hide their association?

Then she'd asked me to dance.

I winced, remembering those sweet moments. Now their magic singed me. Diana had compiled a great deal of intelligence about the nobles at her ball. But she'd already known about Ranjpoot. Her touch upon my hand? I had read it as reluctance to end our dance. Was that also deception? In the goddamn coat room she said she loved me! Those whispered words on the carriage ride home, those embraces!

I went to the earthen pot and drank from the metal tumbler, drink after drink that did not quench. When I proposed using Sutton's boxing match to lure Akbar out, Diana had gone pale, damned me and stormed out. Was it for fear I would be hurt, or concern for Akbar?

"I told you to stay away from my family," she'd cried at the clock tower, as Akbar's blade touched my neck. Had they fallen out, years ago, in a lovers' quarrel? My doubts piled up, burying me.

A knock sounded at my door. Grateful for the interruption yet irritable and off-kilter, I limped across to yank it open.

"Afternoon!" said Superintendent McIntyre, eyeing my battered state.

I swallowed and waved him in.

"Celebrating?" He picked up the metal tumbler from the table and sniffed. His eyebrows rose. "This isn't liquor."

I smiled briefly. "Have a seat," I said, moving newspapers to empty a chair.

"How d'you feel?" he asked, joining me at the window instead, nodding at the bandage around my neck.

"I'm all right. Have you seen them, the Framjis?" I asked.

He sent me a sharp look, then nodded. "Got their statements yesterday. Mostly consistent with yours."

That wasn't what I wanted to know. "Are they all right?"

"Young Framji's recovered." His lips twitched. "Miss Framji looked a bit peaked."

Thinking of her, I hurt. After Karachi, a blessed numbness had taken me. How had I pulled out of that strange fog? The Framji case . . . Adi's letter had brought me back.

Meeting McIntyre's liquid grey eyes, I said, "I need work."

McIntyre asked a couple of questions, then told me to see him at the Constabulary the next morning and left. I continued unpacking, but the sight of my clothes brought to mind the many kindnesses the Framjis had given me. I needed to see Diana, but feared it too, as the end of a dream. I'd been such a fool.

Later that evening, I heard a knock on my door. Expecting no visitors, I opened it, puzzled.

Diana stood there, looking flustered. She'd come to my lodgings alone, risking her reputation, risking ruin. McIntyre had said she looked unwell, but there was more ailing her than that. She had secrets—I recalled how she'd diverted our talk from her time in England.

Looking at her standing red-faced and rumpled on my threshold, I wasn't sure it mattered.

"Do you want me to leave?" she asked.

"God's sake, Diana."

When I'd told her about letting my comrades down in Karachi, she had insisted I must not fault myself for it. She'd believed in me, demanded that I must let it go, move on. She'd refused to accept I was a coward, had insisted she knew me, and it could not be.

She hovered, her face twisted in remorse.

I retreated into formality. "You can't be here."

She shook her head. "You weren't at the hospital." Tears spilled over those satin cheeks.

She was my life. Whatever she'd done, there it was as plain as day. She'd won my affection with her wit, her care—how could I unlove her now? Her anguish, half torment, half fury, told me all I needed to know.

Shutting the door, I scooped her into my arms. Long moments later, when my breathing slowed, I could hear what she was saying. Diana sobbed, "It was awful. The blood! But I had to do it. I had to."

"Yes," I said. The blood. She was talking about Akbar.

"Jim," she whispered into my neck. "How do you live, without this?"

How indeed! I leaned against a wall, holding her, feeling the tension in her narrow body. I was a ship at harbor again, the crossing behind me. Her betrayal, for that's how I saw it, had left me gutted.

But Diana too had suffered, grappling with what guilt and torment I could not imagine. Her body felt birdlike, fragile, yet light and warm. Her arms wound around me with desperate strength. How does one live without this—she'd just told me what was ailing her. That soft admission melted me.

"Find something to fix, something to build," I said into her hair, "and the hours pass."

She peered up at me, fingers on my unshaved jaw. "You look as bad as I feel."

I smiled against her touch. "You look . . . wonderful."

A bitter chuckle burst from her. "Liar," she said, and winced. "Jim, I'm so sorry."

"You knew Akbar," I said, the barb cutting into me, "yet you said nothing."

She pulled back, appealing in her fervor. "Jim, I'll explain if you'll listen."

I swallowed, nodded.

Her mouth twisted. "How can you understand? You're not a woman! Society does not permit a passing acquaintance, do you see? A woman is either innocent or a trollop. There's nothing in between! If I told you I had met him at a ball in London, what would you have read into it? Did he court me? Did I encourage him?"

There it was, what I feared. I searched her eyes. "Did you?"

She burst out, "I thought he was a friend. But, Jim, he threatened me. Four years ago, in London. I told him to go to the devil."

"Threatened, how?"

Her lips tightened. "When I would not agree to his demands, he became irate. Called me a tease. Said he would make me regret it."

"Diana, why didn't you say?"

She shook her head, pleading. "Who would believe it? And Papa was so keen to see me married well—it would have ruined everything. But it's no use. Once Papa's examined the boy's pedigree, his property, family connections, at the khastegari, I find I cannot abide him! He won't speak, or talks too much! He'll pay me ridiculous compliments, but won't talk politics with a woman. I couldn't stand it. Papa's so keen to find me a good match. I couldn't tell him I knew Suleiman and disappoint him."

"You could have told me."

Her voice aching, she said, "I couldn't, Jim! You would see me differently. I couldn't lose you! If I'd been sure of you I could have said. But as it was, well. I hesitated. Then it was too late."

Her explanation, confused as it was, had the ring of truth. Now I understood her worry, that urgent look before she left for Simla, as she tried to bind us with a kiss. I pressed my lips to her forehead.

Diana whispered, "Do you forgive me?"

"Mm." Assailed by the scent of lavender and soap, and my own longing, that thickness overflowing in my chest, how could I not? Quiet moments passed. Yet we could not remain in this place. Time, like a surly quartermaster, demanded action, insisting upon a decision. What could we do, Diana and I, to be together?

She stirred and said, "Is this what you'll do? Keep solving problems, find another mystery?"

I settled her more comfortably against me. "Working for Adi kept me sane. You, sweetheart, you showed me I was wrong about Karachi, how I remembered it. I can go on, because of you."

"Jim," she said. "Is that what I should do? Go on, like nothing's happened?"

Her bitterness cut a familiar slice in me. As I let go of her, she said, "There might be a way. To be together. Can you clean up and come to dinner? I'll wait downstairs in the carriage."

CHAPTER 67

A VERDICT

Over dinner Diana told her parents of her acquaintance with Akbar in London and answered their troubled questions. As the dishes were cleared away, I asked, "Adi? McIntyre asked me who shot Akbar. I didn't say. It was you?"

He shook his head. "I found the revolver by the door. But my hands were tied and quite numb. I couldn't aim it. The two of you were locked together at the wall. I couldn't risk a shot. Diana arrived, and when you cried out, she shot him."

Good grief! "A second later, he'd have cut my throat." I touched my scar, turning to Diana. "Where did you learn to shoot?"

She blushed. "I begged my friend Emily-Jane to teach me. I was hopeless with a rifle—it hurt my shoulder. But her father's Remington handgun was easier to fire."

By God, she'd learned well. I said, "I'm alive because of it. Thank you, my dear." Turning to Adi, I strove for a lighter note. "Well, sir, as promised, we'll have no report for the papers. But Adi, when all this is forgot, perhaps I'll write a book."

"No, Captain, please!" he cried in alarm. Catching sight of my grin, he amended, "At least not for a hundred years."

Burjor's laugh boomed out, and the others chuckled. I grinned. Now all that remained was to persuade Burjor, I thought, watching Diana's glowing smile.

Ganju entered with a tray of desserts and set one before me. A cylinder of wafer burst with clouds of white confection. Dark strokes of syrup glistened upon the plate. I glanced at the delectable concoction, hesitating to demolish it with a spoon.

Watching me gaze at the swirls artistically arranged on my plate, Mrs. Framji explained, "It's melted chocolate—on a profiterole." She sobered, catching my gaze. "Now that this is done, where will you go?"

Adi stilled. I stole a look at Diana. "I hardly know, Marm," I said. "I've not considered anything beyond this matter."

Just then Jiji-bai whispered in Mrs. Framji's ear. She rose, dabbing her lips, saying, "Good night, my dears, I must get the little ones to bed." Seeing me on my feet, she offered her hand in a spontaneous gesture. "Captain, we are so grateful this awful business is over."

I took her hand in both of mine, genuinely touched. "Mrs. Framji, thank you, for everything."

In the quiet after her departure, Adi and Diana exchanged glances.

"Jim, you have many options, you know," Adi offered.

"Yes, Captain!" said Burjor. "Want to run a plantation? We can send you to Ooty. Or would you rather build a hotel in Simla?"

"Papa, Superintendent McIntyre has offered Jim employment," said Diana. "He would remain in Bombay. And we—"

Burjor put down his spoon. "Diana. You know that would be unwise." His somber look passed from Diana to me. "Society has rules, Diana. Breaking them carries consequences. Take your friend Cornelia, twenty-four years old and unmarried. When her father converted to Christianity, his own family disowned him. Our Parsee friends may cut all ties with us. We could lose our livelihood!"

So nothing had changed. Lady Bacha's and Miss Pilloo's reputations were restored. Akbar and Kasim brought to justice. Adi was free from the threat of blackmail. Yet Diana and I were an ocean apart, simply because I wasn't born Parsee. No matter what, that obstacle remained.

I asked, "Sir, what can we do to earn your blessing?"

He dropped his forehead into his hands and groaned. "Captain, it's not just my business. The price is Adi's future, my babies' futures. Adi's an apprentice. Who will give him work?"

Adi straightened up. "Papa, no. Don't do this for me. I'll manage."

Diana said, "Can't we let everyone believe it is against your wishes? You could drop us. In public! Then they can't blame you, can they?"

Burjor glowered. "Child, are you asking me to lie?"

Diana's face was pale, but her chin went up. "Yes! For a good reason, Papa."

Burjor shrank back. His lip curled. "Should I punch the Captain, too? And pretend I don't know you, each time we meet? Think, Diana! What are you asking?"

When she flinched under his gaze, Adi said, "Diana, this is your choice. You don't need permission!"

The implication shocked us all. I stared, astonished. Adi was squarely on our side, Diana's and mine. Against his own father!

"Adi!" Burjor glared. "What are you doing? Setting her against us, against me?"

Refusing to back down, Adi said, "Diana, you could go with Jim. No one can stop you!"

Burjor's face went blank, then creased in bitter lines. I knew that look: he felt betrayed. This was the man who'd seen me shorn of my Pathan disguise and, delighted at my return, had embraced me. The memory of that spontaneous gesture smote me.

"No," I choked out. "No."

The Framjis—I cared for them all. They'd taken me in, given me their warmth, their trust. They were now at loggerheads—because of me!

"Jim," Diana whispered. "Let me fight for us."

"Not like this," I said. "Diana, we can't . . ." Words locked in my throat, refusing to fire.

"We can't build our life upon the wreck of theirs," she said, her voice dull. Our life, she had said. One life.

Diana asked, "Papa, what if it was not a lie? What if I left right now, with Jim?"

I straightened, stared at her. Diana would abandon her family?

She saw my surprise. "Jim, if I came with you, now, just like this, without a paisa, would you have me?"

I smiled at that. Did she not know the answer? When she didn't return my smile, I said, "Always, Diana. Always."

She drew a slow breath. "Right, then. It won't be a lie. If we elope, it's not Papa's fault."

Burjor kneaded his forehead. "Child, what of the scandal, the pain it will cause Mama?"

Diana cringed, biting her lips.

Adi cleared his throat. "I have another solution. If the issue is the Parsees, let's change their opinion. Byram can publish Jim's name, tell his story. The Wadias and Petits will be ashamed to drop you, Papa, for letting Diana marry Jim."

Burjor shook his head. "Adi, it won't work. It's not the Petits, Tatas and such who decree this. Our own people insist upon purity. Race is important to them. Blood matters."

Adi sat up straight. "Well, we don't know who Jim's father is, so what if he were Parsee?" He turned to me. "Jim, is there the slightest chance of that?"

This was a lawyerly approach, but no, it would not do. I said, "Adi, look at me. It's clear that he was English. My name, James, is English."

Burjor nodded. We were alike in that, I suppose, refusing to take the easy way. Truth mattered, and for itself.

"Jim!" Diana's voice was an anguished whisper. She stood abruptly, pressed her fist to her mouth and ran from the room.

Long moments later, I excused myself as well. My feet felt leaden as I stepped down the wide stairs, turning the problem over. Diana loved me. She was everything I wanted. With her, my future was joy and adventure. Without her, it stretched interminable, a lonely, dark road, no matter what I did for a living.

Yet I would not sacrifice anyone, nor ask Diana to. The cost was too great for the Framjis. If I persuaded her to break with tradition and marry me, scandal would swamp them. I could no more hurt this clan than I could harm Diana herself.

Leaving the house, I walked through the rear lane into pitch black, my mind as dark and sightless as the night. Father Thomas's words felt heavy inside me: "Don't let darkness in."

I had traveled between worlds, from army life to Indian villages, feeling at home in each, as though I had two heartbeats. At the Framjis, east and west blended together, suiting me well. Yet here too I had no place. I would have to make my own.

CHAPTER 68

A FAREWELL

Two weeks had passed since I last walked up the drive, my feet crunching gravel in the dusk, remembering the ache of leaving Diana. Ahead, Framji Mansion glowed, radiant with color and light.

Garlands of tuberoses curved around white marble pillars to scent the wide stairway. Adi's brother, ten years old, was betrothed today to a girl from a shipping family. Burjor was expanding his empire.

The door was left ajar for me. Laughter and conversation echoed from the dining room, mingled with Burjor's rumble as he told some story.

I stopped, rooted in the foyer, listening. Mrs. Framji spoke, a softer cadence that caressed my ears. Fingering my mother's pocket watch, I tried to remember my childhood. I still knew the scent of my mother—sandalwood incense and jasmine. I recalled strings of jasmine flowers in her hair. But it was here in Adi's home I saw what family could be. Burjor's hand upon his wife's shoulder, Diana's sharp glance checking Adi when he was about to err. This was family, but I was not part of it.

I recalled Burjor's embrace and winced. I'd have liked such a father, open, honest and tenacious. Mrs. Framji's warm acceptance, her delight in feeding me, her touch upon my cheek. These were precious, partly as they were rare to me, but more so because they were given so honestly, so freely.

The sounds of celebration filtered through the hall: Burjor's booming chuckle, Diana's laugh plucking the strings of a harp somewhere inside me. Her music found a place within and settled there, reassuring in its weight. Our parting had not broken her.

A child's giggle tumbled through the air, pearls of precious sound. I should leave.

Moved beyond words, I sat on the stairs in the foyer and listened. Hearing them soothed a restlessness in me, like watching silver ripples in a stream I longed to touch. In the dining room, Adi's younger brother answered a question. A burst of laughter followed his speech, bringing a smile to my lips.

Joy was made of moments like this, each insignificant in itself, piled together into a monolith, immutable and strong, something to lean against when one's world went awry. Since I'd done my part to keep it safe, might I not enjoy the sound of it?

Footsteps alerted me to the quick stride of patent leather shoes. Adi appeared from the morning room bearing a decanter, and stopped when he saw me sitting in the gloom.

"Captain!" His astonished voice rang out over the marble. "What's wrong?"

I rose to my feet. "All's well, sir. I'm too late for the festivities. I'll go."

"Nonsense, Jim." He caught my elbow and tugged me toward the dining room. When I held back, Adi peered at me in the dim light.

"Come." Hoisting the decanter, he led me to the morning room.

I followed. What I had to tell him was difficult to say. The quiet morning room would serve me better.

He poured out two whiskies as his father usually did. Already he seemed taller and surer of himself than the young man I'd first met.

And I? Although I had funds, having been paid handsomely by the Framjis, I felt worn, far older than the raw journalist I'd been. That battered soldier yet had hope of something better around the corner. Now I saw my path wind through unknown mountain crags. Surprised at my maudlin musings, I faced the window. Adi handed me a glass and joined me, gazing out at the purple dusk.

Very well. I would tell him now, and ask his advice. I cleared my throat to speak.

The door swung open, admitting light and music. Diana entered in a burst of energy. "Adi, how long you've been! Oh!"

She smiled, sunset and moonlight in one elegant package as she pulled the door shut, closing out the dinner talk. Diana stepped into the quiet with the grace of a dancer, confident, beautiful, at ease with herself.

"Jim! Come join us. There's still plenty of dinner."

As she came to greet me, our stillness caught her attention. "How solemn you are, standing there against the night."

She turned up a lamp. Adi's hand stopped her from lighting the rest.

"Miss Diana," I said, "you look . . . radiant."

This time she was not deceived. "What's happened?"

"All's well, Miss."

As I'd expected, she scowled at me. That word separated us, and I had used it deliberately. In the silence we heard a faint clatter of plates, exclamations and compliments on the dessert. I'd hoped to seek Adi's opinion, but it was too late. Instead, I'd seek hers.

"I've had an offer, from the Dupree Detective Agency," I said. "They have a job for me. In Boston."

"America," Adi said. "Will you go?"

"It's for the best," I said to Diana.

"Excuse me," Adi said, starting for the door to give us the room. Then he stopped, grasped my forearm and squeezed. He gave his approval with that touch, telling me he cared, and wished me well.

The door closed behind him. At the center of the floor Diana stood too still, too quiet.

"Diana, we can't go on this way."

Her voice trembled. "You asked me to try. To do my duty. I have."

Why wouldn't she look at me? I went to her. "It's why I can't stay, can't manage your father's land or build Wadia ships. I can't see you with someone else. I can't come to dinner and be 'Uncle Jim' to your children. I won't."

There. I'd said it. It might be enough for her to see me now and again, but for me it was all, or nothing.

She drew a quick breath, and her eyes flickered to my face. "It was awful, this evening. People saying, 'It should be you getting married! Aren't you already twenty-one?'" she mimicked in a high voice.

Ah. She would not acknowledge what I'd finally voiced out loud. Wasn't that an answer, in itself? But again, I was wrong.

"Jim." She regarded me sadly. "I can't marry anyone who isn't you."

I took her hands in mine. "Diana, I have to leave. As long as I'm here, we're stuck . . . in this place. You'll hate your father for coming between us. It will rankle that I won't stand up to him. You might even blame yourself because we didn't elope. Sweetheart, I can't let that happen. I'll go."

Just like that, her composure dissolved. "Boston, Jim? How will I know you're all right?"

Hope flared, ran hot in my veins. To remain in Bombay brought disgrace. But what if we left? Could we truly have a life together?

"Come with me."

I knew it was hopeless before the words left my lips, but I'd regret it for the rest of my days if I didn't try. I caressed her fingers, persuading, trying to believe. "Come to Boston. We could start over, make new friends, build a family. Leave all this behind."

Her eyes widened, a moment locked in time. I waited for the bullet, or the misfire. One smile now, and the path of my life was set.

Instead there were tears. Diana's eyes squeezed shut as they overflowed. I pulled her into my arms. She came easily and folded against me. I felt each sob rack her little frame. I heard a whisper, bent to catch it: "It's tearing me apart."

I knew, then, what it might be like to inhabit two bodies, felt her sorrow like my own. Face buried in my waistcoat, her voice wobbling with hiccups, she said, "They've lost two children. I can't . . . they can't lose another."

"Shhh, it's all right." I touched her hair, so soft and fragrant, brushed away the tears on her porcelain cheek with my thumb. "I'd give anything to have what you've got. Parents who dote upon you. Siblings to love."

"Jim." Her fist clenched in my collar, forehead pressed against my neck.

I said, "I'd sooner lose an arm than hurt them."

"Go, then," she said, rosy and fierce, "but I will have my kiss."

Reckless. I could so easily have pulled back. Yet if this was all I could have of her, I would not back away. Her hands reached up my shoulders, around my neck. Taking charge, she closed her eyes and set her lips to mine.

It shook me, that touch, the warm velvet of her. She deserved better for a first kiss. I gasped against her cheek, held on to my shaking breath. This waiting, too, brought both exquisite pain and exquisite joy. Once I'd mastered myself, I kissed her softly, felt her smile. I'd never had such sweet gentleness, such complete belonging. I tasted salty tears and breathed in lavender, tuberoses and dessert.

"I never imagined I'd envy Adi. Well, not since Bacha . . ." Diana whispered against my jaw. "But I do. They had a year together."

I understood. All this we would not have. Her fingers on my face. Her arm across my chest while I slept. I recalled her fury when I saw myself as less, somehow, than Adi and she. A weight shifted in me, a sense of worth, a substantial feeling. Diana gave me something without measure—she gave me back myself.

A tap at the door broke our solitude. Diana raised her head, regret in each reluctant movement. Adi cleared his throat and entered, sorrow etched into his troubled forehead.

"It's all right," I said, setting her down.

Diana wiped away tears. I watched her sigh, recorded each precious detail. Her dress was pale blue, I saw now. Pearls dangled at her ears and curled around her neck.

"Goodbye, sweetheart," I said against her ear, and pressed my lips to her temple, breathing in the creamy, fresh scent of her.

Then I clapped Adi on the shoulder and walked away.

CHAPTER 69

LEAVING BOMBAY

The next day I booked a berth on RMS *Arcadia*, a British India liner to Liverpool, where I'd board the Cunard steamship Umbria to New York. In the meantime, McIntyre's cases kept me occupied: knotty contradicting evidence, statements twisted with deceit, land records buried in great ledgers. These took my mind off the ache in my chest.

He had demanded my presence at a banquet for the Governor the next evening. Spiffy in uniform, my boots freshly shined, I watched discreetly, seeing Bombay's elite decked out to the nines: old stalwarts in black tails, the Governor's council, Parsee industrialists, their wives in glittering sarees.

I hoped Diana would come. As neighbors of the Sureewala family, the Framjis would be invited. Would she come? A quartet from Portuguese Goa performed familiar British tunes.

She entered in a daring blue satin that left her shoulders bare. Adi, elegant in black tails, spotted me, nodded and murmured to Diana as she greeted the hosts.

Then Diana did something surprising. She crossed the empty dance floor, making a beeline to me. Head high, long neck pale against the blue of her dress, she walked with such composure, graceful and contained, commanding the room.

"Hello," she said, a smile twinkling in her eyes.

"My God, Diana," I said, then gathered my wits and presented the gentlemen to her. She shook hands and made charming remarks. I didn't hear what she said, but my companions' amusement attested to it.

Diana said, "May I borrow you for a bit? Want you to meet my friends."

Without waiting for a reply, she took my hand and started back across the room. Her dash across the dance floor had drawn attention, and now our return caused another stir.

"Diana, what are you doing?" I asked.

As we approached a group of young people, she said, "Burning bridges. Only way to get the army across."

What the devil? Before I could seek an explanation, she began introductions. Miss Ellis, daughter of Colonel Ellis; Mrs. Petit; Mary Fenton—a theater actress; Perin Petit, who went to school with her; and so on. Since we were constantly among other people, I could scarcely bring up her bizarre remark about burning bridges. Had I misheard? Diana calmly discussed the expansion of railways with an elderly civil engineer.

The evening passed in a blur. Diana danced with Smith and another army bloke, returning to me between sets. Smith claimed her for another dance, winking at me. He didn't bother to hide his glee when she accepted, and they swept away.

Across the room, Byram signaled me over. Chuckling, he introduced me to the Governor General of Bombay and his wife. When I snapped to attention, Lord Harris offered his hand with a crooked smile. His wife Lady Harris was utterly charming—I have no idea what I told her about "the situation in the north."

Later, I asked Byram, "Haven't seen Mr. and Mrs. Framji. Are they here?"

When he shook his head, a weight settled on me. I'd have liked to say goodbye, but my appearance at Framji Mansion would only give them pain. Perhaps it was fortunate they were not here. Diana had made rather a spectacle in her marked attention for me, and would surely answer for it. But nothing had changed, had it? So I watched and stored every moment with her, hoarding them like treasures to examine later.

At evening's end, Adi came to fetch his sister. He gave me a meaningful look as we shook hands. Dash it, what the devil was he trying to tell me?

Diana looked demure and untroubled as she gave me her slim, gloved hand.

Jaw clenched, I took it. It was the last time I would see her.

"Well, Jim, bon voyage, then," she said, and was gone.

* * *

I ached, keeping to my rooms, but darned Smith would not let me be. He came by that evening with a bottle of Glenfiddich and we mumbled to each other, emptying it between us. I can't recall what we talked about.

Next day I brought home a sheaf of blank foolscap pages. At the top of one, I wrote, *I turned thirty in hospital, in a quiet, carbolic-scented ward, with little to read but newspapers.*

I wrote to fill my remaining nights in Bombay, when sleep rarely came. I wrote because memories of Diana crowded and jostled me and would not be contained within the narrow confines of my body, because to record my story meant I could dwell on it in some sane way and walk down the street next day and say "good morning," as a civilized person should.

Yet in those foggy, unfiltered moments, when I breathed in the dawn, my mind without defenses, I could feel Diana's touch. I'd find the Rakhee that Chutki had given me, now knotted around my medal, or look up at the sky above, crowded with stars, and turn to tell Diana, look at that, what beauty!—it's like the sky above Simla. Then I'd remember she was not there.

She wasn't there until I picked up my pen again and wrote.

* * *

A September gust hit me as I stood on Victoria Wharf. Despite the light drizzle, neither Adi nor I wore our felt hats, but clutched them against the breeze. The SS *Arcadia* towered over the wharf, her bow rising and falling as she breathed gently in the water.

Adi, come to see me off, had invited me to lunch. In funds now, I offered to pay, but he wouldn't hear of it.

My finances had replenished when Byram came through with the promised reward. With back wages from Adi and my department salary, I now held a respectable balance at Lloyd's. Three trunks at my feet attested to how I'd spent some of it. I signaled a group of coolies to carry them aboard.

Adi fidgeted, in an odd mood today. He scanned the crowd, looked out over the water and back to me. "Captain, why did you undertake this investigation?" he asked. "You were a decorated hero. Why work for me?"

When I paused, surprised, he continued, "You were in hospital, convalescing after an injury. Reading the papers?"

I decided to give him the truth. "I had a head wound. Smith said I was, well, not quite there, for a year. Reading filled the time: Conan Doyle, the papers. Saw your letter in the *Chronicle*. 'They are gone but I remain, sincerely, etc.' That's how you ended it."

He looked puzzled.

Water slapped against the bow of the great ship that would carry me across the Atlantic. "My friends were dead," I said. "They were gone but I remained. Your words . . . echoed how I felt."

"That's why you left the army?"

"I was numb . . . felt . . . dead inside, after Karachi. When I read your letter, well, I got interested in the case. Went to the *Chronicle* for a job—and Byram sent me to you."

"For an interview." Adi smiled.

"Yes." The *Arcadia* gave three long hoots in the windy morning.

I said, "Goodbye, sir."

I reached out to shake his hand, remembering our first meeting—he, a distraught widower; I, a novice reporter.

"Jim." Adi evaded my hand and clasped me in a tight embrace.

I laughed and hugged him back, feeling the bones of his shoulders under my hands. He would do great things, this thin young man with his serious manner and deep thoughts.

In the crowded parapet above, something moved, flapping. Diana leaned over the edge, wrapped in a yellow scarf. One end of it broke free and rode the September breeze, a pennant to mark what I called home.

She'd come to see me off. That cold farewell at the Sureewalas' had left a knot inside me. I could not speak. Adi must have felt me gasp, for he turned and followed my gaze.

Diana pulled back into the crowd. Would I ever see her again? Would

Burjor marry her off to the Wadia chap? Or would she be alone the rest of her years?

"How old is she?" I asked, hoarse, barely coherent. I knew her age, but my mind was blank.

"Twenty-one, Jim."

Old enough to know her mind; young enough to wait.

"Adi," I said, gripping his shoulder, "write to me. If she's not wed in two years, I'm coming back for her."

His smile lit the damp, foggy morning as he said, "Jim. I want to give you something, something that belonged to Bacha. Will you have it?"

Nonplussed, I saw a box in his hand, a ring box.

"When you find a girl to marry, will you give her this?"

He opened it, revealing a square-cut blue stone, encircled by brilliant white diamonds. An heirloom, and Lady Bacha's. I felt like he'd called me "brother." My hand shook as I closed his fingers around it.

"Adi. There's only one girl I'd give it to."

He grinned. "Then, do."

"Hello, Jim," said Diana, behind me.

I swung around. Diana's yellow scarf was wound tight against the drizzle, its fine mist enclosing us in a grey curtain. She smiled. "My trunks are already on board."

I stared. Trunks? On board? She was sailing too?

"What? . . . How?" I gasped.

Burjor came up with Mrs. Framji, saying, "Tell him. For God's sake, girl, tell the man."

Diana's eyes were wide, translucent oceans. "Mama overheard us— that night you asked me to come with you. She'd followed me. She was upset, really, that I said no, without talking to her. We spoke to Papa together."

Mrs. Framji said, in an urgent whisper, "Son, she was miserable. It broke my heart to see it. I couldn't let you leave it like that, not for me."

Diana said, "Jim, you mustn't think we've been idle all this time. Papa and Byram went to the Parsee elders and made our case."

Burjor grunted. "Byram, the old coot. It was his idea. After Diana's display at the Sureewala dinner"—he sent her a hard look—"no decent Parsee will marry her! So we came to an accommodation with the elders."

Adi said, "Papa's being modest. He's got to fund a trust for widows and orphans. And there are several conditions."

"Yes." Burjor nodded slowly. "Diana cannot inherit anything. And your children will not be Parsee."

Children. Diana's children. With me. My breath rattled about. I searched her face, saw it was true. Yet I didn't understand—would they pay an awful price for this generosity?

"But sir, the scandal . . ."

"Oh, some will drop us, of course. But we'll survive. If nothing else, we have the army contract for tea and coffee"—he poked my chest—"that you got us in Simla!"

They would be all right. My heart hammered like a drummer gone berserk. "The younger children?"

Mrs. Framji smiled her sweet smile. "They'll wed, someday. In a few years, the Parsees may forget."

Taking in her warm approval, I asked Burjor, "So we have your blessing?"

He smiled that wide, jowly, unconstrained grin, his dark eyes twinkling.

Diana wound her fingers through mine. "Such a mad scramble to get a cabin! *Arcadia* is full, not a cabin to be had. Can you imagine? Sutton got your friend General Greer to pull some strings. Chief McIntyre called the owner, Mr. James MacKay, himself! So I'm traveling first class!"

I laughed. My God. The Framjis, Byram, McIntyre, Sutton and Greer. A formidable army—resolute, inexorable and in my corner.

Joy overflowed, a deluge, like the rain now beating down on us. Adi shook out an umbrella and held it over his parents. Picking Diana up, I swung her around. A crowd gathered around us, but I didn't care.

"Adi, let's have that ring!" I cried, dropped to a knee, grinning at Diana, squinting up through the rain.

He handed it over. It was perfect. Lady Bacha would approve.

"You're everything to me, Diana. Come with me, sweetheart, marry me, love me," I said. "We've waited long enough."

EPILoGUE

We were married on board two days later. Alone in our cabin, with the slow roll of the SS *Arcadia* Diana whispered into my neck, "Jim? Why did you write this book?"

Diana's face against my skin, I breathed in her fresh sweetness. Catching the curl that bounced against my chin, I rubbed its satin between my fingers.

Those last weeks in Bombay I had tried to give her up. Yet it was giving up a part of me, and that I could not do. Some remnant of my tale should survive, I'd decided. Picking up my pen brought comfort. Precious, short hours slipped through the casements that night and each night after. I'd written to remember, so that something would remain when I was gone.

"Jim?"

"History. It will remember the ladies, Bacha and Pilloo. Adi will likely build something fine and go down in history. But us? History will never know us at all."

Diana pulled up and gazed at me, amused. "History?"

"Mm. It will forget me. And you, sweetheart. I wanted to leave something behind. A record of some sort. To say, 'I was here. I did my part. I loved Diana.'"

"Stop talking, love," Diana said, and carried me away on a wave of pure joy.

GLOSSARY

Afghan: tribal militia in the Frontier province and Pakhtun-khwa princely state, now Afghanistan

Almirah: armoire, cupboard or cabinets of wood to store clothing

Angrez: English, British

Arkati: procurer of slaves and indentured servants for transport to Guyana (also called Guiana)

Arrey: an exclamation like "Oh!"

Babu: minor official

Baith-khana: chamber to meet people, sitting upon cushions and carpets

Bao-di: dialect form of Babuji, a term for an older male, father in some Indian dialects

Bearer: liveried servant

Betho: a directive to sit

Bhayah: brother

Bibi: a suffix for women

Bindi: round dot on a woman's forehead indicating she's married, and a Hindu

Brahmin, Shatriya: names of priestly and warrior castes (in Hinduism)

Burkha: floor-length covering, may cover the face or leave it open

Buss: "Enough!"

Chador: cloth covering for the head

Chaloh Dikra: Gujarati for "Come on, son," may be used for either gender

Chana-wala: vendor of nuts

Chaprasei: peon or clerk, menial worker

Charpai: literally "four legs," a bed or bench with woven seating

Chee-chee: exclamation of disgust, literally "dirt"

Chikki: sweets made with caramelized sugar, nuts or sesame seeds

Chor bazaar: flea market, literally "thieves' market"

Coolies: porters who carry luggage or loads upon their heads

Dacoit: pirate, thief

Dharam: religion

Dhobi: washman, launderer who cleans clothes

Dhoti: baggy trousers formed by wrapping a long cloth about the lower body

Durwan: doorman

Fauji: soldier

Foolscap: legal-size sheets of paper

Gharry: enclosed carriage

Havildar: tower guard, in charge of security, usually locks and unlocks the facility

Hei Bhagvan: exclamation, "Oh God"

Hill station: vacation place, usually on a hilltop

Huzoor: a salutation, "sir"

Inquilab: revolution, rebellion

Jaldi: quick

Janab: a salutation, "sir" (northern India)

Johur: ritual suicide of noblewomen to avoid capture

Kasam-seh: "I promise"

Khastegari: formal meeting between two families to discuss marriage

Khoja merchants: a sect of Mohammedans, often trading families

Khuda-hafiz: goodbye

Kurta-khamiz: long shirt over baggy pants, worn by north Indian men

Maidaan: open field

Maji: salutation for mother

Malee: gardener

Mela: religious fair, festival

Melmastia: Afghan practice of hospitality, part of the tribal tradition of Pashtunwali, a code of honor.

Memsahib: salutation for women

Naag: cobra

Paji: salutation for older male, like Babuji

Parade rest: an army standing position between attention and at ease

Pashto: language of the Afghan province

Pathan: a tall mountain race that live in present-day Pakistan and Afghanistan

Pat-Rani: head queen, first queen

Payal: anklets made of metal links

Pehelvan: athlete, strong man

Poori: fried roti bread

Qila: fortress, village fortification

Rakhee: cloth bracelet given by a sister to a brother

Rakhsha-bandhan: festival in August when sisters tie a Rakhee on a brother's wrist and receive a gift and promise of protection

Rani Sahiba: salutation to address a queen

Rickshaw: carriage pulled by a person

Roti: unleavened roasted bread

Sabzi: a vegetable dish

Sahib: a salutation, similar to "sir" or "Mr."

Sais: groom who tends horses or drives carriages

Salaam, Sahib: a greeting, generally to a superior

Sanad: permission sheet

Saree: floor-length garment worn by Indian women

Sati: ritual immolation of a widow on husband's funeral pyre

Sepoy: enlisted soldier

Shabaash, Sahib: "well done, sir"

Shalwar: garment, clothing

Shama karo: a request to forgive, apology

Shamshan Ghat: cremation ground

Sowar: mounted soldier

Subedar: army rank for native officer

Tonga: two-wheeled carriage pulled by a mule or horse

Tonga-wala: driver of a tonga carriage

Tulsi: plant with medicinal properties

Vada: potato patty

Vada-pav: street food, potato inside a small loaf of bread

Vaid: local physician

Verandah: balcony

Victoria: horse-drawn vehicle or open carriage

Zenana: women's quarters in a palace where upper-class women were secluded from all males other than the king and family members

AUTHOR'S NOTE

Reading Rudyard Kipling's *Kim* in my youth left an indelible impression upon me—its wide landscapes, varied characters and non stop suspense. As children, Mum read us stories by Conan Doyle, "The Redheaded League," "The Speckled Band." With what bated breath we absorbed each winding sentence! To my parents I owe my love of books and reading, a gift more precious because books were expensive in Bombay in the seventies, when we had little—my father often worked three jobs. Having no TV, our family read and discussed books avidly.

To my husband I owe a debt of faith. When, after working twenty years in the corporate world, I grumbled, "When I retire, I'm going to write a novel!" he said, "Why not now?" Giving up an income is scary, more so for immigrants without a family safety net to fall back upon, such as the kindness of aunts and uncles in the old world. He saw the joy that writing gives me, and that was enough. My son Cyrus wrote a brilliant critique that shaped my revisions and steered me away from tired tropes. Thank you. To my early readers, Cindy Simon, Cindy Sapp, Crystal Willock and Khursheed Parakh, who as far back as the nineties told me, "Keep writing. It's good," I thank you.

Above all I'd like to thank my writing group, Marlene Cocchiola, Jay Langley, Mark Snyder, Tony Athmajvar and Evelyn Van Nuys. Marlene focused on emotion, insisting, "But how did he feel, hearing that?" while Evelyn measured pace and emotion, ensuring each page maintained the desired emotional temperature. With decades of editorial experience, Jay reviewed my manuscript twice to tighten up my prose. His wife Catherine pointed out what a reader might misunderstand, which helped me reword key sections.

My agent, Jill Grosjean, a God-send, guided me through the business side of publishing. Each conversation teaches me more about the business. With the calm born of vast experience, she shared industry norms and processes that gave me confidence to proceed.

I am indebted to Mystery Writers of America, to whose contest for unpublished writers I submitted a humongous manuscript of 138,000 words. Despite its length, MWA's judges deemed it worthy, awarding it MWA/Minotaur's Best First Crime Novel. Thank you. I am overwhelmed.

Kelley, Madeline and the staff at Minotaur, I have been blessed to have you midwife this book. Kelley Ragland's unerring instinct for pacing was spot on. Each detailed email helped me see what I could not see before. Her insistence that I trim the mid-section of this book has made all the difference. Thank you, Madeline Houpt, Hector DeJean and Danielle Prielipp, for your professionalism and expertise. No book is written in a vacuum. I was incredibly fortunate to have a magnificent set of colleagues and friends support this one.

I've had the idea for the "secret letter" used in this book, for decades. In 2005 I advertised for a Gujarati translator to translate the 1858 autobiographical poem by my ancestor, Bejonji Ferdonji Jhansiwala, who was a British army mess man during the Sepoy Mutiny. Since it was written in 150-year-old Gujarati, our family could not read it! Fortunately, Mrs. Mani Bhathena of Australia replied, and I mailed her a copy of the manuscript. Lacking a computer, each day she took a single page to her public library to email me the translation. Four months later, I pieced together 123 pages, and at long last, learned of the awful brutality my grandmother's grandfather witnessed. His account contradicts the official version—it would have been dangerous to publish before Indian independence in 1947, so our family kept it hidden. To Mani, I say thank you for your tireless devotion, unlocking my family's secret history.

My book contains two incidents that historians could take exception to: the events I've described in Karachi and Lahore in 1890–1892. Records of Victoria Cross and Indian Medal of Honor recipients describe several skirmishes between tribesmen and British Indian soldiers between 1880 and 1919 (second and third Anglo-Afghan wars). While there is no record of an Afghan occupation of Karachi Port in 1890, there was much civil unrest in the area that is now Pakistan and Afghanistan, between tribes and the British Raj. In the 1891 Anglo-Brusho War, British Raj troops fought the armies of Hunza and Nagar princely states, which are now part of Pakistan's Gilgit-Baltistan province. Hostilities began when the British began building a road through Kashmir, which the Mirs of Hunza and Nagar objected to. The British army won control of Nagar after the 1891 battle of Nilt Nagar (Jangir-e-Laye), and made it a British protectorate in 1893.

True, there is no record of Lahore being burned by Afghan tribes in 1892. In September 1897, Indian soldiers of the British Raj fought the Battle of Saragarhi against Afghan tribesmen. When thousands of Afghans surrounded the British Fort called Gulistan, the Sikh contingent holding this supply post was cut off from Fort Lockhart. Twelve thousand Orakzai and Afridi tribesmen attacked, vastly outnumbering the handful of defenders.

Led by Havildar Ishar Singh, the Sikh group chose to fight to the death, in one of history's most tragic last stands. The outpost was taken back by the British army two days after their death. Therefore, while fictional, the episodes in my book are based on historical events.

To India, land of my childhood that woke so many memories, thank you for inspiring this book. To my Zoroastrian community, this book is for you, to see yourselves through the eyes of those who love you but are apart.

Nev March